FRACTURED FATES

HANNAH HAZE

Copyright © 2023 by Hannah Haze

All rights reserved.

No part of this book may be reproduced in any form or by any electronic or mechanical means, including information storage and retrieval systems, without written permission from the author, except for the use of brief quotations in a book review.

Front cover designed by Covers by Christian

Edited by Buckley's Books

❦ Created with Vellum

FOREWORD

This book is a 'why choose' bully paranormal romance with one female main character and more than one potential love interest. These love interests are ruthless and at times brutally unkind. There are scenes that some readers may find uncomfortable including violence and gore. For more detailed content warnings, please visit my website.

If you spot any typos in this book, please drop me a line so I can make it right: hannahhazewrites@gmail.com (Or just drop me an email anyway. I love to chat!).

PROLOGUE

Rhi

10 years ago

"Wake up."

I open my eyes.

My bedroom is dark, pitch black. It's the middle of the night.

My eyes drift shut.

"Rhianna, wake up, come on, honey."

A cool hand grips my shoulder. It shakes me gently.

I open my eyes again.

A dark figure hovers above me. I squint, features gradually emerging from the gloom.

My aunt, her long blonde hair loose about her shoulders, her face tense.

"Rhi, we have to go. Someone's coming, honey."

I'm awake. My small body already shaking, my heart thumping against my ribs.

I roll up to sit and swing my legs over the side of the bed. The cold air nips at my bare feet as my aunt sweeps me up into her arms.

"You remember what we practiced?" she whispers into my ear as she wraps a woolen cardigan around my tiny shoulders. She's trembling, although her tone is bright.

"Y-y-yes," I say, letting her thread my arm through a sleeve. "Run to the forest and hide in the trees."

My aunt shakes her head. "Not this time, honey. There isn't time."

Immediately, my head snaps to the dark window. In the distance, I hear the roar of engines, lights swinging through the trees.

"It's like my dream," I say.

"Yes, honey," my aunt says, taking my hand and hurrying me out of the bedroom and down the wooden stairs. Her pace is fast, and my feet slip on the steps, but she yanks me upright, tugging me through into the kitchen.

Here she fetches the silver dagger from the shelf above the fireplace before opening the larder door.

She pushes the stacks of boxes to one side, making space for me.

"Who are they?" I ask, my voice trembling. "Magicals?"

In my dream, they were faceless men, angry and violent. I couldn't make out their eyes or their mouths, their noses or their brows. I never can. There's only ever been one face I could and that, my aunt says, is because his face is everywhere. The authorities' enforcer. It's not him tonight though, not him we're hiding from this time.

My aunt motions to the space she's created and I shake my head, clinging to the fabric of her thin nightgown.

"I don't want to," I say, a sob bubbling in my stomach, my body shaking uncontrollably now.

My aunt strokes back tangled locks of my dark hair, holding my face in her hands and kissing my cheeks and my forehead.

"I know, honey, I know you don't. But it won't be for long. It won't be for long and then we'll be safe again."

A noise, half hiccup, half sob, breaks free from my throat. The sound of the engines grows fiercer, echoing among the trees.

"Hide with me," I beg. I've seen what happens in my dream, and hot tears burn in my eyes as I cling desperately to her arm.

"It's going to be okay," she tells me, guiding me in between the cans and the boxes. "Dreams are just dreams. They mean nothing," she adds, knowing the fears in my heart.

I know she's lying. And I don't want to let her go, but soon she's peeling my hands from her arms and pushing me further into the cupboard.

"I love you, my darling. Stay quiet." She kisses me one last time, pressing the dagger into my palms. "Just in case."

Then she piles the boxes back in front of me and closes the larder door. The lock clicks. I hug my knees in the darkness, the knife sliding to the cold floor. The space smells of dried herbs, the homely aroma tickling my nose. Beyond is the stench of gasoline and rancid smoke.

Those engines roar louder. I hear the men shouting, leering.

I cover my ears with my hands and bury my face in my knees.

1

R^{hi}

THE PRESENT DAY

I RETRACE MY STEPS, my knife in hand as I creep through the trees back to the place where I hid my bike.

I buried it under broken branches and dead leaves four days ago and it takes me ten minutes scrabbling around in the undergrowth to find the machine and dig it out. Then I brush it down and wheel it to the ancient track that weaves through the forest.

The track is barely used anymore, and brambles and bushes are threatening to reclaim it as part of the forest. But it's so old it's not marked on any map, and I think it's safe to use. Downside of this whole plan: my bike is noisy.

Gripping the handles, I close my eyes and scan the immediate area. I can't sense any magicals nearby. It's been four days. Maybe they've already given up looking for me out here in the forest and left.

I don't think they can sense me like I can sense them. If they could, I'd already be caught. My aunt said a tracking gift like mine was rare. One that could keep me safe. I hope she's right, because returning home like this is a big risk.

I take a deep inhale.

Am I doing the right thing?

Deep down, I know this is foolish. I'm a young, unregistered magical. Anyone who handed me in would receive a generous reward from the authorities.

But my heart pangs when I think of my pig, back home alone and probably starving. The chickens are freaking hardcore. The last fox that crept into their pen lost an eye. They'll be fine.

Pip, on the other hand, he was the runt of the litter, never growing to his full size, and always one sandwich short of a picnic. I can picture him sitting patiently by the backdoor of the house, waiting for me to return. It probably won't even occur to him to eat the stupid vegetables growing in the yard.

It's a risk, but I'll creep home for just a moment. Just to grab some food, change my clothes and pick up my pig. Maybe even attempt a new bandage on the wound on my arm.

The magicals looking for me must have found my home by now. They must have ransacked it for clues. Surely they've concluded I'm long gone. Any sensible person would have fled. That would have been the logical thing to do.

I take a steadying breath in and kick down on the bike's start. The engine roars to life.

I hold my breath.

Nothing.

I let out a long sigh of relief and wind slowly through the forest, unable to go fast because of all the potholes and debris on the track. By the time I spy the clearing where our house lies, my brow is damp with concentration and my eyes sore from squinting in the dark. I sigh in relief though to see the place still standing, plus I can hear the chickens clucking. I'd half expected to find a flock of chicken carcasses scattered across the clearing and a burned-out shell of a house.

It wouldn't be the first time.

I swing my leg off the bike and kick down the stand.

I can't sense any magicals nearby. I'm good to go.

I'm halfway across the clearing when it occurs to me that the chickens clucking is not a good sign. It's the middle of the night. They should be tucked up inside the hutch, sleeping.

Something isn't right.

I halt, peering through the darkness, my heart hammering.

This doesn't *feel* right either.

I turn back to my bike.

The front door flings open and a man crashes out.

No, not a man, a giant. He fills the doorway, his body wrapped in a black cloak, the hood pulled up so his face lies in shadow.

Why hadn't I sensed him sooner?

Immediately, the aura of his magic fills the air around him, shimmering in a way I've only ever seen once before. Like a litany of stars soaring around his body.

Something tugs deep in the center of my gut, raw and powerful. So strong, I gasp. It pulls me his way, and my gaze is forced up to meet his. Dark, like the night. For a moment, we simply stare at each other and if I didn't know better, I'd fool myself into thinking the man looks as shocked as I do.

But then the expression of bewilderment flickers away. Gone in an instant.

The hook in my belly strains stronger, and before I can react, he lifts his gloved hand and shoots a bolt of magic my way.

It's bright violet, streaking through the space between us like a burning comet. The effect is almost beautiful.

I'm too disorientated to react, and the magic hits me on the shoulder, sending me flying backwards as pain spirals through my body. I scream as I land on the hard earth of the clearing with a thud.

For one second I lie still, too stunned to move.

This is familiar. All too familiar. Like I've seen it before.

I shake that thought away, lift my fingers and send a magic bolt colliding his way.

It's not as pretty as his. Messy, chaotic, but effective nonetheless.

He ducks, the magic hitting the porch above the doorway and cracking the beam. Splinters fall down onto his head. With his arm outstretched, he strides towards me, and I scramble up onto my feet, sending two more bolts his way. They zoom like colorful fireworks through the night, but he twists and turns, avoiding them both.

"Hand yourself in!" he calls to me, his voice deep and gruff, filling the clearing like a thunderclap. "Make this easy on yourself."

I don't respond. I'm too busy struggling with whatever this damn magic is that's hooked inside my belly and is dragging me his way.

When I don't answer, he huffs in annoyance and sends a stream of magic towards me, so fast and nimble I have no time to dodge it. One smacks my left hip, burning my skin. I bite down hard on my lip as I tumble a second time to the ground.

This time I don't pause; despite the pain, I roll away, shooting some of my own magic towards his feet before I jump back up onto mine. He leaps into the air, avoiding my assault and sprints towards me.

"Give yourself in!" he shouts, as another bolt hits my shoulder and my spine. The pain makes my eyes swim with water, and my stomach bubble with nausea, but I grit my teeth, turn and run.

The air smells of burned flesh and singed fabric. I try not to think about the new wounds I've added to my collection.

It's nothing I haven't handled before – my skin a criss cross of scars, each a testament to another time I escaped.

I run as hard as I can. Despite the pain in my body, despite my empty stomach, despite the overwhelming exhaustion. The man is bigger than me, his stride longer. But I'm light and agile. I'm sure I can outrun him. I hear two more magical bolts scream over my head, his heavy boots thundering on the ground, gaining on me and gaining on me until his ragged breath is loud like a siren in my ears. Even the thud of his heart seems loud, beating furiously in time with my own.

Shit! He's going to catch me.

I throw a torrent of magic over my shoulder and he curses, his boots pausing for just a second before they start up again.

He retaliates with magic that spins above me, clever, intricate, weaving nets into the air. I scream as I swerve, avoiding one, two, three, but the fourth connecting with my back with such violent force, I slam forward. I stumble to the ground, the breath gone from my lungs, and when I roll over this time, he's towering above me.

I can see his face now, his eyes dark like the cloak he wears, long jet hair falling around his shoulders, his heavy brow drawn low, his square jaw locked with tension.

The man in black.

I've seen his picture often enough, and yet, that sense of familiarity swims through my mind a second time. Like I know him. Like we've met before.

"Enough," he says. It's not a question, but if he thinks I'm done, he'll be sorely disappointed.

I've been running all my life. They're not about to catch me now. Especially not him.

"I know who you are," I spit. "And there's no way in hell I'm coming with you."

The side of his mouth lifts in a self-satisfied smirk. "We'll see about that."

Smug bastard. He may be known as the authorities' number one enforcer; doesn't mean he's laying his hands on me this easily.

"Yeah, we'll see," I say, and I kick out his legs from underneath him.

His eyes widen with shock, and it would be frigging funny if I weren't running for my life. I watch as the huge man topples like a felled tree and I'm on top of him in a heartbeat, the blade of my knife at his neck.

"Leave me the fuck alone!" I tell him.

He peers up at me with those bottomless eyes, dark and menacing, his chest heaving. He doesn't speak, instead his eyes travel over my face in a way that has my cheeks warming. His body is solid as the trunk of a tree beneath me and I realize I've landed square on the man's groin. It's intimate. I can see the stretch of his ribs through the material of his clothes, the tremble of his lower lip as he huffs in air, the flare of his nostrils, the strange hue of his pale skin.

I've never been this close to a man before. I've lived all my life with my aunt. I never went to school. We've kept ourselves hidden. We kept the hell away from men who only ever wanted to harm us.

Men have been these distant, peculiar creatures, best avoided. I stare straight back at him, noticing the more angular features of his face, the thick stubble brush that runs over his jaw and neck, and the lump that bobs in his throat. His body is different too. Squarer, broader, his shoulders strong beneath his cloak, his body heavy.

That hook in my stomach tugs at me again, like it wants to

drag me as close to him as it can. Like it wants me to press my smaller body against his larger frame.

The man is intriguing.

What the hell kind of magic is this?

I dig my knife more firmly into his neck, the silver blade pinching his skin and he swallows, his pink tongue coming to wet his lip.

"It's not safe here," he whispers, and I find myself caught by the movement of those lips. He hesitates for a moment before his hands find my calves. I should dig my blade into his throat for that. But his touch is electric. The sensation in my stomach spins like a whirlwind. I don't move. My pulse jumps in my throat. His dark eyes flicker across my face. Carefully, as if he thinks I'll bolt like a wild mare, he strokes his gloved hands up to my thighs. The friction of his movement sends more electricity spiraling across my skin.

He's failed to bring me in by force. Is he now going to attempt to do so by seduction?

"I'll keep you safe," he says.

I want to close my eyes and believe him. It would be nice to be safe. It would be nice if someone kept me safe. This past year has been so hard. I'm tired. Tired of running and hiding. Tired of fighting and scrapping. Tired of trying to stay alive. Tired of being alone.

I force my eyes wide open and stare back at him.

Then I laugh bitterly. I won't be safe with him. I won't be safe with the authorities he works for. I won't be safe with the gang of magicals out searching for me either. The only place I was ever safe was with my aunt. And she's gone.

Resting my free palm on his chest, I lean right over him so our faces are only inches apart. His warm breath rushes over my skin and he smells of the forest.

His fingers sink into my thighs and his eyes darken, falling to my mouth.

My pulse quickens in my throat and the magic he's weaving in my gut drags me closer to him still.

It would be so easy to fall into this spell.

"Fuck off!" I tell him, and before he can respond, I've sent a bolt of energy spearing straight into his chest. Then I'm up on my feet and sprinting away. I'm on my bike before he's recovered, groaning and lumbering as he rolls up to stand.

I hear him shout out to me again, but I don't hear his words over the roar of the engine, and I ignore the damned hook in my belly. The bike lurches forward and I speed off, hitting potholes and branches this time and not giving a shit, even as every wound in my body cries out in pain, even though my magic is depleted and my body shakes with exhaustion.

I escaped from the man in black.

That's all that matters.

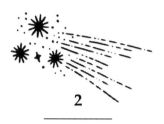

2

The man in black

I STAND THERE WATCHING her go like a damned fool. *A damned fool!*

The blood in my veins thrums and my magic pulsates in my fingers and I let her go.

I never let them go. Ever. I'm the man in black. They never escape my clutches. And I had her, had my hands on her thighs. I could easily have flipped us over, crushed her with my weight. I could have frozen her with my powers. I could send a bolt after her now.

I didn't.

I don't.

She's a scrawny thing with a mane of thick, dark hair and eyes the color of rich maple syrup. At first glance, she appeared younger than she was. Up close, I realized she was older. 19, 20, I guess. How the fuck did she get to 20 and not be registered?

It's near impossible for newborn magicals to slip under the radar. Yet she's been under the radar for two decades.

I shake my head as the forest swallows her up and all I can hear is the dying roar of the bike. A bike that was clearly older than her and about to fall apart.

How has she been surviving out here? The back-ass end of nowhere. Living on the outskirts of a town of normals. How has she gone so long without being caught? How was she never reported?

When I received the call four days ago that there was talk on the underground networks of a young unregistered girl living out here, I thought my job collecting her would involve snatching her from some low-life criminals. Maybe even one of the notorious gangs themselves if they'd heard the news too and gotten here first. I didn't expect her to be on the loose.

I didn't expect to find her at her own goddamn house.

I definitely didn't intend to let her slip through my fingers.

No, that's a lie. I intended it all right. I could have her unconscious and in my arms right now.

The idea has my blood thrumming again and I kick at the earth. What the fuck is wrong with me?

I pull my hood back over the crown of my head and scratch my nails through the stubble on my chin.

What am I going to do next?

I can't leave her out here for the fucking Wolves of Night or the Princes of Death to find. She thinks the authorities' punishment for going unregistered would be severe? She has no fucking idea what those monsters would do.

Anyway, the authorities will probably go easy on her. Probably. She's young. Living the way she has, outcast from her people, probably wasn't her choice or her idea. She's not like some of the stubborn old hillbillies I pick up, the ones who never came forward to be registered decades ago, determined to break the rules and dodge their responsibilities. They're always sent to the labor camps in the North.

What will they choose to do with her? A magical her age should be training at Arrow Hart Academy.

I spit onto the long grass and turn back to the house. There's a tiny pig in there going half-crazy with hunger and a flock of smart-assed chickens that could do with feeding too.

I duck through the doorway, and the pig comes scurrying towards me, snuffling away at my boots. He looks more well fed than the girl, which has anger flaring in my gut. My gut that twisted in fucking somersaults as soon as I stepped into this place. It smells like her, her and at least half a dozen other scents. Obviously, I'm not the first one who's been here hunting for her. The place has been turned upside down, papers, photos, and clothing scattered everywhere.

I reach down and scoop up a shirt lying across the rough floorboards. A thin, cotton thing that's been repaired innumerable times. I bring it up to my nose and inhale. Her scent hits my nostrils and slides down my throat, warming my belly. She smells like fucking sunshine. It has my blood buzzing again.

Buzzing even harder when I remember the feel of her supple thighs beneath my fingers. Remember the swirling color of her eyes. Remember the weight of her perching on my lap.

Shit.

I stomp through to the kitchen, finding a tin of something I tip into a bowl for the pig and some stale bread I crush in my fist and toss outside for the chickens.

Then I slump down at the table and drum my fingers on the surface. Herbs hang, drying, from the ceiling and bottles with contents of all colors line the shelves. It's so fucking obvious magicals live here, it's almost laughable. Sure, it's crude and pretty basic, and the wastelands out here aren't inhabited by magicals, but how did no one spot them? Because there were two. I've already poured over the photos I've found trashed about the house. The girl and an older woman. An older woman who's passed on – the death certificate still lying on the center of this table. I twist it towards me.

Mabel Blackwaters.

That was her name. Died a year ago.

Has the girl been alone all that time?

In the town, they said she was called Rhianna.

I test the name out on my tongue, my voice sounding loud over the noise of the pig chomping down its food.

Then I curse myself. What the fuck?

I tug my phone out of my pocket, and, drumming my fingers again on the tabletop, I call Phoenix. He's more knowledgeable than I am. He always has been. He's also going to love the fact that I am admitting it, and I'm going to have to endure months of his self-satisfied bullshit.

Tough shit. I need his help.

I SLEEP BADLY on the couch in her house. I figure it's as good a place as any to bed down and get some shuteye. She might change her mind and return, hand herself in. Or I might be an unpleasant surprise for any other scumbags breaking into her house.

However, my night's uninterrupted. Not that I sleep one wink. I stare up at the ceiling, my arms folded across my chest, thoughts crashing through my head. Doesn't help that the pig comes to sleep on the rug near my feet and snores the whole damn night.

When the rooster crows just before dawn, and the sky lightens, I'm still brooding. My conversation with Phoenix didn't provide the clarity I'd hoped for. I don't think he believes me about the girl. But he's on his way to help nonetheless. He'll be here later today.

In the meantime, I'm going out hunting for her.

Letting her go yesterday was a fucking mistake. A massively stupid one.

She's young, and though clearly untrained, there are many who would pay handsomely for her. The gangs will be out there searching for her. There is too much money to be made to simply let her slip away.

Do I want her falling into the hands of those monsters? No.

The only place she is safe is with me – until I can get her away from this hellhole to safety anyway. Once she's registered, once she's in the authorities' protection, she'll be fine. Because surely, they won't send her to the camps. She's too young, too much of a potential resource.

I swing my feet to the floor, my soles hitting the floorboards with a thud and jolting the pig awake.

"I already fed you," I tell him before he can start squealing, still mad he's clearly been claiming the lion's share of the food in this house. Maybe she was fattening him up. Then again, judging by the little bed he has in the corner of her bedroom, I doubt it.

I roll my eyes, shrug on my cloak, and stomp out into the forest on foot. The sensible thing to do would be to wait for Phoenix and go in search of the girl together. But I already threw sensible out of the window yesterday and I'm impatient to find her.

I know roughly in which direction she fled, and that sensation in my stomach tugs me a certain way, as if my subconscious believes it knows where she is. As I have nothing else to go on, I focus in on that feeling and follow it through the mature trees. It's cold for an April morning and my breath hangs in a cloud before my face as the birdsong breaks out overhead and the sun's rays gradually penetrate the canopy.

Twigs snap under my heavy boots and branches swipe at

my cloak, but I keep walking, catching glimpses of her scent on the breeze.

This is fucking crazy, but until Phoenix arrives and we form a better plan, it's all I have, stumbling through the forest with my mind a mess.

Stupid. It's fucking stupid, because – as that feeling snags me right and I follow a path that dips down into the belly of the forest – a group of men emerges from the trees to surround me.

It was inevitable. The girl is a valuable commodity. A lot younger than most of the unregistered the gangs pick up.

They're not going to let me swoop in and snatch her without a fight.

And yeah, if I'm truthful, I'm itching for a fight. A chance to swing at these bastards. These bastards who want to abduct her, keep her chained in some lowlife's basement to do their fucking bidding. Even if I'm outnumbered, I'm still keening for this altercation.

They're magicals armed with guns and they don't bother with introductions or negotiations. I am the man in black, after all. A continual thorn in their side. Taking me out would be an even bigger prize than capturing the girl.

The first few shots narrowly miss my head before I react, roaring with rage as I deflect, dodge, and freeze their bullets with my magic, sending a volley of blasts their way.

I charge towards the two men nearest me, taking out their guns. They lunge towards me, synchronizing their blows, forcing me to spin and swerve, but they're no real match for me.

Nevertheless, one catches me on the shoulder, and I hiss at the surge of pain. A lucky hit. I'm not about to be clobbered to death by these clowns. Instead, I hit back with more force, driving deadly magic into one man's chest so that he collapses, lifeless, to the ground, and then lunging suddenly at the other, disarming him and searing his guts.

I spin to face the others, counting four, and send another

battery of fire hurtling back towards them, striking one directly in the face.

Three.

Snarling, I sprint towards the remaining men. Twisting and turning my body, thrusting and driving with my magic, and punching and thumping with my fists.

One sandy-haired fucker secures a lucky hold around my neck, but I wrench around and thump my magic down hard on his neck, snapping it in half.

Two.

I surge on top of a darker man, crashing my magic against his gun. He is larger than the rest and more skilled and, despite my onslaught, he finds his feet, punching me in the gut with such force the wind is knocked from my lungs. As I struggle for oxygen, I manage to dispense of him with a frantic swipe.

Another one down.

Only one left.

But I'm fucked.

The last man towers above me, his weapon pointing straight at the crown of my head.

And this is the end.

Time slows. I close my eyes.

This was stupid and I royally fucked up.

I imagine Phoenix shaking his head, disappointed with me.

I breathe in and wince in anticipation of the bullet.

Then a loud thud hits my ear drums. No pain follows.

I'm still alive.

When I open my eyes, there's a knife lodged in the other man's skull.

The knife that pinched my throat only yesterday.

3

Rhi

I STARE DOWN at my open palm and my entire body shakes.

I killed him.

I killed that man.

I've killed chickens before. Never a man.

Nausea erupts in my gut and I stumble backwards, clutching my stomach and doubling over. I heave into the undergrowth as my body trembles violently. When finally it stops, and I stand upright, the man in black is right in front of me. He stares at me with curiosity.

"You saved me."

My face is damp and I swipe away the tears rolling down my cheeks.

"Here." He hands me a flask from under his cloak and I flip back the lid and take one long gulp. Swilling the warm water around my mouth, I spit it onto the grass and then chug down more. It's been days since I had a decent drink.

When I'm done, I wipe the back of my hand across my mouth and hand his flask back.

"Thirsty?" he asks.

"Yes."

"Hungry?"

I hesitate. "Yes."

We stare at each other. His eyes are black like the midnight sky and I half expect to find stars shining in them.

"You can't stay here," he says.

I frown. I know that. I just don't know what I'm going to do about it.

I also don't know why the hell I just saved the man in black, why I'm still standing here. I should be running.

He tilts his head, and I can tell he's choosing his next words carefully. Like that cautious caress of my thighs in the clearing, he thinks one wrong move and I'll bolt. He's right.

"I don't know what she told you, that woman you were living with–"

"My aunt."

"I don't know what she told you, why she's kept you hidden in this shithole, but it's no way to live."

"I'm perfectly happy."

"But you're not safe. You see that." He points to one of the dead men slumped on the ground. My stomach turns and I think I might vomit again. "See that tattoo on his neck?" It's a huge wolf growling up at us, sprawled across his entire throat. "They're the Wolves of Night. You know who they are?" I bite my lip and shake my head. "One of the most notorious gangs in the underworld. They're after you. They're all after you. And if they lay their hands on you ..."

"So, I suppose you're going to tell me going with you is my only option."

"It isn't. You could stay on the run, live the rest of your life hiding."

I snort. "With you chasing me, as well as them."

"If I wanted to catch you, I'd have done it yesterday." He growls with a smirk and that cocky self-assurance. The bodies of the men he's killed lie at his feet. Five of them. He has every right to be cocky.

Did he really let me go? Is he offering to let me go again?

Is that what I want?

What I want is the wound on my arm to stop throbbing and my belly to be full so I can actually think straight.

"You really are a smug bastard," I mutter, examining his smirk.

"And I can tell you are a bratty nuisance."

I can't help but laugh. The noise, the smile on my lips, seems to startle him for a moment. He looks pretty cute with bewilderment crossing his face and that hook in my belly tugs at me once more, before the look of disdain returns.

"You can't stay here."

"I know," I say, burying my face in my hands. I don't know what to do.

I was always told to hide in the forest if anyone came looking for me, but my aunt never said what to do if the plan failed and they found me.

Now my existence is known, they're not going to stop searching for me. They're not going to give up.

The man in black is right, I have to leave. But where can I go? Do I want to live like those other unregistered magicals who pass through here occasionally, always on the move, never staying in one place more than a couple of nights, constantly peering over their shoulders?

"Your arm."

I lower my hands and peer up at him. I've managed to

soothe the burns he made with his magic yesterday, but the cut is as savage as ever. He examines it.

"Why haven't you healed it?"

"I tried. It won't close. I need to get it stitched."

It's the reason that damn gang found me in the first place. I'd risked a rare outing into the town to visit the clinic. I hadn't made it through the door though, before I was spotted by those strangers, strangers who had somehow recognized what I really was: a magical.

He scowls at me. "I can heal the wound. Come here." I scowl right back. "If I wanted to capture you, we'd already be halfway back to Los Magicos."

I consider him as I chew on my lip. What have I got to lose? I take a step forward. He tugs off his gloves, grips my wrist with his left hand and hovers his right above the gash.

Tingles race across my skin where his fingers curl around my wrist. Apart from my aunt, nobody's ever touched me before. Don't get me wrong, plenty have tried. But none of those touches were consensual.

Occasionally I've imagined what it must feel like to have someone hold me, caress me, want me. Mostly, I've pushed those thoughts aside.

His fingers twitch and the comfort of his touch has my eyelids threatening to drift shut.

Am I simply touch-starved? Is that why it feels this way? Or is it something about him? That hook in my stomach tugs me towards him, and I strain against it to stop myself falling right into his body.

He swallows, eyes locked on my wound. His lips move. Plush-looking lips, rows of perfectly straight teeth stacked behind them.

Warmth radiates from his palm and then I gasp with a sudden sting. He lets go and when I peer down the wound is not only healed, it's gone completely.

"It's a simple spell. One you'd have learned if you lived in Los Magicos with your kind and had been to school."

"My aunt taught me plenty," I snap, running my fingers over the repaired flesh, the pain gone too.

She taught me everything she knew, but, if I'm honest, I've always known it wasn't enough. My magic has always crackled in my fingertips as if it's just itching to be used. I want to test its limits. I have no idea what I'm capable of.

Killing a man.

That's what.

My gut twists again and I frown.

"Come with me, Rhianna," my eyes dart up to his, "and you can learn everything you should have been taught."

It's as if he knows this is the thing that will convince me.

It's tempting, especially when my options are looking severely narrowed.

My aunt told me I wasn't safe with the authorities. It's why she kept me hidden. But what if she was wrong? What if this is my opportunity to learn, to be who I'm meant to be?

I narrow my eyes. He may have piqued my interest, but I don't trust him.

"No one is going to teach me. They're going to lock me in a cell," I say.

"How old are you? 19?"

"20."

"All magicals your age are required to attend Arrow Hart Academy until they reach 21–"

"School? I'm not going to school. Can't someone teach me?" Someone like you.

"This isn't lord of the rings," he says with disgust, his nose wrinkling like he caught a whiff of a bad smell. "We're wasting time here. What's your decision?"

What's my decision?

I stare at his face, into his dark eyes, and there never really was one to make. We both know that. He's playing along, letting me believe I'm the master of my own destiny. But I was always going to go with him. Willingly or forced.

I know when I'm beat. Doesn't mean I won't go down without a fight, without grabbing a hold of some kind of victory.

"I'll come with you," he nods sternly, "on one condition."

"Name it."

"My pig comes too."

His brow crashes down over his eyes. "You want to take your pig?"

"Pip, yes."

"You do know pigs grow fucking massive. They aren't pets."

I scowl at him. "Pip's a runt. He's not growing any bigger."

"They won't let you keep a pig in Arrow Hart Academy."

I shrug. "I'm not leaving without him."

"Fine. But I have a condition myself."

"Okay. What is it?"

"No bolting. You run away and leave me with the pig, I'll be frying up some sausages."

I lift my forefinger to his face and point it at him like a gun.

"You hurt my pig–"

"You run away..."

We glare at each other. Then he shakes his head.

"Come on. Let's get moving. It's not safe out here."

I glance towards my knife, the carved silver handle glinting in the morning's light. I don't want to leave it behind. It belonged to my dad. It's the only possession of his I own. It's kept me safe. But the thought of yanking it from the dead man's skull has vomit crawling up my throat.

I turn away.

"Okay," I say and start walking in the direction of home.

4

R^{hi}

WE WALK IN SILENCE, both on the lookout for another ambush, his heavy boots the only sound in the eerily quiet forest. It's as if the birds and the trees are all frightened of this man. I don't blame them. He looks pretty terrifying, like an avenging angel stepped straight out of hell.

Every now and then I take a furtive glance his way, grabbing my opportunity to examine him further. The leather of his boots is well worn, in contrast to the thick, luxurious material of his cloak. He's pulled the hood up over the crown of his head, but I can see the expression on his face, his brow serious and creased with concentration. I find myself wondering what he looks like when he smiles, if he ever does, and wondering if guilt hangs over his head like mine from all those men he's killed. My gaze drops to the expensive leather gloves he wears on his hands. How many people has this man captured? How many has he killed?

After an hour we reach the clearing and cross to the door of my house, he halts, just as Pip comes skidding out, grunting loudly as he races towards us.

I crouch down and he scuttles up into my lap, licking at my face as I shower him with kisses.

"We need to get out of this shithole as quickly as possible," the man in black says, disgust curling his lips. "You have a backpack?" I nod. "Fill it with whatever you want to take – but be quick about it and you're carrying it so don't make it too heavy."

I tickle Pip's ears and chew on my lip. How am I meant to decide what to take? It's not like I own a lot – we've run so many times, I've got used to traveling light, to abandoning the things I love. But I still have some nicknacks I've collected over the years. I don't want to leave any of it behind.

"Half an hour," he says, and, pushing Pip gently away, I dart into the house, gasping when I see the mess. I peer over my shoulder accusingly at the man.

"You get a kick out of rummaging through a young woman's things?"

"It wasn't me," he says, with indignation in his tone.

"Sure," I mutter, racing up the stairs and into my room. I pull clothes from the wardrobe and stuff them into my bag, along with a pair of sneakers. I run my fingers over the row of books on my shelf and the trinkets I've discovered out in the forest. My heart hangs heavy. It's like leaving another set of old friends behind yet again and my chest pangs.

This home has been one of many over the years. But one in which I was safe up until four days ago. I've been loved and cared for here. Will I ever find a home like this again? Will I ever be loved like that again?

"Are you done?" the man in black calls from downstairs and

with my hand on the handle, I take one last look around my room, and close the door.

He meets me at the bottom of the stairs, handing me a cracker spread with peanut butter.

"Eat it," he commands, and I try my best not to stuff the entire thing in my mouth at once. When I've demolished the first, he hands me two more and I follow him into the living room.

Pip's laid out across the sofa, unmoving.

I gasp and a sudden anger thunders through my veins.

"What the fuck did you—"

"Don't get your panties in a twist. He's only out cold. You think I'm transporting a live pig all the way back to Los Magicos?"

Rushing towards my pet, I run my palm down his body; panic, indignation and rage turning the food in my belly sour.

Warm.

And he's snoring softly.

I sigh in relief, my tense shoulders sagging. I don't say it, but I can see the man's logic. There's no way Pip would consent to be carried or would sit primly on the backseat of a car.

"You should have talked to me first before putting him under," I grumble, turning back to the man in black and taking another chomp of cracker.

"We can leave him behind if you'd prefer," he growls and I decide to change the subject.

"How are we traveling to Los Magicos?"

"On my bike."

"Your bike. Both of us? I can take mine."

He shakes his head. "That piece of shit won't make it all the way back to Los Magicos."

"Oh, and yours will?"

He snorts, picks up my pig, and strides out the door. I've no choice but to follow him again, especially when he's pignapped Pip.

He whistles and an engine roars into life from behind the house, then a bike comes zipping around the building and skids to a stop in front of him. It's sleek and shiny and looks as if it was made yesterday.

I can't help but reach out and touch it, gliding my hand over the soft leather of the seat. I've never seen a bike like it.

"Can I try it?" I ask, unable to hide my eagerness as my palm hovers above the handle.

"No. I'm driving."

I'm about to argue when we hear the far off whine of another engine and both our gazes lift to the forest. I glance towards him, wondering how we're going to handle another ambush. I can't fight like the man in black can. And I no longer have my knife.

"It's okay," he says, opening a box on the back of the bike and laying Pip inside. "It's my friend."

"Friend?"

He slams down the lid on the box, waving his hand across it so a row of breathing holes appear.

"He's come to help me transport you back to Los Magicos."

"Transport me? Jesus Christ! I'm not a crate of apples!"

"No, they would be more cooperative."

"I didn't think you were the kind of man who needed *help*," I snark back.

"Every gang in the underworld is going to be out looking for you. We're going to take the back roads, and he will help me keep you safe."

There's something in his demeanor that tells me he isn't disclosing the entire story. What is he keeping from me? I think of my aunt's warning and apprehension shivers across my skin. Am I making a mistake? He never told me there'd be two of them.

The noise of the engine grows louder and then a bike glides through the trees, crossing the clearing and halting in front of us both.

The rider cuts the engine, swings down his leg and pulls off his helmet. He's another frigging giant and, although I'd guess he's about an inch shorter than the man in black, he's just as broad, a black t-shirt straining across his muscular chest and tattoos tracing down his strong arms. His hair is cut above his ears and a thick beard hides his square chin. Both are the color of willow bark, in contrast to his pale blue eyes.

They lock with mine and just like before, I feel the sensation of being hooked through my middle. I frown, confused by this strange magic. He stares right back at me, his brow creasing, and I can feel the man in black's gaze swinging from his friend to me and back again.

Then the second man blinks, leans away and those pale eyes flick across my face, down my body, then dart up to his friend.

"This is her?"

The man in black nods curtly, before slamming a helmet down onto my head.

"We're not stopping," he tells us both, jumping up onto his bike. He pats the seat behind him and the other man watches me with a frown as I hover in indecision.

Am I making a mistake? Am I trusting the wrong people?

I glance back at my home. One of the bedroom windows has been smashed, and the porch is broken where I hit it with my magic yesterday. The warmth that radiated from the place when my aunt was alive has dissipated. Now it's stony cold.

"One second," I say.

"We need to go–"

I don't hear the rest of the man's words. I race to the backyard and unhook the door of the pen, shooing the chickens out. They'd always wanted to escape, now they're free.

A lump forms in my throat. Unlike me.

I don't know what the hell is going to happen, but one thing's for sure, my fate is no longer in my own hands.

5

R^{hi}

SWINGING my backpack over my shoulders, I hop up onto the back of the man in black's bike. I keep a respectable distance between us, gripping the seat in front of me with my hands.

He peers over his shoulder at me with an amused look, then grabs a fistful of my hoodie and drags me forward until my body slots against his.

"You wanna fall off?" he says, shaking his head and placing my hands on his waist. "Hold tight."

"Aren't you going to restrain her?" the other man says from his bike.

"Restrain me?" I start but before I can protest, a chain of metal coils around my ankles and locks me to the bike.

"Mother fu–"

The man in black revs the engine, cutting off my words of

protest, and slams the bike forward. Instinctively I lean into him, not turning around as we leave the clearing.

A sadness hangs heavy over me. I'm leaving my home behind. Maybe I didn't have the best or the most exciting existence here, but it was my home. Yet another one abandoned. The sadness weighs me down as we weave through the forest, only clearing when we reach the highway and the man in black leans on the accelerator, speeding us along the road.

This bike can go twice as fast as mine and the speed sends adrenaline shooting through my blood. I grip his waist tighter, my fingers digging into hard muscle.

There's something exciting about having the man between my legs, about my body pressed to his. Beneath that scent of the forest, he smells masculine and dangerous and it buzzes in my throat.

I've read enough books to know that falling for your kidnapper is a huge and predictable cliché. I'm not going to do it. I'm not going to crush on the first man who comes crashing into my life. I'm not that pathetic. But I can see that promise is going to be hard to keep when he covers my hand with his and then strays down to squeeze my thigh.

They're simply touches of reassurance. He's making sure I'm okay. But my stomach flutters anyway.

He's good to his word and we take the back roads, avoiding the main ones. The two men ride side by side, occasionally shouting to one another but I can't hear their words over the rumble of the engines.

After a couple of hours, we swing into the parking lot of some run-down diner. My body is stiff and I want nothing more than to jump off this bike, roll my neck and stretch out my back. But I'm chained to the machine. I pull off the helmet instead, shaking out my hair.

"Are you going to unchain me?" I ask. "Or are you leaving me here while you eat?"

The other man swings his leg over his bike and swaggers towards me. He stops right by my side and peers menacingly into my eyes, daring me to say more. Then he lifts his hand and the chains slither away.

With a groan, I slip off the bike, every bone in my body crunching. I'm still sore from my nights in the forest and my first run in with the man in black. I have bruises littering my body and the burns aren't as well healed as the cut.

"Hold out your hands," the second man says.

"What?" I ask.

"Hold out your hands."

"Why?"

With an irritated huff, he takes both my wrists in his grip, forcing them together, despite my attempts to pull them apart, then he conjures a set of handcuffs from thin air.

"You know if I wanted to run," I sneer, "I could do it with my hands bound."

He smirks back at me. "It'll make it harder though, won't it?"

My magic is still depleted from my battle with the man in black, but I call on what little I have to test the strength of these cuffs. They're magical and I don't have the power right now to crack them open.

The man in black jumps down from his bike and, slapping his friend on the shoulder, they turn together and walk in the direction of the diner.

"I'm not leaving my pig out here," I call after them.

"Pig?" the man in black's friend says.

The man in black simply shakes his head and stomps back to the bike.

He opens up the box, scoops Pip out and dumps him in my arms.

The other man's top lip curls in disgust. "What the fuck is that?"

"My pig."

He peers at the man in black. "Why the fuck does she have a pig?" The man in black shrugs. "Is she mentally unstable?"

The man in black looks me straight in the eye. "Possibly."

"I am here, you know," I mutter. "Pip is my pet and–"

"You're gonna need to cover that disgusting thing up," the second man says. "They won't let it in."

"*Him*," I say, resisting the urge to stick my tongue out at him. He tosses his head and strides away.

Shrugging my hoodie over my head – which is fucking hard to do with my hands bound – I wrap Pip up in it and follow suit. I'm only wearing a crop top underneath and the man in black's eyes flick over me before darting away.

The diner door chimes as we step through and a waitress looks up from her magazine at the counter. The place is empty. I doubt it receives much passing business. She eyes us with interest and the man in black lowers his hood. He points to a booth.

"Sit."

I scoot along a bench, Pip resting in my lap.

The other man takes the seat opposite. He's more classically good looking than the man in black. Groomed with those light eyes; his like day, the man in black's like night.

"You always stare at people?" he asks me.

"You're staring at me."

He scoffs. "You're quite pretty. He didn't tell me that. Shame you're deranged and a criminal."

I narrow my eyes. "What *did* he tell you?"

He doesn't answer, swinging his gaze to his friend instead as he joins us at the booth and takes the seat next to him.

They spend the next ten minutes ignoring me and discussing routes to Los Magicos. I fidget on my seat. The smells from the kitchen are driving me slightly insane. My stomach rumbles loudly and I try to rub at it. When the kitchen doors swing open and the waitress strides out with three plates balanced in her hands, I have to force myself to remain in my seat and not rush at her. To my surprise, she places the plate piled highest in front of me and two smaller sub rolls in front of the men.

My jaw drops open and I'm probably salivating, but I can't quite believe it's for me.

"Eat up," the man in black says.

I scowl at him. I have a pig in my lap, my wrists are bound and my hands caught up in my hoodie. Is this some method of torture? Dropping food in front of my face but not letting me eat it? I consider diving my head straight into the plate of food. However, I do have some dignity and, despite what they may think, I'm not deranged.

"Eat," the man in black repeats, this time with venom.

"I can't," I snap. "My wrists are bound, remember?"

The second man throws me another of those irritating smirks. The man in black simply tuts in annoyance, and snaps his fingers. The handcuffs spring open and I untangle my hoodie and lay Pip out next to me on the bench.

The two men watch me as I forget any table manners I ever learned and scoff myself silly, tucking into eggs, tomatoes, mushrooms, hash browns and fried bread.

"You don't usually treat your assignment to a breakfast fit for a king," the second man says to the man in black.

"Look at her." The man in black jerks his head in my direction. "She's malnourished."

I peer down at my body with resentment. Am I? I'm probably a little on the skinny side but I take offense at the description. And at the fact that he wasn't checking me out just now with admiration, more likely disgust.

"When was the last time you ate?" the other man asks.

"I had a handful of crackers before we left. Other than that, four days ago."

His brow thunders down. "They weren't feeding her?"

"They?" I ask with my mouth full.

"*They* hadn't gotten their hands on her. She was on the loose. Hiding out."

"But they were after her? They knew she was there?"

"Yes."

The other man looks kind of impressed at that nugget of information.

"What's your name?"

"Rhi."

"Full name?"

I glare at him.

"Rhianna Blackwaters," the man in black says. I'm not surprised he knows. "Name mean anything to you?"

"No," the other man answers, "you?"

The man in black shakes his head.

"What are yours?" I ask, jerking my chin towards the two men as I chew.

"You can call me Stone."

I nod and peer at the man in black. He glares at me but doesn't speak. Guess he's not disclosing his name.

"Best you call him Sir." Stone chuckles. I roll my eyes. No fucking way. "Why were you hiding out there in Shitsville, Rhianna?" Stone leans forward in his seat. His roll is untouched.

Am I being interrogated? I shift on my seat but don't pause my eating.

"I wasn't hiding out."

The man in black snorts. "Your aunt was clearly keeping you hidden. Why?"

"Some people like the quiet life. Not everyone wants to live in the big city."

Stone examines my face. "Some *people* do. Most magicals live in the city and very few indeed fail to have the children in their care registered. In fact, it's virtually unheard of." He pauses, letting me digest this piece of information. "Why aren't you registered? You do know it's a criminal offense."

"So they are going to lock me up?" I scowl at the man in black. He lied to me. Why am I surprised?

"Like I said, they are likely to send you to the academy."

"Likely?"

"You should consider yourself lucky," Stone says sternly. "All magicals are required to be registered."

I stare at him. "Why?" I know the official answer. But I want to hear what he has to say.

"We could be attacked at any time. At any time from forces in the West. All magicals are required to come forward to be registered and trained. Our nation depends on each generation of magicals to keep us safe."

"There hasn't been an attack from the West in over half a century."

"Because our magical forces are a deterrent. If every magical chose to dodge their responsibilities ..." Anger flashes in his eyes and he trails off.

"My aunt was keeping me safe," I say, sawing my toast in half a little aggressively.

"From whom?"

"People like you I imagine."

"Us? We're the good guys, Sweetheart."

I lower my knife and fork and twerk an eyebrow. "You really look like it."

Stone looks down at his clothes and then at the man in black with his thick cloak the color of coal.

"What did she tell you? Your aunt?" the man in black asks.

"That the authorities were as bad as the underworld gangs. Both would want to land their hands on me if they ever learned of my existence. Seems she was right." I stuff a piece of eggy toast in my mouth. Even if she had told me much more than that I wouldn't be sharing it with these two men.

"She was wrong. You will be safe with the authorities." Stone lifts his roll and takes a large bite.

"In a cell?"

"At the academy."

I hope he's correct, but right now I'm not sure I believe it. My aunt always had my best interests at heart. She cared for me for as long as I can remember. Nursing me whenever I got sick, always forgoing her portion when we were short of food, teaching me all the magic she knew, taking the blows whenever we were attacked.

She said the authorities can't be trusted, and I believe her.

For now though, I'll go along with this situation. Then when the time's right, I'll be gone.

Stone lowers his sandwich and meets my eye as if he knows exactly what I have in mind.

6

Rhi

WHEN I'VE EATEN every scrap of food on my plate and forced myself not to lick it clean, the man in black buys me a pastry. I eat the huge sticky thing in about three bites, licking sugar from my fingertips afterwards. Then, despite my protests, they lock me to the bike and we set off again.

The roads we cruise are empty. One or two beat-up trucks are the only other vehicles we pass. It's not hard to understand why. The tarmac's all broken up and the two men have to weave in and out of deep potholes.

We ride like this for a few more hours, stopping once to drink water, stretch our legs and relieve ourselves. Then we're off again, not stopping until the sun dips low and the sky turns a pink that has my breath catching in my throat. I watch the horizon swallow up the daylight as we follow a side road and stop at a motel that looks as run down as the diner did earlier.

There're a couple of old cars parked out front and some of the rooms have their curtains drawn. A light flickers in the front office and Stone disappears inside, returning a few minutes later with a key.

Only one.

"I'm not sharing a room with you guys," I say, crossing my arms over my chest.

"And I'm not letting you out of my sight," the man in black says, scooping Pip out of the box and following Stone up a rickety staircase.

Damn it! He has my pig. I'm forced to follow. He's always one step ahead. I chase them up the stairs and into the bedroom, swinging my gaze around in search of Pip. He's already hidden him out of sight.

"Apparently, there's a vending machine downstairs. I'm going to pick us out some food," Stone says, leaving the room.

The man in black unbuttons his cloak and slings it over the back of a chair before slumping down into it and scrolling through his phone.

I peer around the room.

"There's only two beds," I point out, relieved there's no double.

"Phoenix and I will take it in turns to keep watch."

"Keep watch? You really think–"

"Someone could ambush us again? Yes." I chew on my thumb. "Don't do that," he tells me, not looking up from his device, "it's a nasty habit."

I scowl at him. "I can take a turn keeping watch too."

His dark eyes lift to mine. "And sneak off in the night? No. Besides, you need a good night's sleep."

Do I? I guess I haven't slept well since all this mayhem started. If truth be told, I haven't slept well since my aunt passed.

"Okay, well, I'm going to take a shower." I stomp towards the bathroom, fantasizing about hot water and soap.

"Wait," he says and I freeze in the doorway as he lumbers to his feet. He sticks his head into the bathroom, peering around. There's one shower, the screen covered in mildew, one toilet and a moldy-looking sink. "I'll be listening at the door," he tells me. "Don't try anything."

"Are you sure you don't want to come in and watch?"

He stares at me with his hard eyes and I slink inside the bathroom and shut the door.

"Good luck," he calls with sarcasm from the other side. "The water is probably cold."

I grimace. That does not sound inviting, but I'm smelly and covered in grime from the forest and the bikes. I need to wash.

Once I've bolted the bathroom door, stripped out of my clothes and stepped under the dribbling faucet, I realize this probably wasn't the brightest idea I've ever had. It wouldn't take much for those two men to break down the door and come at me. It probably isn't a great idea to be sharing a room with them either. But as I massage the rose-smelling soap into my skin, my worries slip down the plug hole.

I'm half way through shampooing my hair, my eyes drifting shut as I scrape my nails against my scalp, when the water snaps freezing cold.

I scream and jump out of the shower, shampoo running down my back as I shiver in the cool bathroom.

"What the Hell?" I mutter, fiddling with the faucet.

"Get out of the shower!" Stone shouts from the other side of the door and I know instantly he is responsible for the water's sudden temperature change.

"Why?" I yell. What is this guy's problem? He's such an asshole.

"You've been in there long enough, that's why."

"I'm half way through washing my hair." I brace myself, ready to brave the cold water and finish cleaning.

"Tough shit!"

The water snaps off.

"Hey," I yelp, but no attempts at wrangling the faucet, or tempting water from the tap with my magic, starts the shower going again.

I curse and squeeze as much of the bubbles out of my hair as I can. Then I step out reluctantly, drying down my body and hair quickly with the rough towel on offer, and trying to warm myself up.

I didn't pack any pajamas so I pull on an oversized t-shirt and a pair of yoga pants. When I step back out into the bedroom, both men peer my way, their gazes straying down my body, lingering fleetingly at my chest. I follow their eyes and find my stiff nipples are visible through my shirt.

Not wearing a bra was another big mistake. I hurry across the room and drop down into a chair. I really hope I can convince the top dogs at the authorities that I can skip the academy because I clearly have a lot to learn when it comes to navigating social interactions. Especially social interactions with men.

"Here," Stone says, tossing me a packet of sandwiches. I catch it from the air and stare down at the label.

Ham.

Pip snuffles from somewhere in the room and I leave the packet unopened, ignoring another of Stone's smirks.

"How far do we have to go?" I ask, acting nonchalant, like the man's games aren't getting to me. I'm not going to give him the satisfaction of asking why he has a problem with me.

"We should be there by nightfall tomorrow," the man in black tells me.

"And where exactly are you going to take me?"

"To the Chancellor."

I nod and tug at my t-shirt. "And who exactly is the chancellor?"

Stone huffs like it's the stupidest question ever asked.

"The head of the authorities." When I stare at him blankly, he adds: "He or she is an elected official, voted in by the council every five years."

"And who votes in the council?"

"No one. The council is made up of the most powerful families among the magical people."

"Sounds very democratic," I mutter.

"It's the way things have been done for the last fifty years, and it's brought stability and peace to our country. Before this system, the world was chaotic."

My aunt taught me to never buy bullshit like that. If something sounds too good to be true, she said, it usually is.

I don't voice my opinion but Stone scowls at me nonetheless.

I watch the men finish their sandwiches and open a second each. Despite the mega meal I ate back at the diner, I'm still starving, and Stone seems to take great delight in eating his sandwich especially slowly, with exaggerated bites. I peer down at my untouched ham sandwich and call the man every imaginable name I can think of in my head.

It makes me feel a little better.

"Time for bed," the man in black announces, watching me. "You have a preference which bed you want?" I shake my head. "Okay, we'll take the one nearest the door. You sleep first," he tells Stone.

"You sure?"

"Yes."

We all remain where we are sitting as if none of us knows what to do next. Pip snores from somewhere hidden in the room and I smother a yawn.

"Bed, Blackwaters," the man in black snaps, balling his

empty sandwich packets in his hand and slamming them in the wastepaper basket.

Although there's nothing I'd like more than to crawl under the covers and lie on a soft mattress – well it doesn't look that soft but it's better than the hard forest floor – I don't like being ordered about. I, therefore, take an exaggerated amount of time to roll out of the chair, stretching as I go, and padding across to the bed. There I fiddle with the bedsheets until I run out of ways to procrastinate and slide between the covers. The bed is lumpy and I can feel just about every spring in the mattress, but it feels divine. I can't help a little moan of satisfaction that has two pairs of eyes shooting my way.

The moan morphs to a yelp as I feel the cold sting of two metal chains wrap around my ankles.

"What the hell?" I say snapping up to sit. "You're chaining me to the bed? You're sick, you know that?"

"We're cautious," Stone says. "And you're a brat. I'm making this job as easy for us as possible. Go to sleep."

"Not until you've unchained me." I peer over to the man in black, appealing to him, but he isn't even paying attention, too busy with his phone.

"Suit yourself. Stay awake all night for all I care. I'm not unchaining you. You're a prisoner. You've broken authority laws."

"You said they'd go easy on me," I say to the man in black. He raises his eyes, nonplussed.

"Probably."

"You fuckers!"

The man in black snaps his fingers and the lights go out.

I spend the next ten minutes tussling on the bed, trying to unbind my ankles with my magic. Nothing works and both men ignore my little temper tantrum.

Finally, I give up, flopping down onto my back and rolling over, my back to them. I try not to imagine what's happening as

I hear Stone unbuckle his belt and drag his jeans down his thighs.

He has a bed of his own. But I'm chained to mine. There's nothing stopping him from climbing into mine.

I screw up my eyes.

I try not to imagine what the man stripping behind me must look like without his clothes. I try not to admit to myself that I'm curious to know.

Eventually I hear him climb into the bed beside mine, the springs creaking. I listen to his breath, to the man in black's too, both loud in the silence.

I try my best to stay awake, not trusting either of these men to behave in the way they should. But I'm tired from nights forced awake, listening for every sound, scanning the forest for those trying to capture me. My eyes are heavy, my body too. Eventually I fall asleep.

I don't rouse again until much later. The room is still dark and I wake to the sound of whispered voices. It takes me a moment to remember where I am – not home in my own bed, not out in the forest – and why I'm here. Then I tune in to what those two voices are saying.

"You feel it too, don't you?"

A pause.

"Yes, I do."

"Do you think she does?"

"Yes, I think she has an awareness but I don't think she understands what it means."

"I think we should keep it that way. For now."

"Agreed."

I wait for them to say more, my ears straining in the dark room.

What do they mean? What can they feel?

But all I hear is the hum of the fan in the bathroom and Pip's soft snores. Finally, sleep claims me again.

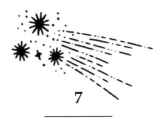

7

Stone

My friend very rarely asks for help. He's been my best friend these last ten years – since we met back in Arrow Hart Academy. He's not the best company. The dude is moody, takes himself far too seriously and is pretty anti-social. I rarely see him these days. But he's also loyal and a damn talented magical – his powers pretty much equal to mine.

So when he calls and says this assignment is different, when he says he needs my help to bring her in, to keep her safe, I don't hesitate.

Not that I wasn't cynical about the whole situation. I'm ashamed to say, I thought he had got it wrong. But I should have known better. My best friend doesn't do wrong.

I drag my hand down my tired face and through my beard. I took the second watch last night and sat in the dark, brooding about this situation.

This morning I'm exhausted, exhausted and slightly pissed off. What is it about fate? Why is it such a miserable bitch? Why can it never land me a break?

And why can't I shake this sense of doom? The idea that this bratty girl is going to lead us into trouble.

At dawn, my friend rises and silently heads for the bathroom. He returns ten minutes later dressed and ready to go. The girl doesn't stir.

"I'll wake her," I say.

My friend shakes his head. "Let her sleep some more."

I raise an eyebrow at him but he ignores me and stomps out of the room, muttering about coffee.

An hour later and my patience is running thin.

This isn't a holiday. I have places I need to be.

I stand and walk to the bed, ignoring my friend, and peering down at the girl. She's out cold. I wonder how anyone in such obvious danger can be so fucking stupid.

We're two men, twice her size, powerful magicals. We could slit her throat while she sleeps, we could rip her in half, we could ...

I clap my hands together, using my magic to amplify the sound tenfold.

Her eyes fly open in alarm and she bolts upright.

"What the fuck?" she mutters, all the hairs on her arms standing on end.

"Morning sleepy head," I say. "Time to get the fuck up. You have five minutes before I drag your ass out of here."

"Shit. What time is it?" she asks, yawning and stretching her arms above her head. She's like a cat, with her big honey eyes and her agile movements. She's almost feline. And she's small like a cat too. My friend is not wrong, the girl's clearly been half-starved.

"Seven."

"Seven? Is that all?"

"Not a morning person, huh?" I ask, strolling back to my cup of coffee.

"Usually I am up with the roosters. But today ... shit I'm stiff." She throws back the covers and stretches some more and I have to look away.

I catch my friend's eye as I do and I know what he's thinking.

The girl is pretty, with those big eyes, curved cheeks, and pink pouty mouth: dark hair all messed up like she's been rolling around in bed for hours.

She's also ten years younger than we are and his assignment. The sooner we hand her over, the better.

Which is why we need to get moving.

Her legs catch on the chains as she attempts to swing them from the bed and she scowls at me like she would like to murder me. Silently, I lift my hands and the chains melt away.

"I'm going to check the bikes," I mutter, turning towards the door.

"Those bikes can drive themselves – I've seen it. They're in tip-top condition. What do you need to check?"

"That they're still there."

Of course, she's right. Once I've ascertained that the bikes are still parked out of sight around the back of the motel, there's nothing else to check, apart from the gas levels. But you couldn't pay me to spend another minute in that room, watching as she moves around the place, humming under her breath in a way I'm sure she isn't aware of, the sweet perfume of her scent filling the air.

Out here the air stinks of gasoline and piss. It's a thousand times better.

I kick at the dirt until finally, my friend comes marching around the corner, the girl trotting to keep up with him, her stinky pig cradled in her arms like it's a goddamn baby.

"Ready?" I ask, climbing onto my bike.

"Ready," he replies, taking the pig from the girl and placing it in the box at the back of his bike. Then he slides onto the bike, the girl following after, her arms wrapped tightly around his waist. He squeezes her hand with his left gloved one and I raise my eyebrow at him a second time. He glares back at me, revving his engine and shooting away before I've had a chance to lock her to the bike.

I mutter a string of obscenities under my breath and follow after him.

I glare at him again when we stop for a late breakfast a couple of hours later and he orders the girl another bumper helping of the most expensive dish on the cheap diner's menu.

He doesn't do wrong and he also doesn't do emotional attachment. It doesn't go well with the job. But I'm beginning to suspect he's making an exception here. The idea makes my head ache.

My friend simply scowls right back at me, the message clear as day – if you dare say a word ...

I'm not going to. Not in front of the girl anyway. We can pick this to pieces once we're back in Los Magicos and the girl is the council's problem.

We skip lunch, stopping to pick up a burger from a truck by the side of the road in the late afternoon. After that the broken roads give way to smoother ones and we start to pass through more towns, eventually reaching the sprawling suburbs of the city.

The eyes of the little cat on the back of my friend's bike grow wide. She's never been anywhere but non-magical dead-end towns like the one we found her in and she takes in everything with wonder and awe. It would almost be cute if it wasn't so abundantly clear how wet behind the ears the girl is. Wet and fucking innocent. How the hell did she survive as long as she did on her own?

My friend says, for an untrained girl, her abilities are pretty efficient. He also said she couldn't even heal a stupid cut on her arm, and she couldn't unlock my chains, so I'm reserving my judgment on that front.

She's got a hell of a lot to learn. And not just about fucking magic.

Finally, we cruise through the center of Los Magicos. It's late on a Monday evening. The sun set long ago. The shops all have their shutters pulled down and the clubs and bars are closed tonight. It's still a sight. Bright lanterns hover above the street casting it in golden light and flowers bloom in baskets along the sidewalks. Unlike the run-down businesses we've been passing for the last two days, here everything is gleaming, clean and new. It looks and smells like money and I'm not surprised the girl's mouth is hanging open in amazement.

Gliding down the main street, the flags of the authorities lining the route and fluttering in the breeze, we near the Council building. It's a huge Georgian building, with magnificent white pillars flanking the front and a huge glass dome covering the whole of the roof.

The gates at the front are forged from a bronze metal and part as we approach, the guards on duty nodding at us in recognition. We circle the building, parking up in a side lot and jumping down from our bikes.

The girl pulls the helmet from her head and shakes out her hair. It's all rumpled from the ride and her cheeks are a vivid pink, her honey eyes sparkling.

"This place–"

My friend cuts her off. "We don't have time to hang about and gossip. We're expected." He points towards an entrance. It's not the main one with its intimidating doors, carved with magical illustrations, but I bet it's the grandest door she's passed through nonetheless. Her head tips back as she walks through and another set of guards acknowledge us before their eyes flick with curiosity to the girl. Instinctively, I step to her side and my friend to her other.

"Am I under arrest?" she hisses.

"It depends what the chancellor decides," my friend replies, his eyes trained forward.

We weave along some side corridors before meeting the main council hallway and climbing the wide sweeping staircase with its red velvet carpet and its golden banisters. Huge paintings hang from the walls depicting legendary battles between magicals from long ago and a huge glass dragon suspends from the ceiling, his ruby eyes gleaming and the fire from its hissing mouth lighting the cavernous space.

At the top, we meet several heavy doors, all carved from walnut wood, each handle formed of a different colored crystal. My friend pauses in front of the first, the handle a deep emerald. Another pair of guards stand either side of the doorway.

He whispers into the wood. Then he turns to me.

"The chancellor will see us now."

"Now?" The girl gulps. She finally seems nervous. The surroundings have intimidated her.

"Not you," he tells her. "Us."

"You? Why doesn't he want to see me?"

"I have to give my report before he will see you."

"Oh great," she says, rolling her eyes.

He glares at her, then, taking her by the elbow, leads her along the hallway to a row of seats. He pushes her down onto the first.

He points a finger in her face. "Stay put." She rolls her eyes again. "I'm serious."

"I'm not going anywhere." Although she's thinking about it.

My friend grunts and marches back to join me. Then we wait for the door to open.

I lean towards him. "Remember that time we got sent to see Principal Jacobs back in Arrow Hart?"

He grunts, his eyes fixed on the door. "We were lucky not to get expelled that day."

"It was worth it though, wasn't it? Just to see the look on old Professor Dickwad's face."

"He always hated us."

"He didn't hate you," I say, glancing down at my mud-splattered boots and jeans. "You had the right mommy and daddy."

"Yeah, but he didn't like the idea of me hanging around with riffraff like you." The corner of my friend's mouth tugs upward.

"Yeah, God forbid I might have led you astray."

"Encouraged me to help turn his precious manuscripts to dust."

"It was all your idea," I grumble. "Seems you're always dragging me into shit."

My friend turns his head, his eyes sharp on me.

"You think the situation we have here is a shitshow?"

"Fuck," I whisper, "you have to admit it's complicated. And you know," I swallow, "that this isn't what I wanted. Ever."

"Me neither," he says, but I don't know if I believe him.

He goes back to staring at the door.

I adjust my wrist watch, running my eyes over the reading it displays on its face. "Do you think we did the right thing bringing her in?"

"You think we should have let her go?" he scoffs. "Delivered her straight into the hands of the Wolves of Night?"

"No," I say firmly. "I'm just ... It's different for you." If the chancellor does as we expect and sends the girl to Arrow Hart Academy, my friend will swan off on his next assignment and never have to see the girl again. Me? It won't be that simple.

"It only changes things if we let it, Phoenix. Besides, since when did we fall in line with conventions?"

I chuckle. I can't argue with that. And maybe he's right.

The bolts on the door clunk and it starts to draw back.

Together we step through into the large office that is the Chancellor's.

I glance towards my friend, wondering just how much he'll tell.

8

Rhi

HEAVY BOOTS THUMP along the hallway, and I look up to find the man in black approaching. Slowly, with Pip in my arms, I rise to my feet.

"What's going on?" I ask.

"The Chancellor and Council have been debating your future."

"Oh, how very nice of them. They didn't think that I might want to be included in that discussion, I suppose?"

Instead of snapping back at me, he sighs, his face suddenly tired. "A piece of advice, keep your sharp tongue under control. Otherwise, all you'll achieve is pissing the Chancellor off and he'll come down on you like a ton of bricks."

I consider bolting. But not only will the man in black catch me in an instant but all the guards roaming this building too. No, escaping is going to have to be a long-term aim. It's clear it's not happening any time soon. That's fine. I will play along. Make them think I'm being compliant. Then when they least expect it, I'll run. Hopefully, by then I may have learned more about magic and I'll be able to look after myself and hide out better.

"Don't you see how unfair this is? Don't you think I should have a say?"

He works his jaw. "It's the way of things. You lost your right to choose when you failed to register yourself."

I stare at him. We both know that wasn't my choice.

"Just take me to them, will you? I want this over with." He opens his mouth to say more, but I'm half way down the corridor, Pip slung under my arm, trying not to appear as petrified as I am. These people I'm being summoned to see will know more than me and will be able to run circles around me with their clever words and superior knowledge.

Then there's the worry that they really will send me to this stupid school. I'm not good in social situations. It's rare I've been in a room with more than two other people at a time. But I've watched enough TV, read enough books, to appreciate the hell that is school. The only consolation I can think of is that at least the others there will be my age and I won't have the humiliation of having to hang out with a bunch of sixteen-year-olds. Perhaps it'll be less hormone-fueled and more sensible.

I stop outside the door he entered earlier, but he shakes his head and takes me down the grand staircase, underneath the dragon made of glass and halts in front of a set of steel doors, their surface decorated with a multitude of jewels. The wealth of this place makes me physically sick. It's literally dripping off the ceilings and the walls, lining the sidewalks. Yet there hadn't even been enough money back in my hometown to fix the park for the kids when it was damaged in a storm or to fund a decent hospital.

"Why here?" I snarl, knowing it's because they want to remind me I'm a nobody in the grand scheme of things.

"The Council has been discussing your future in the chamber. They have reached their decision."

"So quickly," I say with sarcasm.

His shoulders tighten but he doesn't rise to my bait, instead banging his fist against the door. The metal clangs as he does, a noise that reverberates around the large space, and a low voice from within announces 'enter'.

The man in black pushes open the doors and then stands to one side, beckoning for me to go through.

"You're not coming with me?" I say, alarmed.

"No. This is your fate," he says, his eyes darting away from me when he says that. "It has nothing to do with me."

Securing my grip on Pip, I lift my chin and stride defiantly into the chamber. I may be nervous, but there's no way in hell I'm going to show it. My footsteps falter, though, as my eyes adjust to the dimly lit room.

It's not just the aura of dominance that fills the room. There's something else about it too. Something that makes my skin crawl. This chamber is familiar. As if I've been here before.

The faces of at least ten men and women stare at me. They are all a lot older, dressed in expensive clothes, valuable jewels hanging from their ears and looping around their necks. The chamber walls are gilded with gold and above is the center of the glass dome, the night's sky somehow amplified so that the stars and planets appear as if I could reach out and touch them.

The men and women sit in a circle, except for a pale, bald man, his wrinkled skin almost translucent, a heavy chain around his neck and glasses resting on his nose. He is only slightly taller than me, but beside him a woman with much darker skin towers above him. Her silver hair is clipped in tight curls and she's dressed in a tweed skirt and matching jacket. I'm surprised she's not clutching a riding crop.

The man squints at me with shrewd eyes behind his glasses. "Miss Blackwaters."

I shake myself out of my trance and cross further into the room, stopping before the man and the woman.

"I am Chancellor Stermer," he tells me, not introducing the woman beside him who simply stares without blinking. "You are unregistered. Is this correct?"

"Yes," I say.

He waits for me to add more. When I don't, he frowns. "The Council has come to a decision about your fate."

Oh god, I want to make some snarky comment to this stuck-up man, but I bite down hard on my tongue, hard enough to draw blood, and wait for their decision.

"Failing to register your magical status with the authorities is a grave misdemeanor, punishable with a sentence of hard labor in the North of the country. Every magical has a responsibility to this great country to make themselves known, to accept the training the authorities provide and to stand ready to defend our people from attack."

I glare at him some more. I'm not averse to hard physical work and I'm not some coward.

"However," he continues, "given your young age, and what we believe may have been your aunt's influence on your thinking, you will not be feeling the full force of the authorities' hand. Miss Blackwaters, it is important that you understand this. We are showing leniency and mercy here. But do not test our patience. We will be watching you." He squints at me a second time as if to emphasize his words. "You will not be sent to the labor camps, nor will you be sent to the juvenile detention center. The Council has decided that, like other magicals your age, you will attend Arrow Hart Academy until you graduate in the year of your 21st birthday." The Chancellor gestures to the woman. "This is Professor York, principal of Arrow Hart Academy. She has kindly agreed to this unusual request made by the Council even though you are likely to be considerably behind your peers in terms of learning.

"The Council has agreed to loan you the money for your academy fees and board until you graduate," the Chancellor adds. "This loan will then need to be repaid in full after your graduation."

"Loan?" I gape at him. "I don't have any money."

An academy sounds expensive. Something I could never afford.

"After the academy, you will take up a position in the defense forces, like every other young magical, and will be paid a wage accordingly. One which I'm sure will allow you to pay off any debts."

It's not something I actually need to worry about. I'll be long gone before graduation. Just as well. Plunging me into debt seems like a perfect way for the authorities to keep me under their heels. It's looking like my aunt wasn't so wrong about them.

"Fine," I say. The Chancellor smirks. "Just as long as I can bring my pig," I add.

What follows is a lengthy argument between me and the Chancellor, me and the principal, and me and various Council members. Nobody thinks Arrow Hart Academy is a suitable place for a pig. I disagree. If it's suitable for me, it's suitable for him. After half an hour of going round in circles, the Chancellor's face growing redder and redder with frustration by the minute, as if it might pop, he shouts:

"Would you prefer we sent you to the labor camp, Miss Blackwaters?"

"If I could take my pig, then, yes!"

Principal York's lips twitch.

"The pig may come to Arrow Hart Academy, Miss Blackwaters." The Chancellor growls but the principal silences him with an obviously practiced smile. "But he must remain in your room–"

"He needs outdoor space."

"I believe there is a patch of grass outside your dorm room."

I swallow. Dorm?

"Thank you," I manage to mumble.

"But," she adds, "you will be required to undertake additional chores as payment for this exceptional dispensation."

Whatever. I've been running our smallholding alone for the last year. A few chores at some stuck up college will be child's play in comparison. In fact, apart from the gut-wrenching social side of things, I'm expecting my life to be a lot easier at this flashy college than it ever was back home.

9

R^{hi}

"ARROW HART ACADEMY," the principal announces as our car rounds a corner an hour later.

I can't help but press my nose to the window of the car and peer out at the building that will be my home for the next year and a half.

It looks like some old English mansion, stolen from the countryside and deposited here on the brow of a hill. Its walls are a sandstone yellow with turrets circling its roof and manicured lawns running up to its doors. Other buildings crouch behind but I can't make them out yet. What is clear though, is that out here, far from the city, the campus is sprawling and isolated. There are no other houses, not even a farm or some small hovel, in sight.

I'm not sure how I feel about that. I'm used to living far away from everyone else, but it will make it harder to escape when I choose to and, though I hate to admit it, I was rather looking forward to exploring Los Magicos.

"Before we arrive, I will make you aware of some of the fundamental rules of this academy," Principal York says, diverting my attention. "The breaking of which will lead to your suspension and possibly your expulsion, and ultimately grave consequences for your future. You are here as a magical to train with the others as is required by the law set by the authorities. Every magical has a responsibility to protect this country and that is only possible if you have studied accordingly."

I nod. I don't give a shit about any rules, about being expelled or about training for some perceived threat.

"Firstly, it goes without saying that pupils are forbidden from using their magical powers against another pupil or on one another. The only exception to this rule is if you are given permission to use your powers in such a way by a teacher in one of your lessons."

"I understand," I say, somewhat relieved. It hadn't occurred to me that the students might use their powers like that, but now I think of it, it makes obvious sense. Why use your fists when you can use your magic instead?

"Secondly, you are not permitted to leave the campus grounds without permission."

"Seriously?" I say.

"Entirely. Thirdly, student accommodation is split by gender. You will be in a female dorm. You are not permitted to receive visitors into your dorm building, especially those of the opposite sex. In fact, I would advise you to concentrate on your studies while you are here given the fact that you are behind, and put any romantic thoughts out of your head entirely."

"That won't be a problem," I insist.

"I would hope not." She eyes me. "Those are the rules I consider most important. You will find a copy of the academy prospectus in your room with a more detailed list of the other rules you must follow while you are here as well as setting out an expected code of conduct regarding behavior." The principal runs a palm over the tweed material of her skirt. "It's late, Miss Blackwaters–"

"Rhi."

"–and after your long journey, I'm sure you would like to get to bed." I don't know. I doubt I will sleep a wink tonight. "So I will show you straight to your dorm room. You will need a good night's sleep before the first of your classes tomorrow."

"Classes?" I wasn't expecting to be dropped straight into classes. I'd hoped for a bit of one-on-one tuition first to at least give me a fighting chance of catching up.

"Yes, I may have allowed you to bring your pig," her lip curls as she glances down at Pip lying tummy up, with his legs in the air, "but that will be the only exception I will allow you to enjoy. You will be held to the same rules and standards as the rest of my students, all of whom will be attending classes tomorrow. A timetable awaits you in your room."

As she finishes her words, I realize we are already here, parking up outside the entrance to Arrow Hart Academy. But I've no time to take in the towering building, because the principal is out of the car and calling for me to follow, her brown brogues crunching the gravel as she walks around the mansion. I scoot out of the car, slinging my one bag on my shoulder and scooping up Pip. How long will this sleeping spell last exactly because I'm getting pretty tired of carrying his highness everywhere?

It's dark, but as with the Los Magicos streets, lanterns appear above our heads as we walk around the buildings, lighting our path. We weave our way around a huge glass plant house, a squat building with tall chimneys and what looks like a gymnasium, and find our way into what I assume is the student accommodation. There are blocks of rooms; the first few we pass clearly luxurious from what I manage to peek through the windows, huge rooms all done up like palaces. They become less and less luxurious as we walk, until we reach a grotty-looking block at the edge of the cluster of buildings, a forest lurking behind it. Paintwork peels from the building's facade; I can see at least one broken window covered up with cardboard, and the few light bulbs I can spot hanging in rooms inside are all bare.

Seems whatever amazing powers these magicals are learning doesn't extend to repairing run-down buildings.

"This is the accommodation the Council has chosen for you. You will be sharing a first floor room with a student in your year."

"I'm sharing a room?"

"The fees for sharing a room are considerably cheaper, Miss Blackwaters."

"Oh." I guess I'll have to suck it up then.

The principal seems reluctant to enter the block, but she takes a breath in and steps inside, stopping outside the second door and tapping on the wood.

The door flings back immediately and a girl with two long shiny braids and bright pink pajamas bounces out to greet us.

"Is this her?" she says with a wide smile that reveals a heavy pair of metal retainers. Seems these magicals can't fix their teeth either.

"Miss Wence, this is your new roommate, Miss Blackwaters," the principal says with her usual blank expression. The girl practically bounces on her toes, her braids leaping up and down. "I will leave her with you now. I am hoping you will show her the ropes."

"Of course, Professor York," she says, grabbing my wrist and pulling me into the room.

"Thank you. Good night ladies."

"Good night," the other girl calls, shutting the door and spinning around to face me.

I dart my gaze around the room. It's about as run down inside this building as it looked from outside. The room is small, with a large damp spot across the ceiling and a bunkbed pushed up against the wall. On the other side are a pair of rickety desks sitting side by side and one wardrobe, its doors hanging crooked.

"It isn't much," the girl says, watching me take in our room, "but I've tried my best to spruce it up." She has. Fairy lights stream around the window as well as strings of fake spring flowers. Some bright works of art are pinned to the walls as well as a few posters of men and women I don't recognize. "Plus it's the cheapest room the college has." She smiles and flops down on the bottom bunk. "I was beginning to worry I'd have to pay full whack for the room after Saskia left last term. I didn't think I'd find another roommate."

"Saskia?"

"My old roommate."

"Why did she leave?" I ask with suspicion.

The girl's eyes grow sad. "Her mum got sick, and she had to go home to help with her brothers and sisters."

"And the authorities let her? I thought it was compulsory to attend this college."

"She was already 21, and she'd accrued enough points to graduate." The girl twists one of the braids around her fingers. "My name's Winnie by the way. Short for Winifred." She pulls a face.

"Rhi," I tell her, "short for Rhianna."

"Oh, that's a nice name. Your parents aren't cruel like mine. They named me after some pioneering magical from like two centuries ago."

"I don't know why they named me Rhianna. They died when I was young."

Sympathy floods her face. "I'm sorry."

I shrug, walking to the empty desk and lowering Pip and my bag to the surface.

"Where have you transferred from?" Winnie asks as I start to pull my few possessions from my rucksack, "and when do all your other things arrive? We don't have a lot of space for stuff so I hope–"

"This is all I have."

Winnie blinks as I lay out a pair of jeans, a pair of shorts, another hoodie and a couple of tees.

"Well ... we have to wear our uniforms most of the time anyway, so you don't need that much I guess." She looks a little unsure. "Why didn't you bring more? Can't your old school send stuff or something?"

"I didn't come from school. In fact I've never been to school." I hear Winnie's sharp intake of breath as I stroll over to the bed and pull off the spare blanket slung over the end. I use it to make a little nest in the space next to my desk and lay Pip up in it all cozy. I wait for her to ask about my pig, but that last piece of information must have been enough of a bombshell to distract her.

"You've never been to school?! How ... How is that possible? All magicals have to attend school. Were you sick or something?"

"Only *registered* magicals have to attend school," I say, stripping down to my panties and vest. "Is there somewhere to brush my teeth?"

Winnie points to a small sink hidden in the corner by the window. Heaven only knows where there's a toilet and a shower. I run a line of toothpaste over the bristles of my toothbrush and march over to the sink.

"You're ... you're unregistered?" Winnie asks in a voice several octaves higher than it was a minute ago.

"I was. I'm guessing I'm registered now." I shrug and shove

my toothbrush under the trickle of cold water. I notice the basin is cracked and the thin carpet damp around the pedestal. I scrub my teeth, spit, rinse and turn to find Winnie gaping at me like a red alien with ten arms and four heads just landed in her room.

"Unregistered?" she whispers.

"I'll tell you all about it in the morning," I say, jumping up onto the top bunk, the springs of the mattress groaning under my weight as Winnie climbs into the bottom. "Oh my god, is this thing even safe?" I ask as I sink into the soft belly of the mattress. "It's not going to collapse and crush you in the night, is it?"

"Saskia was about twice your size and we never had any problems," she says in a weak voice. Then she snaps her fingers and the light extinguishes, plunging us into darkness apart from a sliver of moonlight that creeps in through the gap in the cheap curtains. "How could you be unregistered?" I hear her mumble.

I sigh. "It's complicated."

"I bet!" I hear her shift on her mattress. "Rhi?" she says after a minute.

"Yes?"

"I'm hoping we're going to be good friends, at the very least civil roomies, so can I offer you a word of advice?"

"Sure." I have a feeling I'm going to need all the advice I can get navigating this new social situation.

"Maybe don't go around telling everyone you were unregistered."

"Why not?" I'm not ashamed of who I am and I don't care what anyone may think of me.

"I'm guessing you haven't been around many magicals. Unregistereds are pretty much despised amongst the magical community – I know you must have your reasons but ... They're considered the lowest of the low."

I chew my thumb. "That's what you think of me?"

"I only just met you. I have no opinion of you yet. But I'm super stoked to have a roomie again and not just to save on the money. Like I said, I hope we can be friends."

I nod into the darkness. "Why do people think like that?"

"Oh gosh," she says. "The authorities have done a pretty good job at telling us all how awful the unregistered magicals are."

"And people believe everything the authorities tell them?"

Winnie laughs, not answering my question and soon I hear her soft snores.

I think I'll be awake for ages, staring up at the moldy ceiling, listening to the alternate snores of Winnie and Pip, contemplating what fresh hell awaits me in the morning.

But I'm asleep before I know it.

10

R^{hi}

I'M WOKEN by the sound of loud snorting and a series of screams from below me. The light snaps on and I shield my eyes, roll over and peer down towards the floor.

Pip is awake and racing up and down the length of Winnie's bed. Winnie is sitting on her mattress, her knees clutched to her chest as if she's about to be attacked by a pack of rabid wolves.

"What the hell is that?" she squeals.

I swing my legs off the bed and drop down onto the floor. "My pig, Pip. Excuse his manners, but he hasn't eaten for two days."

Pip comes trotting up to me, bumping his wet snout against my bare legs.

"Y-y-your pig." She blinks at me like she did before we went to bed, like my words don't quite compute.

"Yes, he's my pet."

"We're not allowed pets in Arrow Hart. If Professor York finds out–"

"The principal gave me permission to keep him here. As long as he stays in my room or on the patch of grass outside our window."

"She did." Winnie's face morphs from pale to green. "He's small now, but don't pigs grow really big? Don't they eat humans?"

"He is fully grown," I say, crouching down and tickling his ears. Usually that action calms him the heck down, but today he's too hungry and snorts at me angrily. "He was the runt of the litter. That's why we named him Pipsqueak and that's why we kept him."

"We?"

"Me and my aunt." The light filtering in from the gap in the window is gray and I'm guessing it's almost sunrise, 6am thereabouts. "It's really early. When do we have to be up?"

"7 am."

"Right, then I'll take him outside so as not to disturb you." And so Pip can relieve himself. He's giving me that cross-eyed look which means he really needs to pee.

Tugging on my yoga pants and grabbing my bag as quickly as I can, I open the window, bundle Pip into my arms and climb out.

"What are you doing?" Winnie demands.

"Going to feed Pip," I say, like duh.

"You can use the door you know," she mumbles, clicking the lights off with a snap of her fingers and flopping back down into the bed.

I close the window behind me and rifle through my bag until I find the bits of leftover breakfast and lunch I managed to smuggle away while I was eating with the man in black and Stone. I drop it onto the floor and, after he does his business, relief flooding his face, Pip skips over and starts to demolish the lot.

I sit down on the grass, damp with dew, and hook out some more of the smuggled food. I was hoping it would last a few meals, but obviously not.

As Pip eats, I watch the sun rise over the looming figure of the distant mansion, painting it a fine gold, and then examine my surroundings in the daylight. We're at the highest point of the hill here and I can see how the land falls away into lush meadows and fields of grass, the occasional copse of trees speckling the pattern and a meandering blue river cutting through it. On the horizon are the tall buildings of Los Magicos, and at my back are the dark trees of the forest.

Pip finishes his food and climbs into my lap, nudging my hand with his snout until I oblige and offer up tummy-tickles.

I'm just bending down to kiss the crown of his head, when I hear the pounding of many pairs of feet. My spine stiffening, I sit up and watch as a line of a dozen girls come running towards me. I brace myself, ready for a fight, until I realize they aren't heading for me after all, just following the path that leads to the woods.

All of them are dressed in matching black velvet shorts and hoodies, the crest of the Arrow Hart Academy pinned to their breasts, their shorts so small I can practically see their underwear. Most of them have their hoodies zipped down low too, displaying their impressive cleavage and their hair is swept up into high pony tails that bounce along with their boobs as they run.

I can't help squeezing my arms against my chest, thinking how painful that looks. But these girls don't seem to feel any pain, in fact, despite the pace they're running, they haven't broken a sweat, all their perfectly made-up faces intact. It looks like someone just broke into the Playboy mansion and ordered all the bunnies out for a race.

As they near me, twelve pairs of eyes, most of them framed by false eyelashes, land on me. Several manicured brows arch, several of the pairs of eyes drop to the blissed-out pig on my lap. Several hands rise to cover mouths and I watch them whispering as they run. Then there's laughing and giggling and the girl leading the pack screeches to a halt right in front of me. She has long blonde hair, so blonde it's almost white, large piercing violet eyes and legs so long they seem to go on and on forever.

She rests her hands on her hips and sneers down her upturned nose at me.

"And who the hell are you?" she demands. Her tone is so damn aggressive, I peer behind me, almost expecting to find someone else lurking there behind me.

"Who? Me?" I ask, pointing to my chest.

"Well, duh!" she says, rolling her eyes. "Who else?"

"Rhianna." She glares at me. "Oh, Rhianna Blackwaters."

"You're new?"

I'm oh so tempted to roll my eyes back at her, but I refrain. I may have a lack of social skills but I've no intention of making enemies on my first day. I stick with a safe, "Yes."

"And what the hell is that?" She waves a painted fingernail in my direction.

"A pig," I say simply. "He's my pet."

Her nose wrinkles and her lip curls. "Were you kissing it?" I don't answer, something in her tone tells me I'm better off if I don't. She turns to her friends. "She was, wasn't she?" Most of the girls nod obediently. "It probably has fleas or rabies or worse." She laughs, cocking her head to one side. "I don't know what backward country you've transferred from, but this is Arrow Hart Academy – an elite academy for magicals – not a farmyard. And people don't bring their 'pets'," she makes inverted commas with her fingers, "to school. You should send it home immediately."

I shake my head and the girl arches her eyebrow.

"I don't want a pig on campus, smelling like shit and ruining my morning run."

"Right," I say, wondering why she would think I care.

"So you'll be getting rid of it immediately," she says, lifting her chin.

"No," I say, "the pig's staying."

The girl's violet eyes narrow. "I'm sorry, you're new, and so you probably don't understand. I'm Summer Clutton-Brock and when I say jump, you say, how high?"

"Why?" I ask her. My interactions with people my own age may have been limited but I've watched enough movies to suspect that this girl is used to the world falling at her feet. That's not really my style.

"Because," she says, flicking her head. "And I don't want that stinky little pig around polluting the air that I have to breathe."

"Then don't breathe the air near him."

She huffs in irritation, her eyes narrowing to fine slits and she takes a step towards me, lowering her voice so the audience can't hear.

"You're going to regret this, Pig Girl."

I simply stare at her, as she straightens up again, a beaming smile of perfectly white teeth forming over her face.

"Come on girls, let's go. Unlike this new girl, I have no intention of smelling like a dirty little pig."

Summer sets off, and her band of girls jog obediently behind her.

"Who is she?" I hear one ask as they run past me and into the woods, several peering over their shoulders to look back at me and laugh.

Finally, their footfall dies away, swallowed up by the wood, and I sit there stunned. What the fuck was that? I feel like I just endured five years of High School on speed setting.

The window opens above my head and Winnie pokes her head out.

"Are they gone?" she asks, her eyes darting towards the wood.

"Who? The bouncing bunnies?" Winnie jerks at my words as if they might land us in trouble. "Yeah, they're gone. Who are they?"

I stand up, realizing the seat of my pants are damp through.

"The cheerleading squad. They run this route every morning. I think they do it just to wake everyone on campus up and remind all the guys how hot they are."

"Ahh they are hoping to imprint."

"What?"

"Like chickens."

"Right," Winnie says, clearly not following my thinking.

I glance back at the woods. "There are so many of them."

"Yep, and they pretty much rule the school so best to keep your head down while they're around unless you want Summer to make your life a misery. She's head cheerleader."

"Right. Well, I'm not particularly interested in joining any squad. In fact, sports aren't really my thing."

"They're going to have to be. Arrow Hart Academy is sports mad," Winnie sighs, "you can't not take part."

We'll see about that. No way in hell someone's making me wear a pair of those shorts and subjecting my tits to that kind of torture.

"Come on," Winnie beckons to me, "we're going to be late for breakfast." I go to climb inside the window and she points at Pip. "How about him?"

"He'll be all right out here. I'll bring him in later."

"He won't run away?"

I chuckle. "Pip? Run away? Errr no." I lean towards her and whisper in her ear. "He's not that smart."

Pip grunts as if he heard me and I blow him a kiss, much to Winnie's obvious disgust.

Winnie leads me down the corridor to the communal bathrooms, passing several other dorms as we do. As we pass one, I notice a bow tied around the door handle, and loud moans coming from within.

"Looks like Pen and Juan are at it again," Winnie mutters. "They are permanently on again, off again."

"I thought there was a strict no-boys-in-the-dorm rule."

"Oh that." Winnie waves her hand through the air as the moans from the room become louder and more high pitched, "Everyone ignores that rule. The teachers never enforce them. It's simply for show – this is an elite academy after all. They don't want people thinking the students are humping like rabbits rather than training to become the future protectors of our country."

A female voice screams out accompanied by a low male grunt and Winnie peers at the door.

"Sounds like they're done."

"Everyone's humping like rabbits?" I ask, feeling a little sick.

"I wish," Winnie says whimsically. "Sometimes it feels like everyone else is and I'm the only one who isn't."

I glance at my new roommate. She's unwound her braids this morning and her dark hair flows in waves down her back. She's also lost the retainer. If she can't get a date, then there is no hope I ever will. Which is a good thing. Those two men set my hormones in a dizzying cartwheel and I am happy for them to calm the fuck down now and leave me in peace.

The bathroom is as moldy as the rest of the building, with water that's barely lukewarm.

"It's not too bad," Winnie insists, as she braces herself and ducks under the torrent, a flowery shower cap balanced on her head. "Besides, it encourages short showers which is better for the environment and student relationships."

"Sure," I mutter, ducking under as well.

When we return to our dorm room ten minutes later, me with dripping wet hair, there's a full college uniform hanging on the wardrobe door.

"Oh," Winnie says, "that must be for you."

"I'm not wearing that!" I say glaring at the tartan pleated skirt, thigh-high socks, white blouse, blazer and matching beret. It looks like someone typed in sexy school girl to the internet and had this delivered – although I have to admit the material and craftsmanship are obviously of a high quality.

"Why not?" Winnie says, opening the wardrobe door and pulling out an identical, if more worn, uniform from within and stepping into her clothes.

"Because I'm a twenty-year-old woman, not a six-year-old girl."

Winnie shrugs. "It's mandatory and anyway I like it," she says. "Green isn't so bad which is some kind of miracle considering it could have been maroon or scarlet."

"I don't care. There is no way in hell I'm wearing it."

I pull out my jeans, a plain t-shirt and my hoodie as Winnie examines my uniform more closely.

"Looks like you're in Venus House," Winnie says, pointing to a small, pink badge pinned to my blazer.

"I'm in a house?"

Winnie smiles. "Of course you are."

"No one told me!"

She points to her own badge. "I'm in Neptune."

"Hence the blue. Are there seven houses, then?"

"No, five. Venus, Mars, Jupiter, Neptune and Mercury. All the Roman gods."

"Why was I put in Venus?"

She shrugs. "They do it before we get here. Apparently they look at your academic records, fitness scores and social profile and decide which house is the best fit."

I don't have an academic record, fitness record or a social profile (that I know of), so why the hell did they put me in Venus and what does it mean?

"Does being in a house actually make a difference? I mean, no one mentioned it at all."

"The sporting events take place between the houses and some academic competitions too. Plus there are mandatory house events each term."

I nod, dressing quickly and running a brush through my tangled locks.

"Aren't you going to dry your hair?" Winnie asks as she straightens her beret on her head.

"I would but I didn't bring a hairdryer with me."

Winnie does that blinking thing again. I'm beginning to realize it means she doesn't understand me.

"Errr can't you just dry it with your magic?"

Now it's my turn to blink. "I ... erm ... I ..." I'm too embarrassed to tell her I don't know how but she figures it out for herself.

"Here, let me." She raises her hands, whispers under her breath, and a blast of warm air sweeps my way, drying my hair almost immediately and leaving it tangle free. "Want me to do your makeup too?" I notice she's added mascara to her light eyelashes and gloss to her lips.

"No, I'm good," I tell her, not wanting her to know I'm a bigger freak than she already does and have never actually worn makeup before. Why would I have bothered? There was never anyone around to impress.

Winnies takes a hesitant look at me. "You sure you don't want to wear that uniform. You'll–"

"Nope. Seriously, I'm happy in this."

"Okay," she says, shaking her head, and picking up a bag with large books sticking out. "Oh, they sent me your timetable before you got here last night. You're in all my classes today which means I can show you around."

"Thanks, Winnie," I say, more relieved than I'd admit.

She steps towards the door and I follow. She peers over her shoulder at me, halts and I walk straight into her back.

"Oof," we both say.

"Have you got your notepad and pen?" she asks slowly like she's addressing a small child.

"I don't have one."

More blinking. Then she rushes to her desk, tugs open a drawer and pulls out a pad and pen for me. She cringes slightly as she hands it to me.

"Sorry," she says. The pad is covered in rainbows and unicorns. "My Grandma got it for me. I think she forgets sometimes that I'm no longer five."

"Thank you, it's fine, honestly."

"Come on, we'd better grab our breakfast, or we'll be late." She pushes me out of the door and I follow her along the path.

The campus is much busier than it was last night or this morning. Other students hurry along the paths, emerging from doorways or call to one another out of windows. All of them are wearing the uniform – the guys dressed in the same green tartan blazers, although they get to wear navy trousers and no silly hats – and I realize I've made a big mistake, because dressed in my jeans and hoodie, I stick out like a penguin in a flock of peacocks. Great! People's heads turn to stare at me as we stride past, and there's whispering and nudging. I try to hide the rainbow pad under my arm, failing miserably.

I'm somewhat relieved when we reach the back entrance of the mansion and duck inside.

"We're eating in here?" I ask.

"Yep, students eat in the Great Hall." She beckons me along a corridor lined with portraits of what I gather are past students and through an internal pair of wooden doors.

The noise hits me first, scores of voices bouncing off the stone walls and high ceilings, accompanied by the clink of cutlery against plates.

By the entrance of the hall is a service station where several women dressed in white aprons are ladling out food onto the plates of waiting students. Beyond them are four long wooden tables running the length of the hall with benches tucked underneath and a final table raised on a slight platform at the far end. Above this high table glitters a multitude of stained glass windows depicting battles including several more dragons and other creatures I've never seen before. Along the other walls hang more portraits and four suits of armor guard the corners of the hall.

As we join the back of the line for food, I realize I was wrong to feel relieved. Every eye in the hall seems to swivel my way and for a few agonizing minutes the hall falls into deadly silence before erupting into that roar of chatter again.

"What was that?" I whisper to Winnie.

"You're new, and, erm, not dressed in uniform, people are curious."

Curious and obviously possessing some ability to seek out new people. It's as if everywhere I go there's a big sign flashing above my head, reading: new girl, new girl.

Talking of senses, my own blare so loudly with the proximity of all these magicals that I'm going to have a raging headache by the end of the day. I need to find a way to tamper down this sense or ignore it. One of my teachers might be able to help me with that. Then again I suspect my ability to sense and track other magicals is probably an ability I want to keep to myself. For now anyway. My aunt said it was a rare gift.

When we reach the front of the line, a large woman with ruddy cheeks glares at me with suspicion, and addresses Winnie.

"Only thing left is porridge."

Winnie answers in an overly high-pitched voice, "Lovely, we'll take two."

The woman slops spoonfuls of a gray sludge into two bowls and passes them over.

As we walk away to try to find some seats, Winnie leans in, "Oh God, the porridge is the worst. I think I may go without."

We carry our bowls down the row between the tables, passing that group of bouncing bunnies again. They're out of the velvet shorts and in their uniforms now, although somehow their skirts seem no longer than the shorts did. They all watch as we pass, Winnie keeping her head down and her eyes to the floor. I take the opposite approach, staring at each one as I pass.

The one with white-blonde hair sneers at me as I meet her eye and elbows the boy sitting next to her. His attention is captured by his phone but he looks up and our gazes lock. He is possibly the best looking man I've ever seen. Chiseled cheekbones, clear, light skin, bright green eyes and a flop of golden hair. He looks like every illustration of a prince in every fairytale book I owned as a kid.

His gaze flips down to take me in and he frowns, his lip curling. I guess he's not as impressed with my appearance as I am with his.

"Look what the cat dragged in," Summer says in a voice so loud the entire hall hears. "I swear I can smell that pig."

I glare back at her, but Winnie grabs my elbow and tugs me away.

"I definitely smell pig. She smells worse than the porridge," Summer calls after me and everyone on her table erupts into laughter.

"Just ignore them," Winnie hisses under her breath. "They're establishing their authority. If you don't rise to it, soon they will get bored and leave you alone."

"Who were the others with the bouncing bunnies?" I ask, unable to help but glance back at the prince. He's back to staring at his phone and I notice the boy sitting on his other side. He's huge, nearly as big as the man in black, his skin dark and his hair clipped short.

"Who do you think?" Winnie says, climbing onto the last seat on the bench. "The popular kids. Insanely good looking, obscenely rich."

I tear my eyes from their little group, noting they've chosen to sit right in the center of the hall where everyone can see them, and take a seat across from Winnie.

I'm starving this morning, but as I drag a spoon through the slop, I think Winnie has a point about this porridge. Could I smuggle it to Pip somehow? He eats anything.

"You have to get here early if you want any chance of finding something half decent to eat," Winnie says, resting her chin in her hand and pushing her bowl away.

"I'm sorry if I made us late," I say, deciding to brave at least a mouthful of the porridge. It's lumpy, chewy and cold. I have to swallow three times before I can force the stuff down my throat.

"It's all right. It was just as much my fault."

"Can we get food from anywhere else?"

Winnie shakes her head. "My mom sends me stuff in the post but I'm out right now. There's the vending machines over by the gym but the jocks from the dueling team guard those like they're crown jewels."

"Dueling team?"

"Dueling team. The normies have their football, we have dueling."

Do I even want to know what dueling involves?

My stomach rumbles.

"Is there nowhere else we can grab food?"

"Nope, we just have to wait until lunch."

Lunch? My stomach growls more violently at the prospect. If I had any money to use in a vending machine, I'd march there right now, jocks be damned.

I rub my stomach and peer around, catching the eyes of several other students staring my way despite the fact Winnie has chosen the end of the far right corner of the table, tucked away as much out of sight as it's possible to be in this hall.

"Am I stopping you from sitting with your friends?" I ask, suddenly guilty that, not only have I deprived my new roomie of her breakfast, but also her usual social interactions.

Winnie's gaze drops towards the tabletop and she scratches her thumbnail over the surface.

"I don't really have any other friends. I mean, Saskia was my best friend, but she's gone now."

"You don't have other friends?" I blurt out inadvertently in astonishment, feeling even more guilty when Winnie's face bleeds bright red.

"Money and power talks here," Winnie whispers over the table. "So if you don't have any like me, if your parents don't sit on the Council, it's near impossible to gain any friends."

"Right," I say, "well, that sounds stuck-up and seriously shitty."

Winnie manages a smile. "It is both, trust me." Then she shakes herself and that air of cheerfulness returns. "But I'm extremely grateful to be here and learning everything I am."

"And living in a smelly hole with damp and a cracked window."

This time she actually laughs, a noise that stops abruptly when her gaze lands on something above my head.

I turn, and find Stone standing directly behind my chair, looking as surprised to see me as I am to see him. No, scratch that, it's not surprise, it's disdain. His gaze travels down my form and then he grabs my upper arm and pulls me to my feet.

"What the Hell!" I screech.

"Come with me please, Miss Blackwaters."

11

R^{hi}

I'M TOO shocked to reply, or to make any kind of fight, my feet moving automatically as he marches me down the row between the tables, out of the hall, and into a corridor. That strange magical hook dragging me after him. Half way down the hallway, I finally come to and regain my voice.

"What are you doing?" I say, attempting to shake off his firm grip with absolutely no luck at all. "What are you even doing here, Stone?"

"Professor Stone."

I jolt to a stop, my heels digging into the carpet beneath our feet, and he's forced to stop too.

"What?! Professor Stone?!" I glance down at what he's wearing. No jeans and leather jacket today. No, he's wearing a very-well-cut dark suit that emphasizes his physique and is at complete odds to the biker I met two days ago. "You work here?"

His eyes dart along the corridor. "Come on," he says, tugging on my arm and forcing me to walk again.

"You never told me you worked here," I hiss as we march up a flight of stairs and down two more corridors.

"You never asked."

"You lied to me."

"How exactly did I lie to you, Miss Blackwaters?" he asks, stopping outside a door with his name inscribed on it. Yep, there's no doubting it. He really is *Professor* Stone, the letters glaring back at me in gold paint.

"You didn't tell me you worked here. That you were one of the teachers."

He yanks a key from his pocket, thrusts it into the lock and waves his hand in front of the mechanism whispering something as he does. I need to get better at hearing so I can copy these damn spells.

"That wasn't a lie," he says, slamming open the door and dragging me inside.

I expect to find myself in an office, but it isn't, it's a small classroom. A giant blackboard lining the back wall, a desk placed in front and then rows of chairs facing that way. Objects hang from the ceiling and are pinned to the walls, but I have no chance to look at them as he pulls me to the back of the classroom and into another room. This seems to be his office – another desk, a leather-backed chair and a large bookcase within.

"It was a lie by omission," I tell him as we finally come to a stop and he spins me around to face him.

He rolls his eyes in that stupidly infuriating manner that tells me he thinks I'm childish.

"Why aren't you wearing your uniform?" he barks at me,

crossing his arms over his broad chest and making the arms of his jacket pull against his biceps.

"Because I didn't want to."

"You want to get expelled?"

I stare at him. "Yes, actually, I would, although I think that would be highly unlikely. You and the authorities have exerted a lot of effort dragging me here. Everyone keeps telling me attendance is compulsory. I can't see anyone expelling me any time soon."

He grunts. "You don't know York. Just because she made a ridiculous exception and let you bring that stinky pig–"

"He isn't stinky!"

"–doesn't mean she's going to go easy on you. Break the rules and she'll have no problem slinging you out of here. Then see where you end up. She doesn't tolerate troublemakers."

"I'm not a troublemaker."

"Really? You see anyone else out of their uniform this morning?"

"It's ridiculous! The skirt is obscenely short," I point to my thighs, drawing his eyes there, "and as for the socks ... It's highly sexualized–"

"It's the uniform. It's the rules. You obey them or you're out."

I shake my head slowly. "I don't care if they expel me."

He considers me, leaning back against the desk. "They'll send you to the detention center, or worse a labor camp."

They won't. I won't hang around for them to send me to either of those places.

Stone tilts his head to one side. "You won't last five minutes on the run."

I suck in a breath. How did he know that's what I was thinking?

"Really? Because I lasted four days last time," I say.

"That was before you killed Marcus Lowsky's favorite brother."

"Me?"

"You." He uncrosses his hands and rests them by his sides. "You know who he is?"

"No," I say quietly, thinking of my knife and that skull.

"He's the leader of the Wolves of Night, and I certainly bet you know who they are."

I nod, chewing on my thumb.

"There's a price on your head now, Blackwaters."

I peer into his eyes, trying to decipher if this is all bullshit to keep me here. "They won't know it's me."

"Your magical fingerprints will be all over that knife. The knife you left in his little brother Joey's head."

I swallow down vomit. "What do you mean?"

He sighs. "You are so ridiculously ignorant. If you'd been to school, you'd know this stuff." I simply glare at him. "A magical who uses an object for a serious purpose like murder leaves their fingerprints with the object. Fingerprints that can never be wiped away, not with magic, not with time. A skilled tracker, some of whom work for gangs like the Wolves of Night, can read those fingerprints and link them to their owner."

He shifts against the desk and smirks at me in that cold manner. "They've already linked the knife to you. They already knew what you looked like. Now they have your name too. Marcus Lowsky has put a price on your head. Dead or alive he wants you to face retribution for the murder of his brother."

"It wasn't murder, I was saving…"

I stare at the floor; unlike the other floorboards we marched across, these are not highly polished, in fact they're scuffed and worn away.

"Why didn't the man in black tell me? Why did he let me leave my knife for them to find?"

"He had a job to do, Miss Blackwaters: to bring you in. And

that's just what he did. What happens to you next is of no interest to him."

Despite myself, my heart drops. Of course. Why would the man in black care about me?

We're silent, his breath and mine the only noise in this small stuffy office that smells far too strongly of his woody scent.

"Don't be a fool. You're safe here. Arrow Hart Academy is one of the most secure and highly protected places in the magical world."

"Protected? We're in the middle of nowhere!"

"Exactly. The next generation of magicals are precious and must be protected at all costs while they train for their futures."

"Funny, a moment ago you said they'd expel me."

"York will if you don't follow the rules. Let me be clear." His eyes roam over my face and down my body, his lip curling in disgust. "You're a nobody. No one's daughter, no one's god daughter, no one's charge. Until yesterday you weren't even registered. You have no unusual powers or abilities that make you worthy of protection. Nobody cares about you, nobody is going to give a damn if you go missing. You run away – you get yourself expelled – it'll be a matter of hours, not days, before Marcus Lowsky lays his hands on you. And then you'll be dead and no longer a problem for the authorities or this school."

I glance away from him, his words stabbing deep in my heart. I used to have someone who gave a damn, who cared about me, so much so she spent her life protecting me and keeping me hidden.

"Why was she keeping you hidden, Blackwaters?"

I'm lost in my thoughts and it takes me a moment to emerge from my reverie and register his words. "What?" I say as his face comes back into view.

"Why did your aunt keep you hidden?"

I stare at him. "How ... how did you know that's what I was thinking about?"

Did I speak my thoughts out loud without realizing?

"No, you didn't but I can hear them anyway." He smirks at me.

"What the fuck? What do you mean?" His smirk somehow grows even more infuriating. I don't think this is some clever confidence trick. I think he is serious.

"I am. It's one of my many talents."

"You can read people's thoughts? That's sick," I squeak, taking a step away from him, trying really hard not to think of all the inappropriate thoughts that have filtered through my mind over the two days we spent together.

Oh God, can the man in black read my thoughts too? Can everyone?

"No, sweetheart. Just me."

"Stop doing that," I snap.

Oh shit, all those things I imagined when I was lying in that motel room. All those dirty ideas I had floating through my mind while I was riding on the bike with the man in black.

Professor Stone frowns, like he just swallowed a particular nasty spoonful of that porridge.

"Don't worry, Blackwaters, I have no interest in rifling through the immature desires of pathetic little school girls like you."

My eyes burn but I'm determined not to cry, not in front of Stone – stone by name, stone by nature. Maybe later, when I've dragged Pip up onto my bed with me.

"Put on your uniform and get to class," he says, turning his back on me to look at something on his desk. "And be thankful I'm not making you strip out of your clothes here and now and sending you back out into the school in your underwear."

I swipe at my eyes quickly before he notices, and suck in air. Regaining my composure, I snap at him: "I would, but you dragged me away from my guide. And I have no map and no timetable and–"

He spins back around to face me, two pieces of paper in his hand: one a map; one a timetable. He thrusts them at me and I snatch them from him and stomp away before he can utter another word.

I don't care what he says, I'm still ditching this place as soon as I can. I'm just going to have to be smarter about it.

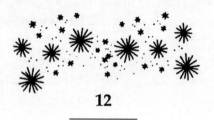

12

R^{hi}

I USE the map to find my way back through campus to my dorm room. It has some kind of magical GPS built into it, a little dot representing me making its way around the buildings. The paths are empty this time. I'm guessing lessons have already started. I'm in no hurry to join them, especially when I'm hungry and a little light-headed. I take my time walking along the paths, and an even longer time stripping off my clothes and climbing into my uniform. It's a tad on the big size, the skirt slipping down from my waist to perch on my hip bones and the jacket hanging loosely from my shoulders. Unlike the bouncing bunnies, I won't be rocking this look.

When I've fixed the stupid beret to my head, I finally have to admit to myself that I can no longer delay the inevitable; I have to get to class. I stare down at the timetable; first up is advanced spells. I used to think I knew quite a few useful spells, that I was actually pretty competent at casting them. How quickly I've learned that is nonsense? I can't heal a wound or even dry my hair.

I drag my feet back through the maze of buildings and duck inside the one with tall chimneys, marked magical labs. I find the correct classroom on the ground floor and hesitate with my hand on the doorknob. I can hear voices within. I brace my shoulders, turn the knob and stride inside.

The classroom looks exactly like I've seen labs look on TV. All gleaming white, sinks lined up against the windows and equipment stacked on shelves. There are also four rows of chairs, all occupied except one right at the front. All the occupants of those chairs as well as a teacher, hovering in front of a whiteboard, turn to stare at me. She's dressed in a white lab coat and sneakers, bright purple glasses matching the bright purple hair piled on top of her head.

"Ahhh Miss Blackwaters, it seems you've finally deigned to join us."

"Sorry," I mumble, even though I'm not. I hope Stone was telling the truth and mind reading isn't common.

"Well, you're just in time. We were about to conduct some practical assignments and I was looking for my first volunteer. Leave your books on your desk please and come to stand at the front."

I do as she says, catching the eye of Winnie who smiles at me with sympathy. It makes me nervous. This is a lesson right? Nothing bad can happen.

I stand next to the teacher, whose name, my timetable informs me, is Dr. Johnson.

"Right," the teacher links her hands together in front of her stomach and surveys the room. "Who would like to go first?"

Nearly every arm shoots up into the air with an enthusiasm that surprises me. An enthusiasm and a definite hint of malice dancing in the pupils' eyes. It makes me even more nervous than Winnie's smile.

"Summer," Dr. Johnson decides, gazing upon the head cheerleader with such clear admiration I wonder if she has a crush.

"Thank you, Dr. Johnson," Summer chimes sweetly as she rises to her feet, all traces of that meanness from earlier vanished.

"The assignment," Dr. Johnson explains to me, "is to see if it's possible to change the voice of another magical. This can be a useful skill when conducting subterfuge activities. Ready?" she asks Summer and not me.

Summer nods, raises her hands, and I know what's coming is bad, the glint in her eyes positively evil. Her lips whisper and I close my eyes, expecting another blast of hot air or something.

Nothing.

Did she mess it up?

I open my eyes. Everyone's still staring at me, Summer smugly like she knows perfectly well she's been successful.

Everyone waits.

Finally, Dr. Johnson says, "If you'd be kind enough to speak, Miss Blackwaters."

I chew my cheek. I don't want to. I don't think this will go well. She's probably made my voice all squeaky, or maybe husky. However, Winnie's right. I need to show her I'm not bothered. Then she'll bore quickly and leave me alone.

I open my mouth to speak, planning to tell them my first name, seeing as nobody has actually asked.

But all that comes out of my mouth is a loud piggy snort.

My eyes dart to the teacher in alarm and I try again, this time a series of squeals and grunts flying from my lips. As I try to speak, I feel an intense pain searing through my nose, as if the skin and bone is being stretched and remolded. My hands fly to my face, desperate to understand what's happening.

The entire class bursts out into laughter and when I stare at the teacher, begging her for help with my eyes, she simply grins back at me and claps.

She actually claps.

"Well done, Summer. Superb. That is some tricky magic indeed. It's much easier to change the tone of someone's voice, class, but to change it entirely like that is extremely skilled. And the snout? What a marvelous touch! Top marks, Summer. Bravo!"

Snout?! I pat desperately at my nose, horrified to discover it's no longer there, replaced by a flat snout with two large nostrils. Several pupils pull out their phones and snap pictures of me before I have a chance to hide my face.

Summer gives an exaggerated little curtsy, before taking her seat.

"Pig girl," she mouths at me as the teacher turns my way and automatically I raise my hands, ready to blast that little bitch right out of the classroom.

However, before I get a chance, Dr. Johnson's hand slaps mine away.

"Miss Blackwaters, might I remind you that using magic against another pupil is strictly forbidden in this school. Now you're new, and still unfamiliar with our rules, so I won't report this attempted attack to Professor York but you will be required to join me in detention after lessons tomorrow evening."

I stare at her in absolute disbelief, unable to argue back because my voice has been turned into a fucking pig's. Summer smiles smugly at me from behind the teacher. And oh, I'm so tempted to blast both Dr. Johnson *and* the head cheerleader into the next classroom.

Instead, I concentrate on breathing, my eyes alighting on Winnie whose obvious concern calms my raging temper.

"Miss Blackwaters, thank you for your help. You may take your seat."

I don't move, waiting for her to reverse the spell, or to ask Miss Sunshine to do it. When it doesn't happen, Winnie finally speaks up on my behalf.

"Aren't you going to change Rhianna's voice and, erm, face back, Dr. Johnson?"

"Not yet, Miss Wence. All voices will be reversed at the end of the lesson. Who's next?"

I slump away into my seat. The changes everyone else makes to their guinea pigs are much tamer. Everyone finds it hilarious when their friends speak with a light accent or with a slight slur. No one else ends up snorting like a pig. No one else's face gets mutilated. And because I can't speak, I can't even practice the spell myself. I'm resigned to sulking in my seat watching everyone else have fun around me, occasionally peering my way, giggling and whispering, 'pig girl'.

I have a really bad feeling that name is going to stick.

13

R^{hi}

LUCKILY, Dr. Johnson returns my face and my voice to normal at the end of the lesson. But only after Winnie reminds her, otherwise I think she'd probably have conveniently forgotten to have done it.

Once I can speak again, Winnie hooks her arm through mine and hurries us out of the labs and towards the gymnasium. I groan when I realize where we're going. My ego's already taken a battering this morning, I'm not sure I can cope with my body doing so too.

"It's not sports," Winnie says as she drags me along. "It's combat training. It's actually pretty fun. Better than cross-country in the rain, or having Summer take aerobics, anyway."

As we draw closer, I grab my first glance of the sport's field, the pitch green and lush and high stands flanking the two sides.

Out on the field several students race around, hurtling magic at one another, laughing and shouting as they do.

"I thought we weren't allowed to use magic on other students," I say flatly, pointing out to the field with one hand, as I rub my nose with the other.

"That is dueling. They're practicing."

I watch as one student strikes another with a magic bolt sending them tumbling backwards, and another student tackles a smaller kid with the force of his shoulder to the ground.

"It looks dangerous," I mutter, "and chaotic."

"Oh, in the olden days, before the official rules, it was. Now there are rules about what spells you can use and what type of force."

I watch some more, unclear what is going on. "But what's the purpose of it?"

"Simple really. Two teams. Objective is to take the other team out. It's popular here, because, you know, one day we might actually be fighting out there like this."

My feet slow, watching some more, but Winnie tugs on my elbow, dragging me into the changing room.

Like this morning, a sports kit awaits me in the changing room, hanging on a peg. A label with my name declares it's mine, but someone has scrubbed that out and written 'pig girl' over the top.

I roll my eyes. Seriously? That's as original as they can get?

Not reacting to the insult, despite all the whispering and giggling, I take off my hideous uniform and dress in the equally hideous sports kit. The shorts are skin tight and so is the top, fashioned from some shiny lycra that clings to every part of my body. It looks great on the bouncing bunnies, emphasizing all their impressive curves. All it emphasizes on me is my jutting out hip bones and the fact that, unlike everyone else, I'm not wearing a thong. Yep, my panty line is definitely on display.

Winnie takes my hand when we're both dressed and leads me out into the huge gymnasium.

"Don't look so scared. Old Coach Hank is actually one of the nicest teachers here, once you get past his bark that is."

"I'm not scared," I tell her, just wishing everyone would stop staring at me like I'm some kind of freak. I glance up into the air wondering if I really do have a sign above my head and touch my nose to ensure that snout hasn't returned.

Winnie leads me over to a group of waiting students. The bouncing bunnies, still styling their hair, aren't here yet, but it looks like the boys are. And oh, I wasn't wrong about this lycra not hiding much. I can see every lump – *every* lump – every butt crack, and every hard-ridged muscle. And oh my lord there are a lot of muscles on display. The men in this college must spend an awful lot of their time working out. I suppose that's hardly surprising since we're here to be trained as elite magicals who can one day defend this country if called upon.

As I glance over all the unfamiliar faces, I spot the huge guy and the prince from this morning, and it seems hideously unfair that two people could look that good in such unforgiving material.

An older squat man, with graying hair, waits in front of the group, tapping his foot and glancing at his watch. Then he spots me and beckons me forward.

He takes me to one side. "You're the new girl."

"Yes, Rhianna."

"Nice to meet you, Rhianna. I'm Coach Hank." He offers me his hand – the first person who has – and I shake it, grimacing slightly as he squeezes my fingers. "I hear you've had no official educational training. Were you taught any combat skills?"

"Yes," I say, happy there's something at last that I can feel confident about.

"And non-magical combat?"

"Non-magical? What like martial arts?" I chuckle.

"Yes," he says, no trace of amusement.

My smile drops. "No, none."

He crosses his arms and nods, clearly thinking. Then he calls over to the group. "Spencer, can you come here, please?"

The huge dude, who looks almost the size of a bear, jogs over to us.

"Yes, Coach," he says.

"Rhianna here has had no physical combat training, which means she can't join in with the lesson today." Spencer glances my way like I must have landed here from an alien planet. Which I sort of did. "I'd like you to run through some basic maneuvers and holds with her."

"When?"

"Now."

Spencer groans. "Really, Coach. It's–"

"You're my best student at this, Spencer. Best member of our dueling team," he says to me before turning back to Spencer. "Missing one or two lessons won't hurt you like it will hurt the others. Besides, I can think of no better person to teach Rhianna here." He slaps Spencer on the shoulder and points towards some mats in the corner. "You can get started over there."

Mats? I don't like the idea of that.

Spencer lets out an irritated huff of air and scowls at me as Coach Hank returns to the other pupils. "Why the fuck don't you know any combat?"

I shrug. "Because I never learned it."

"Fucking ridiculous," he mutters, stomping off in the direction of the mats. Reluctantly I follow, peering over my shoulder and catching the bouncing bunnies scowling at me too. I smile and wave at them sweetly. Then pick up my feet and join Spencer over by the mats.

He peers towards the group of students too, watching as

they file out of the gymnasium with Coach Hank, leaving the two of us alone in the echoey space.

"This is fucking annoying," he tells me, crossing his arms.

"Oh, I'm sorry," I say, "have I ruined your day?" It's not like I asked the coach to pick Spencer to give me one-on-one tuition. If he had asked me, I'd have picked one of the much smaller, skinnier dudes. Someone who doesn't look like he'd crush me to death if he ever fell on top of me.

Spencer's eyes flick down my body, lingering on my hip bones, before returning to my face.

"Why the fuck don't you know this stuff? Didn't your last school teach you anything?"

Remembering what Winnie told me about unregistereds and that my revelation about never going to school had almost made her fit, I decide I'll keep those bits of information to myself this time. Instead, I walk to the middle of the mat, thinking it's likely that's where I'm going to need to be.

"Can we just get started already? The sooner you teach me this stuff, the sooner we can both join the group." Although, I'm pretty sure joining the group is probably a much better option for him than it is for me.

However, in the next moment, I find my body flipped through the air and my back slammed down hard onto the mat.

And I rethink that. Maybe this won't be good for me either.

I groan, the air knocked out of my lungs. My body's still sore from that fight with the man in black. But I think I just gained a whole load more bruises.

I peer up at Spencer. He towers over me, his hands on his hips.

"What the fuck?" I gasp, tempted to send a blast of magic up into his face. There's nobody here to see me do it, after all.

"You said to get started."

"You could have warned me."

"And what would be the point in that? You think an attacker is going to warn you?"

I think of the gang that ambushed the man in black in the forest and the men that found their way to the various homes we lived in over the years. My spine smarting, I climb to my feet.

"I'd use my magic if someone attacked me," I say, raising my hands.

"And what if they disarm you? Then what?"

"Disarm me?" I say, staring at my hands before I lower them.

"Yeah, disarm you," he scoffs, like I'm dumb. "Then all you'll have are your physical combat abilities and skills."

"If I couldn't use my magic against someone like you, I wouldn't stand a chance!"

"You would if you'd actually bothered to learn this stuff."

I don't tell him it wasn't a case of not learning, but of not being taught.

We glare at each other. His eyes are a dark chocolate brown and I swear as I stare into them, I feel that hook, that pull. That same strange magic I felt with the man in black and with Stone. I gasp and my eyes fall to my stomach, just as he lunges for me again, flipping me straight back down onto my back. My spine winces at the impact and my eyes water with the pain.

"Jesus Christ!" I mutter. "Will you cut that out? How is that helping?" I clamber back up. "What am I meant to do? How am I meant to stop you?"

"Fight back, dumbass," he says, lunging for me again.

"How?" I screech, swiping at him. It's no use. I'm on my back a third time. I stare up at the ceiling. This is bullshit. "Do you get a kick out of doing this?"

Slowly, I roll back up.

"Doing what? Coach asked me to show you some moves. And I am."

"That's not what he said. You're meant to be– Argh," I wail as he flips me over again, this time so hard, I swear I see stars.

I lie there panting.

"Get up," he tells me. I shake my head. "Get up!"

"No!" I yell.

He scowls down at me. "You're pathetic. Why the hell did they let you into this school if you know fuck all, pig girl?"

I blanch at the name. Then roll myself up to sit. "I never wanted to be here in the first place."

His jaw twitches. "Then why don't you leave?"

"It's ... complicated," I say, realizing that if I do want to leave, this combat stuff is actually going to be useful, and this giant jacked-up jerk is stopping me from learning it. "Lesson's over," I tell him, jumping to my feet and strolling away.

"You can't leave. Coach will be pissed."

I give him the finger and keep walking.

Collecting my uniform from the changing room, I head straight back to my room, picking up Pip from where he's snoozing on the patch of grass as I do.

I saw a laptop on Winnie's desk this morning. I'm hoping she won't mind me using it.

Sinking down onto the floor, I drag the computer onto my lap as Pip curls up beside me. It takes me a few attempts to guess Winnie's password. Once I'm in, I search for instruction videos on self-defense. If that meathead won't teach me, I'll teach myself.

After half an hour, the door bursts open, and Winnie comes hurrying inside.

"Rhianna, I've been looking for you everywhere."

"Well, I've been right here," I say, shrugging.

"What happened? Spencer said you skipped class because you couldn't do the moves."

"Bastard," I mutter. "He wouldn't teach me so I decided to come learn myself."

"Coach is going to be mad, Rhi. He's on the war path. He's usually really sweet, but when you get on the wrong side of him ..."

"Great," I mutter. "Seems all the teachers in this place are already pissed off with me – Johnson, Hank ... Stone."

"Oh, you mean earlier? What was all that about?"

I don't answer, returning my attention to the laptop.

Winnie drops down on the floor next to me. "I don't mind you borrowing my laptop, but don't you have your own?"

I shake my head. "Left it behind."

"Could someone send it to you?"

"There is no one." I peer up at Winnie. "I lived with my aunt. But she's gone now."

"You don't have any other family?"

I shake my head.

"Oh ... I'm sorry," Winnie says.

I suck in air through my teeth and close the lid to the laptop. "What about lunch? Don't tell me, we'll be eating road-kill or something if we're late to the hall."

Winnie chuckles. "Lunch tends to be a little better." I jump to my feet, offering my hand to Winnie and pulling her up. "I'm sorry your first day isn't going so well," she says.

"I wasn't exactly expecting it to, you know."

Winnie smiles at me. "Next time, though, if you get pissed off like that, don't storm off. Come find me. Seriously, I've been searching for you everywhere. I was going to just call you but I realized we never swapped numbers."

"I don't have a phone."

"Did you leave that behind too?"

"No, I've never had one."

Winnie's face spasms. "N-n-n-never had one. How? How can you live without a phone?"

I give her a hard stare. "You can't live without your phone?"

"No, not really."

"Why? What's so vital about it?"

"It's ... well ... I need it for ... it just is, okay? And we're going to need to get you one. We'll swing by Trent's after lunch. He's got all sorts of gadgets for sale. I bet he has an old phone or two."

"How much is that going to cost me?" I think of the piddly allowance the authorities have deemed to give me each week. It's barely going to be enough to buy a bag of sweets and I'm going to have to find food for Pip.

"Don't worry about that. Trent's one of the nice guys." She says the words a little misty-eyed and I wonder if she likes him.

Lunch is pretty similar torture to breakfast. Everybody stares at me and whispers as I walk past with a large cheese baguette and bowl of soup, only this time there's the added bonus of my new nickname: Pig Girl.

Plus, someone has kindly printed out pictures of me with my snout face and pinned them around the Great Hall.

I ignore it, wolfing down the soup and a few bites of my baguette and saving the rest for Pip.

"Aren't you going to eat that too?" Winnie asks as I stuff bits of bread into the pockets of my blazer. "I'm starving after skipping breakfast."

"I am too but I need to save some for Pip." Winnie stares back at me blankly. "My pig."

"Oh, yeah, right," she says. She chews on a carrot stick. "Shouldn't you be feeding him pig feed or something?"

"And where am I going to get my hands on that around here?"

"Well," she grabs my elbow, "that is something we can solve right now."

Trent's room is in a similarly grotty block as our own, although he must have more money than Winnie and me, because he's not sharing a room.

Several boys stare at us with suspicion as Winnie knocks on

Trent's door and we wait for an answer. However, no one actually tells us to get out. So much for those rules.

After a long minute, Trent opens his door. He's tall and skinny with a mop of hair that falls over his eyes which I don't think he's combed today. In fact, he looks like he just got up.

"Hey Winnie," he says, scrubbing his hand through the tangles, "I was napping."

A nervous smile hovers on her lips. "Sorry, we can come back if–"

"Nah, I had to get up for class in five anyway. What's up?"

"This is Rhi. She's new."

"Hey," Trent says, jerking his chin my way.

"Hi," I reply.

"She needs a phone."

"I don't *need* a phone," I mutter.

"Everyone needs a phone," Trent tells me, "you don't have one?"

"No, and I don't have any money either so I don't think I can afford–"

"I have an old one I'm not using. I was going to take it apart and use the parts to build something."

Winnie leans in and whispers with clear admiration: "That's what he does. He's like a genius."

The top of Trent's ears, poking out through his hair, sizzle red. "Anyway, you can have it if you want."

"That's kind but–"

"Hang on. I'll fetch it for you." He ducks inside the dark gloom of his room, blue lights from several devices illuminating a rumpled bed, and returns several minutes later with what looks like a brick, a charging cable wrapped around it. "You'll need to charge it. And don't worry, it's already wiped."

"Erm, thanks." I take the gift from his hands. It's the first gift I've ever received from anyone who wasn't my aunt. If you exclude the food the man in black bought me. That, however, was him doing his job. This is actual generosity. From someone I just met. A sensation I can't describe swims in my belly, half discomfort, half gratitude.

"Thanks, Trent," Winnie beams at him, "see you in class."

"Yeah, see you in class."

He closes the door and Winnie insists we return to our dorm to plug in my new phone before next class.

Coach is waiting for me outside the classroom.

"You left my class without permission, Missy."

"I did. Spencer wasn't teaching me–"

"No one leaves my class without my permission." His tone is calm and measured. He doesn't sound angry, but that somehow makes him more menacing. "You have a problem, come and see me about it. Now, as you missed half an hour of my class, you can make up for it this evening. Be in the gym at seven on the dot. Do not be late."

He turns and storms away. A second detention. Yeah, I'm totally rocking this whole school thing.

The next lesson is Magical History and Politics and the little old lady teacher, Mrs. Hollyhill, quickly realizes I know about as much as a newborn babe. She sends me off to the library with a long list of books to read, and tells me to come back when I've caught up.

Armed with my map, I find the library back in the mansion. It's almost a similar size to the Great Hall, its ceiling nearly as high. Only here the space is filled with shelf after shelf of books, all towering up towards that ceiling. I've never seen so many books in my life before. Small paperbacks, giant journals, tatty old looking things, and brand spanking new volumes. Some inscribed with gold lettering down the spines, others with illustrations or plain simple text. The place smells of dust and old paper and the aroma is somehow welcoming. Armchairs and squidgy sofas are dotted about the place as well as desks with lamps.

I show the librarian my list and she helps me navigate the maze of books until I have a pile so high I can't see where I'm walking as I search for an armchair. I sink into one in the corner, finding its belly must have given way with the weight of all the students who have sat here over the years, and start flicking pages.

Most of it's dull historical accounts of battles and political negotiations that happened hundreds of years ago, mostly on the other side of the ocean. I yawn, debating whether to skip ahead to more recent history, attempt to fill in some of the blanks in my knowledge. But my eyes glaze over and my eyelids droop.

"Sent to catch up too, huh?" I jolt awake and find a boy my age staring down at me. He has neatly cut brown hair, a plain face and slightly crooked teeth.

"Huh?"

He lifts his arm, showing me the three books he holds in his hand.

"Yeah," I say, rolling my neck and sitting up straighter.

He grabs a chair and drags it towards me, taking a seat and resting his forearms on his knees. "You're new?"

"Yep."

"Me too. Been here about a term."

"You're new?" I was under the impression I was some kind of anomaly.

"My family moved over from Aropia. Some of the stuff they taught us over there is different from here. I'm trying to catch up."

"Tell me," I ask him, "how long until the 'new kid' label wears off?"

"The 'new' label or the 'pig' one?" He grins at me, although I can tell it's good natured.

"The pig one's never going to go, is it?"

He shakes his head. "And my 'new' boy label lasted until the next new kid showed up and that was you." His grin widens. "I am officially no longer the new kid."

"Congratulations ... erm ...?"

"Andrew."

"Rhi," I tell him. "So do you prefer it here or over in your old school?"

"Actually here. They teach much more practical stuff. We were never really allowed to test our abilities and skills in my old school. Here it's encouraged."

For the first time today, a sense of excitement sparks in my stomach. That's what I want. To test my capabilities. If I'm going to be stuck here, I at least want to find out what I can do.

"I like the sound of that."

From out of nowhere, the librarian's voice reaches us. "Quiet, please. This is a library."

Andrew rolls his eyes and leans closer to whisper. "Nice to meet you, Rhi. See you around."

Then he gets up and disappears around a bookshelf.

Did I just make a second friend?

I grin to myself and sink back into the chair. Maybe school isn't so bad after all.

14

R^{hi}

IT IS BAD. It's really bad. Because the punishment coach Hank decides to dole out is nothing short of torture. I think he looked at me and found my ultimate physical weakness. Laps of the grounds, sit-ups, press-ups, even burpees. They might hurt like hell but I can give them a try. This. This is dead-on impossible.

Of course, I didn't realize this at first. He led me over to a rope hanging in the gymnasium and pointed to the ceiling.

"Climb that and ring the bell at the top, then you can leave."

I thought I'd be back in my dorm after ten minutes. After all, rope climbing would be like tree climbing, right? No problem.

Uh uh. Big problem. Big, big problem.

I can't do it for shit. I coil my hands around the rough rope and haul myself up, but I only get about a foot off the ground before I slide back down, the fibers burning my palms and my thighs. I try again, gripping harder with my feet and my hands. It makes not a jot of difference. I try jumping for the rope and pulling myself up. But with an agonizing squeal, I just have further to slide back down. I look around the gym searching for help.

Where is the coach? He could have given me some hints on how to do this. There must be a technique I'm not getting right.

I try once more, my arms and legs screaming with pain. They give way and I tumble to the floor, landing splat on my stomach in the most undignified manner possible.

Laughter fills the gym and I lift my head to find both the bouncing bunnies and a group of jocks strolling past.

Fucking great.

"Look," Summer calls out to her cronies, "it's pig girl. Is she rooting around for truffles? Oh no, she's trying to climb the rope. But the poor little pig can't do it because she has trotters instead of hands."

Everyone laughs.

I want to retort back but I'm too damn out of breath. She swings her pony tail at me and jogs off with the rest of the cheerleading squad to the corner where they promptly start forming pyramids.

The jocks head off to the opposite corner of the gym where a circuit has been set up. I catch Spencer's eye as he files past.

"Want a hand up, little piggy?" he asks me.

"From you, no," I snap, dragging myself up, which is damn hard when my arms are made from jello.

He smirks at me, giving me an infuriating wink and I find the strength to unfurl my finger and offer it up to him once again.

The audience I now have in the gym though, gives me the extra boost of energy and determination I need to climb this damn rope.

I tip my head back and squint up at the distant ceiling.

Funny how it didn't seem that far away when I started this task. Now it seems about as far away as the moon, the bell a tiny, twinkling dot in the distance. I rub the sweat from my palms down the front of my shirt and puff out three lungfuls of air. Then I take the rope in hand, and try again.

And again.

And again.

This time I seem to climb a tad higher with each try but I'm still the length of two elephants away from the ceiling. The accompanying sniggers and sarcastic shouts of 'Go Piggy go!', do not help.

I fall onto my backside for the millionth time, realizing that I've spent quite a bit of my first day this damn way. I roll down onto my back, close my eyes and scream internally, so loud I burst my own ear drums.

"What are you doing?"

My eyes flip open and I meet the dark gaze of the man in black. Instantly my body seems to melt like butter.

I open my mouth. Close it. Then open it again. It's probably a very attractive view from where he is up there. He can probably see my tonsils.

"Are you all right?"

"What are you doing here?" I groan.

He shifts his weight from one heavily booted foot to the other.

"Visiting Stone."

He's not wearing his cloak today. Instead, he's dressed in dark jeans and a dark t-shirt. Short-sleeved so that my eyes can't help flicking to the raised veins and elaborate inks that spiral down each of his arms towards his hands. Hands that ...

I swallow.

"I'm trying to climb this stupid rope and ring that bell."

"Then why are you lying on the mat?" He frowns.

Groaning, I roll up, resting my forearms on my knees. "Because I can't do it."

"Then you're not trying hard enough."

I snort – stupidly because I can hear the bouncing bunnies giggling. "I really am. I can only get a few feet off the ground. And now my hands are shredded to smithereens." I hold out my palms, red and raw and blistered.

Without warning, he grabs them in his own and hauls me onto my feet. I open my mouth to complain, but then I'm distracted. Partly by the way his touch has my stomach flipping somersaults, and partly by the way he closes his eyes and starts whispering. When he lets go of my hands, they are completely healed.

"There," he says softly, before his expression hardens, "you need to learn that fucking spell."

I swear my legs are shaking and it isn't from muscle soreness any more.

"Thank you, but it isn't going to make much difference. I'm never going to make it to the top."

"Coach said you couldn't use magic?"

"Wh-what?" I mutter, feeling about as dumb as it's possible for one person to feel.

"Did coach tell you that you couldn't use your magic?"

"No." I hang my head.

"Hmmm," he says, and when I lift my gaze I find he's strolling away.

Damn it. Magic. I could have used my magic all along.

Not that anyone was kind enough to tell me.

I stare at the stupid bell and consider sending a blast of magic its way, just to make the fucking thing ring.

But, no, I'm determined to reach it myself.

With my eyes fixed on the ceiling, I call on my magic, letting it soar from the center of my chest, along my limbs, to my fingers and toes. I step forward and take the rope in my hands.

Then I climb, using my magic to support me, to lift me through the air. This time I climb higher and higher, soon level with the top of the cheerleaders' pyramid, then up to the windows and finally, finally, to the ceiling. The bell hangs right above my head and, concentrating with all my might, sweat pooling along my brow and trickling down my spine, I grip the chain in my hand and ring that bell so loud everyone in the gymnasium looks my way.

I grin down at them. At Summer. At Spencer. At all their minions.

Then I let go of the bell, of the rope, and float down to the floor, this time landing gracefully on my feet.

I can't help a little squeal of delight when I'm down safely, punching the air. I spin on my toes, hoping coach is here somewhere now and witnessing my triumph. Instead I spy the man in black, hovering by the door, watching me. When I catch his eyes, he looks away, turning his back to me and walking straight through the exit.

Did he stay to watch?

And why does that make my insides flutter?

It takes me a while to track down Coach, who I find outside, timing sprints. I'm practically buzzing when I tell him I've done it, and even the way he looks at his watch and asks why it took me so long, isn't enough to kill my good mood.

I skip off to the changing rooms, sweaty and stinky and aching everywhere, but elated nonetheless.

My mood takes a serious tumble in the opposite direction when I find there's someone else already in the changing room. Not just anyone.

Summer.

I've known this girl less than a day and I already hate her.

At least she's alone and not surrounded by her adoring fan club.

She hears me enter and peers over her shoulder.

"Oh, it's you," she says, her lip curling in disgust.

"Yep, it's me."

"I wondered what that smell was."

I can't help dipping my nose near my chest and sniffing. "I probably do smell pretty bad right now. Is the water actually hot in these showers?"

"You're going to take a shower?"

"Erm, yes."

"You can't." She spins around to face me.

I fold my arms over my chest. "And why not? You don't own this school, Summer."

"Debatable, but actually everyone knows Tuesday nights are my nights. No one else gets to come in. Didn't your little friend tell you that? Or perhaps you're a pervert as well as a pig."

Staring at me, she reaches down to her waist, grips the lycra material of her top and whips it straight over her head. She's not wearing anything underneath and I receive a full on flash of her impressive tits before I look away.

"I'm meeting Spencer here. So scram, okay?" From the corner of my eye, I see her step out of her shorts and underwear. "Okay?"

I peek her way, she's completely naked, not even attempting to shield her body. In fact, she stands face on, her hand resting on her hip, her long blonde hair loose around her shoulders.

It's obvious why she's popular. The girl is stunningly beautiful. And it's obvious why someone like Spencer would be meeting her here in the showers.

"Get out, little piggy, now!" she snaps.

And suddenly shame floods through me. Shame and something I don't think I've ever felt before, self-loathing.

I grab my bundle of clothes and flee, hearing the shower roar into life as I swing back the dressing room door and walk straight into a very solid wall.

Spencer.

He's topless, his chest gleaming with sweat under the changing room lights, and his scent deeply masculine.

He grabs my arm to stop me tumbling and for a moment we stare open-mouthed into each other's eyes. And god what is wrong with me, because all those flutterings in my stomach start up all over again.

"I ..." I begin.

But I don't finish because he slams me out of his way without saying a word.

I stumble through the door, trying to block Summer's purrs of delight from my ears as Spencer joins her in the shower. I hurry out of the gymnasium and down the path. It's dark and empty and after several paces, my heart is racing so erratically, I stop and lean against the cool trunk of a tree, trying to catch my breath.

What is wrong with me? I hate them both. Really, really hate them. So why is my head spinning with thoughts of the two of them? Together, underneath the showers, kissing, and caressing and ...

Why does that make me want to vomit? Why does that have the blood in my veins heating?

What is wrong with me?

"Everything if you ask me."

I jolt and open my eyes. I need to stop closing them, because every time I do some fucker creeps up on me. This time I find Stone passing me on the path.

"Professor Stone," he corrects.

"Get out of my head!" I yell.

"You think I want to be swimming down there in the gutter with all your dirty little thoughts and secrets? You really are a bratty little pervert, Blackwaters."

My cheeks burn so hotly I'm surprised they don't catch fire.

"You're the pervert!"

"No, in this case, it's most certainly you." He sneers at me and keeps walking.

And oh god do I want to send a bolt of magic hurtling straight at his head.

"Don't even think about it, Blackwaters. Not if you treasure all your limbs."

I stamp my foot and scream into the night's air.

I hate it here. I really do.

IT'S ONLY the idea of Pip waiting for me in my dorm that persuades me to return to my room. Otherwise, I'd be out of here. Fuck this college. Fuck the authorities. Fuck Marcus Lowsky and the Wolves of Night.

When I stumble through the door, probably looking a physical and emotional wreck, I find Winnie and Pip engaged in a Mexican standoff. Winnie sits on her bed in one corner of the room, Pip in the other.

"What's going on?" I ask, my gaze swinging between them both.

"I caught him snuffling my 'Magical economics notes'. I told him off. Now he's sulking."

"He ate your notes? Shit, Winnie, I'm really sorry. I need to find him some proper food." I glare at Pip and he lowers his head to the floor and whimpers.

"He's been doing a lot of that."

"He doesn't like it when people are mad at him."

"Hmmm." She diverts her attention away from my pig and

back to me. "Anyway, I got your phone working so I think you will be able to order him some food."

"What do you mean?"

She doesn't blink this time, instead she pats the spot on the bed next to her, and talks me through how to use the phone Trent gave me, including how to order pig food on the internet and have it delivered to our dorms. I have to use Winnie's credit card to set it up but we make a deal that I'll pay her back, as well as rewrite all the notes Pip ate.

When she's finished her lesson, she sinks back against her pillows and looks me over. "You don't look so good. What happened?"

Should I tell her about my encounter with the man in black, how he has butterflies dancing in my stomach? Or about my run-in with Summer and Spencer in the locker rooms?

I decide to go with Stone and the thing that's bothering me the most.

"I had another altercation with Professor Stone. Please tell me he's the only one who can read minds in this place?"

"There are one or two others but he's the best by far. In fact, everyone says that's why he got the job here. It's pretty useful to have a member of staff who can read pupils' minds, find out who's lying about stuff, who's cheating on tests."

"It's so annoying though. So invasive." I shiver when I think of all the dirty things he saw in my mind out there on the path.

"Oh God, Rhi. How much did he see?" My cheeks redden again. "Can't you keep him out?"

"No ..." I stare at my new friend. "Is that possible?"

"Yeah, you need to work on your mental shields. I mean, Professor Stone is pretty effective at breaking through them when he wants to, but at least it stops him casually walking into your thoughts when you don't want him to."

"Yeah, that does sound good. But how do I learn it?"

"Ahh, that would be a problem." She grimaces. "Professor Stone would be the one to teach you."

"Oh crap."

"I could try, but I doubt–"

"I'd be grateful for any help."

Anything to keep that creep out of my thoughts.

15

R^{hi}

UNFORTUNATELY MY FIRST lesson the next day is with the creep himself: Professor Stone.

"Ancient Magic. It sounds pretty dry," I tell Winnie as we file into the classroom with the rest of the students. There's no sign of Stone. His classroom was unlocked, but it's empty.

"I guess it's one of the harder subjects but I like it," she shrugs, then leans in to whisper, "most of the girls do, and several of the boys as well."

"Please tell me that's because he makes the topic interesting and entertaining."

Winnie grins and shakes her head. "Most of the teachers here are older than our parents. Stone's the one piece of eye candy on campus and pretty decent eye candy too."

I roll my eyes. If they knew Stone was as much of an asshole as I do, I'm sure they'd think differently.

I take a seat next to Winnie, peering at the ancient-looking scripts pinned in frames on the walls and the equally ancient-looking brass instruments lining the shelves.

I think of Stone in his leather jacket riding his bike and it's hard to imagine him teaching such an obviously academic subject. Then again, his office had been rammed full of books. Maybe he's more of a nerd than I realized.

A hot nerd if Winnie is to be believed.

I glance at the clock. It's already gone nine but nobody seems particularly bothered that the professor is late. Everyone is chatting and nobody has started any work.

"Is he actually going to show up?"

Winnie jerks her chin towards the door as Stone comes strolling in like he has all the time in the world and isn't nearly ten minutes late.

He shrugs off his jacket – a blazer today not leather – and drops it on the back of the chair. Then turns to face the class as everyone falls silent.

His eyes travel over all the faces trained his way, lingering on mine for a fraction of a second longer than the rest. Then he lifts his hand and a piece of chalk flies towards the blackboard behind him, hanging in the air.

I open my unicorn notepad and fold back a new page, ready to take notes.

It still feels strange sitting in a classroom after all these years of avoiding them. I keep expecting to wake up and find myself in my bed back in my house in the clearing.

"Today, we're going to examine the existence of magical fingerprints," the professor says and I glance up and meet his eyes. "Why they come about. How we can avoid leaving them. And how they can be tracked."

Summer, sitting front and center, and leaning forward slightly in her seat so the professor has a clear view straight down her shirt, shoots up her arm.

"Yes, Summer?" Stone says, in a friendly manner that has my guts twisting strangely with jealousy. I don't know why I'm surprised. I bet Summer is every teacher's favorite student.

"I thought we were going to be covering fated mates and the bonding process today, Professor?" she says sweetly.

Several other students murmur their agreement.

The professor waves his hand and the chalk begins to scribble words across the board.

"A change of plan."

There are several disappointed groans and I lean towards Winnie. She senses my curiosity.

"We've all been waiting ages for him to teach us about it. Although, everyone knows that stuff already." I look at her blankly. "Well, most people," she says with a sympathetic smile. "It's still a favorite topic among everyone though because you know everyone's hoping it'll happen to them. That their one true mate, or mates, are out there somewhere."

I pull a face. "That sounds like a load of bullshit."

"It's not," Winnie says earnestly, "just rare."

"So rare, nobody actually knows of a fated pair in real life, I bet."

"Oh, I do. It happened to my cousin," Winnie says, resting her elbow on the table and her chin in her hand. "Lucky bitch."

"Really?" I say cynically. "Because anyone could claim they're fated mates, doesn't mean they are."

"That's not true. There are signs. And a blood test. Ways to know for sure."

"Signs?" I scoff.

"Miss Blackwaters," the professor calls from the front and I snap upright automatically. "If your conversation is so pressing, perhaps you'd like to share it with the whole class."

I grin at him. Seriously? That's the best he's got?

I shake my head.

"Then pay attention. You of all people have the most to

learn." Several people swivel in their seats to glare at me and the professor frowns. "In fact, let's test how much you do know."

Internally, I groan. I was taught enough to survive, to get by. Okay, I didn't have a conventional schooling, and okay it's becoming clear that there was a hell of a lot my aunt missed out. But she did the best she could while keeping us safe and fed. She didn't have a whole lot of time for reciting the various fucking battles of what stupid wizard attacked which dumb witch. We were too busy feeding chickens, harvesting vegetables and keeping our true nature hidden.

"You're wrong, Blackwaters. She failed you. She left you ignorant and exposed."

"Tell your friend that."

The gazes of the other pupils swing between the professor and me as if they're watching a tennis match.

The professor leans back against his desk and surveys me.

"All right then, Miss Blackwaters. Please tell me how we consider ancient magic to differ from modern?"

I stare at him, opening and closing my mouth like a goddamn fish, then I smirk. "One's old and one isn't."

No one laughs.

"Summer?" the professor asks.

Summer stands up addressing the professor directly. "Ancient magic is considered the base of all other magic. It is the most powerful and fundamental. A magical who doesn't understand how to wield such magic is likely to fail." She peers over her shoulder at me with a look of self-satisfaction.

"Some examples of ancient magic, please, Blackwaters?"

I glare at him.

He sighs. "Summer?"

"Life, death, love, sex." She practically winks at the professor. "Some examples would be the creation and destruction of life. The giving of one life to protect another. The donation of magic from one magical to another. The combining of two lives together to create a fated b–"

"Yes, thank you, Summer," the professor says with sudden irritation. "Take a seat."

The chalk continues to scribble notes on the board behind him. "Summer is right. You may never wield ancient magic but you need to understand what it is and how it works. You need to understand the marks it will leave on this earth and on your soul if you ever do choose or need to use it. You need to feel it thrumming in your fingers if you hope to ever successfully perform more modern and complex spells."

His words seem to spark electricity in my fingertips and I close my eyes and see the knife lodged in that man's head. I wish I'd never done it. I wish I turned away and left the man in black to his fate. Although, as I think those words in my head, I know that isn't true. I couldn't leave him. I couldn't let him be killed. That hook in my stomach had driven me straight to him and in that moment I would have done anything to save him.

The magic in my fingertips sparks more violently and I feel that tug now deep in my gut.

When I open my eyes, everyone is bent over their desks copying notes from the board. But the professor, he's staring right at me.

I drop my eyes immediately and pick up my pen, attempting to follow everyone's example. The words I'm copying seem meaningless though and I can't think of anything but that man and my knife.

I'm relieved when finally the class turns to something more practical.

The professor splits the class into four groups and hands out several old artifacts – a mirror, a purse, a book and a pipe.

"Each of these objects," he explains, "were used in the wielding of ancient magic. All have been marked with magicals' fingerprints. I want you to examine the artifact and see if you can find the fingerprints. Bonus points if you are able to identify the magical who used them."

Some muttering follows. The other students clearly believe the professor has set an impossible task. But as I sit back and let the others work, I'm not so sure. Somehow over the last two days, I've managed to subdue that power of mine that senses the presence of other magicals. After all, now I'm surrounded by other magicals 24/7, the alarm in my head would be ringing off the hook if I didn't.

However, as I sit watching the others turn the mirror over in their hands, that sense stirs into life and for a moment I almost imagine I can see the hand that held the mirror, that wielded the ancient magic.

The mirror's glass is dull and the frame made of a white porcelain that's lost its shine and its decoration. The handle starts thin, growing fatter by its base and the hand that grips it is young, bedecked in several golden rings, the fingers long, and the nails short and well kept.

"How are you doing that?" the professor asks right by my ear, and I jolt, dragging my gaze from the object to him.

"Doing what?"

"Are you imagining that hand or seeing it?"

I shake my head, unable to explain, not sure if I want to.

"You're seeing it."

I simply stare up at him, trying my best to clear my mind.

He scowls at me and moves on to the next table.

Over the remaining half an hour of the class, the students don't make much progress in identifying the fingerprints. One tall skinny boy insists he can feel the presence of lingering prints and another claims the name Angus springs into his mind every time he holds the pipe.

The professor seems unimpressed by these efforts though and declares that no one in the class has shown any real talent.

However, when he dismisses the class, he grabs my arm as I scuttle past.

"Not you, Blackwaters."

"I have another class."

"Then you'll have to be late."

Winnie lingers by the door, waiting for me, but the professor strides towards her and slams the door shut.

"In my office, now," he says, picking up the mirror from one of the desks as we walk through.

Once we're in the office, he shuts the door and I notice the pile of open books on his desk that weren't there the last time we met in here.

He catches me looking and comes to stand in front of his desk, blocking my view.

He holds up the mirror.

"Can you do it again?"

"Do what?" I ask, feigning innocence.

"Blackwaters, I saw what you saw. I can tell when you're lying. Your thoughts shimmer in this uncertain manner."

Crap.

"It wasn't anything special," I mumble, "just my imagination."

He examines my face and I stare at his shoes. The boots he was wearing when he came to collect me in the forest, hidden under the hem of his pants.

"You're lying again."

Crap crap crap.

"It's never happened before," I say, then quickly add, "not that I remember anyway, not that I would have known what it was if it had."

He nods like he believes this bit of information.

"Try it again."

He holds the mirror closer to me. I don't like the way the

object makes me feel. Shivers creeping across my skin and my stomach turning over.

"What was it used for?" I whisper.

"Why?" he says.

I glance towards the door. "I'm going to be really late for my next class and I've already had two detentions."

He scoffs. "Tell me, Blackwaters."

"I don't like the way it makes me feel. It's eerie. It was used for something bad, wasn't it?"

He nods but doesn't tell me what and for once I wish I could read his mind like he can read mine.

"That takes skill, Blackwaters, and you clearly don't have any."

"And yet you've dragged me into your office because you seem to believe I have some kind of ability."

"Do you?"

I slam shut my mouth.

He shrugs. "Have it your way."

I step towards the door.

"But know that powers like that would be useful when you're on the run. You should consider refining them."

I spin to face him. "I thought I wouldn't last five minutes on the run."

"With powers like this you might last ten."

I hover on my toes, for one long minute, considering his offer. But that smirk hovering on his lips tells me everything I need to know. He won't help me. Not really. He'll use it against me.

"Probably," he agrees, "besides, it's only a matter of time before I pilfer that secret from your mind, Blackwaters. You'll end up telling me whether you want to or not."

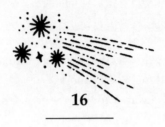

16

Spencer

I WAKE up with a fucking cloud hanging over my head. I swear it's freaking visible to everyone around me, because everyone, all the kids in the hall at breakfast, all my duel team mates, even Summer and the other cheerleaders, leave me the fuck alone.

They know the score. Piss me off – piss me off more than I already am – and live to face the consequences.

I eat my breakfast – scrambled eggs cooked just the way I like them – in silence and it's only goddamn Tristan who's brave enough to utter a word to me.

"What the hell's got your panties all in a twist?" he asks, as he drops down on the seat next to mine and observes my tight jaw and thunderous brow.

"Fucking gym class," I mutter, scooping up eggs with my fork and shoveling them into my mouth.

"Gym class? You live for fucking gym class, man. What's the problem? Coach not licking his tongue far enough up your ass?"

I snort. "Coach has got me teaching defense moves to the new girl."

Automatically, my eyes lift to the corner of the hall. The spot where the new girl hides during every meal. Tristan's eyes follow mine and I swear something in his own face stiffens when his eyes land on her.

"And ..."

"And it's fucking dull. She doesn't know what the hell she's doing, and it means I'm missing out on all the fun." And the one class I truly excel at. The one class in which I whip Tristan Kennedy's butt every time.

Every. Single. Time.

It feels good to be better than him at something.

I know he hates it. That's half the fun.

But now that stupid girl's come along and ruined it all. I know I shouldn't care. I know I should teach her the stupid moves and be done with it. But she irritates the hell out of me. Ever since that first day on the mats. It's like she's a rash, slowly spreading across my skin, becoming harder and harder to ignore. Plus more infuriatingly irritating. I swear every time I lay eyes on her my entire body itches.

Tristan flops back against his chair like this topic of conversation already bores him. "So what's the problem? Don't teach the girl."

"Don't worry," I tell him, slamming the last piece of egg into my mouth, and letting my fork clatter onto the plate. "I don't intend to."

I stalk back to my room, watching as other students leap out of my way, flattening themselves against walls. No one wants to end up on my wrong side this morning. I'm guessing my foul moods are legendary.

Unfortunately for him, at least one scrawny little first year didn't get this memo. He's so engrossed in his conversation with his friend, he fails to see me coming, walking the middle of the path and not moving out of my way.

I plow straight into him, sending the little squawk flying to the ground with an oof. He blinks up at me in shock, mouth hanging open.

"Move," I tell him, and when he doesn't scrabble out of the way quick enough, I give him a helpful kick to his ass. Then I haul him up by the scruff of his collar, lifting him right off the ground.

"Do you know who the hell I am?"

I'm not always like this. Most of the time, I'm the life and soul of the party. Guaranteed to make a classroom laugh. Guaranteed for a good time. But sometimes, sometimes, this fucking dark cloud consumes me like a mist seeping into my blood and everything makes my head hurt.

"Y-y-y-yes," the boy says, and I can feel his body trembling under my fingertips.

There's a rumor circulating among the lower years that I sent some dude to the infirmary for an entire month. It's not true. It was a week. But I haven't been quick to correct that piece of misinformation. Not when it means pipsqueaks like him treat me with respect.

"Then why the hell were you blocking my path?"

He doesn't have an answer. Not one he's willing to give me anyway. "I'm sorry," he splutters. "It won't happen again, I swear."

"Too goddamn right it won't, because if it does ..."

I open my hand and let him fall through the air, hitting the ground a second time.

He's on his feet and scurrying away like a mouse before I can grab him again.

I close and flex my fist. Usually, taking out my bad mood on some unsuspecting victim, makes me feel a lot better. Not today. That darkness still sits in my veins.

I roll my shoulders and my neck, listening to the vertebrae click. I've been cooped up too long. I need to get out of here and stretch my legs. It'll be weeks before my chance to do that though, and the darkness inside me strains to break free. I screw up my eyes and beat it down.

Back in my room, I swallow twice the number of pills I'm meant to take. I swear they're not working any more. I swear this cloud, this darkness, is becoming harder to control. Especially when some pissy little girl provokes it. Like it's met its fucking match and wants to come out and play.

Of course, she's in my first class this morning. Practical magic.

After what Summer did to her last week, she's one of the first there, cowering at the back like everyone will simply forget she exists.

I wish I could.

I wish it were that easy.

I fold into my usual seat, second row from the front, and dump my bag on the floor. Then I sit there with my arms tight across my heaving chest and tune into what the professor is demonstrating to us – how to conjure fire from our fingertips.

I may not be as skilled as Tristan Kennedy – winning every fucking academic award going – but I've been able to do something as simple as conjure fire since before I grew my first freaking pube.

I focus on listening anyway. I do not let my eyes flick to the new girl in the back row.

I do not watch as she scribbles notes in some damn stupid shiny notepad like her life depends on it. It probably does. She seems incapable of defending herself and ignorant to a point it's actually ridiculous. I know it's mandatory for every magical her age to attend the academy but for her they should've made an exception. We don't need liabilities weighing down our ranks.

When the professor asks for any volunteers to have a go at the fire conjuring, I slam my hand into the air. The other students who have done the same, see mine go up, and quickly lower theirs.

"Mister Moreau," Dr. Johnson says carefully. She knows as well as anyone else to tread cautiously around me today.

I lumber to my feet, my eyes flicking to the girl although I don't turn my head.

I lift my hand and let my magic lick hot through my veins, fire springing to life in my fingertips.

Several of the students gasp in amazement. One or two of them are likely genuine.

"You make it look easy, Mr. Moreau."

"Because it is," I tell her, surveying the room, meeting every pupil's eyes, reminding them I'm more powerful than any of them.

Then I drop in my seat.

"Would anyone else like to try?" Dr. Johnson asks.

Nobody's as eager after my show of dominance, but one hand rises.

I almost laugh.

"Miss Blackwaters." The professor nods in her direction.

She uncurls herself from her chair and lifts her hand up for everyone to see like I had done. Her eyes meet mine and holding my gaze, she frowns in concentration.

I smirk at her. What the fuck is she playing at?

She frowns harder. Her fingers begin to smoke and then a bright red flame dances into life in her palm.

No one speaks. The classroom is silent, only the quiet flicker of the fire in her hand.

"Thank you, Miss Blackwaters," Dr, Johnson says, turning towards the whiteboard.

The pig girl closes her hand and the flame extinguishes with a hiss. She smiles at me in triumph, her pretty honey eyes sparkling, and the black cloud resting over my head just got a hell of a lot darker.

I TAKE my time strolling to the gymnasium, letting the other students rush about me like deranged ants. If I'm late, coach won't give a damn. I'm his star. It makes me all the more angry that he picked me to teach the pig girl.

The locker room is silent as I strip off my uniform and tug on my kit, people eyeing each other anxiously and everyone trying to avoid catching my attention.

I'm dressed and out the door before anyone else and then I'm striding next door, crashing through the door and into the girl's changing room.

High voices scream, squeal and yelp, and I catch the sight of flesh, tits and panties. I swing my gaze around, most of the girls trying their best to cover themselves with arms or blouses, a few standing there for me to admire. Finally, I find the pig girl. Right in the fucking corner as usual. Standing in her mismatched fucking bra and panties. The girl needs to eat more. She's all skin and bones.

She turns around to see what all the fuss is about and stares straight into my face. For a moment, that connection penetrates deep inside my chest and my breath hitches in my throat.

My eyes dip to her chest and I smirk at her. Surprisingly, she actually possesses a nice-looking rack. Despite her titchy size, her tits are a perfect handful.

Then before anyone can say a word or attempt to shoo me out of the locker room, I dip my shoulder and charge at her. She screams, the noise of her alarm only making me more determined. I bundle her up into my arms and stuff her, kicking and cursing, into the nearest locker.

I struggle for a moment to cram those long spindly arms and legs of hers inside the locker, her nails scraping against my skin in a way that's almost goddamn erotic. But then I succeed, slamming the locker door shut, blocking out the sounds of her yells. I twist the lock and lean panting against the door, my heart hammering against my ribs.

Behind me, the girls' locker room is nearly as silent as the boys' was two minutes ago. You could hear a pin drop.

Slowly, I turn to face the room, my brow drawn low in a scowl.

"Anyone lets her out, they'll have to answer to me. Understood?"

Several girls nod. Some simply drop their eyes to the floor.

I wait for anyone to speak up for her. Nobody does and I charge away, ignoring the sounds of her tiny fists thundering against the locker door.

17

R^{hi}

10 YEARS *ago*

I can't breathe.
    I can't breathe.
    My lungs rasp. Warm air burns my throat.
    My knees are jammed under my chin. My arms folded into my chest.
    There's no room. There's no light.
    I close my eyes shut tight.
    Pain pierces through my lungs and into my chest, through my gut and into my limbs.
    Can't. Breathe.
    I gasp. I gasp again. Faster and faster. It feels like someone's gripping my throat. Gripping my throat and squeezing.

I can hear her screaming. I can hear the men laughing. I can hear the thumps as they hit her. As they throw her across the room like a rag doll.

I want to help. I want to go to her. But I'm only tiny. Nothing compared to the three large men who stormed into our home.

And she told me to hide. She told me to stay quiet.

I screw my eyes up tighter. My hands form steely fists. I count in my head. One. Two. Three.

I try to breathe. I try to block out the sound.

I don't know how long I'm in there. I don't know how much time passes.

I only know that when the cupboard doors finally open, it's my aunt that opens them. Her face is swollen, a clump of hair is missing from the crown of her head, and there's blood in the corner of her mouth.

"Come on, Rhi," she says anxiously, reaching out her hand to me. "Time to go."

18

Rhi

Present

I'm not quiet this time. I scream with all my might. With all my lungs. I hammer my fists on the locker door and kick at it with my feet. I scream so damn loud the entire school must hear.

I don't care. The sound keeps the other noise from my mind. Those noises from long ago. My aunt. My aunt taking punches for me over and over again. I don't want to think of it. I don't want to be reminded. So I keep screaming, if only to keep the air sucking into my lungs.

I'm shaking, my bones rattling with the violent movements, and I'm caked in sweat. A terror swims in my belly and threatens to overtake me entirely.

I won't let it. I won't let some stuck-up dickhead do this to me. I won't let him force me back there.

Fury begins to simmer in my belly and I focus on that emotion and none of the others as I continue to scream. Soon that fury is pulsing through my veins and with all my goddamn might, I send a bolt of powerful magic crashing from my fingertips and thudding hard against the locker door. It rips the metal from its hinges and the thing flies across the changing room, crashing into the wall opposite, plaster splintering everywhere.

I stop screaming. I close my eyes and take a steadying inhale. Then I squeeze out of the locker, trying not to think of her hand, trying not to think of her face, trying not to think of it at all.

I don't look at the other girls gathered in the room, but I know they're all staring at me open-mouthed.

"Rhi!" I hear Winnie gasp and I lift my gaze to find her pinned between two cheerleaders. There's sympathy and concern brimming in her eyes and I can't stand to look. Instead, I grab my clothes, pick up my heels and run. I run the hell out of here.

I don't stop running until I'm back at my dorm, until I have Pip gathered up in my arms.

He squeaks and squeals, alarmed at my sudden appearance. I bury my face against his coarse skin and soon he's licking my face.

"I hate it here," I tell him and he snorts as if he's agreeing with me.

I miss my aunt more than ever.

I wish I'd been switched on enough to ask her more. I wish I'd demanded more answers. I realize now, I don't even know who those men were that night. I don't know who any of the men that terrorized us over the years were. I don't know how many we escaped by luck and skill, and how many men my aunt killed to keep us safe. She kept all that hidden from me, so much on her shoulders. I owe her more than I ever realized. She was stronger than I ever understood.

I don't know if I can be like her. I thought I could. I thought I was.

But one stupid boy locks me in a locker and I'm almost hyperventilating.

My aunt wouldn't have let someone do that to her.

She would have fought back. She'd have blasted her way out of that locker and then she'd have blasted the man next.

I sink to the floor, Pip still gathered in my arms, and peer up at the mirror.

My aunt always told me I had my mom's eyes. A caramel that in some light appears more brown and in others golden. But now as I examine my tear-stained face, I see they are my aunt's eyes too.

We weren't alike in any other way. She had long fair hair I always admired that she wore braided around her head. Plus she was tall and willowy. It was no surprise she caught the unwanted attention of men. She was beautiful. Beautiful and strong. Strong and courageous.

I drop my eyes from the mirror and find Pip staring up at me. His snout ripples and I feel like he's trying to tell me something.

Probably that he's hungry.

He snorts like he's dismissing that notion and keeps his gaze locked with mine.

"You're telling me not to give up, aren't you?" I say, tickling his ears. "You're telling me not to be such a baby. You're telling me to get my act together."

Pip's eyelids drift shut as he leans into my touch.

I don't think he's actually telling me anything. But I know all that is true anyway.

I am my aunt's niece. I am the woman she raised. I am no pushover. I'm made of stronger shit than this.

Spencer Moreau can go to hell and I am going back to gym class.

Ten minutes later I stroll right up to him in the gymnasium. He's crunched over his knees, mid sit-up. He frowns when he sees me.

"You're late," Coach calls over to me.

"Yes, but I'm here now and I'm ready to go."

"Spencer ..." Coach says.

Spencer rolls back down. "Can't someone else babysit her today?"

"No," Coach replies simply and Spencer takes his merry time lumbering to his feet and strolling to the corner where we've been practicing.

Over the next half an hour he doesn't mention the locker and neither do I. In fact, we don't speak at all. And I endure another thirty minutes of being tossed to the ground.

"You're still fucking useless at this," he snarls at me as we near the end of the class. Which is pretty true despite the one or two times I've managed to dodge him and the three successful times I've snapped out of his hold.

"And you're still teaching me fuck all."

"You're not even trying!"

"I am," I snap, digging my nails into my palms and grinding my molars.

He scowls at me and then without warning comes at me, tossing me high up into the air like I'm nothing more than a lettuce leaf, and then slamming me down hard onto the mat.

Stars twinkle in front of my eyes as I blink up at him.

He reaches down and picks up his towel from the mat, then flings it over his shoulder.

"Next time, stay in the locker where I put you, Pig Girl."

"No," I tell him simply, wishing I had the strength to drag myself to my feet. "No way."

I'm my aunt's niece. That's all I need to remember.

19

R hi

I NEED to remember it plenty over the next week and a half, even if I manage to dodge Spencer, Summer and their minions. I'm massively behind in all my classes and the subject of much ridicule among my peers who find it utterly hilarious that I know fuck all and can do even less.

Still, despite the daily humiliation, I fall into a routine. I wake early, feed Pip and spend time with him. Then head off for the day with Winnie. I really like that girl. She's kind, sweet and when she's not feeling too self-conscious, funny. I don't understand why she doesn't have more friends. She's also prepared to spend her evenings helping me in my bid to catch up, showing me, among other things, how to dry my hair.

"But your aunt taught you some magic, right?" she says as we both stand in front of the mirror with soaking wet hair. "Like the fire conjuring?"

We haven't talked much about my home life, mainly because Winnie looks a little nauseous every time she's reminded of my previous unregistered status.

"Yes, but we had to be careful about practicing. If anyone spotted we were magicals, they would have shopped us in to the authorities. It kind of limited what she could teach me I guess."

"I think you're picking it up pretty quickly all things considered," she says, slowly demonstrating the movement of her fingers as she tempts warm air over the strands of her hair.

I copy the motion, concentrating on the words she's taught me in my head. I can feel the air brushing against my fingertips but it won't bend to my will. I huff in frustration.

"You know it's much easier than fire conjuring," she says. "That is really difficult stuff."

"I don't even remember my aunt teaching me that. I must have been really little. Maybe these things are easier to learn when you're younger."

"Doubt it. You should try being around little magicals with no proper training. It's chaos. Mom had to ban me and my sisters from using magic in the house. She got sick of finding frogs in the fridge and fish in the bathtub."

I laugh. That sounds a lot of fun.

I try the spell again, this time managing to encourage the lightest of breezes to waft across my head.

"There!" Winnie says. "But don't force it. Just feel it, beckon it."

But as soon as I stop forcing it, the breeze dies away.

"A bit of practice and you'll get it."

"Humph," I say, turning to find Winnie's already dried and styled her hair.

"We'll try again tomorrow and if you like we can go over the mind blocking again too."

I've been even more hopeless at that but I appreciate all the help Winnie's been giving me, plus the fact she's let me borrow her cover-up and mascara every morning and shown me how to apply it.

"Would you also show me healing spells? My aunt did try to teach me those, but I'm pretty useless."

"Probably because you have no patience."

"Me?"

Winnie gives me a look.

"I'm just keen to catch up," I mutter.

Catch up so I can leave.

Although, despite my first few shitty days at Arrow Hart Academy, I think being here – I think having friends – might not be so bad. I find I'm not the hermit I always thought I was. I enjoy Winnie's company and Andrew's too.

I let more wisps of air brush through my hair.

"We can spend the weekend practicing if you want," Winnie says.

"Really?"

The first weekend here at the school I spent catching up on sleep and orienteering myself around the college. I'm hoping this weekend might be a little more exciting.

"There has to be more to do on the weekend than that?"

Winnie slumps in her chair. "Not really."

With all these young people in one place?

"I assumed there'd be tons to do."

"Oh, there is if you're popular or on one of the sports teams. Then there are matches, and parties pretty much on repeat. But, I hate to break it to you, we're not going to get invited."

"That sucks."

"You don't really seem the partying type, Rhi."

"I don't know. I've never–"

"Been to one." Winnie shakes her head and smiles. My strange upbringing no longer makes her break out into those manic blinking attacks. "Then we're going to have to make it our mission to get invited to at least one party this term!"

"So what do you usually do on your weekends?"

"Saskia and I used to go for walks, catch up on our assignments and read books."

"Oh my God, Winnie," I say, sending an impressive blast of warm air towards her. "We're twenty-year-old women living in the twenty-first century. Not old spinsters living in the nineteenth."

"True, but don't you start your chores for York this weekend?" Winnie says, peering at Pip who's scratching his ear.

"Not until Sunday."

"Honestly," Winnie says, "there isn't much else to do."

I don't believe that for one minute. Having lived hidden in the back-end of nowhere for the last two decades, I'm determined my first real weekend in civilization will be fun.

"What are you doing this weekend?" I ask Andrew later that afternoon in the library.

"Meeting a friend in Los Magicos on Saturday afternoon, then going to drink some beers with my boys later."

"Hang on," I say. "One, I thought we weren't allowed into Los Magicos. And two, you're underage."

Andrew grins at me and raises his index finger. "One, you can go into Los Magicos if you have permission." He raises his middle finger alongside the first. "Two, there are bars that will let you in if you look old enough."

I glance down at my body. Could I look old enough? Maybe with the right hair and makeup.

"How does one go about obtaining permission?"

"Why? You want to come with us?"

"Maybe, if I can bring my friend, Winnie."

"Winnie ...?"

"The girl with the long black braids."

He grimaces a little but I glare at him so hard, he quickly says, "Sure, the more, the merrier."

"So, how do I get that permission?"

"Apply to your head of house."

"Head of my house?" I had no idea there was such a thing. "And who is the head of my house?"

"Venus? Tristan Kennedy."

The Prince Charming I'd spotted on my very first day. Little did I know back then how much of a prince he truly was. The dude is treated like royalty in this school, everyone practically bowing and kissing his feet wherever he walks.

"Tristan Kennedy?! I thought it would be a teacher or something."

"Nope."

"Shit.

"Yeah," Andrew says, leaning back in his chair. "A piece of advice, if you want to make your life easy, don't fall out with the head of your house."

I TELL Winnie that we're going into Los Magicos on Saturday night with Andrew and his friends. She looks exactly like she did standing outside Trent's room – half excited, half sick.

"I've never been to a bar before."

"Ha," I punch the air.

"What?" she says, glancing at me.

"Finally, something that you haven't done either."

"If we get caught my parents will actually skin me alive."

"We won't get found out. Andrew says they go to that bar all the time. Besides, we have something Andrew doesn't. Makeup."

Winnie's eyes light up. "You'll let me do your makeup? I've been dying to lay my hands on you from the moment you stepped through our dorm door." I tilt my head. "Wait, no, not like that, I mean, I want to give you a makeover."

"Hmmm."

"Pleeeeaaase," she begs, linking her hands together.

"If you promise not to turn me into a bouncing bunny."

"Eww, no. Although you will have to borrow some of my clothes. Jeans and hoodies won't cut it."

"Your clothes will be too long on me. I'll look like a walking scarecrow," I protest.

She bumps her shoulder against mine. "Magic, remember, Rhi."

Yep, magic. I was only permitted to use it at home in cases of emergency, when we really had to. My aunt was worried too much magic would light up the sky above our house like a firework display and have the town folk talking. I'm not used to being able to use my magic whenever I like. It's going to take some getting used to.

"Andrew says we have to seek out permission from our head of house to go into Los Magicos."

"Yep. That won't be a problem. Fiona's a bit of a bitch but she's so preoccupied with being popular, she can't be bothered to toy with the likes of me."

"I hope Tristan will be the same."

"I've never actually spoken to him," Winnie whispers with reverence. "He's like a living god in this school. His parents own half of Los Magicos. His dad's on the council and Tristan has won every academic prize going for the last two years. He's extremely talented and–"

"Good looking. Yeah, I noticed. You're not helping, Winnie." I don't want to feel intimidated going to speak to some other kid my age, but Winnie's building him up to be some superstar.

"Do you want me to come with you?" she asks, not so convincingly.

"No, I'll be fine. But where am I likely to find him?"

"In the Venus common room."

I roll my eyes. There's a common room? That would've been nice to know.

Before dinner, Winnie sets off to find Fiona and I go in hunt of Tristan. I expect to find the Venus common room somewhere in the mansion, but when I study my map, it's hidden in the gardens behind. I haven't walked through them before, and the floral aromas of the blossoms hanging in the trees and the flowers littering the beds has me thinking of home. Is it homesickness then stirring in my belly as I approach what looks like a summer house tucked under trees and out of sight, or is it that eerie feeling of déjà vu?

I consider turning around. Déjà vu never works out well for me.

Before I can make up my mind though, the door flings open and a group of the bouncing bunnies come trotting out, all giggling excitedly and muttering Tristan's name. My eyes flip to the open door and the dim gloom inside, sultry music weaving its way from within. I wonder what the hell I would've interrupted if I'd rocked up ten minutes earlier.

One of the bouncing bunnies, Aysha, spots me hovering outside. Her face immediately descends into a frown.

"Eww, pig girl, what are you doing here?"

"Visiting the common room," I state, even though that's obvious as hell.

"I doubt you'll be welcome. Tristan won't want your stench infecting the place."

I give her a cool stare but she simply swishes her hair over her shoulder and the girls move as one, like a pack.

I remind myself how badly I want to go into Los Magicos tomorrow, and knock on the door frame, even though the door's open. It's quiet inside apart from the music.

"Aysha, I thought I dismissed you," a voice drawls from within.

I peer into the gloom, taking a cautious step inside. The room is like some hippy love shack. There are big floppy sofas and cushions all over the floor, colored gauze shrouding the windows, lanterns hanging from the ceiling and a haze of smoke drifting in the air. Over by one wall a double bed dominates the space, dark cushions and throws draped over the mattress, and Tristan Kennedy resting against the headboard.

His shirt hangs open and he's wearing dark blue chinos, his feet bare, his outstretched arm resting on one bent knee, a joint burning in his fingers. His golden hair is ruffled around his head and I swear he has a bite mark on his right pec.

"It's not Aysha," I say, stepping further into the room. "I'm Rhianna, Rhianna Blackwaters."

He lifts the joint to his mouth and takes a long suck between his plush lips, the tip glowing red and embers darting from the end. Then he blows the air out slowly from between his parted mouth, gray smoke curling upwards.

"And?" he drawls.

"I'm a member of your house and–"

"And you finally decided to make the effort to come and show yourself. How gracious of you. Didn't think about presenting yourself earlier?"

"Presenting myself? Excuse me?"

"To your head of house." He jerks his thumb his way. "I like to check out the new meat."

I remember what Andrew warned me about staying on the right side of my head of house. Although this dude is an asshole. A hot asshole. But still an asshole.

"Right," I say, ignoring his words, as his gaze crawls down my body, lingering on the bare flash of thigh between my skirt and my stupid socks. Damn this ridiculous uniform. Damn the stupid way his gaze warms my skin. "I've come to ask for a pass to go into Los Magicos this weekend."

He rolls the joint in his fingers and considers me. "And what will you give me in return, pig girl?"

I grind my teeth together. "My understanding is that that isn't how this works."

"Your understanding is incorrect. You want me to give you a pass, you have to give me something in return."

"What exactly do you want me to give you?" Maybe I'm reading this situation wrong. I wouldn't be surprised. My social interactions have been few and far between. Perhaps I'm ill-practiced at reading signals. Maybe the creepy feeling in my stomach is not what I think it is. He's probably just stoned.

But when the corner of his mouth lifts in a sly smile, I'm less convinced.

I scowl at him. "You're sick."

He chuckles, leaning over to the table by his bed and flicking ash from his joint into a tray. "Don't worry little piggy, I'm not interested in anything like that from you. I mean look at you." He chuckles. "There's no meat to you." He leans forward. "You need fattening up, little piggy, before anyone will sink their teeth into you."

His words smart. Until I met the man in black, until I arrived at this school, I never had to consider my own attractiveness. I never gave it much thought. My face seemed fine enough and my body let me do all the things I needed it to do. What else did it matter?

Now it seems to matter. Where you sit in this school hierarchy is determined by how hot you are, how much money you have and your last name.

Well, at least my plainness means this creep won't be expecting any ... any whatever favors he was implying.

"Just give me a pass."

"After you've done a few jobs here for me. Those girls messed this place up. You can empty the bins and change these sheets. I'm going for a shower." He stubs his joint out in the tray and slides off the bed, padding across the room to a door on the far side. "When you're done, I'll sign your pass."

I go to ask one of a million questions, but he's already slammed the bathroom door in my face and a moment later I hear the water running.

Huffing, I glance around the room. There's a large trunk tucked up against one wall and when I open it up I find clean sheets inside. I carry them over to the rumpled bed. It stinks of musk and masculine odors and there are several damp spots I don't want to think too closely about. Irritated, I yank the sheets from the mattress, trying not to touch any of those spots, trying really hard not to imagine what caused them, thanking my stars Stone isn't here to read my thoughts. I throw the dirty sheets onto the floor, then battle with the clean ones.

When I'm done, I hunt down the bins. They're all empty apart from the one by the bed. As I bend down to pull out the trash bag, I get an unfortunate glimpse of what's inside and I almost vomit. A used rubber accompanied by that masculine scent again.

Quickly, I tie up the bag and toss it onto the pile with the sheets. Tristan hasn't returned yet, so despite the fact that I already hate the guy, I spend the next few minutes collecting up dirty glasses and straightening cushions.

He emerges from the bathroom just as I've exhausted all the jobs. A billow of steam follows him as he pads over to inspect the bed, his hair damp, and a white towel tied around his waist. He bends over to inspect my work and the muscles in his back ripple in a way that has me sucking in breath.

Unfortunately, I think he must hear, because he snaps his head around to smirk at me.

"Good job, pig girl. Perhaps I'll get you to change my sheets every day." I don't answer, and he sits on the bed. The towel hangs low on his hips and two deep grooves cut from his hips down below the material. I drag my eyes away, my cheeks warm, as he opens the drawer in the bedside table, and pulls out a slip of paper.

It's a blank form, but as he waves his hand over the paper, words appear along with a looped signature.

There goes any hope of faking a form next time.

He holds it out for me. "Here."

I walk towards him, reaching out to take the piece of paper. He snatches my wrist and pulls me in close, so close I can smell the dark notes of whatever soap he used in the shower and see moisture sliding down his sculptured chest.

"What's your phone number?"

"Why?" I ask, tugging on his grip.

"Because there are rules and expectations you need to follow in this house and I need to be able to get in contact with you."

He stares into my eyes, his gaze flicking left and right, my cheeks so hot they're blazing and my stomach fluttering.

I hiss the numbers at him, and he smiles with amusement at me, releasing my wrist. I grab the paper from his hand before he can taunt me with it any more.

"Enjoy your Saturday," he says pleasantly.

As I pass through the door, I realize the bastard has filled the form out for Pig Girl.

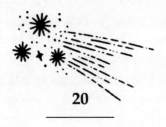

20

Tristan

SATURDAY NIGHT. Same old same old. Some girl whispering into my ear, her fingers trailing down towards my lap. Same girl giving me eyes from the other side of the table, even though she's been dating my friend Max for the last month. Same group of friends relaying the same old stories around the same table.

I smile at the girl opposite, and take another sip of my beer. Warm. With too much head.

This place sucks.

I'd rather be at one of the private clubs down by the harbor. But though my name alone would carry me through the front doors, half the rest of this rabble wouldn't get within ten feet.

So we're stuck here. As always. Same old same old.

I'll drink some more beer. Dance with one of these girls,

finger her in a dark corner of the dance floor and then take the other one home to my bed.

Next morning, I'll wake up with a pounding head, a dry throat, and will throw out whichever girl it was who ended up there the night before.

It's Cassandra whispering into my ear which has her friend Aysha pissed. She's throwing daggers at her from a table two feet away. It makes this evening a little more entertaining. Maybe tonight will end in a cat fight. Maybe it'll end in me taking both of these girls home.

I yawn, not paying attention to whatever bit of gossip Cassandra's relaying down my earhole, and think of the latest message from my father. He wants me to go meet him tomorrow, says there are things to discuss. The idea irritates me and I push Cassandra away and stumble through the maze of seating and people towards the bar.

Immediately, some new woman, older, not from the academy, attempts to strike up a conversation. I turn my back on her and stare at the mirror behind the bar. Bottles are lined up along its length. Behind them I can make out my reflection and the door of the bar.

Because there is one thing that would make this night different. That would shake things up.

That girl.

That fucking stupid pig girl.

The one who marched into my common room like she owned the place and …

I drum my fingers on the bar top. I haven't told anyone. It could have been the weed. It could have been the post-coital buzz. It could have been my fucked-up imagination.

Because her? *Her*?

I think not.

The girl may have had an attitude, but that's about all she

has. No manners, no respect, no name, no education and not even a fucking figure worth looking at.

Still.

My reflection snarls back at me. There is no 'still'. I'm fucking Tristan Kennedy. There's talk of me being a future Chancellor once I join the Council. I was born to lead, born to rule.

The barman skips past the other people waiting at the bar and comes to serve me next.

"What will it be, Kennedy?"

"Two shots of whisky."

"Add to the tab?"

I nod and watch as he scoops ice into a tumbler and then pours the liquor in free hand, giving more than the double I'll end up paying for. If he charges me at all.

He slides it along the bar and I twist the glass in my hands before taking a long sip. The alcohol burns my throat and warms my belly.

But it's not satisfying. Nothing much is these days. Nothing but the unleashing of my powers and I'm not permitted to do that as often as I'd like. I can't wait to ditch this place and show this world what I'm really capable of. Far more than sitting in boring council meetings, discussing politics, deciding how the authorities will bring the underworld gangs into line and sifting through intelligence from the West. Screw that. Give me a free hand and I'll bring those gangs to heel, will show those bastards in the West they are nothing compared to us.

I lift my glass to my lips and freeze. It's that feeling. That hook in my stomach, tugging me in a certain direction.

I close my eyes and concentrate on that sensation, bringing all my attention to focus on it. Is it real? Is this how it's meant to feel?

I flick open my eyelids and stare in the mirror.

A group of students hover by the door, looking nervous and

conspicuous as hell. If it weren't for me and my influence, most of the students at Arrow Hart would never get served here. But the cops are never going to raid this place, not when they know this is the favorite spot of kids like me, Spencer and Summer.

I examine the group. There's that new boy who transferred here last term, some boys from the athletics team, that tall kid with the black hair and, yeah, her. Pig girl.

For a moment my breath catches in my throat, until I huff it away in annoyance. Because she looks different tonight. Not dressed in the ridiculously sexed-up excuse for a uniform and not drowning in an oversized hoodie. No, she's wearing a little black dress. One that hugs every inch of her lithe body, emphasizing her tiny waist, her full tits and her rounded hips. Her black hair falls in waves over her shoulders and her lips are painted blood red.

If she'd come looking like that to the common room last night, things would have gone a hell of a lot differently.

I watch as the group looks around the bar searching for a table, and she leans in to talk to her friend, her eyes alive with excitement.

Then her gaze sweeps the bar again, and she spots me leaning against the bar. With my back to her, she can't see that I'm watching her. But I am. I watch as her lips part slightly, her tongue sliding over her white teeth, how she trails one hand up her bare arm, her skin peppered with goosebumps.

She may look good, but she also looks damn awkward. Especially when she follows the others across the bar to a table in the corner, wobbling on her too-high heels like any minute she's going to fall.

Which gives me the idea. I don't know why I do it. Except that I'm irritated. Irritated and bored and her presence is both interesting and an annoyance.

And so I lower my arm down to my side, and twist my hand

around, then silently I send a gust of wind rolling her way, silently, deceptively, so that no one else feels it or hears it.

The gust hits her and for a moment, she waivers, her body swaying one way, then another, before she loses her balance and I topple my tree.

She yelps as she falls, landing unspectacularly on her ass and flashing half the school her little black panties.

There's a shocked squeal from her friend as well as a few peals of laughter from those close by and then people are pushing and fighting to see what's happened, several people lifting up their phones to take pictures as a roar of laughter sweeps through the bar.

She snaps her head over her shoulder, peering my way, looking for the culprit. Her gaze locks with mine in the mirror. I stare back at her blankly. No guilty look of admission, no smirk of triumph.

The Andrew dude reaches down to help her up and I don't like the way his hand curls around her waist, squeezing her there.

Yeah, I don't like that at all.

I down the rest of my whisky and slam the empty glass onto the bar top, then I turn and march back to my group. Finding the first girl I bump into, I grab her wrist and lead her onto the dance floor. She's so fucking excited she doesn't know what to do with herself, her hands all over me as she giggles uncontrollably. I'm guessing I haven't slept with this one before. I don't even remember her name.

I grab her ass, and pull her tight against my body, letting her grind up against my cock while I try not to think about that flash of black panties. About Andrew's hands. About why the hell I'm thinking about either of those things.

I'm half hard and it's making the girl even more wound up thinking it's for her.

"Want to go back to my room?" she hiccups.

"Not really," I tell her flatly.

"Oh." A pause as the tiny cogs in her tiny mind whirl. "We can go back to yours if you want, or the ... or the bathroom?"

"I'll pass," I say, unhooking her arms from around my neck and walking away. I don't know where I'm going as I walk through the bar. Except I do know. Going for another peek. Going to check up on her. Disappearing into the shadows, I watch the pig girl from afar.

She sits sandwiched between Andrew and her roommate, two bottles of beer lined up in front of her. She shouldn't be drinking. She's tiny. One drink and she'll be flat on her ass again or face down in the gutter. It's probably what Andrew has planned. I see how he takes every fucking opportunity to touch her. I also see she doesn't return those touches, and observe how she's enraptured by both her friends and yet her eyes keep darting around the bar. Like she's restless. Restless like me.

I have to talk to her again

I pull out my phone and type her a message.

I need to talk to you. Outside now.

The message sends. She reaches down into her purse and scoops out her ancient-looking phone, pressing the buttons like she doesn't know how to use the thing. Eventually, her friend helps her and they read my message, whispering to each other. They're clearly discussing what to do.

I message her again, my patience waning.

I'm waiting.

Agonizingly slowly she types out a response with one finger.

And? Can't we talk at school tomorrow?

My phone nearly cracks as I squeeze it tight and hammer out my response.

When your fucking head of house asks to speak to you, you don't say no.

The little piggy actually has the nerve to roll her eyes, like I just requested she trek across the Salbian desert to come see me. Then she messages me again.

Fine, I'm coming, your highness.

She rises to her feet, pushes back her chair and wobbles her way to the exit.

I give it three minutes then follow her out. I'm not having her hanging around on the street alone dressed like she is.

I crash through the door and march out into the steamy night air, the door slamming shut behind me. She's waiting six feet away, her arms wrapped around her middle like she's trying to shield herself from my gaze.

"You look like a fucking hooker," I tell her.

"You pushed me over."

I ignore the accusation. "Where did you come from, pig girl?"

"What?" she says, full of incredulity. "That's what you want to talk about?"

Maybe it is. Maybe it isn't. Maybe I just wanted to talk to her, that hook yanking in my belly.

Is she feeling it too? There's no sign of it. No hint in her eyes, in her demeanor. In fact, all her eyes and her demeanor tell me is that she's mighty pissed off.

"Yes. Where are you from?"

She mumbles some place I've never heard of.

"Where is that?"

"Two days' drive south from here."

I shake my head. "No, pig girl, where did you transfer from? I'm not interested in whatever swamp they dragged you out of."

"You know this is none of your business."

She spins unsuccessfully on her heels, and I grab her arm before she tumbles again. Her skin is soft under my palm and warm.

She attempts to shake off my hold but I won't let her go.

"There's something up with you. I know it. You come from one of those batshit schools in the North of Aropia."

"No."

"Then where?" I grip her harder.

"Ow, you're hurting me," she says, and then to my utmost surprise, she sends a jolt of her magic straight into my hand.

I yelp and let go, the shock stinging through every finger.

"Did you just electrocute me? You know you can get kicked out of school for that," I thunder.

"You used your magic to knock me to the ground. So I guess we're both getting expelled."

"No, little pig, they're not expelling me."

We glare at each other under the orange lamplight and I notice her cheeks are flushed and her shoulders rising and falling.

"I didn't go to school," she finally snaps. "Until last week I was unregistered."

"What the fuck?" I mutter, stumbling away.

I knew she was different. Unusual. Not anyone I should be looking at, not someone who should have piqued my curiosity. But unregistered? This is not good.

This is ... ending.

"You kept that quiet." I scowl at her.

"I didn't. I'm perfectly happy with who I am. I don't give a shit about any of you and what you think of me or my pig. Because you know what I'm learning? You people are fucked up and miserable. And tucked away in my 'swamp'," she makes little inverted quote marks, "I was perfectly happy."

"Then why the fuck did you come? Why the fuck did you come here?"

To fuck up my life. To ruin everything.

"It wasn't my choice," she says, and she's clearly had enough of this conversation because this time she strides away and straight through the door of the bar.

Unregistered!

She was unregistered.

I drag my hand down my face. My hand still stings from that shock.

It doesn't matter. I'm probably imagining the whole fucked-up situation anyway.

My father always says I'm teetering on the edge of self-destruction, so maybe I'm inventing a way to implode my life.

There's a way to confirm it for once and for all: have our bloods tested. But how could I do that without someone finding out? This news would leak faster than a boat hitting an iceberg.

No, best to keep this quiet. Hidden.

Best not to tell a living soul. Least of all little pig girl.

21

R^{hi}

I WAKE up on Sunday morning with what I assume is my very first hangover. The room is spinning, my stomach sloshing and my head pounding.

I groan, too scared to roll over and hide my eyes from the sunshine pouring in through the gap in the curtains in case I vomit.

The pounding in my head only intensifies until I realize it isn't in my head at all. Someone is pounding the door.

"Urgh, who is that?" Winnie groans from below.

"Blackwaters!"

I close my eyes and wince.

Stone.

"Get your ass out here now!"

"Why?" I yell back, my own loud words making me wince.

"Chores! You're fucking late."

Chores. The ones Professor York said I'd be required to undertake if I wanted to keep Pip with me at the college. I'd forgotten all about them.

"It's early!" I groan.

"I'm giving you to the count of twenty to haul your ass out here or I'm coming in and doing it for you."

Asshole! I think as loudly in my head as I can, knowing he'll be able to read the thought.

"Takes one to know one, Blackwaters."

"You'd better get up," Winnie whispers up to my bunk. "Stone isn't known for his empty threats."

I groan again and slowly slide off my bunk, trying not to make any sudden movements or I'll disturb my stomach.

I hobble over to the wardrobe and pull on a pair of jean shorts and a t-shirt, ignoring Pip's angry snorts around my ankles.

"Would you feed him for me?" I ask Winnie.

She eyes my pig but nods her head. I think she may be beginning to soften towards him.

I shut the wardrobe door, the bang making me yelp and take a quick peek at myself in the mirror.

I have rings of mascara under my eyes and my hair is a mess around my head.

"I'm waiting," Stone yells, and I scowl at the door before opening it gingerly. "Fuck," he says, staring down at me, "I didn't think it was possible for you to look any more awful, Blackwaters, but you seem to have managed it."

"I need to pee," I tell him, pushing past him and stumbling down to the bathroom.

"Hurry the fuck up," he tells me and I consider giving him the finger. "Do it and I'll double the number of chores you have for today."

After I've used the toilet, I scrub my face at the sink and wash my pits, taking a long drink of water straight from the tap.

Then, I dry myself on the thin paper towels and go to find Stone waiting for me at the dormitory door.

"You're hungover," he says, with disgust, his nostrils flaring like he can smell the alcohol I can still taste on my breath.

"Yep," I say, "I really need to eat."

"Tough shit. You think this is how I want to be spending my Sunday morning?"

I glance towards the horizon. The sun hovers above and it's clear it's only just risen.

"Is it morning?" I grumble. "It's so fucking early."

Stone shrugs and stomps down the path and I'm forced to half sprint to keep up with him. He doesn't need to read my mind to know how sick that makes me feel. I'm sure the retching noises I'm making are damn obvious. But it doesn't slow the bastard down, instead, he picks up his pace, weaving around the buildings. The campus is quiet this morning. No bouncing bunnies, no football team, and I'm grateful for it when I'm forced to stop, hunching over my knees and heaving into a flowerbed.

When the sickness passes, I don't move, panting and staring down at the ground.

"Are you done?" Stone asks with annoyance.

I wipe the hem of my t-shirt around my brow and over my mouth.

"If you weren't walking so damn quickly–"

"If you hadn't been so fucking irresponsible and drunk so much last night."

I stand up straight and glare at him. "I'm twenty years old. This was my first chance to explore the city."

Stone takes a pace towards me, his jaw hardens. "You went into the city?" I nod. "Are you fucking stupid?"

"No," I tell him.

He scoffs. "Then why the hell would you go into the city?"

I don't understand why he's so outraged. "Everyone else was going into the city!"

"Everyone else doesn't have a bounty on their head. A bounty placed there by the Wolves of Night. You want to get yourself killed?"

"I was with my friends. They're not going to come after me when I'm surrounded by magicals and–"

"You don't know Marco Lowsky, Blackwaters. He'll come for you whenever and wherever he likes. *Your friends,*" he says the words with disgust, "aren't going to stop him or his men. The only place you're safe is here, in the academy. I don't know how many times I have to tell you." He glares at me, then shakes his head. "Come on, I've got places to be."

I follow him to the back of the mansion and into the garden. I peek at the Venus common room. The windows are all dark and the place silent. Whatever orgy took place there last night, they're probably all sleeping it off this morning. They won't be woken up by some asshole professor in a bad mood.

"I'm in a bad mood, Blackwaters, because I drew the short straw and am having to babysit you on my day off."

"Babysit me?"

"Professor York wants to be sure you actually complete your chores. Seems she doesn't trust you very much."

"I'm perfectly capable of carrying out a couple of chores and I always keep my word."

"Really? Excuse me if I don't believe an unregistered."

He marches me further into the gardens and stops in front of a giant flowerbed that runs the length of the fence that circles the gardens. In one corner, sits a pile of steaming manure, so tall it reaches over my head.

I've shoveled plenty of manure in my time. I've cleaned out chicken pens, and cleared up pig shit. But today, with my insides churning and my head aching, the smell is so pungent, I'm bending double and spilling my guts all over again.

I'm never drinking again. Never ever.

"I thought you were made of stronger stuff, Blackwaters."

As there's nothing left in my stomach to throw up, I conjure the most revolting image I can imagine into my mind and hear the professor mutter a string of expletives under his breath.

"You are fucking revolting," he snaps.

"You don't want to see it, then stay out of my head." Maybe I've finally found a way to keep him out.

"Trust me, I don't want to keep stumbling into your pathetic schoolgirl thoughts, but you make it so fucking easy."

"Then teach me how to stop it," I say, rolling back up to stand.

The professor doesn't say anything, just tosses me a pitchfork he's now holding.

"I think you can guess what you'll be doing here today."

"Running assholes like you out of town?" I ask hopefully, lifting the pitchfork over my head.

"Nope. Shoveling shit. The Head Gardener wants it spread over all his flowerbeds."

I peer up at the tower of manure, and then the never-ending rows of flowerbeds. It's going to take me all day.

"Let's hope not," the professor says, yawning and conjuring a deck chair out of thin air. He sinks down into it and next a newspaper appears in his lap and a cup of hot coffee in his hand. "The sooner you're finished, the sooner we're out of here."

I stare longingly at the coffee, wondering if I asked nicely enough whether he'd conjure me one too.

"No," he says, not lifting his eyes from the front page of the paper.

I huff out a breath through my teeth, then stroll over to the tower of manure. Might as well get started.

An hour later, I've shifted several pounds of manure but I've hardly made a dent in the tower and I realize I'll be working well into the night at this rate.

The sun's risen higher in the sky and the shadows have retreated. I'm sweating and parched and my head hurts even more than it did when I woke up.

I lean on the handle of my pitch fork and swipe my arm over my brow, then peer at the professor. He's immersed in his newspaper, and I don't think he's realized I've halted until he shouts:

"Not time for a break yet, Blackwaters." I jump about a foot off the ground and the pitchfork clatters to the ground. "Careful with school equipment."

I send him another disgusting image.

"You want me to make that shit pile higher, Blackwaters?"

"I'm dying of thirst over here. I need something to drink."

He looks up from his paper and examines me. Maybe he realizes I'm close to fainting on him, because he rolls his eyes.

"Go get some water from the Venus common room. I'm giving you two minutes. If you're not back–"

"The Venus common room? Can't I–"

"You're wasting time."

I scowl at him and sprint off in the direction of the common room. As I arrive at the door, I can hear the murmuring of voices within.

No, scrap that, whoever is inside certainly isn't doing any talking.

I decide that actually I'd rather die of thirst than walk in on *that* looking and smelling like I do right now.

But my feet don't seem to be in agreement with my mind and that strange sensation in my belly keeps me grounded right where I am. Right where I am and listening to the high-pitched moans of some girl, the squeak of mattress springs, the thud of a headboard and deep male grunts.

I may have been a recluse all my life but I know what that

means. I don't want to stand here and listen but I can't seem to move, my stomach a strange concoction of nausea and fluttering. I remember the last time I was here, Tristan in that towel, his toned body glistening with water, his golden hair damp from the shower, his eyes intense.

I remember the power that seemed to radiate from his body, a body and power he's now using to ...

The room hangs heavy with that masculine scent and a lighter one that turns my stomach.

My eyes adjust slowly to the dim light and I can make out the outlines of two bodies: one laid out on the bed, a woman, the other stood by the end of it, a man. Legs are wrapped around his waist, his hands tight on her thighs. The bodies crash together in a rhythm that seems to match the beat of my heart and the body on the bed writhes in pleasure. Both seem oblivious to my presence, lost in each other.

Their panted breaths become more frantic, the girl cries out, the bed bangs against the wall with more force.

I want to leave. I don't want to be here. I don't want to see this. But my feet won't move. My body won't obey and to my shame my blood seems to heat.

Then there's a loud grunt. Someone swears.

Tristan, definitely Tristan.

I need to leave. Now.

But I'm too late. His head turns. His cheeks are flushed, his hair a mess, sweat on his brow, his eyes fierce. He peers over his shoulder. At me. Right at me.

"Pig girl," he growls, and finally my body responds. I sprint out of the common room as quickly as my legs will carry me.

Stone's waiting for me on his feet.

"That was longer than two minutes."

"I bumped into a couple of assholes," I mutter, keeping all those revolting images hovering in my mind so the professor won't see what I just have.

"You ever wondered whether it's you that's the asshole, Blackwaters?"

I ignore him, picking up the pitchfork and sticking the throngs into the mound of manure. I could toss a nice lump of it straight over the professor's head. I linger on that mental image next, not giving a shit whether he sees it or not.

"Try it, and you'll find yourself buried face down in that pile," he says darkly, dropping back into his seat and taking obvious delight in torturing me, by picking up a bottle of cold water from by his feet and gulping the stuff down.

I lick my dry lips, and grit my teeth.

Another two hours pass, other students filter into the gardens, lying out on the grass in the sunshine or kicking a ball about. Several of them stop to stare at me, whispering behind their hands or being less subtle about it and laughing out loud at me. To my surprise, the professor growls at them and sends them on their way, telling them not to distract me.

Finally, when the sun is high and scorching in the sky, the professor rises to his feet and stretches.

"Break time," he says, tossing his paper into the seat of the deck chair.

I drop the pitchfork and collapse onto the ground, breathing heavily.

The professor peers down his nose at me. "You need to improve your fitness."

"Seriously?" I say. "It's like 500 degrees out here and I'm hungover as fuck." I point towards the pile. "I've moved nearly half of that stuff this morning. I'd like to see you do better."

"You would?"

"Yes, I would."

His mouth twitches and I know I'm going to regret this.

He turns in the direction of the manure pile, waves his hands in a circular motion and I watch in horror as the muck glides through the air and sprinkles perfectly over the flowerbeds.

I screw up my eyes and cycle through every curse word in my vocabulary. How could I have been so stupid?

"It seems to come naturally to you," Stone says, and I open my eyes just in time to see a large clump of manure falling through the air in my direction. I try to twist out of its path, but most of it lands over my head anyway.

I cough and splutter, shit in my mouth, in my nose and in my eyes. My stomach heaves again and I try to spit the dirt away.

The professor leans over me, his hands on his knees. When he speaks his voice is so quiet only I can hear him and none of the spectators, who have gathered to take photos of me.

"And you think you'd last on the run, Blackwaters? Think again."

By the time I've made it back to my dorm room, the photos of me lying on the ground and covered in shit must have circulated around the entire school, because Winnie's waiting for me with a look of sympathy and she seems to know some version of the story.

"Professor Stone?" she asks.

"Who else?"

"Honestly," she says, taking a step away from me because I stink to high heaven. "It could be any number of assholes in this school."

I laugh, because she's right.

I grab a towel from our room and stomp down to the bathroom. People cower away from me as I pass down the corridor as if I'm diseased and they may catch something. One girl from the year below shouts after me, "You better not leave the showers covered in shit!"

The water's cold when I duck inside, but today I'm not bothered. I'm sweltering hot anyway and the cool water is a relief. When I've scrubbed the shit from my eyes, my nose and my mouth and cleaned my face five more times, I tip my head right back to let the water flow straight into my mouth and down my throat. It's glorious and I stand like that pretending that the rest of the world doesn't exist, imagining I'm back home standing in the meadow with rain battering my face and not some shitty shower.

My moment of peace is soon broken though, when someone hammers on the door and tells me not to waste up all the water.

I scrub the rest of my body, scouring my hands and fingers until they're red raw. It's no use though. My fingernails seem to be stained a permanent black and I can't get all the dirt out from underneath them.

It feels like the universe is punishing me. Yesterday, I felt amazing. Once Winnie had altered one of her dresses for me, styled my hair and made up my face, I'd felt like someone else. Someone who could almost be considered presentable, if not beautiful. I felt like maybe I did belong here. With these people. In this school. And despite Tristan Kennedy's attempts to disrupt my evening, I'd had fun. With my friends. *Friends.* Something I've never had before.

It felt good.

But just like Cinderella, I went to the ball. I had my special moment. And now the magic has most definitely faded and I'm back to being a nobody. A dirty nobody who smells like shit.

A nobody who is most definitely not going to land herself a prince and a palace.

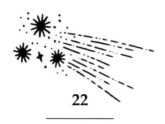

22

Stone

I hate Sundays.

I hate them even more when I have to give up half my day to babysit the Blackwaters girl.

Not that my Sundays are filled with entertainment. That's the problem. They're a weekly reminder of how fucking terrible my life actually is. Usually I lie in, go for a run, lift some weights and spend the rest of the day scanning the paper, wondering what the hell the authorities aren't telling us behind all those carefully crafted and manufactured headlines. In the evening, I hit the bar, usually alone.

That's the problem with the entire fucking day. I spend it alone. Have done for a year now since I ended things with Jessica.

Today, though, my friend's in town. It's not like him to hang around the city so much. But I have my suspicions as to why he's here. Even if he'd never admit it to me.

I find him already sitting at the bar, nursing a bottle of beer.

I signal to the barman to fetch me one too as I take the stool next to him.

"You stink of shit," my friend says.

"Nice to see you too," I say, handing a banknote to the bartender and taking a long swig of my beer.

"No, seriously, Stone, you smell fucking awful. What the fuck have you been doing?"

That's because I didn't shower after the morning I spent with the Blackwaters girl. That's because after I sent her on her way, I headed straight to my office and my books.

There has to be a way around this. A way to undo it. Not that I've told my friend about my little bit of research. He wouldn't approve. There are some rules he doesn't believe in breaking.

"You don't want to know," I say, taking another long gulp of my drink.

My friend stares at me, examining my face, then lowers his eyes back to the bottle he's cradling in his hands.

"Have you discovered anything else about her?" he asks me.

We're both searching for more information on the girl. Me in her head, he through his network of sources.

"She's a tracker. A good one. Can sense the presence of magicals and," I flick my gaze towards him, "she has the ability to see the remnants of ancient magic." My friend nods like those types of powers are everyday occurrences. "Not that she wanted me to know that. She tried to keep it hidden, but ..." I shrug with a smirk.

"Anything else? About her background?"

I spin the beer bottle in my hands, watching the liquid swish against the sides. "She had a tough upbringing."

"How do you mean?"

He saw how she was living back there in that forest. I don't know why I have to spell it out.

I sigh.

"No money. Scrabbling to put food on the table. Hiding her true nature." I take a swig of my beer. "Harassed by dickheads." I scowl.

My friend is quiet and I can feel his eyes still examining me.

Of course, I've shared the bits of information I have found out about her with my friend. I'm not so open to sharing my failures. There's always been this quiet competition between us, the need to impress one another.

And while it's been easy as fuck to stroll straight into her mind and peruse all her thoughts like I'm window shopping, there are some memories she's keeping locked away. Memories I can't reach without strapping her to a chair and invading her mind. Memories I'm not sure the girl even knows she possesses.

I'm not ready to admit I've been unable to unlock them. Not yet.

"You don't like her?" my friend says, after several moments of silence.

"I never said that."

"Phoenix–"

"She was unregistered."

He doesn't have anything to say to that. He knows how I feel about those who shirk their duties.

"There may have been a good reason," he says finally.

I stare at my friend. Is he out of his mind? The authorities' enforcer? His very job is to collect those unregistered and hand them in for the punishment they deserve.

"There is never a good enough reason," I snap.

The girl may have some talent. There are even times I catch myself captivated by her because she's goddamn beautiful, those big honey eyes of hers, too mesmerizing for words. But she's also a brat. A brat who has every intention of fleeing as soon as she gets the chance.

"She reminds me of you," my friend says. "How you were when we first started at the academy. Always bristling for a fight – with the teachers as well as the other pupils."

I scrape my fingers through my beard. That's because I'd learned the hard way always to strike first. If I'd let them, those rich kids and snotty teachers would have ground me to dust.

It's a lesson the girl needs to learn. And quickly. The Academy, Los Magicos, the society in which we live, is not one of unicorns and rainbows.

"How about you?" I ask. "What have you learned about her?"

He lowers his beer bottle to the bar top.

"Nothing so far. There were whispers about a woman and a girl a few years ago. Somewhere down South. They disappeared. It was thought to be a false rumor."

"And the name? Blackwaters? Did you find out anything about that?"

He spins in his stool and taps the beer bottle on the counter. "There are no files with that name. No official ones, anyway."

"What do your sources say?"

"The name's familiar to them but nobody can quite remember the story that goes with it."

"Have you asked your father?"

My friend looks at me like I suggested he dip his cock in a pool full of piranha. He avoids his dad as best he can. Unlike me, my friend comes from a family with a reputation and connections. His father had planned on a political career for his son. His son had other ideas.

"If I turn up and start asking him about some family name, he's going to want to know why and that isn't a conversation I want to have."

I scrub my hand over my chin. "Yeah." We're the only ones

that know. The girl, she seems utterly oblivious. It gives us options, choices. It gives me time to find a way to undo this mess. It's best we keep this knowledge to ourselves.

"You need to keep prying. See if you can find anything more out about her family," he says.

I grimace, lowering my bottle of beer. "Her mind is a cesspit."

My friend laughs. "I thought you were used to delving into the minds of teenage delinquents."

"No, seriously. It's a cesspit. Her way of trying to keep me out. You should have seen the images she was conjuring up this morning."

"This morning?" my friend says, all innocent like, but I see the way his spine stiffens ever so slightly.

"I drew the short straw and had to oversee her undertaking her chores for York."

My friend downs the last of his beer and pushes his stool backwards.

"Let's go for a stroll. There are other matters we need to talk about."

IF SUNDAYS SUCK, Mondays are far worse. The students are always in a bad mood and mine is no better.

Usually, I lounge around in bed until the very last moment, rocking up to my lessons five minutes late. Today, I'm in my office early again, reading through the old tomes I've stolen from the library, searching for a fucking solution to our current dilemma.

The students won't expect me in my classroom until five minutes past nine, so I'm fucking surprised when there's a knock on the door. I stare at it with disdain and return to the paragraph written in the old magical scripture that I'm trying to decipher.

Whoever it is standing the other side of the door is pretty persistent though, rapping their knuckles a second time against the wood.

But who am I kidding? I know exactly who it is. I can tell by that tug deep in my stomach, the one pulling me towards her.

Blackwaters.

I slam the book shut and stomp to the door, flinging it open.

I woke up on the wrong side of the bed this morning. I'm pissed off. About this situation, about our inability to find anything out about this girl, about my failure to find a fucking solution, about my life in general.

I never wanted to be a fucking teacher. But people like me have limited options. Something the authorities and my best friend's father reminded me of when the offer was made.

Her presence outside my classroom door pisses me off a thousand times more.

"What?" I bark right in her face, satisfied when she can't disguise the way that makes her flinch.

Good, I'm not here to be the fucking girl's friend. I need to make that clear.

"Good morning to you too, Professor," she says with a sarcastic smile.

Yeah, the brattiness is half the fucking problem. It isn't just irritating. It also heats my blood.

"Lessons don't start for another hour. This is my personal time that you are interrupting, Blackwaters, so get on with it, what the fuck do you want?"

Her face cracks. Her usually steely countenance falters. I take an automatic step towards her. "What is it?"

"My pig."

Her pig? She's fucking knocking on my door at eight in the

morning, looking like her world ended, because of her stupid pig.

I don't understand her. I don't want to understand her.

I should slam the door in her face but I'm weak and so I can't help asking, "What about your damn pig?"

"He's missing."

"He probably ran away. Arrow Hart Academy is no place for a pig."

She shakes her head vehemently. "He would never do that."

"He's a pig. He has no logic or reason. You have no idea what he would or wouldn't do."

"It's been me and him for a year. Just the two of us and the chickens. I know exactly what he would and wouldn't do."

I look away from her. She could have been here, at the academy, learning from me. Instead, she chose to live like that. Hiding. Alone. Barely surviving.

Her choice.

"I can't help you. I don't know where the hell your pig is."

"I think someone pig-napped him," she murmurs, and the way she cares so much about the dumb animal has anger boiling in my gut for no logical reason.

"Why *do* you have that stupid pig?" I say unable to stop myself from swiping at her. "Is it because you're socially awkward and incapable of forming relationships?"

Her eyes snap up to mine and she frowns. "You can talk! You're 40 and living on your own in a school with no wife and no family?"

"I'm thirty-fucking-two and I could be gay."

"With a loving husband...wait are you gay?"

Images of me with some dude swim through her head.

My knees almost buckle.

Fuck this girl's fantasies.

And thank god she can't see mine.

"You think that's an appropriate question to ask your

professor?" Her gaze doesn't flinch from mine. "I'm bi. And you have a dirty mind. Is it because you are sexually frustrated? You should do something about that." My mouth twitches as she frowns harder. "But not with the pig." She snorts. "See? You're even beginning to sound like him."

Her stern facade cracks for a second time and she laughs, sunshine momentarily flooding her features and making her caramel eyes dance.

I stare at her, that tug straining in my stomach, my blood so hot it's scorching.

I grip the edge of the door.

"Get out before I kiss you," I snarl through my teeth.

She stops laughing and looks at me. Her cheeks pinken.

The air seems to crackle with electricity and I can hear her breath hitch.

I grip the doorframe so hard my knuckles bleach.

"Maybe I want you to kiss me," she whispers in her head and more images flood her mind, images of me bending down to press my mouth to hers, images of me lifting her up and pressing her against the door, images of me laying her out across my desk.

I stand there watching them all, my arms shaking, my heart pounding. Then I get a fucking grip on myself.

"Get out!" I yell at her, pushing her backwards and slamming the door.

The door rattles in its frame and for what must be several long minutes, I stand there, catching my breath, staring at the grain of the wood.

Then I return to my books.

The quicker I can solve this situation, the better.

23

Rhi

SOMEONE HAS TAKEN HIM. Someone has *stolen* him.

I feel it in the pit on my stomach. I know it by the way the other students stand and laugh at me, as I dash about campus in a frenzy, searching everywhere I can think of for my damn pig.

He's not in the garden, my dormitory, the Great Hall or the gymnasium, and to be honest most of the buildings in the campus he wouldn't be able to enter without someone's help anyway.

No, someone took him.

Someone took him to mess with me.

But I have no fucking clue who.

Scrap that. I have several ideas who it could be.

That's the problem. It could be any number of people. I've

been here two weeks and I already seem to have built up an entire army of people who hate my guts.

I don't understand why. I didn't do anything to provoke their dislike, other than being myself. Maybe that was enough.

Winnie tries to calm me down, grabbing me by both hands and pulling me to sit on her bunk when I return to our room to search the cupboard yet again.

"He's probably just wandered off. He was probably bored of hanging out in our room, wanted an adventure. I'm sure he'll be back for dinner."

I shake my head, telling Winnie the same thing I told Stone. "Pip wouldn't do that. He never wanders off. He's too fucking stupid."

"Exactly," Winnie says, ignoring my scowl. I am allowed to criticize my pet, nobody else is. "Perhaps he got lost. Let's get to class and if he's not back by lunchtime, we'll go out looking for him again. He probably wandered into the forest or–"

"Someone took him!"

"Why would someone take him?"

I give my friend a hard look.

"To fuck with me."

"Oh," Winnie says, realization dawning over her face.

"I need to get him back before they do something horrible to him."

Winnie turns slightly green. "It was probably Summer," she says.

"Or Tristan. I tried the Venus common room – it was empty. And so were the locker rooms."

I wish I could track him like I can track magicals. I wish I'd thought of placing a tracking spell on him. Fuck it, I wish I'd put an actual chip in him. But it never, in one hundred thousand years, occurred to me that someone would steal my pig.

After all, the students here spend their entire time making snide comments about how filthy and smelly he is.

"You could go to Professor York?" Winnie offers, although she doesn't sound convinced.

We both know Professor York isn't going to give a shit about my pig.

"I already went to ask Professor Stone for help," I mumble.

"You did?"

"I was desperate! And I thought, seeing as he's so damn good at reading minds–"

"He'd be able to identify the culprit."

I nod.

"And?"

"He basically slammed the door in my face." I neglect to mention the part where he threatened to kiss me and how that had set my heart racing like a freight train. I can't think about that now. When I find Pip, then I'll think about why the idea of kissing that asshole had been, in that moment, so appealing.

Winnie squeezes my hand. "Let's split up and be methodical about searching this place."

I try not to sob. Campus is freaking huge and Pip could be hidden anywhere.

"All the other students will be in class soon so it'll be easier to search."

I agree and Winnie sets off towards the Great Hall as I set off to the gymnasium for the second time this morning.

As I reach the main entrance, I come face to face with Summer still dressed in her shorts and hoodie from her morning run.

"Ewww Piggie, what are you doing here?"

I ignore her and do my best to push straight past. She steps to the side, though, blocking my path.

"Are you deaf as well as stupid?" she says. "I said, what are you doing here?"

"None of your business."

"It is my business if you're going to go snooping about the

locker rooms. I know you don't have any money, Blackwaters, and I don't want you pilfering our stuff."

I take a step towards her. "Are you sure it isn't you who has taken something of mine?" I hiss. I don't want to give her the delight of seeing me squirm about Pip. And if it wasn't her who took him, I don't want her finding out and taunting me with this. But I can't help myself.

She looks at me, all innocent. "I don't know what you're talking about. Speak some sense for once, pig girl."

"Where is he? What have you done with my pig?"

She screws up her nose in disgust. "Ewww your pig. I wouldn't touch your filthy, diseased little pig if you gave me a ten-foot pole." Then she pauses and tilts her head to one side. "Wait, is he missing?" She bursts out laughing. "Oh my god, pig girl, you're so pathetic even your scummy little pig has run away from you. That's hysterical."

"He didn't run away," I say, trying to hold in my anger. All I want to do is punch this girl right in the face with a fistful of my magic. It's practically sizzling in my veins just asking to be unleashed. "Someone took him."

"No one would want your pig."

"If it was you ..." I hiss.

"You'll what?" she tosses her hair. "You don't know the first thing about magic. Professor Stone is right. You're an ignorant little pig. You should head back to whatever hovel you crawled out of. You don't belong here and I'm going to make sure you're gone before Christmas."

My fingers twitch and she seems to register the anger on my face. She smiles and goes to step around me, then at the last minute she barrels straight into me, her shoulder hitting mine and causing me to fly backwards onto my backside.

"Ooops, sorry," she chimes before bouncing off in that infuriating way she does in the direction of the Great Hall.

I sit there in the dirt, yelling a few choice names in her

direction. I'm tempted, so tempted, to send a bolt of magic her way. But it's what she wants. She's trying to get me expelled. I can't rise to the bait. Not yet anyway. Not with Pip missing.

※

I SPEND the whole day searching for Pip. Winnie helps me despite muttering under her breath about how much trouble we're going to be in for skipping class. I don't care. I don't trust the assholes in this school not to harm him, whether intentionally or not.

It's my fault he's here and my responsibility to keep him safe.

By dinnertime and three circuits of the campus later, I have to finally admit defeat though.

He's not anywhere I'm going to find him. I need a different tactic.

Winnie hugs me as I slump down onto our bedroom floor.

"Maybe if you went and asked Summer nicely …"

"I'm not even sure Summer has Pip. It could be any number of her minions. Or Tristan. Or Spencer. Or half the dueling team. No, wait, probably the entire dueling team." I slump over my knees. "Even if I groveled at their feet, I can't see them handing him over."

"Not without torturing you first," Winnie concedes. "Maybe you should go to Professor York, after all."

"Maybe," I say, chewing my thumb, although I think ratting on the other students will do nothing to increase my popularity and will probably double the likelihood that they'll hurt Pip.

There's one other person I could ask for help. I really don't want to. It would be awkward and weird. But I've already swallowed my pride once today; for Pip I can do it again.

I tell Winnie I'm too stressed out to eat and when she leaves the room to go for dinner, I fetch my phone and stare down at the number.

I don't exactly know how or why I have his number, but when I was adding one of Andrew's friends to my feeble list of names in my contact list a day ago, I noticed it was there.

It could be another prank. Maybe I'll phone it and it'll put me through to some sex line.

I'm kinda desperate though so anything is worth a try.

With sweaty palms, I hit connect and lift the cellphone to my ear, listening to the long drawn out rings. I screw up my eyes, half wanting him to answer, half hoping he doesn't.

I'm about to give up and disconnect, when the rings halt abruptly and I hear his voice in my ear.

It's him.

The man in black.

"Rhianna."

"Hi," I say.

Silence.

"Did you call for a reason?"

I swallow. "Yes ..."

His voice sounds quizzical when he speaks again. "What?"

"My ... my pig's missing. I think someone stole him."

More silence.

I feel so stupid. I want the ground to open up and swallow me whole.

This is the authorities' Enforcer. I shouldn't be calling him about my lost pet.

I shouldn't be calling him at all.

"And?"

And ... I don't know. I don't know why I thought he would be able to help me even if he could. He's probably halfway across the country right now tracking down another unregistered like me.

"Nothing," I mumble, disconnecting the call and tossing my phone across the room.

I screw up my face and sink down to the floor, hugging my legs to my chest and resting my forehead to my knees.

I'm not sure I can do this. I'm not sure I'm cut out for human interactions and navigating people. I'm an idiot with no social skills and pretty feeble magical ones to boot.

I thought I could come to this school, soak up as much information as I wanted and then disappear into the sunset. Now I don't know what the hell to do. I wish I had my aunt here. To guide and advise me. To tell me what to do.

But I realize, for all her preparation, for all her teaching, for all the times she kept me safe, she still failed me. I don't know enough about this world and I don't know what the hell I'm doing.

And now to top it all off, I've lost Pip.

The one being in the world who would make me feel better right now, who would climb into my lap, snuggle in my arms and lick my face. He'd make me laugh with his silly little snorts and he'd remind me there is at least one being left in this world who likes me.

My phone starts to buzz from the other side of the room. It lights up and vibrates across the worn carpet. I ignore it. It's most likely the man in black calling to berate me for disturbing him with my ridiculous nonsense.

All I want to do is run away. Right now I'd risk the stupid Wolves of Night just to be rid of this place. But I can't. I'm trapped. I can't go anywhere without Pip.

I wipe my face with my palms and watch as the lights on my phone die and it lies still on the floor once more.

Then I jump up. I can't sit here feeling sorry for myself. Not when Pip is missing. I need to find him.

There's one place we haven't searched properly. The forest behind the dormitory. Mainly because I was convinced my pet had been stolen and wouldn't go bumbling off into the scary woods without me. Winnie hadn't exactly been keen to go snooping about the forest either.

"It gives me the serious creeps," she'd whispered in my ear as we'd searched the perimeter. "There're all sorts of tales about goings on in there."

I'd rolled my eyes at her then and I roll my eyes again now, as I switch on the torch on my phone and walk around the dormitory building and through the first few trees of the forest.

Once I'm under the heavy boughs, though, the light of the moon hidden and the sounds of campus muted, I'm not so sure of my earlier skepticism.

This place is pretty darn spooky. I've spent years living in various forests. I've camped out and hidden in them multiple times. I've never felt afraid before.

But it's the pitch blackness and eerie silence of this place that I don't like. Plus the feeling that I'm being watched. Perhaps even followed. I spin around suddenly, the beam from my phone swishing through the trees, sure there is someone behind me, certain I heard the snapping of twigs underfoot.

There's nobody there though.

I'm letting this stupid college and these people crawl inside my mind and mess with me.

I cup my hand around my mouth and call Pip's name. The sound of my voice reverberates off the solid tree trunks, echoing back at me and for a moment I'm stunned by how much my own voice sounds like my aunt's. It's almost as if she's calling me now, like she did multiple times, calling me in for dinner, calling to me to tell me the coast is clear.

I close my eyes. I can't lose them both. Not my aunt and Pip. He's my only connection to home now, to the family I've lost.

I trek deeper through the trees, trying not to notice how they become denser, crowding closer and closer together until soon I seem to be squeezing through the gaps in the trees.

Bark scrapes against my legs and branches catch in my hair. I keep going, calling Pip's name over and over again.

My phone beeps twice in my hand. A message from Winnie most probably. I ignore it. If she'd found Pip, she'd know to call me.

As I trek deeper, the silence that had drowned me is pierced by the creatures of the forest. An owl hoots low over my head and something scrabbles in the undergrowth near my feet. The wings of a bird crack and I could almost believe I hear the distant howling of a wolf.

I stop, leaning my weight against a tree. I haven't eaten all day and I'm hungry and light-headed, my footsteps heavier and requiring more effort than normal.

"Pip," I call out desperately. "Pip, are you here?"

What if I'm wrong? What if it wasn't a human who stole him? What if it was one of the creatures who live in this wood?

I should never have left him outside on his own. Unguarded, defenseless, gullible as hell.

In desperation, I tap into my power. It won't help me find my pig. But I'm desperate. Maybe I can bend it, manipulate it, force it to find Pip for me.

As soon as I release the doors holding my tracking power, it floods into my mind and I know immediately there's someone here, someone with me in the darkness.

Without warning, I spin my torch around, pivoting 360 degrees on the spot. The light flickers through the trees. But once again there's no one there.

Except there is. I can feel them. Close. Close enough that the beam of my torch should pick them out.

"I know you're there!" I call out, lifting my hand, ready to shoot my power at whoever is lurking there in the shadows.

Immediately, I'm slammed hard against a tree, my back and my head thumping hard against the solid bark.

I grunt and try to struggle free, but I'm caged, caged by a warm solid body.

I blink, all I can see are the dark trees of the forest. There's no one there. Yet I can feel them, feel their body pressing against mine, feel their presence buzzing in my magic.

"Get off me," I say, struggling against the body restraining me, but they grip my wrists, pinning them above my head, and I can't twist my hands around to blast them with my magic. Something sharp tugs in my stomach as I try to wriggle free, the fingers at my wrist only gripping tighter, digging into my flesh.

"Who are you?" I snarl, peering up into nothingness.

The body leans into me, solid flesh warm against mine, hot breath whistling over my cheek.

I can hear them now, too. The panting of their breath, the thundering of their heart.

They hold me tight against the tree.

The forest is silent. The dark oppressive.

They inhale, right by my ear, sucking in my scent. I hear it rush through their mouth. Hear them wet their lips with their tongue.

The hook hums in my stomach, the sensation shivering through my body.

I shudder as sharp ridges of teeth brush against my throat and warm lips press against my skin. Then a wet tongue slides over the point where my pulse thrums and a mouth sucks gently, tenderly, almost like a kiss.

My eyes flutter shut as my head tips back, the pair of lips trailing lower and lower, to the base of my throat, along my clavicle, down to the neck of my top.

I should be struggling. I should be demanding they stop. But to my shame, it feels too good.

A needy sigh escapes, unbidden, from my mouth.

And then just as suddenly, I'm free. The grip at my wrists releasing, the body stepping away.

Immediately, I lower my hands and, despite the fact I'm shaking and confused, send magic shooting through the dark. The bolts hit a tree in the distance, sparking and splintering the bark. I curse, drawing my arms wide and firing again, hoping in my wildness I'll hit whoever the hell that was.

My magic flashes through branches and overhead but after a few minutes I have to admit defeat. I'm fighting blind here and that tug in my stomach, the magical awareness I possess, grows weaker. Whoever that was, has gone.

24

R^{hi}

I STUMBLE BACK through the forest, dazed and confused and determined to leave this goddamn place as soon as I can get my hands on my pig.

Soon the trees start to thin and that eerie silence returns. I'm nearly at campus. Nearly at campus, when my senses tingle all over again, that tug in my stomach pulling like mad.

I lift my hands ready for them this time.

"If you try anything you mother fucker ..." I yell. "I swear I'll–"

"You'll what?" a deep voice says. A familiar one. I strain my eyes through the darkness in the direction of heavy footfall.

Then the man in black comes crashing through the trees.

"It's you," I gasp, my arms still raised.

He glances at them with disdain. "Are you planning to attack me again?"

"Again? It was you?" I say, confused. I have a feeling I'd have known if it was him. Besides, it doesn't seem like his style. He's more of an attack-you-face-on kind of man, not a sneak up on you.

"What?" he says.

But before I can explain, my gaze has dropped to his arms and the squirming bundle he's cradling.

"Pip?" I gasp, darting through the trees towards him, forgetting altogether that this might be the man who attacked me only moments ago.

"Yes," the man in black says, passing him to me with a look of clear disgust. Once he's safely in my arms, snuffling madly at my face, the man in black wipes his hands on his cloak. "That thing needs a bath. He stinks."

"Wh-wh-where did you find him?" I pepper my pet with kisses, letting him lick at my face in excitement while I search his body for any signs of harm. With relief, I find there are none.

"Not me. Stone."

I peer up at him.

"Stone?"

He nods. Then frowns. "What the hell are you doing out here in the woods alone?"

"Looking for him," I say, burying my face against Pip's.

"It's not safe." He marches towards me, gripping my elbow and pulling me through the last remaining trees and onto campus.

When we're back on the path, I peer up at him with suspicion. "How did you know where I was?"

"Your roommate said you weren't there and then I saw bolts of magic in the forest. Looked like your brand of magic."

"My magic has a brand?"

He shakes his head like I'm the dumbest person on earth.

"You're lucky the teachers are all up at the mansion. If you got caught out in the forest, using magic–"

"Let me guess. I'd be expelled. Funny how everyone here can treat me like shit and not face any consequences but anything I seem to do, is threatened with expulsion."

I lower Pip onto his patch of ground and he shoots straight in the direction of the bowl of food I'd left out for him.

"Where did Stone find him?" The man in black's jaw hardens in answer, like he doesn't want to answer that question. I cross my arms and glare at him. "Was it Stone who took him?"

"Why would Stone waste his time hiding your pig?"

"To mess with me."

"He has better things to do."

"Are you sure about that?" I ask and the man in black shuffles on his feet.

"He was found in the cellar in the mansion."

"Who took him?"

"Unclear. Stone is looking into it."

"He is?" I say, utterly surprised.

"Yes."

I drop down onto my haunches, stroking along Pip's back when he comes trotting back to me.

"I really fucking hate it here," I mutter.

I can feel the man in black gazing down on me, his heavy boots visible on the periphery of my vision. The tug in my stomach yanks me his way, but I tense every muscle, forcing myself not to move.

"You want to get out of here?" the man in black whispers.

I glance up at him.

"Wh-what?"

"I said, do you want to get out of here? Go for a ride on my bike. Clear your head."

"You're offering to let me ride your bike?"

He chuckles. "No, I'm offering you a ride."

"Are you sure it's safe? I hear there's a price on my head," I say with a serious lacing of sarcasm.

The man in black's jaw stiffens again. "Where did you hear that?"

"Stone told me. I guess he saw how desperate I was to leave this place."

"Come on then," the man says, holding out his hand to me. "Let's go."

I take his hand in mine, ignoring the tingles his grip ignites on my skin and let him pull me to my feet. Studying him, for one long minute I debate what to do. Escaping the college grounds, cruising on the back of his bike, is severely tempting. I can't refuse it.

I probably need permission to go off campus with him, but I'm already in shit for skipping classes today so screw it.

"Okay," I tell him, gathering Pip up in my arms and depositing him safely inside my dorm room. I make Winnie swear on her grandmother's life that she won't let him out of her sight. I can tell she isn't best pleased about me heading off with the fuck-off scary-looking man lingering at my shoulder, but she's too petrified to voice her qualms.

Not until he's stepped out of the dormitory. Then she grabs my arm and whispers in my ear, "That isn't ... that isn't the man in black, is it?"

I simply smile at her and then I'm at the door and following him down the path before anyone can stop us.

At his bike, he tries to force his helmet on my head, but I wave him off.

"Suit yourself," he says, casting it to one side, "but don't come complaining to me when your brains are omelets on the side of the road."

"Are you planning to crash?" I ask him, resting my hand on my hip.

His dark eyes sail down my body and I repress a shiver. Two

weeks of regular meals plus the latest batch of goodies sent from Winnie's family, means there's more meat to my bones. Does he notice?

"I'm planning on going fucking fast. You're going to need to hold on to me. Tight."

I look away from him, not wanting him to know how much the idea of that turns me on.

My aunt was right to keep me away from men. It seems I am attracted to completely the wrong ones. And judging by whatever just happened out there in the forest, lacking a serious amount of self-control.

He kicks the stand away from his bike, righting it with his right arm and swinging his left leg over the saddle. Then he glances over to me, jerking his head in an invitation to join him.

Every part of my body stirs. The way he looks at me – fuck, the way he looks full stop – makes me feel as if electricity is pulsing through me.

I stroll up to the bike, knowing he's watching me, and climb up behind him, scooting forward so I'm flush against his back and wrapping my arms around his wide chest, his heart beating beneath my palms.

"Why were you using your magic tonight? Out there in the wood?"

"Someone – or something – attacked me."

"You don't look hurt."

"It didn't hurt me ... it .... I got away."

"What was it?"

"I don't know."

"You never saw whatever it was before?"

"No, that's it, I couldn't see it at all. It was invisible."

"Hmmm," he says, then revs up the engine and we're away. He weaves down the wide driveway of the college, down the hill and then we're out on the road that brought me here two weeks ago. The stars are bright above my head, and when I tip my head back to look at them more and more appear, one by one by one, until the heavens are a blanket of twinkling lights.

The man in black leans on the gas and the bike darts forward, shooting us along the road. I grip him tighter with my thighs and with my arms, feeling him warm against my skin. The wind batters through my hair, assaulting my face so that tears run down my cheeks.

I don't care. It's exhilarating. I feel alive. Like nothing could touch me. Nothing could hurt me. Not out here. Not with him.

We swoop around bends, the bike leaning right down low against the road, the tarmac almost scraping my cheeks. I close my eyes and scream, the noise muffled by the roar of his bike.

I want this ride to last forever. I want to forget about all the problems hanging over my head. I want to forget that my aunt warned me magicals like him, men who work for the authorities, could not be trusted.

I want to simply feel.

But before too long, he's slowing the bike down and swinging into a pull-over by the side of the road.

He cuts the engine and for a moment we both sit there, my arms still clinging to his body, his chest heaving.

Then he twists his body around, taking a hold of my waist and dragging me over his lap, lowering me onto the saddle in front of him.

My heart bounces in my chest, knocking against my ribcage.

Because I don't know what he's doing. I don't know what this can mean.

He doesn't say a word, and he doesn't meet my eye. Instead, his gaze is locked on my mouth. He slides his rough hand into my hair, cupping the back of my neck and then he leans down and presses his mouth to mine.

I've imagined this. Lying in my bed, I've imagined just this. His warm mouth against mine, his lips caressing first my top lip, then my bottom.

I close my eyes, that sensation of electricity sparks violently in my gut, buzzing along every nerve in my body.

My hands find his chest, bunching into fists in his shirt, clinging to him like if I don't I'll float away.

"You going to kiss me back, sweetheart?" he murmurs against my mouth and my eyes flutter open.

I've never kissed anyone before. And I guess it's another thing I need to add to my growing list of things I need to learn.

"Kiss me back," he murmurs again, this time with more of a growl, half way between a plea and a command.

I swallow down my embarrassment and for once I don't argue with him. I do exactly as he says, copying the way he'd moved his lips against mine, mimicking his movements.

As I do, he growls a second time, his grip on my neck tightens, his kiss grows hotter, his tongue plunging into my mouth. He tastes me completely. It makes my body wilt and my panties wet.

The hand at my waist slips under my shirt, stroking up my body, and squeezing at my tit through my bra.

I whimper, my back arching, an ache building between my legs.

All of a sudden, I want it all. His hands on my body, my hands on his. To taste every part of him, to have him taste me too. To feel what it's like to be wanted. To understand what it's like to want someone back.

I press myself more closely to him, feeling the outline of something hard and big even through the layers of denim between us.

That ache between my legs beats more incessantly and I can't help but grind my core against his, chasing something – friction? Movement? Relief?

He groans, pulling down the material of my bra and rubbing my stiff nipple between his finger and thumb until I'm whimpering. Then his hands are gripping my ass, yanking me more firmly against him, encouraging me to wrap my legs around his waist and grind a second time and a third. Harder. Firmer. Along the whole girthy length of him.

His mouth finds mine again, and he kisses me hungrily, swallowing all the noises that slip from my throat as the sensation between my thighs becomes more potent.

No one had touched me intimately. I am the only one who's made myself come, and even then I don't think I'm so good at it.

This feels utterly different. The heat of his body, the peculiar buzz in my stomach, his strong hands gripping me, moving me, forcing all these sensations from my body.

I lose the ability to kiss him back, he's winding me so high and I'm so close. I sink my nails into his chest as my legs shake around him and my core tenses.

"That's it, pretty girl," he whispers and I open my eyes to find him staring right at me. I don't feel embarrassment or shame. Instead, I stare deep into those midnight eyes of his and I fall apart completely, a long twisted sigh falling from my lips as my whole body sings with pleasure.

It's never felt like this. So all-consuming. So complete. So devastating.

He kisses me again as I'm jolted through aftershocks of ecstasy and then I collapse against him, panting.

I want to make him feel that good too. I want him to touch me, really touch me. My hands stray to the buckle of his belt.

But then something changes. His body snaps rigid. He pulls away from me, his hand sliding from my hair, his other removing my hands from his shirt.

"We shouldn't be doing this."

"What?" I say, dazed, my head still spinning with the effects of his dizzying kiss and my earth-shattering orgasm.

"We shouldn't be doing this, Rhianna."

"Why ... why not?"

"You're a hell of a lot younger than me." I scowl at him.

"So?"

"I'm complicating matters," he says sternly, a frown forming on his brow.

"How is this complicated?"

Nothing about this felt complicated. It felt like the least-complicated thing I've experienced in weeks.

But he's in no mood to argue. He takes my waist in his hands and maneuvers me back to my seat.

"I don't want to go back," I tell him. "I want to stay with you."

I could become addicted to the way he makes me feel.

His shoulders stiffen, then he relents, his hand covering mine.

"You don't have a choice."

"I'm safe with you."

He shakes his head. "No, you're not. You're not safe with me. Not one little bit." And I sense there's more to his words than I understand.

I want to argue with him, tell him he's being a jerk. But I'm tired and confused and I have no idea how this works. Maybe this is what a hook up is like.

He kicks out the stand and soon we're turning in the direction of the academy.

I can't help but lean my chin against his shoulder and watch as the old mansion draws closer and closer and closer.

When he drops me outside, I slide reluctantly from his bike, and stand in front of him, suppressing the need to bite at my thumb.

"Will I see you again?" I ask him.

"No," he says, eyes trained straight in front of him. "No, I don't think that would be a good idea."

And as I watch him sail away, I wonder how it is possible for my heart to feel so elated one moment and so fractured the next.

25

R^{hi}

WINNIE'S WAITING for me with questions when I sneak back into the dormitory later.

"Oh my God, Rhi, where have you been?"

"I told you. Out for a ride."

"With the man in black?"

I yank my shirt over my head and nod.

"You were gone ages, where did you go?"

"Nowhere."

Winnie gives me a skeptical look as I step out of my jean shorts and into my pajamas.

"We just went for a ride," I say.

"They are going to kill you if they find out."

I shrug and jump up onto my bunk. "They won't find out." I peer down at Pip, out cold in the corner. "How's Pip been?"

"Fine. He ate his body weight in potato chips—"

"You fed him potato chips?"

"I thought he deserved a treat after his ordeal."

"He's growing on you," I say, peering over my bed to grin at her.

"He is not. But I can sympathize with anyone who suffers at the hands of the psychopaths who attend this college."

"When I find out which of those psychopaths it was ..." I say darkly.

"Anyway," Winnie says, changing the subject. "He ate my stash of chips and then passed out in some salt-induced haze."

"He seemed okay?" I say, suddenly feeling guilty for abandoning him so quickly after he was returned to me. And for what? A chance to hang out with the man in black. I am one bad friend.

"He did." Winnie kicks my mattress from below. "How about you?"

"I'm fine."

"Want to tell me how the jiggins you know the man in black?"

"He was the one who brought me in. Who found me."

"Ahhh," Winnie says, "I thought that would mean you hate him."

"I do, I guess," I say, chewing on my thumbnail. "And I don't."

I sigh dramatically.

Winnie pokes her head up over the side of my bed and peers at me. "Is something going on between the two of you?" she asks, clearly scandalized. "He didn't try anything on or force you to–?"

"Too many questions." I breathe in and out.

"But ..." Winnie prompts.

"But perhaps, maybe, I don't know, I'd like it if there was something going on." I cover my face with my hands. "Does that make me fucked up? I mean he's at least ten years older than me."

"Yes, and dangerous and mysterious, and renowned for being ruthless ... huh," Winnie says.

"What?" I ask, peeking at her through my fingers.

"I can understand why you find him so hot. And I mean, the man is freaking hot."

I sigh. "He is." I cover my face. "I've never had a crush before. I mean, there was never anyone around to have a crush on. But trust me to pick the two most inappropriate men to crush on."

"Wait? *Two*?" Winnie asks.

"Crap," I mutter. "I meant one."

"You said two."

"No, one."

"Definitely two. Out with it, Rhianna," she says. "You owe it to me after today."

I twist my head to look at her and she scrambles up onto my bed and lies out beside me. The bunk creaks and I hope it can support our weight.

"Thank you, Winnie," I say, taking her hand in mine, "for all you did for me today." A second wave of guilt sweeps through my body. There I was bemoaning everyone in this place, completely disregarding Winnie. Winnie, who gave up her day to help me, despite the consequences coming her way. I'm not alone. I have her as well as Pip and I should start being freaking grateful for it.

"That's what friends are for," she says.

"I've never had a friend before," I admit in a whisper.

"I kinda figured," Winnie smiles. "Or a crush." She smiles wider. "Two crushes. Come on, spill the beans."

"Stone," I say quickly and quietly.

Winnie stares at me like I lost my marbles. Truth be told, I'm not sure I ever possessed them.

"You hate Stone," she says finally.

"Yep. The dude is an asshole. A really hot asshole who makes me feel things I cannot control."

"Oh," Winnie says.

"That's bad, isn't it? Really bad."

"No, no," Winnie says, shaking her head. "I think you're just ..."

"Just what?"

"A twenty-year-old woman with, you know, needs."

"Needs?"

"I think you're just horny." Winnie turns over, tucking her hands under her cheek. "I think you need to get laid." She sighs. "I think we both need to get laid."

"I'm sure Trent would be more than willing," I say, waggling my eyebrows at her and watching as she morphs a beetroot red.

"I'm not sure about that," she mutters. "But you, you have more options than me."

"I don't think so, Winnie. I—"

"Andrew," she says.

"Andrew?"

"Yes, Andrew. He clearly likes you."

"No, Andrew and I are just friends." As nice as Andrew is, he doesn't make me feel things the way Stone and the man in black do. And I can't see that changing anytime soon.

"Sure, now you are but if you wanted to be more, I think he'd be up for it."

I shake my head. "I'm not into him in that way."

"What? The decent dude who treats you nicely and definitely has the hots for you—"

"He does not!"

"No, you'd rather go for the two older, unattainable and slightly psychopathic guys."

"Do you think Stone is psychopathic?"

"Honestly, sometimes I think he's on the verge."

I stare up at the ceiling. "I'm screwed."

Winnie giggles in my ear.

"What?" I ask, elbowing her in the ribs.

"That's your problem. You're not!"

✺

EXCEPT I AM. Well and truly. Because if I think I might get a moment to breathe before my punishment for skipping class is doled out, I'm once again wrong.

When Winnie and I open our dorm room door in the morning to head to the showers, we find a note pinned there. The letters are typed in a deep and foreboding red.

I snatch it off its pin and open it up gingerly.

"It's a summons," I tell Winnie, reading the typed-out text inside the folded piece of paper.

"Oh Jeez," Winnie says, paling. "I've never got one of those before. If my mom finds out …"

"It's bad then?" I ask.

"Being summoned to see the Principal? Yeah, that's bad. When do we have to go?"

I scan the text.

"Nine o'clock."

Winnie looks as if she might throw up.

"At least it means we'll be missing Stone's lesson," I remind her.

"And here I was thinking you'd be keen to attend," she says, managing a half smile.

Winnie unbraids and re-braids her hair and insists on inspecting both our uniforms, straightening my beret for me and sending me to scrub my shoes in the sink.

"We need to look spotless," she tells me, but I think she'd be fussing like this anyway, simply to distract herself from her nerves. I'm gathering Winnie has never been in trouble before.

She's perfected the art of keeping her head down and staying invisible. Now I've come along and landed her in serious shit.

I apologize for the one hundredth time as we walk along the path towards the college mansion and for the one hundredth time she waves me off, assuring me I'm her friend and she'd do it all over again if I needed her to.

"Maybe save that judgment until we find out our punishment," I hiss as we climb the stairs and make our way along to the principal's office.

It's Winnie's first time here as well as my own and we knock on the door at precisely nine o'clock and wait outside.

Several minutes tick past and we glance at each other anxiously, wondering if we messed up the time or something.

What the hell punishment is the principal likely to hand out? She already has me shoveling shit as my obligatory chore for Pip's presence at the college. What other treats will she have in store for us? I peer at Winnie's face, white as a ghost now, her skin almost the same color as her teeth. I hope she has the stomach for something nasty.

Finally, just when I'm beginning to consider knocking a second time, a voice from within calls out, "Enter."

Winnie seems frozen stiff, so I reach out, push down on the handle and open the door, stepping inside and dragging Winnie in behind me.

The principal's office is large and grand with a wide fireplace adorning one wall and a giant-sized landscape painting the other. Unlike Stone's office there are no books stacked on shelves and every available surface. There's just a laptop resting on her desk and a round globe spinning slowly on its axis in the corner. The principal stands in front of her desk and to my dismay is flanked by not only Professor Stone but Tristan Kennedy and Winnie's head of House, Fiona, as well.

It seems this is going to actually turn out to be a million times more hellish than I expected.

"Hello, girls, so nice of you to actually join us this morning. Your presence was missed yesterday," the principal says without a hint of amusement. She's dressed in her usual tweed suit, her hair twisted up into a French knot.

I keep my eyes locked on her face, not wanting to meet the eye of the others in the room.

"Perhaps you could explain to me why you chose to miss your lessons yesterday, lessons that I might hasten to remind you are absolutely mandatory to attend."

Winnie's eyes flick towards me in alarm and I can tell she's too petrified to speak.

"I'm sorry," I say. Tristan snorts, but I ignore him and continue. I'm not sure how best to lay out our case but I decide to go for the facts, plain and simple. "My pig went missing and we were searching for him."

The principal rolls her eyes. "That pig!"

"Is very precious to me," I say earnestly.

Fiona smothers a giggle. And from the corner of my eye I see Tristan leer at me.

I bet it was him who stole Pip in the first place.

"That he may be," the principal continues, "but his temporary disappearance does not excuse the two of you from missing lessons. This isn't a holiday camp, girls. We don't get to choose what we can and can't do. Lessons are mandatory."

"Yes, Professor York," Winnie mumbles.

I stare down at Professor York's shoes. Sensible black heels. She doesn't need them. She must already be verging on six feet without them. I don't say anything, waiting for the forthcoming punishment, but I sense Stone staring at me, can feel that familiar tug in his direction. Is that what it's like to have a crush? To want someone even when you shouldn't. Even when you know they are totally unsuitable and most probably out of bounds. Even when you hate their guts.

It's only as that last thought flits through my mind that I remember the goddamn professor can read them.

Crap.

My cheeks sizzle and I can't help raising my eyes and catching his for the briefest of moments before he looks away to the principal.

"Principal York, Miss Blackwater's pig didn't simply disappear. He was taken."

"Taken?" The principal frowns. "That's rather a wild accusation for Miss Blackwater to be waving around."

I don't speak. I'm not about to snitch and land myself in even more shit.

"It isn't an accusation, it's a reality," Stone says and I don't know what his intentions are here. Is he trying to help me or forcing me into the shit I'm trying to avoid?

"And you know who did this?" Principal York asks him.

"I'm looking into it," he says.

"Well," Principal York straightens her jacket, "when you have answers, let me know."

Stone nods and then he looks at Tristan pointedly. Like he suspects him too. Tristan, however, smothers a yawn like he couldn't give less of a damn.

"I am sorry this happened, Miss Blackwaters. And we will look into the matter," – inwardly I groan. No one will know it was Stone who told the principal, everyone will assume I went blabbing. Great! – "However, this still doesn't excuse the skipping of classes. I have brought your heads of house here so that they are aware of the serious nature of your indiscretions and so that they are both aware that you are banned for a month from leaving school premises. You will also both be required to attend kitchen duties for the next week."

Winnie nods gravely and I suppress a sigh of relief. Neither of those punishments sound that bad, especially considering the other crap that I've endured since I've been there.

"Mr. Kennedy, Miss Hayes," the principal continues, "I ask that you ensure both Miss Blackwaters and Miss Wence complete their kitchen duties."

"We will," Tristan says in a serious tone that makes him sound like the principal just asked him to guard the holy grail.

"Well, thank you, that will be all."

Winnie's shoulders sag in relief and we both step towards the door.

"There's something else I need to make you aware of, Principal York," Tristan pipes up, just as I'm reaching for the door handle.

"Yes? What is it?"

"It concerns Miss Blackwaters."

Principal York nods and motions towards Winnie and Fiona. "Miss Wence, Miss Hayes, you may leave. Miss Blackwaters please remain."

I glance at Winnie whose shoulders have stiffened again with concern. But she doesn't get a chance to say anything to me before Fiona ushers her out of the room.

I turn back to the others, this time staring Tristan square in the eye. I don't know what he has to say but I sure as hell don't like the cocky look on his face.

"What is it?" Principal York asks, this time with a note of irritation.

"Miss Blackwaters was seen leaving campus last night. After hours and without permission."

"Alone?"

Tristan glares at me, not saying a word.

The principal sighs and I feel Stone's eyes on me again.

"You hadn't granted permission for this excursion?" the principal asks Tristan.

"No and nor would I have."

The principal doesn't bother to ask me if all this is true. It's obvious she considers an angel like Tristan incapable of lying.

Stone snorts and I turn towards him, just as he strolls towards the window.

"Miss Blackwaters," the principal says with exasperation, collapsing onto her chair. "I am at a loss ... I know you have had an unusual upbringing and I can empathize with how you must be feeling – a fish out of water indeed. But the authorities have shown you real leniency. This academy has bent its rules for you. And you in return ..." She shakes her head. "I am very disappointed in you, Rhianna. I had real hopes for you."

I don't know if I'm meant to feel shame or regret. I don't. I feel annoyed. All I did was skip a few classes and went out for a ride on the man in black's bike.

Stone spins around from the window and folds his arms tightly over his chest.

"You may consider them trivial rules, Miss Blackwaters," he snarls, "but if everyone chose to disregard them like you, this place would descend into chaos, our country would be left vulnerable to attack."

"It's also about respect," Tristan says, clearly loving every minute of this. "Respect for this school, this institution."

"Quite right," Principal York says, resting her arms on her desk and clutching her hands together. She examines my face. "I really don't know what to do with you." I open my mouth to speak but she lifts her hand to silence me. "But I do know this much, Miss Blackwaters, you are now on an official warning. Any more behavior such as this and I will have to consider more serious consequences."

"Expulsion," Stone says, making it abundantly clear for me.

Tristan struggles to cover his tiger-like smile.

"As for your punishment ..."

"I have a suggestion," Tristan pipes up. In my head I spiral through my entire vocabulary of curse words. Stone frowns. "The dueling team has recently had to let go of our helping-hand. She wasn't up to the job. I think Miss Blackwaters would be a perfect replacement. I would be able to keep more of a watchful eye on her and she might also benefit from becoming more involved in school activities."

Principal York examines my face. I try to keep it neutral, suppressing all the pissed-off energy bubbling in my veins from my features. What the hell is a 'helping-hand'? Do I even want to know?

Principal York looks to Tristan next and taps her fingers on the desk.

"Okay," she finally answers, "Miss Blackwaters, you will be helping-hand to the dueling team for the remainder of the term. Mr. Kennedy will be able to fill you in on what that entails as well your duties."

"And will I be doing this as well as my kitchen duties?" I ask with a serious dollop of sarcasm.

"Yes," the principal answers, turning her attention to her laptop screen. "You are dismissed."

Tristan makes no move to disguise his grin this time. His smile is wide. He looks just like a tiger that's caught the prey it's been toying with.

Stone strides from the room, his boots banging angrily against the floor.

And I follow him out. I don't want to hang about either. It looks like I'll already be spending more time with Tristan Kennedy than I want to. I certainly won't spend a second more than I have to.

26

R^{hi}

THE LOOK on Winnie's face when I fill her in about my additional punishment tells me everything I need to know. She actually turns green and swallows hard.

"Is it that awful?" I whisper to her. We're meant to be reading a passage from the book Stone placed under our noses. But as our professor is currently engrossed in messaging on his phone, we're taking the opportunity to talk.

"Worse," she leans in closer to whisper in my ear. "I mean, lots of girls would give their right arm," she pauses, "and probably several sexual favors," I pull a face, "to be the dueling team's helping-hand but you're basically their slave. At their beck and call, answering their every wish and their constant demands."

"Why would anyone volunteer to do that?"

"Because most of the school is in love with the dueling team and it's one way to attract their attention. A lot of girls seem to believe that if only one of those dudes would notice them, they'd fall hopelessly in love with them and they'd live happily ever after."

"That's incredibly sad."

"This is the problem with crushes," Winnie says with a smirk. "They tend to warp your judgment and common sense."

I elbow her in the ribs but my eyes can't help straying to Stone. Is it my imagination or does he look especially hot today? He's lost his jacket and rolled up his sleeves revealing the inks that run down his arms.

I practically drool. Yes, my mind is definitely warping.

Didn't I kiss his best friend last night? Why am I crushing on two men? Isn't one enough?

Stone glances up from his phone and frowns at me.

And I remember for the second time today that my mind is an open door to this man.

"Eyes on your book, Blackwaters," the professor snaps.

And, if all my free time wasn't already occupied with my new various duties, I'd give him the finger. But I decide it's not worth the risk. I don't want to add toilet duty to my kitchen and helping-hand ones.

I concentrate on the words in front of me instead and try my best not to relive my meeting in the principal's office, try not to imagine what Tristan will have in store for me. Probably washing their sweaty jockstraps. I almost gag.

It turns out, Professor Stone has no desire to teach us this morning and we spend the remainder of our lesson reading passages from the book until finally the bell sounds. I pack up my bag along with everyone else, but when I stand to my feet, the professor is by my side.

"A word please," he whispers, and a shiver spirals unexpectedly through my body.

It's his proximity. The dense growl of his voice. And his woody scent.

Shit.

"This is beginning to become a recurring request," I say, as the last student steps out of the classroom.

Except this time he doesn't lead me to his office. He simply scowls at me, standing there right in the middle of the sea of desks.

"What did you do to piss Tristan Kennedy off?"

"Oh you know, just sharing my usual sunny personality with him."

"There's nothing sunny about you, Blackwaters," he says with a darkness that almost has me shivering again.

I shrug. "Well, beats me."

"You must have done something. Kids are skipping out of college grounds all the time. I've never known Kennedy tell on anyone else."

"What can I say? Most of the student faculty hates my guts."

"Because you were unregistered." I glare at him. He takes a step forward. "I know all about Tristan Kennedy. I know what bullshit he gets up to in this school. I know how he treats girls and ..."

His words falter off as I stare at him aghast.

"Are you asking me if I've slept with him?"

He doesn't flinch. "I'm asking if you haven't and that is why the asshole is giving you grief." He folds his arms across his chest.

I cock my head to one side. "You don't need to ask me anything. We both know you can just stroll inside my head and look for yourself."

"Your mind is a cesspit. I don't want to go anywhere near thoughts about your fucking sex life."

What sex life? I think. Then curse in my head. Third time today.

The professor smirks at me with satisfaction, like hearing I have no sex life is the best news he's heard in a long time. I don't want to examine too closely why that may be, especially when he's standing right in front of me ready to read every one of my theories.

"Can I go now?" I ask with my voice dripping in contempt.

"You may," he says, still grinning as I spin around and storm off, heading in the direction of the gymnasium.

Coach has had us running sprints in the last few classes which means I've actually been allowed to join in with the others and haven't had the pleasure of being partnered with Spencer again.

Not today though. Today it's back to combat training and back to the mats with the dueling team star. Today, however, I find I don't mind. Today I'd quite like the opportunity to take some of this pent-up frustration out on someone. Especially a dickhead like Spencer.

Unfortunately, his mood seems as black as mine this morning. As I hurry over to the mats, he scowls at me so hard I'm surprised sparks aren't flickering out of his nostrils and his ears.

I don't even receive a hello before I'm flipped over and slammed onto my back.

As usual the wind is knocked from my lungs, but I push at his chest hard, kicking at his legs and shoving him off me.

"Asshole," I mutter.

He wipes his hands on his shorts and rolls up onto his feet. Smacking me down on the mats has done nothing to improve his mood, in fact it only seems to have made it worse.

I don't even make it to my feet before he flips me over his shoulder and down hard this time on my stomach. I try to clamber upwards but he leans the entire weight of his body down on top of me, pinning me to the mat.

"Break free," he spits. I don't move. "Break free," he repeats, this time louder.

"We both know I can't."

"So you're just going to give up," he says. "Is that what you'll do if you're attacked?"

"Just let me up," I mutter.

He doesn't move and for several seconds I hear his angry breath puffing in my ear.

I'm not playing his games. Not when we both know I have no chance of winning.

"Are you dating him?" he growls finally.

I frown. "What? Who?"

"He's twice your fucking age."

My heart stops beating in my chest. Stone. Does he know about my crush? I am seriously bad at this crap if it's that obvious to everyone around me. Not that I'm going to admit it. Like ever!

"I don't know what you're talking about."

"You were seen, Pig girl. It's why we're going to have the displeasure of you as our newest helping-hand."

The man in black.

He means the man in black.

"You have Tristan to thank for that," I mumble. "Trust me it's the last thing I want to do."

Spencer snorts loudly in my ear and rolls off me.

I flip over onto my back and glare up at him.

"It's sick," he says, scuffing the toe of his sneaker along the mat. "He's old enough to be your dad."

Now I snort. "He isn't. He's like ten years older than me."

"What the fuck were you doing with him?"

I roll up onto my knees, place one foot onto the mat and then stand up, brushing my hands together.

What is it with everyone and my sex life all of a sudden? First Winnie, then Stone and now Spencer.

It would be concerning if I actually had anything to tell

anyone, but it's laughable considering I don't. Nothing more than a kiss and some dry humping.

I rest my hands on my hips and meet Spencer's eyes. Swimming with anger and darkness and about a million other emotions I can't read.

"Why do you even care?"

He doesn't answer me, instead he comes charging at me again. And as I hit the mat, I vow to lace Spencer Moreau's jock strap with chili powder just as soon as I land my hands on it.

THERE'S a note waiting for me on my dorm door when I return at lunchtime to feed Pip. It's from Tristan instructing me to meet him in the boys' locker room just as soon as I've finished kitchen duties.

My evenings so far have been occupied by homework, a little bit of magical tuition from Winnie, followed by watching old movies. She was completely scandalized when I confessed I'd never watched a movie like *Pretty Woman* or *Clueless* and she's been making me watch them with her ever since. Maybe that's why my brain has become warped by ideas of romance. I need to encourage her to show me some movies about revenge, about surviving on the run. Not that I'm going to be able to watch a movie anytime soon.

Kitchen duties consist of scrubbing pots and pans with Winnie in the kitchen after supper. After the hour's up, my hands are red raw. I suspect it's going to be nothing compared to the punishment Tristan has waiting for me.

Out on the path, Winnie gives me a long hug and wishes me luck.

"There are limits to what they can ask you to do. Just ..." she gazes warily towards the gymnasium, "just be careful."

I square my shoulders, trying to demonstrate I'm not

cowered. Really, I'm pretty apprehensive, but I'm determined not to show it.

As I draw closer to the gymnasium, I find the field flooded by light and what can only be the dueling team practicing out on the grass. Bolts of magic of all descriptions, colors and size whizz through the air, as ten men – five dressed in red bibs, five in blue – race underneath them, spinning and ducking out of each other's way.

I see Spencer, larger by far than all the rest, chase down an opposing player, diving for him, catching him around the knees and crashing them both to the ground. I see Tristan, firing magic from his palms so quickly it's dizzying, striking two of the opposition square between the eyes.

Then I watch as Coach Hank blows on his whistle, and the men freeze, their magic whistling away through the air. Spencer climbs to his feet, heaving the other player up with him, and saying something that makes them both laugh. Tristan sweeps his bib and then his jersey over his head, wiping his shirt around his brow as he leads his team mates through the doors and into the gymnasium.

I feel more apprehension than ever. It's clear that, if they wanted to, any of these men could destroy me.

Once I think it's safe, I make my way to the boys' locker room, hearing the sound of several low masculine voices, whoops of laughter and the slamming of locker doors.

I hover outside. I don't want to walk in on a load of half-naked jocks. Even if I am a tad curious.

I've been there for about five minutes when the door swings open and Tristan pops his golden head out. He spots me immediately.

"You're late," he barks.

"I'm not. I've been here ages."

"Then what the fuck are you doing out here? I said to meet me in the locker room." He grabs a fistful of my shirt and drags me along behind him. His hair is wet from the shower and he's wearing a pair of shorts and nothing else. I'm treated to the sight of his muscular back, a dark tattoo sweeping over his left shoulder. I'm so busy puzzling over what it is that I don't think to drop my gaze to the ground as he pulls me inside. As a result I see way more male flesh than I want. Flesh that includes toned ass cheeks and more male genitalia than I've seen in my lifetime.

Who am I kidding? I've never seen any male genitalia in my lifetime.

Despite my best efforts, my cheeks burn and I drop my eyes down.

The room stinks of sweat, hot showers and deodorant, and steam hangs in the air, clinging to my skin. Tristan swings me around to face him.

"Do you have any idea what a helping-hand does, Pig Girl?"

"No," I say, eyes focused on his face because I do not want to be treated to a front view of his chest, a chest I know from previous experience is as golden and well sculpted as his back.

"You didn't think to ask? To do your homework before rocking up here?"

"No," I repeat.

"We usually start things off with a blow job," some dude from the corner shouts out. "Want to drop to your knees, sweetheart, and we'll all line up."

I open my mouth to tell him that if he comes anywhere near me with his nobbly dick, I'll split it in two with my magic, but instead Spencer beats me to it.

"Shut up, dickhead." I look up and find him scuffing the other dude around the back of the head with his hand. I feel something akin to gratitude in my chest until the asshole goes and ruins it. "You want to end up with some swine disease on your cock?"

"Is she sucking off her pig?" Another of the men laughs.

Tristan captures my gaze. "Don't get your hopes up, Pig Girl. You're going to be doing nothing nearly as exciting as sucking my cock."

"Can we just cut the bullcrap and you tell me what it is I have to do?"

He takes a step towards me and the room falls quiet. "A little more respect please, Blackwaters." He reaches forward and clasps my chin in his hand. I try to twist my face away but he holds my head still. His fingers are calloused and his face so near to mine I can see the pores in his perfect skin and the dancing pulse in his throat. "You don't talk to me like that, okay? You don't talk to anyone on the team like that. You're ours now, Pig Girl. You do as we say. If I tell you I want a glass of freshly squeezed orange juice there on the pitch while I'm training, you make it happen. If Spencer tells you he wants his helmet spotless, you spend all night and day scrubbing and buffing it until it sparkles. If Joe here says the team needs new laces, you thread new pairs through every single boot."

I stare straight into his eyes. They're the color of clear morning skies. But now up close I see the ring of darkness circling his irises – dark like night.

His breath smells like weed and peppermint.

"I'm not doing all that crap," I say simply.

"You want to be expelled?"

I shrug. I'm less certain about leaving. There are some parts of this school I'm loving – having friends, learning how to use my magic – something I'm getting better at each day I'm here. However, there are other parts I don't love. If I'm honest, it's only the price on my head that's kept me from bolting six days out of seven.

His blue eyes flicker from side to side as he examines my face. The malice in his expression has melted away and now there's only curiosity. I don't know if that is worse or not. The strange hook in my belly has me wanting to step closer.

"Come on, man," Spencer moans from the other side of the locker room. "Just give her the goddamn list. We're meant to be meeting Summer in five."

Still gripping my chin, Tristan holds out his hand and one of the other jocks, already dressed in shorts and a t-shirt, hands him a scroll of paper.

Tristan shakes it in my face. "This scroll outlines your role and responsibilities. Read it carefully, little piggie. I'm going to be watching you closely."

He stuffs it into my hand and releases me.

I want to rub at my face, my skin burning where he gripped me, but I don't give him that satisfaction. Instead, I sit on one of the benches and unroll the scroll, reading the words as if I'm not surrounded by a locker room of leering and half-nude boys.

As I scan the list of chores I'm expected to carry out, it's clear the dueling team want me acting as their own personal maid around practice and games. There's nothing too horrendous on the list, although I groan inwardly when my suspicion about the jock straps is confirmed.

I glance up at Tristan. He has his back to me and he's rubbing a towel through his golden hair. This is the official role. The one they're prepared to commit to paper. The one signed off by the teachers. I know they'll try to push it. I know Tristan, Spencer and the others will use this opportunity to torture me more than they already do. Well, let them try. I'm doing what's written on the list and not a damn thing more.

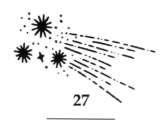

27

Tristan

I'M FUCKED.

I knew that the moment this stupid girl crossed my path. Knew it instantly and completely.

Didn't mean I was going to lie back and accept the freaking situation, though, was it?

Yet the more I struggle against this, the more I pull away, the tighter the noose around my neck becomes, the more entangled my limbs become in the rope.

She's an addiction. An unhealthy one.

I didn't have to tell the principal about her little night time escapade with the authorities' enforcer. I sure as hell didn't have to suggest she become the team's helping-hand.

What was I thinking?

I was thinking I wanted her close. I was thinking I find the damn thing more and more fascinating. A thing I want to poke and prod just to see how she'll react. A thing I want to provoke just to see how far I can push her before she breaks. A thing I want to rip apart.

I should stay the hell away from her. Far, far away. There is no need for our paths to cross.

But I can't help myself.

I find myself lingering in the locker room, as the little thing starts work on her first chore, gathering up gym kits and dirty towels from around the locker room. Strictly she's not allowed in here when it's occupied, but it's not like the teachers actually enforce those rules, and it's become a ritual. We drag the helping-hand in, give them a fucking eyeful they won't forget, one they'll probably be dreaming about. Dan makes his crude fucking joke about the blow jobs and half the time our little helpers drop to their knees without a word of complaint.

She was never going to do that though. We all call her Pig Girl, but she's more feline than swine. Like a scrappy little cat, hissing, claws out, fur flying.

"Are you coming, man?" Spencer asks me, slinging his gym bag over his shoulder.

"Yeah," I say casually, "in a minute, I'll catch you up."

His gaze flicks between me and Pig Girl. He frowns. He had some choice words to say when I told him she was our new helping-hand. I didn't tell him that was down to me. I don't know if he suspects I have an infatuation.

Is that what it is?

I've never been infatuated with anyone before. Or anything. Girls have always been distractions. Fun. Entertainment. Nothing more.

The idea I, Tristan fucking Kennedy, could have an infatuation with a girl like her is laughable. Unthinkable. Ridiculous.

But it isn't an infatuation. It's more. And that is the fucking problem.

"Summer's going to be pissed if you're late."

"Summer can kiss my ass."

Spencer grins. "I hear she already has."

I smile lazily. He wouldn't be far off. That girl would do just about anything for me, would let me do anything to her, if it meant she could say she was 'Tristan Kennedy's girlfriend'.

Most of the girls in this school would do the same.

They think that title will give them everything they've ever dreamed of. That it'll lead to some high-society wedding, a mansion in Pale Heights and a pack of sons as gifted as I am.

That's because their imaginations are about as limited as their intellects.

Spencer slumps out of the locker room, glancing at the girl one more time, and I drop down onto the bench, pretending to tie my shoe laces. Soon the last few guys follow Spencer out and it's just her and me.

My eyes drag down her body. She's not as skinny as she was. There's more meat to her now, more curves. Her cheeks aren't as hollow and there's more color to her skin. Peaches and cream. Lips like strawberries. Eyes like caramel.

She's a sweet fucking feast. I can almost taste her on the end of my tongue.

I soak her in.

I'm not sure she's even aware I'm still here, still here and watching her, until she says over her shoulder, "Are you going to sit there and glower at me all night?"

I jolt. If she only fucking knew.

"I want to check you're doing a satisfactory job."

"I'm not," she says back. "I'm going to be the worst helping-hand this team has ever had. Expect odd socks and bobbly jock straps. Oh, and I'd be careful getting in and out of the showers. You may find the floor is always slippery."

Half of me wants to laugh. Instead, I frown.

"Just try it, Pig Girl ..." I snarl instead.

She doesn't even flinch at my tone.

Does she actually know who the fuck I am? Does she know what I'm capable of?

She tugs a towel out of a half-open locker and throws it in the laundry bin, then she spins and faces me.

"Why?" she says.

"Why?" I repeat, my eyebrows rising up my brow.

"Why did you tell the principal I sneaked off campus? Why do you enjoy torturing me?" She cocks her head to one side. "No, don't answer that. Let me guess. Poor little rich boy. Did your parents not buy you enough ponies? Did they not fly you out on enough exclusive holidays? Did the nanny fail one day to give you her complete and undivided attention?"

This time I can't keep the smirk from my mouth. "You think I haven't heard those lines a million times, Little Pig? You think you're actually being original."

"Maybe not original, but not wrong either."

I stand up, drawing myself to my full height and step towards her. I tower above her smaller frame but she doesn't back away. She lifts her chin defiantly and fuck, I thought I liked my girls all submissive, backing away, doing as I say, whimpering my name, but no, this turns me on a million times more.

This defiance makes me want to push even harder.

"You don't know the first thing about me, Blackwaters."

"No, I don't. Because I don't come from a world like yours, *Kennedy*," she hisses my name, mocking me. "I wasn't born into a world of privilege and money, I didn't have everything handed to me on a glittering silver platter. I've spent every day scrabbling to survive, something I bet you've never had to do."

To my utter surprise she reaches out and takes my hands in hers. Her touch is electric, awakening every single nerve in my body, the hairs on the back of my neck standing on end. The hook in my stomach strains towards her. She turns my hands over, revealing my palms.

"I bet you've never gotten your hands dirty in your whole entire life," she says.

I don't answer her. Instead I stare down at her, my hands in hers. My heart thumps against my ribs. Thumps like it wants to break free and claim her.

I need to get the fuck out of here. Now.

I don't move.

I can hear the whistle of her breath. See the way her slender shoulders rise and fall. Notice how soft the skin there is.

I curl my fingers around hers, capturing her hands in mine. "You're wrong. I have. Just not in the way you think." I lean closer, lowering my mouth to her ear. "And you're wrong about something else too, little pig. We do own you."

I drop my hold of her hands and push her backwards.

"No one will ever own me," she hisses. "Least of all you, Tristan Kennedy."

I smile lopsided at her, a look I know has girls creaming their panties. "You said I'm spoiled, little Pig. And you know what, you're right about that much. I'm used to getting what I want. And do you know why that is?" I don't wait for one of her bitchy retorts. "I'm the most powerful magical in this school."

She rolls her eyes at me. "Because Mommy and Daddy own half the city–"

I lower my voice. "I'm not talking about influence and politics here." I don't know why I'm telling her. I've never told anyone what I suspect. Never told them that I have all this power screeching around my body. Limitless. Unrelenting. Bottomless. Raw.

She holds my eyes and whispers, "Are you sure?" I smirk at her. "Are you sure, *I'm* not more powerful?" And as she says the words, I feel something crackle against my skin, taste electricity in the air. Those hairs on the back of my neck don't just stand up, they bristle.

For the briefest of moments, I wonder ... I wonder if ...

Then I remember she's a nobody. From nowhere. An unregistered with no real education and no formal training.

She can bullshit all she wants. She has about as much power as a fucking lightbulb.

"I'm sure," I say smugly. Her fingers flex. She wants to blast me across the room. She's spoiling for a fight. All I need to do is push her that little, little bit more ...

Then she'll be out of here faster than you can say expulsion. Gone. Disappeared. Out of my life forever.

I'd probably never see the girl again.

This problem, this headache, would be over.

I can't do it, though. I'm too damn addicted.

Automatically I take a step away from her. And then another, watching her the entire time. Her fingers twitch.

I want to ask her a million questions. What was she fighting? Why was she running? Why was she fucking unregistered?

But I can't. The more I know, the tighter that damn noose grows. Strangling, keeping the blood from my brain and the oxygen from my lungs.

She won't defeat me like that.

"It needs to be spotless," I tell her. "So fucking spotless I could eat my dinner off the floor."

SUMMER OPENS her door to me ten minutes later. Displeasure dances in her eyes and Spencer's right: she's pissed off I'm late. A movie's playing in the darkened room behind her and the smell of freshly popped corn wafts my way. She won't say anything though. She wouldn't dare.

"Hey," I say, and when she steps aside I make my way inside her room.

Summer's family isn't anywhere near as rich as mine, but

she's still fuck-off wealthy and owns one of the nicest rooms on campus. In fact, it's not really a room, it's more like an apartment with a bedroom, a guest-room, two bathrooms, and a large living area.

That's where everyone is, sprawled over the sofas and lying on the plush carpeted floor. No one's actually watching the film. Dan and Lily are making out, Spencer has some girl sucking on his neck and a group of the girls from the cheerleading squad are gossiping in the corner.

"Want some popcorn?" Summer asks me, holding out a bowl as she places a sugared piece between her pink lips. If I told her to coil those lips around my cock right now, she'd do it. Even in front of all our friends gathered here. But despite that electricity buzzing through my nerves, that warmth simmering in my blood, I don't want that.

I plunge my hand into the bowl, the corn warm, and grab a handful.

"What we watching?"

"Some action movie Dan wanted – not that he's actually watching it." She motions her head in my teammate's direction, just as he pulls Lily into his lap. "Get a room," Summer squeals with obvious delight. Sometimes she whines about everyone hanging out in her place, but I know that's all part of the plan. She likes to be the conductor, spinning the music around to her pace, her rhythm, having everyone dance to her tune.

I don't need that kind of control. I'll let them use the Venus common room but I wouldn't let these losers within one foot of my actual room.

"Kyle and Aysha are already using the spare bedroom," Dan mutters.

"Can we use your room, Sum?" Lily asks, peering up at us, her cheeks all pink.

"No, you fucking can't," Summer says, throwing a piece of corn at Lily's head. "Go back to your own place."

Lily glances down at Dan and in the next moment he's tossed her over his shoulder, squealing, and is hauling her out of the room.

"Why does he have to be so dramatic?" Summer says, although I bet she'd give her right arm for someone to do that to her. She hates that Lily's captured the attention of the room for that millisecond.

"He's pretty taken with her."

"For now!" Summer places the bowl on a coffee table. "He was following Petra around like a lost puppy two weeks ago."

I watch Dan slam the door behind him, winking at me as he does. He's perfected the 'I'm madly in love with you' routine down to an art. For that one week of dating, he'll make any girl believe she's the love of his life. Until he dumps her and moves on to the next that is.

"You want to watch something else?" Summer says, grabbing my wrist and leading me to the spot on the sofa Dan and Lily have vacated. Her long nails pinch into my wrist and her expensive perfume tickles my nose (and not in the good way) as she pulls me down into the cushions with her and curls up against my side like I'm her damned boyfriend. I snag my arm away from her and lean forward, resting my forearms on my knees.

"The news," I say as she flickers her fingers in the direction of the TV, the guide appearing on the screen.

"Are you kidding?" She giggles, leaning forward too and resting her head against my shoulder. Her hair smells worse than the perfume. All sweet like processed candy.

"No." I swipe my hand in the direction of the screen and a news presenter sitting behind a desk fills the screen.

"How was practice?" Summer asks, stroking hair back behind my ear.

"Good." I lean my head away from her in irritation, keeping my eyes locked on the screen.

She leans towards me, whispering in my ear, "They really should have made you captain."

I ignore her. She rests her hand on my thigh, stroking it up my leg as she pretends to watch the report about a series of killings out near the borderlands. She sighs quietly as her hand strays closer to my groin and up to the waistband of my sweatpants. It's all an act. I bet she finds the idea of holding my junk in her hand about as appealing as I do.

She dips her fingertips under the waistband and for a minute I think about letting her do it.

Why not? She could jerk me off. Maybe it would feel good.

I swallow. That sweet scent catches in my throat.

"Don't," I tell her.

"Want to go to my room?" she asks, leaning back into me.

"No," I say firmly, gripping her wrist and returning her hand to her own lap.

"Fine!" she snaps, tossing her head in an irritated manner and stalking off.

I keep watching the news. Eyes locked on the screen like I'm engrossed. I want to know what's happening out there. I need to know.

But the picture blurs and the words hum.

There's only one thing on my mind tonight.

That damn pig girl.

28

R^{hi}

JUST WHEN I was beginning to actually possess a social life, it's been firmly snatched away from me. What with kitchen duties, dueling team chores and a ban from leaving campus, my social life has permanently stalled. I caught a glimpse of the ball. And now I'm back to rags in the cellar.

At least I have Winnie to share in this misery.

"It's really unfair," I tell her as I scrub yet another giant pot with some unrecognizable food stuff smoldered to its surface. "Someone pignapped Pip and we're the ones being punished."

"I'm sure they'll be punished too once they're caught," Winnie replies, her hands lost in a bowl of bubbles.

"I doubt they'll even *be* caught."

"Stone said he was looking into it," Winnie says with a teasing tone. I ignore her and scrub harder.

I don't know why he'd bother. Not because he actually

cares. Obviously. The man cares about nothing – except maybe his bike and his books. I scrub harder not knowing why that makes me angry.

Winnie lifts a frying pan from the bowl, runs a sponge over its base and drops it onto the draining board. "I'm just relieved my mom hasn't heard about this. If she knew I skipped class, she'd string me up by my braids."

I pause my scrubbing. "Would she really?" I ask skeptically. Winnie's family sounds utterly lovely, confirmed by the fact her mom sends her packets of home-baked goods in the post every week.

"Well ... no," Winnie admits, "but the lecture would be pretty horrific and the disappointed face my mom makes is a killer."

I toss my sponge at Winnie and she ducks.

"What are we going to do this weekend, though?" I moan. "I've spent my entire life entertaining myself." I was damn good at it. I didn't have a choice. "But now I've had a taste of more, going back to darning socks and rearranging my books does not seem appealing."

"Are you really worried about having nothing to do, Rhi?" Winnie asks. "You're going to have so many chores to do, you'll barely have time to sit down."

"But the evenings ..." I mumble. "Everyone else will be going out."

The hangover may have been hellish after last time but I enjoyed myself more than I ever had that night. Even the dressing up proved fun.

"We can play Scrabble," Winnie suggests and I groan. "Or watch another movie."

"Yeah," I mutter, heading off to find my sponge. "Another movie."

✺

"You're banned for a month?" Andrew asks me the next day in the library.

"Yep," I say with a pout. "No leaving campus for a month."

"That sucks."

"Uh huh."

"I was going to suggest the pool hall Saturday night. It's quieter than the bar and I'm a bit of a pool shark." He grins.

"Well, I won't be joining you."

"Another time."

"Yeah, another time," I say, picking up my book and resuming my reading.

Except come Saturday night, as Winnie and I are holed up in our room listening to everyone else getting ready for a night out, there's a knock on our door.

We look at each other and I gently push Pip's sleeping head from my lap and go answer the door.

It's Andrew.

"Hi," he says.

"Hi," I reply, surprised to see him. "Aren't you meant to be at the pool hall?"

He shrugs. "Yeah, we decided not to go."

"Why?" I tug at my sweater wishing I hadn't opened the door in my PJ bottoms. "I'd give anything to get out of here."

"Mikey's got no money. Couldn't afford to go out tonight. We've ordered a pizza, going to play video games instead. You want to join us?" I peer over my shoulder. "Oh … yeah … and Winnie too."

I screw up my nose. "I've never played video games before."

Andrew leans against the doorframe. "You haven't?"

"No. We only had one rusty old laptop at home. It took an age just to load a webpage."

"This could be life changing, Rhi. You need to come have a go."

I turn back to my roommate. "Winnie, you want to eat pizza and play video games?"

"Sure," she says, rolling Pip onto his bed.

"Give us five," I tell Andrew, closing the door and going in search of my jeans. Winnie scurrying up to me as I do.

"See, I told you, he likes you."

I scramble through the pile of clothes on my desk. "He does not. He's just being friendly."

"You really do know nothing about men."

"Evidently," I say, sliding on my jeans.

Winnie does the same and then we walk over to Andrew's dorm. His block isn't swimming in luxury like some of the others but it's in much better condition than ours. He has a room to himself and there are no damp patches or cracked windows. In fact, the carpet looks pretty new as well as all the furniture and it looks like someone actually cleaned in here recently.

A couple of boys who went with us to the bar in Los Magicos sit on Andrew's bed, controllers in their hands, eyes locked to a computer screen resting on a desk. Several pizza boxes lie stacked up on the floor.

"Take a seat," Andrew says, pointing to his desk chair and a beanbag. Winnie grabs the chair first and I sink into the bag as Andrew drops down onto the floor.

He opens the first pizza box. "Margarita or Hawaiian?"

"What's Hawaiian?" I ask, peering towards the box.

"Jeez, you really did live in the far end of nowheresville," one of the boys says from the bed.

"Yep, and we never got take out."

"It's a pizza with ham and pineapple," Winnie explains.

"Pineapple?" I wrinkle my nose. "A pineapple doesn't belong on a pizza!"

"Exactly!" Andrew says. "That's what I always say. But Dane loves it."

Dane holds out his hand and Andrew slaps a large, greasy piece of pizza into it.

"Thanks, man," he says, stuffing it into his mouth, his eyes never leaving the computer screen.

"You should try it," Winnie tells me. "It's really good."

I shake my head. "I'm sticking to plain."

Andrew hands Winnie the box with the Hawaiian and opens the next one, taking a piece for himself and then handing it to me.

I chew on my slice, the grease staining my fingers yellow as we watch his friends play. From what I can tell, it's some game with elves and trolls and a quest for gold. Andrew explains how it works and after another ten minutes, he turfs his friends off the bed and insists me and Winnie have a go.

Winnie's obviously played before because she doesn't immediately end up with an arrow through her head.

She streams through the magical world on screen, firing arrows of her own and collecting parcels of gold.

I take five minutes just to make my character walk in a straight line.

I'm not sure how fun this can be. I'd rather be having my own adventures out there in Los Magicos and beyond. Not pretending to have one back here in the dorms.

"Here," I say to Andrew, handing the controller to him after I fall down a hole and kill my character for the tenth time in a row. "I think you'd better take over. I'm useless."

"You shouldn't give up so easily," Winnie says, slaying a dragon as it comes swooping towards her. "It's really fun once you get the hang of it."

I shake my head.

"How about we try something more straightforward," Andrew says. "Winnie, do you mind?"

"No," Winnie says, resting the controller on the mattress beside her and sliding down onto the floor to join Dane and

Mickey as they demolish the rest of the pizza. "I've completed this game already."

"You have?" Dane asks, sounding impressed.

"Yep." Winnie shrugs and I think she just added another admirer to her list.

Andrew snags her spot on the bed, and loads up a new game on the computer.

"This one's easier," he says, "you see your puzzle piece at the top of the screen? All you have to do is fit it into the puzzle below. Use the arrows to move it left and right and that key there to rotate it."

"Sounds technical to me."

"We'll start on an easy level." He picks up Winnie's discarded controller and I take mine. Five minutes in and I actually seem to have the hang of the thing. Soon, I'm utterly hooked, whooping as my score climbs higher and higher.

"Rhi," Winnie calls from the floor, stretching, "it's twelve."

"It is?" I say glancing at my watch. I had no idea so much time had passed.

"Yep, I'm going to head back to the dorm. Are you coming?"

I begin to lower my controller.

"You can stay a bit longer if you want," Andrew says. "I never get to bed before one anyway."

I glance at the screen. The game's gotten harder, the music more frantic, the puzzle pieces descending at speed.

"Are you sure?"

He nods.

"I'm going to stay a little longer."

Winnie clambers to her feet, thanking Andrew for the pizza. Two levels later, Andrew's friends follow her out.

"You're really good at this," Andrew says, after I beat him at another level.

"I spent a lot of time completing jigsaw puzzles as a child." I grin. "Seems those skills have finally come in useful."

The screen explodes in confetti, trumpets blaring as I complete another level.

I fist pump the air, catching a look at the clock on Andrew's shelf.

"Shit it's one thirty. I'd better go."

"You don't have to," Andrew says. "You can stay a bit longer."

"I think I should call it quits while I'm ahead. Besides, I'm starting to go cross-eyed."

"Yeah, me too."

Andrew exits the game and switches off the machine, the screen fading from bright white to a dull gray and then a midnight black.

I lift my arms above my head, stretching and uncurling and edging towards the side of the mattress.

"Thank you for the piz–"

Andrew grabs my wrist and tugs me backwards.

"Don't go yet," he whispers.

"Oh but I–"

I don't finish my words because before I know what's happening he is leaning towards me, lowering his mouth to mine. I smell his breath. Cheese and oregano.

He's going to kiss me.

I've only been kissed once before.

I'm curious. I want to know if that kiss with the man in black was special or if all kisses are like that.

But do I want my second kiss to be with Andrew? Do I want him to kiss me at all?

I mean, I like the guy. He's my friend. I don't, however, like him in that way.

I turn my head. His wet mouth lands on my ear with a smack.

"Sorry," I mumble, as heat crawls up my neck.

"It's okay," he whispers, cupping my chin and attempting to move my mouth towards his.

"No," I say, leaning away and pushing my palm against his chest. "I like you." Andrew grins, his mouth dropping to my neck, where he sucks my skin sloppily. Quickly, I hasten to add, "But not in that way."

He lifts his head to look at me. His grin drops to a frown.

"You don't like me in *that* way," he says with a light petulant hiss to his tone. He's still pressed over me, making no effort to move.

I cringe. "No, not in that way."

"Are you kidding me? Is this some ploy to play hard to get because–"

I frown too. "No, I'm not playing at anything."

"But no one else is interested in you."

I frown harder. "So what?"

"Are you frigid or something?" I push at him, my fingers crackle with magic. "Come on, don't be such a prude. It's just a bit of fun."

I push him off me with all my force and slide off the bed. Am I a prude? I have no idea. More heat crawls up my neck.

I grab my jacket from the floor, but he's there blocking my path to the door.

"You're not really going? I bought you pizza. I bought you all those drinks the other night."

"Well, thank you for that but, yes, I'm going."

I stand up, squaring up to him. I don't care what the rules say, if he tries anything more, I'll blast him with everything I have.

"I can buy you other things too. A decent pair of shoes." He points at my worn pair of sneakers. "Clothes that actually fit you."

Seriously?

"You're such a jerk!" I say, dodging around him and racing towards the door before he tries to stop me.

"And the best offer you're going to get!" he yells after me as I jog down the hallway and out into the night.

It's late but the campus isn't sleeping. It's a Saturday night after all. I can hear hoots of laughter, shouting and music. People elsewhere having a much better time than me. The air nips at my skin and I shrug on my jacket and, with my head down, walk back to my dorm.

Both Winnie and Pip are snoring when I creep into our room, and start to strip off my clothes but Winnie stirs, rolling over and yawning.

"Hey Rhi," she whispers. "How was the rest of your evening? Did you complete the entire game?"

I manage a limp smile in the darkness. "Not quite."

Winnie yawns again. "Oh, there was a parcel waiting for you outside our room when I arrived. It's on your desk."

"A parcel? Where did that come from?"

"Special delivery. You must have a secret admirer."

"I very much doubt that." I snap on my desk lamp and examine the square parcel wrapped in brown paper. My name is printed in a scrawled hand across the top, followed by my dorm number and the academy's details. I turn the parcel over in my hands. There's no return address and the postage stamp is blurred.

"I don't know who this could be from."

"Maybe the Council?" Winnie suggests, folding her pillow under her head.

I shrug and tear back the brown tape and the cardboard flaps. Inside the box is full of shredded plain white paper and, a tad hesitantly, I plunge my hands inside and pull out something wrapped in layers of cellophane.

"What is it?" Winnie asks.

I prod it a bit. "No idea."

"Is there a note?"

I plunge my hand back inside but I can't find anything more.

"I don't like it," I say with unease.

"It won't be anything bad," Winnie reassures me. "The postage service check for hexes and jinxes and that kind of thing."

"You're not making me feel any better." It hadn't even occurred to me that this thing could be cursed.

"Just open it," Winnie yawns. "Then we can both go to sleep."

I nod and gingerly peel open the cellophane. Immediately, I'm hit by the smell of something rotten. So pungent, it makes my eyes water and I drop the object, stepping away automatically.

"Ewww, that is revolting," Winnie screeches, bolting upright in bed and waving her hand in front of her face. The smell wakes Pip too; he begins to grunt angrily. "What the hell is it?"

"I'm not sure I want to know," I say, but my curiosity gets the better of me and, pinching my nose and trying not to breathe, I venture closer, stripping away more of the cellophane. It makes the smell worse and Pip races around the room, squealing, as tears roll down my face.

I examine the object.

Ham.

It's a ham.

A rotten ham.

My stomach turns and I peer down at Pip.

"Can you tell what it is?" Winnie says.

"Yes," I tell her, wrapping the plastic back around the slab of meat and marching with it to the door.

I walk out of the dorm, around the building and towards the communal trash cans, opening the first lid and dropping the package inside.

The smell still hangs in the air, following me. My stomach twists and I run inside the dorm, racing straight to the bathroom and vomiting into the toilet bowl.

After I wash my face and swill water around my mouth, I return to my room. Winnie's opened all the windows and is dashing around squirting perfume into the air.

"It still stinks in here," she moans, Pip squeaking his agreement. "What the hell was that thing?"

"A ham," I say, and my friend freezes in her tracks.

"A ham?"

"A rotten ham."

"Maybe it wasn't rotten when they sent it." I stare at my friend. "Yeah, I suppose not. But why would someone do that?"

"Because the people in this school are assholes – present company excluded."

"You think it was someone from the school?"

"I can't think who else it could be." I reach down to stroke Pip's head, calming him down and guiding him back to his bed. He licks at my hand and snuggles up in his blanket.

"You should tell Stone," Winnie says.

I shake my head and shrug off my remaining clothes. "No, I don't need his help."

I snap my fingers and extinguish the lamp.

"I'm really sorry, Rhi," Winnie says. "I don't understand why they can't leave you alone."

"Yeah," I mumble, lying flat on my back. But I know why. It's because I'm different. Because I was an unregistered. Because, rather than groveling and begging for forgiveness for my very existence, I've not cared what they think of me, my past or my pig. I've made myself a target and it's a matter of pride for them now. They have to win this battle. They have to see me put in my place. They won't stop until I am. The whole thing is exhausting.

But despite how tired I am, despite how late it is and all the chores I need to complete tomorrow, sleep won't come.

So much for getting the hang of things around here. So much for thinking I could belong.

A week ago I could actually see myself staying. Could even see myself enjoying myself. How quickly all that has turned out to be garbage.

No life. No frigging clue. And one less friend.

I've screwed everything up. I'm not cut out for people, for friends, for fucking civilization.

I'd be better off on my own with Pip somewhere no one can find me.

29

R^{hi}

EXCEPT THERE'S no way I can leave yet. If there is one thing this stupid academy has taught me, it's that I don't know as much about magic as I thought I did. If I have any chance of surviving out there on my own, with the Wolves of Night and the authorities chasing me, I need to keep my head down and learn as much as I can.

I know I have potential. I wasn't bluffing back there in the locker room with Tristan Kennedy. I can feel this power sparking in my blood. I know it could be enough. If I could just learn how to use it, to unleash it, to bend it to my will.

So no more attempts at a social life, no more trips into the city, no more hanging out with friends. I'm spending every waking hour I can in the library and I'm going to concentrate like hell in every single one of my classes.

Starting with gym class.

On Monday morning, I arrive at the gymnasium early, taking my spot by the mats and waiting for Spencer. I ignore the snide comments the other students make as they filter past me. They're especially vicious today, half the dueling team deciding to either leer at me or toss out innuendos. To my surprise though there's nothing about the ham, about my special delivery or bad smells.

Perhaps whoever sent it hasn't told their friends about it yet.

I ignore all their jibes, my jaw set, my shoulders stiff.

I reckon my determination is written all over my face because Spencer does a double take as he strolls towards the mats.

"I want you to stop fucking about and actually teach me," I say folding my arms as he approaches.

"There's no point. You're so far behind everyone else, you're never going to catch up."

"I would if you actually taught me," I snap in annoyance. "This stuff might actually save my neck one day, did you ever think of that? Did you consider that, by failing to help me, you're putting my life at risk?"

He shrugs off his sweater, his vest lifting as he does, and flashing me a strip of toned abs. I avert my gaze. His abs aren't just washboard, they're marble.

"You expect me to believe you're actually worried about that stuff?" he goads and I register for the first time that his mood is about as black as mine today.

I see him fooling around all the time, making all his little football pals roll around in laughter nearly every single day. And yet, whenever he's here on the mat with me, it's like he's had a personality transplant. Like the school joker's been replaced by the prince of darkness. I don't understand why I get treated to this special side of him.

"Why?" I ask him, meeting his scowl with one of my own.

He darts towards me and I yelp, springing to one side, slipping out of his grip.

I'm not playing this time. I'm not going to let him toss me about like a sack of potatoes and teach me precisely zero.

He grunts and lurches for me a second time. I dodge him again, although this time his fingertips brush over my stomach causing unexplainable sparks to burst into life there.

I shake my head.

"Cut it out!" I yell. "Cut it out and teach me."

"I am teaching you, Pig Girl, I'm teaching you just how fucking hopeless you are."

He charges for me again, ducking his head like a bull that's seen a red flag.

I spin and run. Like I said. Not playing.

But he doesn't give up. He doesn't halt like I expect. He keeps coming for me.

I pick up my heels and keep running. Our footfall catches the attention of the other students in the hall.

"Go Spencer," I hear Summer call out, while others hoot and cheer.

His thundering steps seem to draw closer.

I huff out air, and drive my legs and arms harder.

He's not going to catch me. No fucking way.

I don't care about the rules. I don't care about the lesson. I wasn't learning anything anyway.

I keep running, crashing through the gym doors and out onto the pitch. There's no one out there; the grass and the stands empty.

I run right across the center of the field, spying the perimeter fence in the distance. If he doesn't give up, I'm leaping straight over it.

But he's not the star of the dueling team for nothing. He may be huge but god dammit he's fast.

I hear the thud of his feet. I hear the pant of his breath.

I grit my teeth and run with everything I have. It's no good.

He hooks his arm tight around my middle and tackles me to the ground with ease.

I hit the hard grass with a thwack, my face meeting dirt, and the heavy weight of his body mushing me into the ground once again.

"Get off me!" I yelp, squirming underneath him, despite every bone in my body crying out in pain.

He only presses me deeper into the dry grass.

"Do you know how I know?" he snarls.

"Know what?" I snarl back.

"That you're not taking any of this stuff seriously." I don't answer him. I'm pretty sure it was a rhetorical question anyway. "First, the authorities' enforcer. Now Andrew Playford."

I freeze. "Huh?"

What is he talking about?

"Firstly, you're fucking around with the man in black. And now a week later, Andrew Playford," he spits right in my ear.

"I'm not fucking around."

He laughs hollowly. "And you don't even have the guts to own it. If you want to be the school slut, at least wear that shit with pride."

"You're such a misogynistic asshole," I hiss. "I'm not ashamed of who I am. But I'm not having jerks like you spreading rumors about me either. Andrew and me, we're just friends." At least we were. I'm not sure if we still are. "And me and the man in black we're ..." What the hell are we? Friends? I don't think so.

"You expect me to believe that!"

"I don't give a flying crap what you do and don't believe. I'm telling the truth!"

His body turns rigid. He's silent, his heavy panting dying away to a whisper by my ear.

"If it's not true," he says sinisterly, "then why was Andrew telling all the locker room about how you went around to his room on Saturday night, let him eat you out, before he fucked you on his desk?"

Now it's my time for my body to tense, my next words faltering in my throat. "He ... he didn't say that."

He wouldn't. It isn't true. Why would he make something like that up?

Spencer is quiet again. I can hear the gym door banging in the breeze and feet in the gymnasium pounding the sprung floor.

"He did," he finally says, more quietly now.

"He didn't. You're just trying to fuck with me like always." Andrew is my friend. He was angry with me on Saturday night but that is because I hurt his feelings. I'm sure he'll come around. I know he wouldn't say that stuff about me ... would he?

I think about the way the boys leered at me this morning. I think about how several of them invited me to see their desks.

Spencer rolls off me and onto his back on the grass. He looks up at the cloudless sky, and then turns to look at me. The irises of his eyes are like two dark spheres floating in an ocean of light. That sensation tugs deep in my gut.

"I'm not fucking with you, Rhi. That's what he said."

I know he's telling the truth.

I choke. Because it hurts. Of all the things they've done to me here, all the cruel stupid bullshit, this hurts the most. I twist my head away from Spencer so he can't see the water swimming in my eyes.

We lie there, the wind kicking up dirt from the track that rings the pitch, the sun warming the back of my neck, until finally Spencer jumps up onto his feet.

"You can't even run properly, Pig Girl," he snaps.

And I can't take it anymore.

I can't take it!

My magic sears through my body, hissing and fizzing, dark and angry. My body shakes with it.

I lift my hand and I blast him.

It hits him right in the center of his gut. His eyes go wider than saucepans as he flies backward and hits the ground with a thud.

I roll up onto my knees, lifting my hands, ready for the counterstrike.

He stares down at his stomach in shock as his body twitches and jerks, his bones seeming to strain inside his body, his shape distorting and reforming before my eyes.

I gasp as he staggers to his feet, grunting and shaking his head, his hands flexing and balling, fighting whatever the hell this is.

Then as suddenly as it started, it stops. He stands, panting, and lifts his gaze to mine.

"What the hell are you doing?" he yells, "have you lost your mind? Do you want to get yourself expelled?"

Want to? Because I'm pretty certain I just did. I used my magic on another student. Hell, I'll use more on him if he comes at me again.

I'm out of here.

"I don't care," I spit. "I don't care what you tell Principal York. I don't care if she kicks me out. I don't care at all."

He scoffs at me, his face turning sour. "I'm not Kennedy. I'm not a snitch. I'm not going to tell on you." He rubs at his stomach, peering down at it with confusion. "Fuck, that actually hurts." He glances back up at me, frowning. "You're fucking lucky no one saw that, Piggie."

"What?" I say. "Saw me whip your ass?"

He lifts an eyebrow lazily at me. "Whatever. You know if I wanted to, I could snap your skinny ass in two, with or without my magic." He takes a step toward me. "One time, Pig Girl. You get to strike me like that one time. Try it again and ..."

"What? You'll blast me back? You'll tell on me?" I don't care. I'm beyond caring.

I don't stick around to hear him finish his threat, instead I storm past him, straight through the gymnasium and into the locker room.

I feel eyes on me the whole way. I can hear them whispering about me and I wish I was anywhere else but here.

※

I DON'T SEE Winnie until kitchen duties and another round of pot washing. My hands were beginning to soften after a lifetime's rearing chicken and working in our vegetable plot. Now they're red raw and painful every time I plunge them into yet another bowl of piping hot water.

It doesn't help my foul mood.

A mood which must be written all over my face.

"Bad day?" Winnie asks, carefully removing the pan I'm scrubbing from my hands before I rub away the sponge.

"You could say that."

"Want to talk about it?" she asks.

"No," I say, sulking as I pick up the next pot. It reeks of gone-off fish and my stomach lurches.

"Talking helps."

"I don't see how."

"Well, bottling this up and destroying cook wear," she says, snatching this pan off me too, "definitely doesn't."

I sigh, resting my hip against the sink.

"It's Andrew."

"Oh," Winnie says, trying her best to keep her face neutral. I haven't told her about what happened after I left his room on Saturday night. Half of me thinks she'll confirm I was a bitch to him. The other half suspects she'll be marching around to his room and giving him a piece of her mind. I have no idea which is the correct half.

"He ..." I stare at the point above her head, avoiding her eyes. "He tried to kiss me on Saturday night."

"Oh," Winnie repeats, examining my face. When I don't add anymore, she prompts, "And ..."

"And I told him, I don't like him in that way. That I want to be friends."

"Okay," she says, the skin between her brows pinching. "How did he take that news?"

I chew on my thumb. "Well, not exactly great."

Winnie rolls her eyes and harrumphs. "Asshole."

"Wait until you hear the rest."

Winnie shifts her weight from one foot to the other. "I may have heard about the other stuff."

I stare at her. "What do you mean?"

"He's telling everyone that you–"

"Slept with him, I know." I bury my face in my hands. "I thought he was my friend. I was so stupid."

"You weren't stupid. Men pull this kind of crap all the time, trust me. Pretend to be your friend, pretend to respect you, pretend they're one of the good guys. Then as soon as they figure out they're never climbing inside your panties, wham," she whacks the pan onto the countertop, "they turn sour quicker than an apple that's tumbled from the tree."

"But to say that stuff about me! And then Spencer, in gym today, was at my throat about it all, calling me a slut."

"Oh," Winnie says in a way that makes me peek through my fingers at her.

"What?"

"Did you ... did you tell him it was all lies and bullshit?"

"Of course I did, not that it's any of his business, not that I would be ashamed if it were true, but it's not and that seems ... what?" My best friend is chewing on her bottom lip.

"Andrew's walking around school with a black eye and a busted nose. I saw him heading off to the infirmary."

"Good!" I snap. Winnie's brows pinch again. "I'm not going to feel sorry for ... what?"

"Guess who gave him that black eye?"

"I don't know but I wish it had been me."

"Spencer Moreau."

"Spencer Moreau gave Andrew a black eye?"

"You don't suspect it was because–?"

"No," I snap, "no. Spencer Moreau hates my guts about as much as Summer does. He must have done it for another reason."

Although, I'm still here aren't I? There's been no summons to the principal's office. I think Spencer Moreau may be true to his word. He won't be snitching on me.

What the hell do I make of that?

30

R^{hi}

IT SEEMS EVEN my plan to retreat to the library is now screwed up, because Andrew is likely to be in there and I really, really don't want to bump into him right now. I've already gotten away with blasting one asshole with my magic today, I'm not sure I'll be so lucky a second time.

There's no dueling training this evening so I avoid the indignity of having to head to the locker room. Winnie suggests another movie, but I'm fed up with being cooped up. Irritation spirals through my body and I need to burn it off.

"I'm going for a walk," I tell Winnie as we step out of the kitchen and onto the campus paths.

"Where?" she says, clearly concerned I'm going to run off again.

"Around campus."

She looks at me like I've lost my mind. "Do you want some company?" she asks, a little unsure.

"No, I need to think and walking helps."

"Are you sure you don't want to talk about it some more?"

I shake my head. "I'll see you back at the dorm later."

She gives me a hug and I watch her walk down the path, before choosing one in an opposite direction. One of the quieter routes because I can't stomach the idea of another encounter with one of the assholes around here.

I should be in that library studying everything I can get my hands on. I should have done that from the start. There's so much I don't know, so much I don't understand. And here's my chance to learn it all. I can't believe I got distracted by dresses and video games and crap like that.

Since the man in black found me and brought me into the authorities, everyone's been asking me the same thing: Why was your aunt keeping you hidden?

I don't have an answer for that. From a young age, I just knew we had to keep hidden, had to keep moving. I never thought to question why. I never thought to ask about my parents.

Now, as I meander along one of the paths, gravel crunching under my feet, the moon casting silver light over the ground, I wonder why.

I want to know.

I want to know why I wasn't sent to school like everyone else. Why we never lived like everyone else. Why my mom and dad aren't here.

I glance up in the direction of the library. Maybe the answers are in there, lurking in some book. Maybe my parents will be in some history book, or recorded in the columns of a newspaper article. Maybe if I knew what happened to them, I'd know why my aunt kept me hidden.

But the library is out of bounds. And the irritation in my stomach simmers all the harder. I want to know. I want answers.

I twist my head and look up at the mansion. I'm pretty sure there's one person who *can* give me answers.

I spin around and march in the direction of the mansion. It's late, the Great Hall all shut up and the corridors dark.

I don't know if he'll even be there. I have no idea where he lives. On campus? Another question I never thought to ask.

But as I draw closer, along the hallway that leads to his classroom, I feel that all-too-familiar tug in my stomach. And I know he's there.

The hook pulls. It's so familiar now I hardly notice it. Another thing on my long list I've failed to question.

I knock on his door and wait. No one answers. I crane my ears, listening for sound. I know he's in there. Perhaps he's asleep. Tough shit.

I bang harder.

"Stone!" I cry out.

It takes a while but eventually I hear the creak of furniture and footsteps approaching the door.

"It's nearly ten o'clock," he mutters from the other side of the door. "Come back tomorrow morning."

"I need to speak to you. Now."

"Speak to me tomorrow," he says with irritation.

"No," I say. I wait. I rattle the door handle. I hear him mutter a string of curse words. Then the door creaks open. Only a fraction. I see him through the gap. No jacket, no tie, shirt undone at the collar, his sleeves rolled up. His feet bare.

The way he looks makes my stomach swoop.

"What do you want, Blackwaters?"

"To talk." He scoffs and starts to close the door. "I lied," I say quickly.

He stares at me, his features unchanging. "You lie to me all the time."

"I lied to you about those objects. I could ... I could see the fingerprints."

He keeps staring, and I notice the multitude of different colors in his beard. "Come in," he says finally, pulling the door back and stepping aside.

The classroom is dark except for the moonlight penetrating the window and the light from his office falling across the floor.

He shuts the door and rubs his fingernails across his chin, the noise rough. I have an urge to do the same, to run my fingers through his beard.

He frowns at me and drops his hands.

"Why did you lie?"

I shake my head, dropping to lean against one of the desks. Then remembering the rumors currently circulating about me, I jerk upright.

"The boys in this school are pathetic scumbags. I could have told you that."

"I've not come to talk about that," I snap.

His eyes flicker across my face and he nods. "Why did you lie?" he repeats.

"Because ... because it felt safer to conceal the truth."

"You don't trust me."

"I don't trust anyone ... except for Pip and Winnie."

"That's very sad, Blackwaters."

I shrug. I'm bored with feeling sorry for myself. I want answers. I want answers so I can get the hell out of here.

Stone drops onto a chair, resting his forearms on his knees.

"This again?"

"I don't belong here. That much is clear."

"Yeah," he says, involuntarily rubbing at his chin again. "Yeah, I don't think you do." I take a step backwards, like he slapped me and he looks up, as surprised as I am. "What? You think I'm going to spout a load of bullshit to you about how you do?"

I stare down at my sneakers. There's a hole forming over one toe and the laces are fraying.

No, Stone doesn't deal in bullshit. But I realize deep down, deep, deep down, buried away, I wanted to belong. I wanted to fit in. I want something more than chickens and a pig. More than a home which only serves for as long as the next potential threat. I want safety and belonging. I want it more than answers.

"You don't think we all want those things?" he says.

"Everybody else has them. You have them!"

"Me?" He laughs. "You think I belong here?"

"You're a teacher."

"Because I have this one goddamn skill they can make use of. I don't belong here anymore than you do Blackwaters." He holds my eye. "We're not like them."

My forehead crinkles in puzzlement. "Are you telling me you were an unregistered too, because I find that hard to–"

"Never mind," he snaps. "The point is, whether you belong here or not, you're stuck here, just like I am. So stop making things difficult for yourself, stop making enemies, stop making friends with the wrong people, stop ..." He lifts his arm in frustration. His gaze travels over my form. He frowns. "Stop lying to teachers."

"Why is it important?" I ask him. Because I'd sensed it was, could taste his eagerness that I had the power to see magical fingerprints. It was why I'd kept it from him.

"It's a rare power, Rhi. Very rare. Don't get me wrong, it's one skilled magicals can learn over time. But an untrained one, one with little formal education ... I've never heard of that before."

I stare at him wide-eyed.

"Did your aunt teach it to you?"

"No," I say.

He hesitates.

"Why was she keeping you hidden, Rhianna?"

"I don't know," I say, "but I want to find out."

He nods slowly. "And you think I can tell you?"

"Can you?"

"No, but ... we've been looking into it."

"The authorities?"

He hesitates then nods a second time.

"And what have you found?"

"At this point, nothing."

"You must have found something."

"We're finding it hard to even determine the names of your parents."

"I don't know–"

"I know. You think I haven't rifled through your mind for answers, Blackwaters?"

I scowl at him. "You couldn't see into my mind about the magical fingerprints though, could you?"

"No, you're finally learning some goddamn control." He leans back on his chair, staring up at me. "There are other parts of your mind I haven't been able to unlock as well."

I shift my weight on my feet uncomfortably, an unease prickling over my skin. "What ... what do you mean?"

Until recently I thought my mind had been an open book to him, one he could pick up and flick through the pages whenever he liked.

"There're some memories deep down in your mind that I can't penetrate."

Good, I think. Then shift again. "What memories?"

"I don't know what memories, I can't see them." He holds my gaze. "I'm not sure you are even aware you possess them."

"I ... I don't know what you're talking about ..."

He stands up and stalks towards me, pausing when he's standing right in front of me. I tip my head back staring up into his face. The hook in my belly shimmers with his proximity.

"If you let me, I could open them. It might provide the answer you want."

"And the answers the authorities want too."

He shrugs.

Are there memories really locked inside my head? Ones I wasn't even aware of? And if it's true, what the hell kind of memories are they? Ones I've hidden from myself?

"Perhaps. Or ones your aunt kept hidden from you."

"What?" I say, blinking, his pale eyes coming back into focus.

"Your aunt may have stored these memories in your mind for you to find one day. Or ..." His eyes flick across my face. I can feel the warmth of his body and the tickle of his breath, gentle on my face. That tug pulls me toward him. I was going to ask him about that too. But now, I find I can't bring myself to do it.

"Or?"

"Or ... she may have hidden your own memories from you in order to protect you from them."

I swallow. I don't know what happened to my parents. I don't remember a single thing about them. My earliest memory is of my aunt. Of her face, her laugh, her voice.

"Because they're painful," I whisper.

"Perhaps, or maybe because whatever they are is a danger to you. A threat."

I close my eyes. I have a Pandora's box inside my head. One it would be severely tempting to open. But I know how that went down for Pandora. I have enough pain in my heart, enough doubts lingering at my shoulders, enough axes hanging over my head. Do I want to add to those? Do I really want to know?

"I won't open them," Stone says softly, "I won't open them unless you ask me to."

I open my eyes. Whatever this hook is in my belly, I think

it's hooked him in, too. He leans over me, our faces merely inches apart.

"If I let you ... if I let you open those memories, do you promise not to tell anyone what's inside?"

I hold his gaze. The power of the connection is intense, like I can feel his power longing to connect with mine. I hold my breath.

He steps away, shaking his head.

"No, Rhi, no, I can't promise you that. I don't know what the hell your aunt was up to. I don't know who your parents were. I can't make you that promise."

Because for all that connection I just imagined – that I stupidly believed I felt – I'm just a nobody, a nothing. Didn't he tell me that on my very first day here?

"Yes, I did. Don't get the impression that just because I'm curious about your past, that I possess any interest in you, Blackwaters." He frowns. "That I'd make concessions and allowances for you. I'm not in the habit of making promises to students. No matter who they are."

"And yet despite the late hour, you opened your door to me. Why do I have the suspicion you don't do that for just anyone, Professor?" He scoffs. "And also," I continue, "despite your lack of interest in me, you threatened to kiss me. Or do you make moves on all your students?"

"You want answers, Blackwaters. I'm not the one to give them to you."

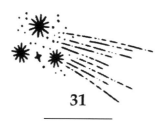

31

The man in black

It's midnight by the time Stone reaches the bar. But who am I kidding? It's not like I've been sleeping much the last few weeks. My fucking body and my fucking mind won't let me. I'm restless, aware that there's only one damn thing that will cure that.

I'm beginning to think Stone is wrong. That this isn't something we can ignore. Isn't something we can forget. Sure as hell isn't something we can reverse.

But perhaps this late night plea to meet will prove me wrong. Perhaps he's found the answer to our problems.

Jesus Christ, I hope so. It's becoming harder to resist. Harder to ignore.

I've already faltered once. I know I could do so again.

However, as soon as I catch sight of him in the mirror

behind the rows of liquor bottles, strolling toward me, I know he hasn't.

He looks as tired as I feel. Dark rings lining his eyes, his beard unkempt.

He slumps down on a stool.

"Two times in one month. This is becoming a habit."

He's not in the mood for banter and small talk. He picks up my beer, takes several long swigs, then slams it on the bar top.

"She came to see me tonight," he says, rubbing his fingernails through the bristles of his beard.

My eyebrows leap up my forehead, and I try to ignore the sensation of jealousy that pokes at my chest.

"She did?" I say, although the words leave my mouth in an aggressive growl.

Stone's eyes flick up to mine. "It wasn't like that, asshole." His eyes narrow. "I'm not about to bundle her onto my bike."

"Are you sure? It's growing stronger, you know it's growing stronger."

He scrubs his hands over his face.

"She wanted answers."

"Answers?"

The girl doesn't understand, shows little signs of awareness and no curiosity at all. If it had been any other way, she'd have showed up at Stone's office long ago, demanding answers ... and more. But it was only a matter of time. She was always going to work it out eventually.

"She wants to know who she is, who her parents were, why she was being hidden."

So it wasn't that. I'm not sure if I feel relief or disappointment.

I lean back on my stool. "You think she was serious? You think she really doesn't know those things?"

"She's getting a little better at shielding her thoughts," he frowns, "but only a little. She was being truthful."

"Why now? Why ask now?"

He shrugs, signaling to the barman for a drink of his own. "She's not happy. She wants to leave."

I lean forward. "With a price on her head?"

"Yeah, with a price on her head."

"She won't last two minutes."

My friend side-eyes me. "She got away from you."

"I *let* her get away from me."

"You're going soft in your old age."

I stare at him. We both know that my age isn't the reason I'm turning soft.

"You need to keep an eye on her, Stone. You need to make sure she doesn't leave."

The barman smacks a bottle of beer down in front of him, twisting off the cap and Stone takes a gulp.

"I don't know. If she went, she'd be dead sooner or later. Maybe that's our way out of this shit."

I grab a fistful of his shirt. "You want her dead?" I spit into his face.

His body flags, gaze dropping with shame to the floor. "No," he whispers.

I stare at him hard. "And I thought you were a fucking professor. Do you actually read any of those books in your fucking office? You know what would happen …"

He lifts his head and glares at me. "I've seen it first hand," he growls through gritted teeth, "remember?"

Guilt floods my body and I let go of his shirt. "Shit! Phoenix, I'm sorry. I–"

"It wouldn't be like that for us," he says, his hands gripping the bottle so tightly I'm surprised it doesn't shatter. "I'd make sure of it."

I shake my head. He thinks we're special? He thinks we're different?

Maybe in some ways we are. Maybe in more ways than anyone else will ever know about.

But in this? We won't be.

"I'm serious, Stone. It's ancient magic. Existed since the beginning of time."

"I want her gone."

"Sure you do," I say, my voice laced with sarcasm.

"She's a nuisance."

"Women always are," I say but my joke falls flat.

He spins the bottle in his hand. Then sighs, his shoulders slumping in defeat.

"I'm not going to let anything happen to her. You know that. But I'm not going to be nice." He scowls. "And she can fight her own fucking battles."

That's good enough for me.

"So what answers did you give her?"

Stone spreads out his hands. "What answers do I have?"

It's true, despite our continued investigation, we've turned up nothing. "I can't help feeling the council has information it hasn't shared with me." I lift my beer bottle to my lips and finish the remaining liquid.

"What makes you think that?"

"The fact they sent her to the academy, let her keep that dumb pig. I've never seen the council be so lenient before."

"Every magical is precious. They wouldn't waste an opportunity to train another for the force."

"She's one girl, and the Chancellor likes to set an example. Not every mother wants to hand over their precious child to become a soldier. He needs to prevent them from getting any ideas."

"So they showed leniency. Why would that mean they have information about her?"

I shrug. "Beats me," I say with annoyance. "It's just a theory."

Stone glances at me from the corner of his eye and I know there's more.

"What is it?"

"There are memories in her mind, ones I can't access. She wasn't aware they existed." He swallows more of his beer, swiping his tongue along his bottom lip afterwards. "I think they were locked there by another magical."

"Can you get in?"

He snorts. "Of course."

"So did you?" My body tenses. Whatever memories are buried deep inside the girl's mind may hold the answers to all the mysteries that exist about her.

"No. I asked her if she wanted me to open them and she said no."

"Why?"

"Doesn't trust me not to hand her secrets over to the authorities."

I freeze, turning my head slowly towards him. "You couldn't keep shit like that–"

"I know. I know." He spins the beer bottle in his hands. "But I can't get in unless she lets me and fuck I'm curious."

The barman points to the clock above his head. He wants to close up soon.

I examine my friend. I've known him a hell of a long time. He may seem like this laid-back professor, content with his career, no ambition, no drive. It's all a load of bullshit. Stone's driven all right. A man with that many books isn't coasting. He knows that sometimes tough choices have to be made, that sometimes we do the unscrupulous thing for the greater good. That's never phased him before.

"You could have lied to her. Told her you'd never tell a soul just to get inside her head. You still could."

"It had occurred to me."

"So what stopped you?"

"It ... it wasn't a conscious decision." He turns his head to look at me and I know for all the bravado and sulking, he cares about the girl. More than he's willing to admit. "I don't trust this situation," he continues. "I don't trust that there's no record of this girl or her parents. I don't trust that her aunt kept her so well hidden. I don't trust the fact she has powers a girl like her shouldn't. Fuck, I want to know what's in her head. But I'm damn scared I'll regret it."

His words weigh on my mind as we say our goodbyes and go our separate ways.

He's right. None of this smells right. And I'm pretty certain I'm right too. The Council knows something about this girl.

I meander through the streets of Los Magicos on my bike, only realizing where I'm heading when I arrive.

The Council building.

The guards let me through the gates without a word. It's late but I'm often coming and going at strange times given the nature of my work.

I park my bike and take one of the back entrances.

The Council building is dark and quiet. It's the middle of the night and the only people hanging around are guards, although judging by the number of them, none of the council members are here in the building tonight. Good.

I pass a set of guards at the base of the sweeping staircase, nodding to them all. They let me pass, not even blinking. At the top of the stairs I look down at them. Their eyes are trained ahead, searching for any danger that may be coming their way, unaware of the potential mischief I'm up to behind them.

The corridor is empty. The Chancellor's personal guards aren't here tonight; most likely they're with him at his personal residence in the luxurious part of the city.

I stare at the door to his office, examining the emerald crystal in the door handle.

There'll be all sorts of charms and magic keeping this door

locked and intruders out. It's why those guards aren't interested in what I'm up to. They don't think I can enter anywhere I shouldn't.

They're wrong.

I hover my palm in front of the door, and close my eyes, reading the spells there. This ability is one of the reasons I'm so damn good at my job. It's also an ability I've never revealed to anyone but Stone. Not even to my father. Keeping it a secret has made it far more useful than it would otherwise be.

As I predicted, there are several spells by two different hands. The Chancellor himself and his head of security, Janice Pierce. Two of them are hexes designed to harm anyone who attempts to open the door by force.

Those are easily removed, a few whispered words and the magic dissolves into the air.

The next one is more challenging. It's an alarm, designed to sound if anyone tampers with the spell. I peer at the intricacies of the magic with my mind, peering at it from every angle. Every piece of magic has its weakness. A way in, a way to destroy it.

Finally I find this too, a switch buried in its midst placed there by its creator to disable the alarm if necessary. I flick it, holding my breath, prepared to sprint if the alarm sounds.

Nothing, simply silence and my own breath, loud enough in my ears.

I shake my head. A thin film of sweat forms along my brow.

I peer down at the guards. They're talking softly among themselves, still unaware of what I'm doing.

The two last pieces of magic are the most complex. They twist together, tangling and combining to hold the door locked.

Of course, there must be a way to undo them, otherwise the Chancellor would never be able to enter his own office.

Again I examine the magic. On closer inspection, I see the magic is not as sophisticated as it first appears. It's flimsy and simple. I scoff. So very like the Chancellor himself: all show and no substance.

Carefully, I unbind the magic, unraveling it a strand at a time, making a mental note as I do of how it was entangled. I will need to replace these spells when I'm done. Otherwise they'll know I was in here.

Finally, the last strand of magic uncoils and the door clicks open.

I wipe my brow and rub my eyes. Then with one final check on the guards, I slip inside, shutting the door behind me.

There's a security camera blinking in the corner, but I send a wave of magic its way, ensuring the only pictures it records are that of an empty office. Then I swing my gaze around.

Moonlight casts the room in a hue of silver, making the place look older and more ghostly than it is.

The Chancellor's laptop isn't here and I realize I'm clutching at straws. Why would the Chancellor keep any records in his office? They'd be stored elsewhere, locked away in archives or in some administrator's filing cabinet.

Still, I'm here now. I may as well look.

There's a stack of papers resting on the Chancellor's desk so I start there, rifling through the pages one at a time. They're all neatly typed briefings and minutes from meetings. The topics range from a trade deal with the Eastern Isles to proposed changes to the school curriculum. There's certainly nothing about a scrawny, unregistered girl from the wastelands.

I straighten the pile, waving my hand to remove any traces of my scent, magic or fingerprints.

I look to the shelves next. They're lined with ancient leather-backed tomes and not much else, except a small statue of a fairy spinning on her toes. I flick through the books. I check the index for Blackwaters. Nothing.

This was a futile visit. One I should have planned out better.

I rub at my forehead. What the hell is going on with me? I'm not impulsive like this. I don't pull risky stunts that would ruin my reputation, end my career and land me in the Northern labor camps.

Except that's the reason I am here. I'm not myself. And if I ever hope to be so again, I need to understand.

My eyes flick to the bust on the desk. My grandfather's cold eyes stare back at me. I barely remember him, just another ancestor in a whole long line of them with famous names and towering reputations.

I step closer towards him.

He was ruthless, crushing an uprising in the East, a state that had wanted to break away and form a republic of its own. He'd have agreed with Stone. Not only would he have let the girl run, he'd have encouraged her to do it.

The bust is made from walnut like everything else in this overdone office, but his eyes weren't brown, they were dark like mine. Soulless my mother once called them, screaming at my father.

I drop my gaze from my grandfather's face and my eyes land on the drawers that line the underneath of the solid desk.

There won't be anything of interest in them, but I drop to my knees anyway and open the top drawers. Gold-plated pens, a stamp and a wrist watch.

The second drawer has more but they are similar briefings to the ones that lie on the desk's surface.

The third is much the same.

The fourth one though ... the fourth one contains a stack of files. I halt, my breath catching in my throat.

I lift the first one and flip open the folder. It's full of pages, notes and information, all about one magical. I don't recognize the face or the name, but I make a mental note of both, my heart beating faster.

The second, third and fourth files are the same. Another face, another name. None familiar.

I begin to despair.

There's one more file in the drawer. I lift it out and onto my knee. I flip back the cover.

The picture of a young woman stares up at me. The photo faded but the details clear.

For a long moment, I think it's her. The color of the eyes, the angle of the jaw. But then slowly I understand that it isn't. The nose is wrong, the hair too light, the forehead too broad, the lips too thin.

It's not Rhianna. But those are her eyes.

32

R^{hi}

WHO AM I?

Now I've allowed myself to ask that question, it's a question that won't leave me alone. It buzzes around my head as I lie in bed, Winnie and Pip snoring in unison, and won't let me sleep.

I recount every conversation with my aunt, every nugget of information she'd relayed. I strain hard to remember. The exact words. The precise phrasing. I try to conjure in my mind's eye all the things she'd shown me and all those she hadn't as well. The photo she kept by her bed, the map she drew from memory, the locket around her neck ...

The locket. She always wore it. Never removed it. It hung there, the silver oval resting against her clavicle. I never saw it opened and when it came to burying her, I couldn't bear to part her from it, even though she'd told me to take it.

I flip onto my side in irritation. How stupid could I be?

I didn't keep that locket like she asked. Apart from the money in the tin and the herbs in the jars, she left me no other hints. No diary, no journal, no letters. Nothing. That necklace was my only clue.

I picture that locket. Silver with a pattern of faint flowers engraved around its perimeter. Flowers that looked like ... I crinkle my forehead, forcing the memory back. But it's too buried and it changes as I force it into existence. I never looked at it properly, never held it in my hands and studied it, traced my thumb over the engraving.

Winnie's wrist watch ticks in the darkness and outside the wind rushes through the tall trees. I burrow down under my covers.

I miss the clearing and the wood. I miss the freedom. I miss my aunt.

I can almost hear her voice in my ear, her footsteps in the hallway, her hand twisting the door handle ...

I freeze.

The door handle? Did I hear that for real or was I dreaming?

I hold my breath, certain I can hear the door of our dorm creak open. The noise is faint, hardly audible. I peer through the darkness.

The door stands ajar and yet there's no one there. The doorway is empty.

Am I really awake?

I stare at the space, at the empty room, at the darkness, and I swear I hear the floorboards creak, the whispers of a stranger's breath.

I remember the woods. The thing that attacked me unseen.

I breathe in, hunting for a scent, any sign or clue, my fingers taut under the bedsheets, ready to defend myself if I need to.

But there's only silence again. Silence and darkness.

"I know you're here," I whisper, but there's no reply. No

other sound until the door clicks shut and I'm left there with even more questions swirling through my mind.

When finally, the darkness retreats and the room slowly brightens, I'm still awake. Doubting that I really heard or saw anything. Still without an answer to that question.

Who am I?

☀.

I DON'T PARTICULARLY WANT to emerge from bed when Winnie's alarm finally sounds. But she doesn't leave me much choice.

My friends prods me on the cheek.

"You can't let the assholes win, Rhi. Come on, up."

When I groan and tug the cover over my head, she dives straight for my weak spot, depositing Pip in the bed with me. My pig snuggles under the covers, licking at my face and squealing loudly.

"See, he wants you up too. You're not setting a very good example to him by hiding away in your bed."

"Fine," I say as Pip grunts angrily at me as if he's agreeing with everything Winnie is saying.

Winnie and I are halfway pulling on our uniforms when there's a knock on our door.

We look at each other, Winnie slightly alarmed. I know what she's thinking: another summons to Principal York.

I have a suspicion she could be right. Visiting hot teachers late in the evening is probably not allowed.

"Who is it?" I ask anyway, hopeful we have a visitor and not a note.

"It's Andrew."

Winnie gapes at the door. "Go away!" she says, before I can even open my mouth. "We have nothing to say to you."

"I'd like to talk to Rhi ... I'd like to apologize."

Winnie scoffs. "Well, Rhi doesn't want to hear your pathetic

"..." She trails off as I walk towards the door and reach for the handle. "What are you doing?" she whispers tersely.

"Hearing him out," I whisper back.

Winnie shakes her head in disapproval and slams her beret on her head.

I draw the door open, finding Andrew standing outside with a large, elaborate bouquet of daisies in his arm and a very black eye on his face.

I cross my arms and glare at him.

"These are for you," he says sheepishly. I don't say anything. This guy spread rumors about me. I'm not going to make this easy for him. "To apologize."

"For ..." I prompt.

The look on his face grows even more sheepish and he stares down at his shoes. "I'm sorry," he repeats. "The banter in the locker room got out of hand and–"

"Out of hand?!" Winnie hisses, coming to stand next to me. "You were bragging to all your boys. You said all that stuff about Rhi and it wasn't true."

Andrew shakes his head frantically. "No, that's not how it was. They were teasing me. Someone had seen you leave my room. Everyone started jumping to conclusions, debating about what we'd been up to and–"

"You didn't put them straight."

Andrew looks me in the eye. "Not with enough force, no. I'm sorry, Rhi. I should have shut it down straight away. I should have–"

"You totally disrespected her, dude," Winnie says. "You trashed her out. All because she doesn't feel the same way you feel about her."

"No," he says, "it wasn't like that. I respect you and your decision about ... well ... you don't know what those guys can be like!"

I sigh. "I do. I do know what they can be like."

"Then you understand."

"Not really," I say sternly, "I'd never do that to a friend."

"You're right. I screwed up. But I care about you, Rhi, and I'd like us to still be friends."

"You also said some pretty mean stuff to me."

"I know. I was a jerk and I'm sorry. Can you forgive me?"

I examine his face, searching for signs of sincerity as I chew on my thumb. His face is hard to read.

"I'll think about it," I say finally.

"That's probably as much as I deserve," he says and I nod.

"I'll see you in class," I add, closing the door, wanting to end the conversation.

Before the door slams shut, Winnie ducks her arms through the crack, grabs the flowers and pulls them inside.

The door shuts.

"You're not really going to forgive him?" she asks, carrying the flowers over to my desk.

"Like I said, I'm going to think about it."

I think about it all through my next few classes. At least it gives me something other than my identity to mull over.

By dinner time, I'm wondering if I could.

"Really?" Winnie says, shaking her head as she dips her fork into something that is meant to be mashed potatoes but looks more like a gray lump of slime.

"Remind me why we can't conjure up real, decent food?"

Winnie peers up at me and quirks an eyebrow. "It's the fundamentals of magic, Rhi. There are some things that just aren't possible. Creating food and precious metals, making someone fall in love–"

"Yet, you can kill someone with your magic." I lower my voice. "You can torture them until they go insane."

"There are some things we do not have the power to do. Changing water to wine, stone to bread, straw to gold – not possible."

I grimace and lift the slime into my mouth. It tastes like cardboard.

"Stone conjured coffee from thin air."

"Stone is special," Winnie says with a tease.

"Humph."

Winnie brings the slime to her mouth, then changes her mind and lowers her fork.

"So you're really considering forgiving Andrew?"

"I think he was genuinely sorry." Winnie snorts. "A lot of people have been shitty to me since I arrived," I continue.

"But this was–"

"He's the only one who has actually apologized. Who actually seems remorseful for what he did. The only one who's brought me flowers."

"I suppose so."

"Besides, I can see how it happened with those jerks from the dueling team."

"At least everyone seems to realize what he said was garbage now. A lot of kids are laughing at him for making up shit." I frown. "He deserves it!"

"Yeah," I say, "I suppose he does."

Although I've decided to forgive him, I let Andrew stew for a few more days until I actually tell him this.

We end up in the library together on Thursday afternoon. As I enter and take a seat at a separate desk, he eyes me nervously over the top of his book. I pretend I haven't noticed him, opening another fat book of my own and leaning over to focus on the words.

After half an hour, a shadow falls over my page and when I peer up it's Andrew, the corners of his mouth turned down, his face tired.

"Rhi," he says, "can we talk?"

I signal towards the chairs around the table and he takes a seat.

"I'm really sorry–"

"I know," I say. "And I forgive you."

His mouth falls open and he gapes at me like I just agreed to marry him.

"You ... you do?"

"Yes, if you promise never to do anything that dumb to me or any other girl ever again."

He lays his hand over his heart, relief flooding his heart. "Believe me, I promise I never will."

I wag my pencil at him. "I'd still like to hear you swear it."

He smiles at me shyly. "I hereby swear never to make crap up like that again."

"Good, and if you ever betray our friendship like that again–"

"You won't forgive me a second time."

I stare at him darkly. "I won't forgive you and I'll curse you and all your future children."

"I wouldn't expect anything less."

His shoulders relax and he sinks back into his chair.

"I was thinking," he says, "as another way of showing you how sorry I am ..."

I chew the end of my pencil. "Uh huh?"

"That I could lend you that video game you like so much."

"Really ... but I don't have anything to play it on."

"Dane has an old console I can pinch. He won't mind."

I grin. The flowers were a nice 'I'm sorry gift'. This is freaking amazing. I loved that game.

"Thanks," I say with a smile. "I'd like that."

Winnie groans when Andrew and Dane come round that evening and set up the new console in our room, Andrew loading up the puzzle game.

"You know this game is seriously lame, Rhi," she mutters.

"I like it," I tell her, hovering around the two boys as they plug in wires. "And it gives us something to do this weekend when we're stuck on campus again."

"Maybe I'll ask my mom to send me some of my games from home."

When the boys leave, I switch on the game and sink down onto the floor ready to play.

"You know this makes us official nerds with no life," Winnie says, shooing Pip away from the wires. "Home playing video games while everyone else is out partying."

"We'd be out partying if we were allowed."

"I guess," she says, "and it's not like I had this amazing reputation in the first place."

She sinks down beside me and takes the other controller.

A weight lifts from my shoulders. I feel lighter even though that question of who I am hangs over my head like a rain cloud.

※

THE FINAL TWO weeks of our punishment pass in a blur of pot scrubbing, dueling-kit laundry and helping the gardener on the weekends. In between my classes and video games, I spend most of my time holed up in the library or practicing magic with Winnie in our dorm room.

Winnie doesn't seem to question my need to study in the library. She can see how far behind I am and thinks I'm trying my best to catch up.

She doesn't know I'm scanning every book in there for answers about my identity.

I start in the modern history section, reading about events that occurred in my lifetime for any hints of me and my aunt. When I find none at all, I go further back, searching for clues about my parents. Nothing.

I find some ancient tomes about old magical families,

searching for anything about Blackwaters, then resorting to reading every page when that name isn't listed.

I read up more about this power that I possess that interested Stone so much. I learn the power to track fingerprints and other magicals was once common but over hundreds and hundreds of years was gradually lost so that now only a handful of scholars are true experts. I also begin to understand why a girl with my power would be so attractive to gangs like the Wolves of Night.

When I ask the librarian for instructional books about this power, I learn all the books the school owns on this have been taken out on long-term loan by Stone.

I decide I'm not going to go begging for his help again and resort to pulling out books on mind reading instead. I learn Stone's skill is about as unique as my own and more difficult to defend against than others have let on. Still, I read up about how to shield my thoughts and practice with Winnie in the mornings as we're getting dressed.

"Being able to read someone's thoughts is a pretty powerful skill according to what I've read," I say to my friend as she picks out of my mind what I want for breakfast.

She shakes her head. "Everyone can do it just a little bit if they try," I imagine my friend's being modest, "but it takes real power and skill to do it properly. Stone's the only magical I know who can."

"Am I meant to be impressed?" I ask, rolling my eyes.

"And here I was thinking he did impress you."

I whack her on the arm. "Some things about him impress me–"

"Like his biceps and his pecs and his–"

"Winnie! No, most things about him piss me off." I frown. "Actually nearly everything."

Especially the fact he may be the solution to solving the

riddle about my identity. If I let him into my head ... If I let him open that box of memories ...

It's so darn tempting. But so far, it's a temptation I've resisted. I don't trust him not to use what we find inside my head against me.

In fact, I'm almost certain he will.

No, I'm just going to have to continue my scouring of the library in search of my answers.

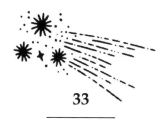

33

Spencer

SOMETIMES I COULD THROTTLE Tristan Kennedy.

Most days I could throttle him.

He's been my best friend for as long as I can remember, our mothers are connected through their high society circles and close acquaintances. Our friendship was encouraged. Our rivalry too. We've been competing for as long as I can remember. Still there isn't anyone else I trust to have my back if I needed them to.

Which is why the fuck-up with the girl is ten times as bad.

It isn't enough that half my gym classes are disrupted by the brattish little thing, now she's there at every dueling match and practice too.

And in my head. The moment she blasted me across the pitch playing out over and over again on repeat.

I watch her mopping the locker room floor after another

practice that dragged on thirty minutes longer than it should have because Dan couldn't get a play down. That knuckle-head has had his head turned by pussy and he's not focusing. I'm going to have to speak to him. Make him see that fucking his new girlfriend isn't a priority.

"Shouldn't she be doing that after we've cleared out," I grumble to Tristan under my breath.

Tristan drags his eyes from her. "If she's not doing the job properly, then talk to her about it," he says with a frown.

"I miss Cassie and the little cupcakes she used to bake us."

"Well if you hadn't shouted at the girl, she'd still be here."

"My shirt was wet. On the day of the match," I growl.

Tristan holds up his hands. "Hey, I'm just saying."

"And I'm just saying, we need someone else."

Tristan combs his fingers through his golden hair, his eyes flicking back to her. "I like having her where I can see her," he says in a low voice and I turn my head to look at him.

"What does that mean?"

"There's something about her ..."

I scoff. "You can't be serious, man. The girl has no ass and–"

"That's not what I mean," he says in irritation, although his jaw tightens in the way it does when I've hit a raw nerve. "Her powers ..."

I grab the collar of his shirt and pull him behind the open door of my locker.

There are only a few of our team members still lingering around, but I don't want them hearing this. I don't want her hearing it either.

"What does that mean?" I hiss and Tristan looks up into my face in that lazy way he does. It's an act. I see how alert his eyes are. I've known him long enough to see the tells behind the mask.

"It's a feeling I have ... power."

I hesitate, weighing up whether to tell him or not.

But we've always had each other's backs. One day we could be on the front line together. He needs to know.

"She attacked me," I whisper. "The other day out on the pitch. Blasted me right across the fucking field."

I wait for him to laugh at me, to at least grin. Instead his eyes are more alert than ever.

"A lucky shot?"

"Maybe, a little. She caught me off guard for sure. I had no time to defend myself. But ..."

"But ..."

"Her power ..."

I lift my shirt, showing him the dark mark sitting in the center of my gut, the size of a fist.

Tristan looks up at me, then back to the injury.

"You haven't healed it?"

"I've tried. It was twice this size a day ago."

"Did you show it to the nurse?"

I blink. "If I did, then there'd be questions and ..."

"I thought you wanted her gone."

"Out of the fucking locker room, yes, but ..." I trail off. Who am I kidding? I have no idea why I made that decision. Why I decided not to tell on her. Why I let her stay.

No idea, except that maybe she intrigues me as much as she does Tristan.

"I think it's time we had a serious word with her," Tristan says, the curiosity in his eyes and that laid back attitude dissipating, and the calculating man I know him to be showing himself.

I drop the hem of my shirt.

"Yeah, I think we should."

We wait until there's no one else left in the locker room but us and her.

She's busy packing away her cleaning supplies, but looks up, frowning when she senses the two of us approaching.

"What?" she asks with suspicion.

"You know every other helping-hand we've had has been a hell of a lot more cheerful and welcoming than you."

She shrugs. "I never asked for this job. I'm quite happy to hand over the washing of your kits to you."

Tristan shakes his head and sits down on one of the benches.

"Where do you come from, Pig Girl?" I ask her.

She flinches, it's barely perceptible, but she does. I dart my gaze to Tristan and he frowns.

She flicks off her rubber gloves in irritation and glares at Tristan. "If I recall, we already went over this."

"Yes," he says with that lazy smile the girls go wild for. "But if I recall, you told me fuck all."

"It's none of your business. You're not my friends."

"No, we're not," Tristan says darkly. He's always enjoyed playing with his food. I guess I have too. But tonight I want answers.

"Cut the bullshit and answer the question."

She stuffs the gloves into the bucket with the rest of the cleaning materials.

"She was an unregistered from the wastelands," Tristan says quietly.

This time she doesn't flinch, she doesn't show any reaction at all, like Tristan didn't just launch a freaking bomb.

"Unregistered?"

My gaze flicks between the two of them, trying to determine if this is some joke. But I don't see any humor in either of their faces, all I see is a mirrored tension. The air is thick with it.

Tristan says he can feel her power and I don't think he's kidding. I feel it too. Sparking and fizzing in the air.

"That doesn't make sense," I say.

"Have you seen her in any lessons, Spencer?" Tristan says.

"The girl knows nothing. She's not been educated or trained. She barely knows how to tie her own shoelaces."

"I was trained just fine," she snarls.

"By who?" Tristan snaps.

She looks away from him. "None of your business."

"You're making it our business."

Her head snaps back our way, her jaw falling open in astonishment. "Are you serious? I want nothing to do with you meatheads–"

"Careful," Tristan warns with another amused smile.

"You're the ones poking around in my life, unable to seem to leave me alone."

I glance at my friend. Is that true? This is the first time we've discussed the Pig Girl. She's a nobody. A nuisance. Why would we bother?

Except he's been keeping this scandalous piece of information quiet. Unregistered. If the other pupils in the school knew that, she'd be even more of an outcast than she already is. Usually, he'd be trading information like that all over the school. Usually, I'd be the first person he'd tell. Why the hell has he kept it quiet?

"You aren't telling us something," Tristan says. "You materialize out of nowhere. With a fucking pig and an attitude. You know nothing and yet ..."

"And yet, what?"

Tristan points towards me. "Show her, Spencer."

I scowl at him, but do as he says, lifting my shirt, this time for her to see.

She stares at the dark bruise on my stomach, her eyes widening in astonishment. "I didn't do that," she mumbles.

"What? You think I did it to myself just to fuck with you?"

She lifts angry eyes to mine. "Do you want me to show you all the bruises I have littering my body from all the times you've slammed me on the mat?"

"You want to get undressed, Pig Girl, you go right ahead."

"It won't heal," Tristan says, having no patience for my games. "He's tried and it won't heal."

"Then maybe," she says, "he's not as good at magic as he thinks he is."

I throw my head back and laugh, Tristan's chuckles joining mine.

"Oh the thought that you might not be as good at something as your big head would have you believe is amusing, huh?"

"No, your ignorance is."

She doesn't like that answer. Probably because it hits the mark. We're always going to know more than this weedy little girl. That's what a proper education at prestigious schools with the best teachers in the land will give you.

Her mouth clamps shut but I can see in her eyes how desperate she is to know, to understand.

I'm prepared to leave her wallowing in her own pool of ignorance but Tristan has other ideas.

"Only deeply scarlet magic can do that to someone so much bigger than you."

Her jaw twitches but she refuses to ask us the next questions clearly spinning in her mind: what's scarlet magic?

"Look it up," I snap before Tristan can indulge her again.

"Where did you learn that," Tristan says, "because it's not something they teach just anyone here at the academy?"

"Maybe I'm one of the lucky ones, maybe they did teach me."

"Like I said, you can't even tie your own shoelaces, they're not about to teach you highly complex and potentially lethal magic like this."

She shrugs, although I can tell how interesting this information is to her.

"Who taught you it?" I growl in irritation.

"No one," she says.

I stalk towards her. "You know what happens to you if I tell them what you did."

"Yes," she says. "I get expelled, another thing we went over already, Spencer."

Tristan shakes his head. "If Spencer, here, shows them that bruise, Pig Girl, they're going to do more than expel you."

Her eyes travel over his face, then mine, determining whether we're bluffing.

"So," I say, towering above her, "if you don't want me to go show Principal York, I suggest you start talking."

"Who taught you that magic?" Tristan adds.

"I told you already, no one."

"You think I'm messing about here, Pig Girl—"

"I just told you what you want to know. No one taught me anything. I ... I didn't know what I was doing ... it wasn't deliberate ... it just ..."

"It just what?" Tristan says, and the tone of his voice, eager, yet strained, excited, yet cautious, has the hairs on the back of my neck prickling.

"It just happened."

"Do you buy it?" I ask Tristan as we walk along the darkened pathway on our way back to our rooms.

"No," he says, "no, I don't. You don't just conjure magic like that from thin air. You don't just 'feel' it. It's bullshit. She's hiding something."

I chew on that for a moment, adjusting the gym bag on my shoulder. "I don't know, man. I think she was telling the truth."

"Spencer, it isn't possible."

"What do you know about her?"

"What do you mean?"

"She's in Venus, man. I know you look into every student who joins your house."

"Her files are empty."

"Empty?" I say skeptically, wondering why the hell he'd be keeping things from me.

He shakes his head. "The crap that's in there is all the stuff we already know."

"And that didn't arouse your interest?" I know my best friend. I know that it would.

"I asked someone who works for my father to look into her." I nod, it's nothing short of what I'd expect him to do.

"And?"

Tristan stops on the path outside the apartment block which houses our rooms. He rests his hand on the door knob. "Jack shit."

"This man, is he any–"

"Good? One of the best in the business."

"I don't understand it." I rub at my belly.

"You want me to have a go at it?" he asks, with a smile teasing his lips. He fucking loves that he's just that bit, that stupid smidgen of a bit, better than me.

"No point."

"It could fester."

I swear under my breath. "Fine."

"Let's go up to my room."

There are about a dozen notes pinned to his door, most of them in handwriting I recognize. The same notes get pinned to my door daily, invitations to join girls in their room.

He ignores them all, unlocking his door with a wave of his hand and stepping inside.

A low lamp flicks on and I gaze around the room. It's rare he lets anyone up here, even me, and the place always fascinates me.

It's not like any other room on campus. No posters pinned

to the room, no trophies resting on the shelves, not even any books scattered across the desk. It's empty. Bare. Like he doesn't want this room to reveal anything about him.

"Take your shirt off and lie on the bed," he tells me, walking to a floor lamp, switching it on and dragging it over to shine down at me.

The circle of light illuminates my skin, making the bruise all the darker. Like a fucking black hole right in the center of my gut.

He leans in closer, his blonde hair flopping over his face, and examines the bruise.

"Can you just get on with it?" I say, I've never enjoyed being the patient. Other people's hands on my skin irritates the hell out of me. It has the monster inside me itching to break free, to shed this weak pathetic form and adorn something harder, stronger, more magnificent.

Even when I'm with a girl, I won't let her touch me. They can keep their hands firmly to themselves.

I bristle now, the monster inside stirring, my eyes locked on Tristan's hand. He'd better not touch me.

I growl and his eyes move lazily up to meet mine.

"It doesn't look like a bruise to me," he says.

"No, I know that asshole. It's scarlet magic, we know that."

Tristan shakes his head. "No, look closer." He reaches out his hand and I flinch away.

"Don't," I warn him.

"It's like … it's like she's torn back a layer of your skin …"

I shake my head. That's the other thing that reveals itself when he drops the bored act. He has a fucking poetic way with words. It left me captivated as a kid, now it pisses me off.

"What do you mean?"

I gaze down at the wound. And I see. I see what he means.

It's like she's torn back my skin to reveal the darkness lurking within.

34

R^{hi}

IT'S OFFICIALLY the end of our month of punishment and our first evening of freedom. The sun is warm and low in the sky so after dinner Winnie and I lay out on our patch of grass, Pip snuffling around our feet, and let the rays fall across our faces.

"If I never see another saucepan in my life, it will be too soon," Winnie grumbles.

"And I never understood the appeal of sports but now I can tell you I officially hate them all. And what is it about boys? Do you know how bad they smell? And the state they leave the toilets in?" I gag.

"So you're off boys then?"

"I was never 'on' boys."

"Your crush?"

"Just a stupid phase. I'm over it."

"Hmm," Winnie says, picking the petals off a daisy. "So you won't be asking anyone to Founders' Night."

I rest up on my elbow. "What is Founders' Night? Is it a school dance, because I've seen how those things play out in movies? Either you end up heartbroken by a douchebag or you're one of the ones who's slaughtered in the zombie massacre."

"There have been no zombie sightings in centuries." I gape at my friend. "Not since they banned the use of resurrection spells in the 18th century."

"You're kidding me? We can use our magic to resurrect the dead?"

"Yes, if you want to spark a plague of zombies and/or land yourself in the Northern Labor camps for the rest of your life."

"I assume you'd be safe from zombies up in the North, though," I muse.

"Anyway, Founders' Night is nothing like that. It's actually a lot of fun."

"Fun like you said *Pretty Woman* would be fun."

"I love that movie, it's one of my favorites."

"The love interest is an asshole."

"I thought that was your thing."

"I haven't decided what my thing is yet ... and is it me? Or do a lot of men appear to be assholes? Even the ones who seem nice," I say, thinking of Andrew.

Winnie sighs. "Not all of them are assholes," she says wistfully and I know she's thinking of Trent.

"So what's fun about this Founders' Night?"

"It's in celebration of the founding of the school by Sterling Hart and Morgan Arrow. Each House hosts a party – each trying to outdo the other. It's pretty wild. Do you know what Venus has picked for a theme this year?"

"Nope, I didn't even know it was happening."

Winnie gives me a sympathetic look. "Fiona is holding a

meeting tomorrow morning to hand out jobs to everyone in preparation. I'm hoping I end up on the decoration committee again."

"We only just finished our chores and now we're going to have more?"

"But these ones are fun."

"Your idea of fun is different to mine, Winnie."

She throws a handful of petals at my face. "Says the girl who is addicted to *Puzzle Masters* and until a few months ago considered watering her vegetables the highlight of her day."

"Okay, you got me there." I giggle.

I roll onto my side, tucking my hands under my cheek. "So, are you going to ask Trent to Founders' Night?"

Winnie's face blushes a deep beetroot red. "Me?"

"Yes, you."

"Oh ... I ... don't ..."

"You like him?"

"Perhaps ... maybe ... okay, yes, majorly."

"Then ask him out."

She takes a panicky inhale. "Just the thought of it makes me want to puke."

"What's the worst that could happen?"

"What's the worst? He laughs in my face, then picks a girl a million times prettier than me to take and completely shatters my heart." She rests her palms over her chest dramatically.

"You said this dance includes no broken hearts."

"Every dance includes some broken hearts. It's the way of things."

"Count me out."

"We can go together."

"And cement firmly in everyone's minds that we're dating."

"I don't care about that."

"No, me neither I suppose."

I twist my head up and look at the sky, turning slowly purple as the sun dies away.

"Winnie, what do you know about scarlet magic?"

"Probably about as much as you do by now – you're spending an awful lot of your time in the library."

"Yes, but I haven't come across this type of magic before."

"I guess that's because it's pretty rare."

"That's what I heard."

"It's a type of ancient magic – it was used a lot in ancient times, but the knowledge died away."

"Died away?" I think about what Professor Stone told me about the tracking of magical fingerprints. Is this same or something different?

"Yeah, some magicals can still conjure it, but it takes a lot of training and study and it's pretty dangerous. Its use, a bit like the resurrection of dead people, is highly regulated so most people don't use it. Although, there are always rumors going around that one or two students are chosen each year to be trained in its use. Personally, I think that's bullcrap though." She brings a daisy head to her nose and sniffs. "Why'd you want to know?"

"Oh, I just heard someone talking about it and I didn't know what it was."

"You should ask Professor Stone," Winnie waggles her eyebrows, "and while you're at it, you could ask him to Founders' Night."

"Like that would be allowed."

"True ... I read in the school rules that relations between students and teachers are strictly forbidden."

"You read all the rules?"

"Yes, didn't you?"

I shake my head.

Winnie rolls her eyes at me. "So that's why you keep breaking them all."

I stick my tongue out at my friend.

"Do you think you'll volunteer for decorations too?" Winnie asks. "We could help each other out if you do."

I laugh. "I doubt very much that Tristan and his band of limpets will want me anywhere near their party."

THE NEXT MORNING there's a note pinned to my door and I learn I'm wrong about that. I'm commanded to attend a planning meeting in the Venus common room and the tone makes it clear attendance is mandatory.

"Remember, if they give you a choice, go for decorations," Winnie says as we part ways on the path – she heading for Neptune common room and me Venus.

As I enter the gardens, I can hear the murmur of voices, voices that grow louder and louder as I approach the common room. When I reach the door, I can tell it's heaving. My assumption confirmed when I find every available chair, cushion and piece of floor taken. I squeeze in at the back, closing the door behind me and meeting the eye of Tristan Kennedy, standing on top of an upturned crate, Aysha hovering on one next to him.

"Now, Pig Girl has finally deigned to join us, we can start," he announces, several heads swiveling around to gape at me. Aysha glares my way, before sweeping the frown off her face and replacing it with an excitable smile, all her pearly white teeth on display.

"Thank you, Tris," she says, resting her hand on his upper arm. "The organizing committee has been in discussion with our head of house and he has approved our theme for this year's Founders' Night." She looks out at the crowd with excitement. "It's going to be ..." she pauses for effect, drawing in breath, "Angels and Demons!" she squeals, clapping her hands together. Several of the girls around her squeal too and applause ripples through the common room. Several of the people standing with me at the back of the room groan under their breaths.

"We're going to decorate the common room as Hell with our Head of House as the Devil himself, of course." Tristan does a little bow, winking at us all and I swear several of the girls seated around his feet swoon. "And we've also been given permission to decorate the gardens as our very own slice of Heaven."

"It's going to kick ass," Tristan interrupts. "We're going to blow the other Houses out of the water and host the best goddamn party in the history of the academy!"

I roll my eyes at the hyperbole but it seems most of the common room love it, even those who were groaning earlier. There's lots of cheering and fist pumping.

"So it's all hands on deck," Aysha continues, "we're all going to need to work hard if we want to pull this off–"

"And beat those pussies!"

Aysha giggles. "So you'll find notices pinned up around the common room assigning everyone responsibilities and tasks for the party."

"We don't get to choose?" someone asks from the middle of the room.

"No," Aysha says cheerily, "it's all been assigned by Tristan and the organizing committee."

Those around me start groaning again and this time I'm inclined to join in. If Tristan and Aysha have assigned the roles, I'm bound to be head of 'cleaning toilets' or 'garbage disposal' or something equally glamorous.

I wait patiently at the back of the room for the crowd to circle around the room, stopping at each of the notices. There are lots more excited squeals from the bouncing bunnies. It seems Aysha has given all her friends the best jobs.

"Hey," Tristan says, as the first students begin to leave. "It goes without saying that the theme of our party is top secret. Anyone caught disclosing the theme to members of other houses will be severely punished." His eyes assess me as he says this, which for once seems fair enough. I was all for telling Winnie everything.

When there's finally space enough in the common room for me to wander around, I scan each notice looking for my task. I'm not on cleaning and garbage after all, neither am I entertainment or food and drinks. I hover in front of the final notice, listing all students required to help with decorations. My name is top of the list.

I blink. This can't be right. Tristan and Aysha wouldn't pick me for something like this, not when they can use this party as another way to humiliate me.

"Is there a problem, Pig Girl?"

I turn my head and find Tristan right behind me.

"No?" I say, a little unsure.

"Good. Because I want this party to be awesome." Something glints in his eyes and, if I didn't know it already, I'd see just how much Tristan Kennedy enjoys winning.

It only takes me three days to wish I'd been assigned to garbage duties after all.

Hanging out with Aysha and her cronies while they obsess over crepe paper and streamers is a form of torture, especially with Tristan Kennedy lurking in the background finding the whole thing amusing. I see him smirking to himself from his position sprawled out on the bed, like a king observing his servants as they fuss about. Not that he shows his amusement to Aysha and the others. Whenever they ask for his opinion on something, he adopts a deadly serious expression, pausing to consider his answer like he actually cares. Is it only me who sees the mischief dancing in his eyes?

As well as actual physical decorations, Aysha wants us to create special magical effects to add some 'pizazz to the affair'.

I wonder how my life went from shoveling dirt in the middle of nowhere to sitting in a stuffy common room debating whether lanterns or magical orbs would be a better look.

I tune out of the conversation as Aysha and her friends discuss the magical effects they're going to create for the common room to make it look like the real dungeons of hell, and only tune back in again when I realize Aysha's addressing me.

"Pig Girl!" she says, snapping her fingers in my face. "Are you listening?"

"Huh?" I answer, blinking.

Aysha tosses her hair in annoyance. "I'm leaving the heavenly magical effects in your hands." She leans in to whisper in her friend's ear. "Hell is going to be where it's at, nobody's going to care about outside."

Inwardly I roll my eyes. "Fine," I say.

Aysha's eyes snap back to mine. "You need to run all your plans past me first."

"Right."

"I'm serious, I don't want you messing this up. Tristan's counting on us."

Which makes me severely tempted to make heaven as shitty as possible.

Only, once I'm on the path back to my dorm, all these ideas start whizzing about my head; ideas about how to bring the garden to life as a heavenly paradise. I actually feel excited about the prospect.

I've been working so hard these last few weeks, what with chores and all my time in the library and practicing, maybe a chance to be creative would actually be fun.

Checking nobody else is on the path, I flicker my finger through the air and conjure up cotton candy white clouds that hang right in front of my nose. Next I sweep my hand and paint a rainbow through the air.

I've never used my magic like this before. I've always used it to defend myself or while practicing and studying more serious concepts in class.

I laugh, clapping my hands together and watching as both the rainbow and cloud melt away.

Perhaps I could create little cupids to fly around the garden shooting arrows into the sky. Perhaps I could hang little silver stars in the branches of the trees.

Perhaps this could be fun.

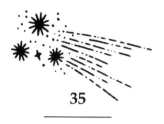

35

Spencer

I SPRINT ALONG THE PATH, earbuds in, beat of the music pounding in my ears.

I feel good. Coach just put me through my paces, a one-on-one that pounded every part of my body and pushed me right to my very limits. It's quietened all that restlessness simmering in my blood.

I want this feeling to last. That's why I'm not done yet. Despite the shaking in my legs and the exhaustion in my muscles, I'm out here running. Pushing harder and further. Maybe this is all I've needed.

It's the most peaceful I've felt in weeks, the most peaceful since the pills stopped working and the girl started at the academy. Nothing gnawing at me, scratching at me, scraping at my insides. Just peace.

It lasts until I round the path, gravel crunching under my weight, and I feel it, that all-so-familiar tug in my gut.

Immediately all that peace vanishes like smoke on the wind. Every fiber in my body is taut. My insides alert with awareness and interest.

Shit

Pig Girl.

Does she have to ruin every fucking thing?

I force my feet to halt, even though my instincts want me running right towards her.

That's bad.

I should turn around and run back the way I came. Try to reestablish that sense of calm.

The music continues to thump in my ears and for a minute I'm not sure if it really is the notes of the bass or my own heart. I yank out my earbuds and stay right where I am. I don't move. Because I can hear. I can hear her laughing.

The sound is genuine and free and makes my insides buzz.

What the actual fuck?

I frown, lifting my shirt to gaze at the bruise on my abdomen. Tristan's handiwork has helped. It's not as large or as vivid as it was. But it's still there. Reminding me. Of her. Of this fucked-up situation. Of what I really am.

I drop the hem of my shirt and look up.

She's right there on the path in front of me now. I hadn't heard her draw closer and she hasn't seen me yet. She's too engrossed in what she's doing, waving her hands in front of her face and creating fluffy white clouds and bright curved rainbows. The kind of things little kids do when they first start magic school.

It's making her smile in a way I've not seen her smile before. All curved cheeks and bright eyes. Excitement and pleasure flickering in her expression.

I stare at her. Transfixed, like she's something special.

I want to knock that smile right off her face. I want to throw her into the air and slam her down hard on the ground.

I want my hands wrapped tight around her throat.

Before I know what I'm doing, I pick up my feet, running again, running at her. I'm right in front of her before she realizes, lifting her face to me in alarm.

"Don't you–" she starts, the clouds streaking away.

I grab a hold of her throat with my right hand, my fingers right where they want to be, the thing inside me purring with pleasure.

I stare down into her face. Her expression is all outrage and suspicion.

I wait for her to grapple at my hand. She remains perfectly still, her pulse jumping against my palm.

"What are you doing?" she growls.

"This," I tell her and then I'm leaning down to kiss the girl.

Kiss her! I don't even like fucking kissing. Too close, too intimate. But in this moment, it's all I want to do. I'm all instinct, all want.

I want to taste that smile. Consume everything she was feeling. I want to make it mine.

Mine.

She tastes of mint gum and black coffee.

Her mouth is warm. Her lips soft.

She smells of fucking fluffy clouds and rainbows.

She pushes against my chest and her touch does not repulse me. It never has.

I pull away, keeping my hand wrapped around her throat.

"What the fuck?" she says, looking so utterly confused it's cute. "What are you doing?"

"Kissing you. Are you so fucking ignorant you don't know what that is?"

"And are you so ignorant you never heard of consent?" She scowls at me. "Ever thought to ask first?"

I frown. I don't usually have to ask. I take. I'm given.

But though I note the pissy tone in her voice, I also note she's not pushing me away.

And though this is seriously fucked up, I want to kiss her some more.

"Can I kiss you?" I mumble.

"Why? Why do you want to?"

"Is that a yes or a no?" Her body so close to mine is making me dizzy, I can't think right. I want to slam her to the ground and do more than kiss her. I want to destroy her.

My fingers dig into her neck and maybe the pissy little pig girl – with her superior attitude, pretending she's different, pretending she's better than the rest of us – is just the same, because her pupils blow wide and her breath turns that tiny bit panty. I can hear it.

She wants me to kiss her all right.

"Yes or no?" I say more firmly.

"No!" she says, even as her body melts towards mine.

"No," I spit out in disbelief.

There's more to her now. Less bone, more curve. More soft flesh. More tit.

"You're an asshole," she says.

"And you're an unregistered brat."

"So I should be grateful that yesterday you were throwing me around the mats and refusing to teach me, and today, all of a sudden, you want to kiss me?"

"Most girls like me throwing them around."

She swallows in a way that tells me she doesn't hate it as much as she claims.

"I want this out of my system," I growl.

"What out of your system?"

My gaze travels over her face down her throat to her cleavage. A gaze that's fiercely hot.

Is this all this is? Lust? Do I want it simply because it hasn't been offered up to me on a plate?

If I had her, would this all stop?

She still hasn't pushed me away, hasn't zapped me with that magic of hers.

"You're seriously fucked up," she says. Yeah, she doesn't know the half of it. Doesn't know just how fucked up I am.

I jerk my hand away.

"You really are as frigid as they say you are."

"Just because I don't want to kiss you."

I manage a smile. "Because you do want me to kiss you, but you won't admit it to yourself." I take a step away. "Well don't worry, your precious virginal reputation is not in danger. Not from me anyway."

I shove my earbuds back in my ears so I don't have to hear whatever snarky retort is coming my way. Then I turn and start running.

All that peace has gone. My insides scream as loudly as they've ever done and it's only a matter of time. Only a matter of time.

36

R^{hi}

I watch the academy's dueling hero's retreating back. Is this what men are like? Confusing? Fickle? Fucked up?

One minute ignoring you, the next hating on you, and then finally trying to kiss you.

I touch my lips.

No wonder my aunt wanted to keep away from them. They are all insane. Even the man in black. Taking me to heaven, making me feel things, then disappearing into thin air. I haven't heard a peep out of him since.

Is it all just a game to them? It must be with Spencer because he hates me, really hates me. The dude can barely look at me without hatred spitting out of his eyes. And yet that kiss didn't feel like he hated me.

Shit, it felt intoxicating. It certainly felt way too good, something I should dismiss from my mind, not be reliving. Not be reliving in a way that has my body stirring.

I walk through the entrance of the dorm building and arrive at our room.

Immediately an unease rattles through my bones, any other sensations darting away.

The door hangs open, the room beyond dark.

"Winnie," I say, lifting my hand in defense.

There's no reply.

I step forward, nudging the door open with my foot.

"Who's there?"

Nothing.

I snap my fingers, flicking on the light.

I scream.

Something is pinned to the side of my bed.

Something organic and dripping onto the floor.

The stench is rancid and I cover my face with my sleeve trying not to gag.

I step closer.

What the hell is it?

I lean forward.

It's pink and fleshy with coarse hairs. Dark red blood. The white blur of bone.

It takes a while for my brain to process, to unjumble the mess, to see the object for what it is.

A pig's trotter.

I scream again, Jumping away.

"Pip!" I scream, "Pip!"

They wouldn't. They couldn't.

Would they?

Could they?

"Pip!" I sob.

Biting hard on my sleeve, screwing up my eyes as pain splinters through my heart. "Pip!"

Grunt.

I jump a mile up into the air.

Grunt, grunt.

I swing my head around desperately.

"Pip?"

My pig comes wiggling out from under Winnie's bed, grunting all the time.

The space is small and, with his newly rounded tummy, he only just fits.

I drop down on my knees and tug him. He emerges with a pop, and I tumble backwards onto my behind, Pip coming with me, snuffling and grunting and licking my face.

"Are you okay?" I say desperately, checking each of his legs and sighing with relief when I find all four untouched.

I hug him to me.

"Did you hide? Did you hide under the bed?" My pig snorts in reply. "Good boy. Clever boy."

I squeeze him tight, trying not to peer up at the severed limb.

"Who was it? Did you see them?" He grunts again, meeting my eyes with his own beady black ones. "It doesn't matter. I'll find out. I'll find out who it was."

And as I say the words, I realize Spencer was a part of this. That's why he stopped me on the path. That's why he kissed me. It wasn't anything else. He was simply delaying me, preventing me from returning to my room too soon.

37

R^{hi}

SETTLING PIP IN HIS BED, I pace with caution towards the disfigured limb. Pip squeals and ducks his head beneath his blanket. I consider doing the same. But I need to know who did this and maybe there's a way I can find out.

I step closer, approaching the thing with caution and trying not to vomit. I hold my hand out, hovering it above the trotter and closing my eyes. My mind sits empty and I reach for a memory, a clue with my magic.

It had been easy, almost instantaneous, with those objects in Stone's classroom. The magical fingerprints had appeared in my head without me even trying.

But this time there is nothing.

Perhaps it's because the magic used this time wasn't powerful enough to leave a trace.

My eyes open.

Or perhaps it's because I'm not touching the object.

I gulp.

I don't want to touch it.

I really, really don't want to touch it.

I've handled dead animals before. Rats in traps. Chickens after the chop. This is different. My belly churns with nausea.

But I want to know who's toying with me so I swallow and, before I can chicken out, reach out and touch the limb.

It's cold and both stiff and squidgy. I force myself not to think of that and instead reach for any fingerprints.

Yet again my mind is blank and I huff with irritation, straining with my magic to find something, anything. Slowly, an image appears in front of my eyes. But unlike before, it's not clear, it's not vivid. It's blurry, hazy, barely visible.

I press harder, trying to force the picture into focus. It doesn't work. The picture simply splinters, falling away, and I curse.

It was a hand. A man's I think. Although I couldn't be sure. Heavy rings on every finger. Inks across the skin.

Not a hand I recognize. Not one I know at all.

※

BY THE TIME Winnie returns from decoration making, I've removed the pig's trotter from the bed and disposed of it in the outside trash cans. But I'm still scrubbing the worn carpet.

Winnie comes bouncing into the room and stops dead when she finds me on my knees, Pip shuffling nervously around me.

"What's going on?" she asks as Pip squeaks at her.

I fall back on my haunches, dropping the soiled rag I'm holding to the floor and running my wrist around my damp brow.

"Removing a blood stain."

Winnie drops to the nearest chair. "Wh-wh-what? Blood? Are you okay? Is Pip okay?"

I swivel around to peer at my friend. "We're both fine. But some sick bastard pinned a bloody pig's trotter to my bed."

Winnie loses all color in her face and blinks at me rapidly.

"I'm guessing it was some kind of prank." I start scrubbing again.

"Or ... or a threat," Winnie offers in a wobbly voice.

"A threat?" I say with a scoff. "There wasn't a message, Winnie. No words painted over the wall in blood."

Pip squeaks and covers his head with his trotters.

"Are you sure he's okay?"

I stroke my hand over Pip's head, scratching at his ears.

"He was here, hiding," I whisper, meeting the beady eyes of my pet. I know what it's like to hide. How frightening it is. How lonely. "I think whoever it was gave him a scare."

"You need to tell York."

"No, I'm not letting them win, Winnie. I don't want them to think they can rattle me this way."

"But it's sick," Winnie says, "really sick. And next time they might hurt Pip for real."

I gather Pip up into my arms and hold him close. "I know they might. But I won't let them do that. From now on he goes wherever I go."

Winnie looks at me skeptically. "They aren't going to let you take Pip to class."

"I don't care. I won't go."

"And York will expel you."

I shrug.

Winnie drops off her chair and comes to sit next to me and Pip on the floor, eyeing the blood stain with revulsion. "Rhi I love you and," she tickles Pip's ears, "I'm even beginning to like

Pip here too. I don't want you to leave. You're my only real friend."

I sigh, feeling guilty for never having considered Winnie's feelings in all this. I rest my head against her shoulder. "I'm sorry. I didn't mean it." And it's the truth. Winnie's friendship means more than I could ever express. The price on my head, the ability to learn more magic, are not the only things keeping me tethered to this school. Her friendship is too. Without her, this experience would have been a million times worse.

"But I'm serious about Pip, Winnie." I chew on my lip. "I had this feeling that someone was in our room the other night. And it's happened before."

Winnie lifts her hands to her mouth. "In our room? At night? Rhi, you need to tell York."

I shake my head a second time and Winnie hugs me close.

"Then if not York, how about Stone?"

"Stone?" I almost laugh. "Why would he care?"

"He was looking into who took Pip last time."

"And he found nothing. It was all bullshit. He doesn't care."

"I still think you should tell him."

"No, Winnie. I don't want him involved." He's already in my head more often than I'd like him to be. I don't want him knowing everything. "Besides, it could be him who did this."

"Stone?" Winnie says, drawing away from me and peering down into my face to see if I'm being serious. "He's a teacher."

"A teacher who hates me."

"Stone doesn't hate you."

I laugh, thinking of the way he chained me to the bike when they brought me to the city, the way he'd thrown that ham sandwich at me in the motel, the way he'd dumped a load of manure over my head in the gardens. "Oh, he hates me all right."

"Hmmm," Winnie says, "I don't think he does. The way he looks at you sometimes ..."

I laugh again. "Oh God, you are way too invested in my crush, Winnie."

She smiles, although it doesn't quite reach her eyes. "Maybe ... Anyway, I don't like the idea of people entering our room and leaving these ... surprises. They shouldn't be able to unlock our door. They must be using some kind of magic to do it."

"Yep."

Winnie twists a braid around her finger, thinking. "I know another spell *we* could use. I use it to keep my little sister out of my room. I've never used it here because I didn't think I needed to," she sweeps her hand around our shabby room, "it's not like I have anything to steal."

"Do you think it would work?"

Winnie grins. "My sister has invested a lot of time trying to break that spell, even roped my Grandma into helping her, and they've never gotten in."

"And it would keep Pip safe?"

"Yes," Winnie says, "I think it would."

I grin at my friend and then wrap her in a tight hug. "Thank you," I say, "for everything."

"That's what friends are for, Rhi. Now, tell me, what's Venus' theme for Founders' Night?"

I WAIT FOR THE TAUNTS. I wait for the posts on social media. I wait for whoever pinned that pig's trotter to my bed to capitalize on their sick trick. But like the ham, there's only silence. Maybe they're all laughing at me behind my back. But I doubt it. This feels personal.

Tristan. Spencer. Summer. Even Stone. They all hate me. They've all tried their best to make my life miserable.

I eye them from the back of the classroom. I watch them.

But for once they pay me no attention. For once there isn't a single dirty look, nor one taunting word.

I don't understand. I thought they'd bask in the pleasure of watching me squirm. Of making me uncomfortable. And yet they don't seem to care.

At the end of lessons, Winnie jabs me in the ribs.

"Are you done staring?"

I spin my pencil around my fingers. "I'm trying to work out which one it was."

Winnie drops her books into her bags. "Maybe they feel guilty, ashamed. Maybe they don't want anyone to know."

I lift an eyebrow. That doesn't sound like Tristan, Spencer or Summer. I doubt any of them have ever felt a miniscule of remorse in their entire lives.

I'm still stewing about it as I shovel food into my mouth as quickly as I can at dinner time. Despite Winnie's spell, I'm nervous about leaving Pip on his own for too long and I want to get back to him. In fact, I'm so busy side-eyeing the bouncing bunnies' table in the Great Hall, I totally miss Trent approaching our end of the table and only realize he's hovering next to Winnie when he says, "hi".

Winnie instantly morphs into the color of the tomatoes on her salad but despite her glowing color, she manages to squeak out a "Hi" of her own.

"Is this seat free?"

Winnie gapes at him and I force down my mouthful and nod. "Yes, it's free."

He drops his tray to the table and climbs onto the bench beside Winnie.

"How's the phone?" he asks me, his hair falling over his face as he leans over to poke at his noodles.

"Working really well. Thank you again," I say as Winnie stares into her salad.

I kick her under the table and she yelps.

Trent glances towards her and then continues: "If you have any trouble with it, then just bring it round to my room. I can fix most things."

"Thank you," I say again, venturing a glare at Winnie. She stares at me bewildered and I mouth 'talk to him' at her.

"Erm ... how are the noodles?" she says after several long minutes of silence.

Trent pokes at them with his fork. "Better than the porridge."

I snort. "That's not hard."

"Did you work out how they manage to make the food so bad?" he asks, turning his head to peer at Winnie through his curtain of hair.

"Huh?" she asks.

"Weren't you on kitchen duty?" he asks, the tops of his ears turning a similar color to Winnie's cheeks.

"Oh, yeah, but they only let us do the washing up. We never got to see what goes on with the cooking."

"I swear they try to make it disgusting," Trent says and Winnie giggles.

"I once had a slug on my lettuce," she says, holding up a leaf on the end of her fork.

Trent chuckles and quietly I pick up my tray and tiptoe away. They don't even notice me go.

I'm reading at my desk, Pip curled up on my lap, when Winnie returns almost an hour later, looking slightly shocked. She walks into the room and drops down on her bed, her mouth ajar, her eyes wide.

"That was a long dinner," I tease. "Did you go for seconds and thirds?"

"He asked me out," she mutters.

"Who, Trent?" I say, my lips curling into a smile.

"Yes, Trent asked me to Founders' Night."

I lower my book and cock my head to one side. "You don't look very happy about it. What did you answer?"

"Y-y-yes."

I giggle. "So why do you look like you saw a ghost?"

"It can't be real, can it? It must be a trick. Or maybe I'm dreaming." She pinches her arm.

"You're not dreaming. And it isn't a trick. The guy clearly likes you, Winnie."

"I don't know."

"Oh, come on, he's always finding a reason to come over to you in lessons and ask you a question."

"That's just because he needs my help."

"The dude built his own computer, Winnie. No offense, but he doesn't really need your help."

"Oh," Winnie says. She sits there quietly for a moment before a wild smile dawns across her face. "You really think he likes me?"

"Well, duh!"

She flops back onto the bed, then screams, kicking her legs and hugging her arms to her chest.

"Is that a happy scream?" I ask her.

"Oh my gosh, Trent asked me to Founders' Night."

"Of course he did," I say, rolling my eyes and returning to my book. "As if it was in any doubt."

I RARELY DREAM ANYMORE. When I was a kid, my head was full of them. I'd wake up in the night, screaming, my body shaking with terror.

It's funny. I remember the fear, how frightened I felt. But these days, I don't remember the content of those dreams that left me so petrified. I don't remember why they scared me so much.

The dreams stopped long ago and I haven't had one – good or bad – in all that time.

Tonight though, things change.

For the first time in years, I dream.

I dream of that hand. Still blurred, still shifting, still dim. Yet I know it's the hand. Those rings line the fingers. Those black inks scribbled across the skin.

The hand hangs in front of my face and then slowly the fingers flex, flex and then reach for me, following the line of my jaw, stroking over the curve of my cheek, tracing the line of my lips. The touch of the fingertips are warm yet cold, soft yet hard. Fear and longing collide in my stomach.

I lift my own hand to bat this hand away and the fingers flex again. Flex and dart for my throat. Curling around my neck, fingers cutting into my flesh.

The hand squeezes.

I scramble to pull it away, I toss and turn trying to dislodge it.

I gasp for air.

I wake up, panting.

My skin is covered in a fine layer of sweat. My heart races in my chest. My body is paralyzed with fear.

It wasn't real. It was only a dream.

Only a dream.

It doesn't mean a thing.

And yet when I glance at myself in the mirror the next day, I swear I see the faintest of bruises on my throat.

I step closer. It's a trick of the light.

Not real. Only a dream.

I shouldn't dwell on it.

Yet, it bugs me even more than the question of who left the trotter. It felt so real. I can almost feel the fingers still pressing at my throat.

I consider going to Stone like Winnie suggested. I ponder whether to tell him about the trotter, the hand and the dream.

But Stone doesn't care about me. As much as something deep inside me would like him to, he doesn't. He's made that clear. I'm a nothing. No one of importance.

If I told him, I suspect he'd laugh in my face.

He'd tell me, "You're a silly girl with silly dreams."

I wish I could believe that. Instead, I can't shake the feeling that it's a warning.

38

R^{hi}

PIP GRUNTS AT ME UNHAPPILY, his brow pulled down in what looks like a scowl.

"What?" I say. "You can't expect me to leave you here alone." While I'm sure Winnie's spell is keeping any unwanted visitors out of our room, I'm not taking any risks. Pip has been accompanying me whenever the opportunity allows. No one can complain about his presence out in the gardens.

"Besides," I tell him, "you look adorable."

Pip shakes his head, then his behind, trying to dislodge the halo and matching pair of wings I've dressed him in.

"Look," I wag my finger in his direction. "If I have to wear a stupid costume, then so do you."

I'm dressed in a white nightie that I've borrowed from Winnie with a halo and wings that match Pip's. I know all the other girls in Venus have opted for slutty demon outfits – I've seen the sequined hot pants and devil horns – but Aysha insisted that someone had to go as an angel, and Tristan had backed her up.

So everyone else will get to look hot while I look like a schoolgirl in a nativity play.

Luckily, Winnie's already left to hang some last-minute decorations in Neptune common room, otherwise I'm sure she'd be trying to sex up my outfit.

"Come on," I say to Pip, bending down and beckoning him into my arms. "Aysha keeps reminding me nobody's going to care about Heaven so it'll just be the two of us hanging out in our ridiculous costumes anyway. Although, I have to say dude, you are pulling this look off way better than me."

Pip gives me a disgusted snort and attempts to take a chunk out of his wing.

I cradle him in my arms and make my way to the gardens.

The campus is alive with excitement this evening. I can hear chatter and laughter, music and song from every dorm room and several of the school buildings. The pathways have all been lit with strings of colorful lanterns and the gravel enchanted so that it glows beneath my feet.

Even Pip seems genuinely impressed as he quits wriggling and stares at the lights.

When we step off the path and into the gardens, he snorts with satisfaction. He's been with me the entire time I've been decorating, but neither of us have seen my handiwork in the dark.

I have to admit, it looks pretty good. Not nearly as good as the Venus common room I'm sure – there was talk about burning torches and a bottomless pit – but I'm pretty proud of my handiwork.

I went with the stars hanging in the branches as well as glowing moon flowers circling the base of the trees and sparkling fireflies flitting over the flowerbeds, chased by cheruby cupids. Clouds linger around my feet and hover in the air above my head and I've decorated the fence with a pearly gate.

If the real Heaven looks as magical as this, I think I could be content there.

The music committee wasn't interested in planning a playlist for Heaven, focusing all their attention on tunes for Hell. So some of my cupids are doubling up as harpists.

I've been told I have to stay in Heaven for the evening 'to make sure nobody ruins the decorations' which is the reason I suppose I was given this job. I'm going to miss the real party. There aren't even any drinks or food out here.

But I have Pip safe and sound and my very own piece of Heaven. I'm not sure I care.

It's half an hour before the first few students come hurrying through the gardens in search of the Venus common room. They pay little attention to my decorations, although one points at Pip and laughs.

My pet peers up at me scowling as if to say, "I told you so."

"You look cute," I remind him, pulling out my new phone and snapping a photo despite his grumpy expression.

After that, the flow of students to and from the common room is pretty constant and I start to see the themes the other houses have chosen.

Superheroes, Alice in Wonderland, pirates and circus.

Winnie's arranged to meet up with Trent in the Neptune common room, and only Andrew and Dane stop to admire my handiwork and talk to me, bringing me a cup of warm beer on their way out.

By ten o'clock with the music growing wilder and the people passing through drunker, I admit to myself that this really sucks.

My first real party and I'm stuck on the outside looking in. I peer up at the fluffy cloud above my head and consider morphing it into an angry storm cloud that could strike the freaking Venus common room with lightning.

"I'd like to see you try," Stone says from somewhere behind me.

I drop my gaze and find him standing on the lawn, a cupid dancing around his feet. He follows my gaze and kicks at the little angel. In retaliation the cherub fires a tiny arrow at him.

"What the fuck?" he says, waving his hand at the arrow and watching it evaporate into smoke.

"You like him?"

"Did you make that little goblin menace?"

"He's not a goblin. He's a cherub."

"Doesn't look like one." The cherub sticks its tongue out at my professor and flutters off before he's kicked.

"Why are you lurking about out here …" His eyes trail down my body. "In your grandmother's nightdress."

"I'm an angel."

Stone points to Pip. "He is no angel."

Pip grunts, turning his back on the professor and snuffling about in a cloud.

"So, why are you lurking about out here?"

"I'm required to guard the decorations."

"Required by whom?"

I roll my eyes but don't answer.

The professor steps forward into the starlight. He's dressed in dark chinos and a shirt.

"I see you're embracing tonight's festivities."

The professor snorts, leaning against a tree trunk and crossing his arms. "Hanging out with a bunch of drunk and horny students is not my idea of fun."

"Hmmm," I say. "What is it about this party? Everyone seems high on pheromones and love potions." I've already been a rude awakening for five different couples and one threesome who hoped to sneak off into the gardens for what I can only assume is a rendezvous.

Stone rubs at his forehead. "Rumor has it you've been spending all your free time in the library and yet you still know fuck all about fuck all. Doesn't your little friend tell you anything?"

"She's been rather occupied with decorations." And Trent asking her out.

Stone lifts his eyebrow and I immediately slam down the meager defenses I've been practicing. I'm not sure Winnie would appreciate me revealing information about her love-life to our professor.

Stone shakes his head in a manner that tells me he isn't impressed by my feeble attempts.

"Well," he says, "when a boy likes a girl, or a girl likes a boy, or maybe a boy likes a boy and a girl, and a girl likes a girl ..."

I can't help laughing. "Oh god please, you're a bad enough teacher most of the time, I do not need a sex education lesson from you!"

The professor's eyes flash dark and I feel heat crawl up my neck.

"I mean ... I thought ... I thought you were going to say the influence of the full moon and the tides was influencing people's behavior."

"No, just the regular old influence of alcohol and teenage hormones."

"Disappointing."

"Disappointing?" A smile hovers on his lips.

"The full moon stuff would be more romantic."

"It isn't."

"You sound like you're talking from experience."

He cocks his head to one side. "Are you digging for information about my love-life again, Blackwaters?"

"No, I'm not sure I'd like what I'd find."

He tips back his head and laughs, the sound making my stomach spin. "Yeah," he says finally, "it isn't very pretty."

"A trail of men and women who've left you heartbroken?" I smirk at him. "No wait, that would require you to own a heart."

He lays his palm over his left pec, and my eyes drop there automatically, unable to help but notice the way his muscular chest strains at the fabric of his shirt. "Blackwaters, you've wounded me."

I laugh myself and he smiles at me, the starlight catching in his pale eyes.

"And you?" he says softly.

"Me?"

"Have you ever been heartbroken?"

I shake my head slowly. No, I haven't, not in the way he means anyway. I swallow and force a more jovial expression back onto my face. "Oh well, we'll both have to hope there's a fated mate out there somewhere waiting for us both."

The smile on his lips falters before he seems to check himself.

"You believe in that stuff?"

I shake my head. "I don't know what to believe half the time." I think of that deep bruise on Spencer's stomach, of what they'd told me about scarlet magic.

"What?" the professor says, suddenly right in front of me, grabbing at my wrist. "What was that?"

"Nothing," I say, attempting to shake off his grip as I focus all my mental energy on raising my shields.

"It wasn't nothing. Tell me."

"Honestly, it was just something I read about in a book."

"It looked like a memory." He examines my face, his grip on my wrist tight, his fingers pinching my skin. "Did you do that?"

"You're hurting me," I hiss, attempting to twist my arm away.

"Rhianna, I'm not fooling around here. You need to tell me if–"

"I did tell you. I read it in a book."

"You're lying."

The hook in my stomach twists and for a moment I think I might vomit.

"Get off me," I hiss. "Get off me before I scream!"

"No one's going to hear you even if you do. No one is even missing you. Do you see that?" He jerks his head in the direction of the common room. "They're all in there. And you're out here."

"If you're going to tell me I don't belong here, you've already told me that countless times." I glare at him. "But I'd wish you'd make up your mind. Do you want me to stay or do you want me to go?"

"I want you to tell me the damned truth!" He tugs me close to him and the hook in my stomach spins with excitement. I can feel the heat of his body, the whisper of his breath by my ear. I can taste his scent. Masculine. Woody. Deep.

I gasp as I feel him pushing against the shield in my mind, trying to force it down.

"Don't!" I gasp, pain piercing through my skull. "Please don't."

"I don't want to," he pants. "But I need to know this, Rhianna."

I screw up my eyes, rocking my head from side to side, clinging to the shields with everything I have.

I don't know why I don't want to tell him. Why I don't want him to see the truth. But every part of me screams to keep him out.

"No, please, no," I whimper, tears pooling in my eyes.

The pressure in my head falls away and his fingers snap open, releasing my arm. He stumbles away from me.

"I'm ... I'm sorry," he stutters. "Rhi ... I'm ... sorry."

I clasp my head in my hands, my brain still thumping hard against my skull.

"Fuck you," I hiss, tears racing down my cheeks. "Fuck you!"

I hear Pip grunting angrily, snapping his jaw and when finally I can open my eyes, the professor is gone.

I wipe the tears away from my cheeks, conscious that most of my mascara must now be smudged down my face, suddenly aware the halo I was wearing has fallen from my head.

The pain sings in my head but it isn't as intense.

I need water. My throat is parched.

"Stay here," I mumble to Pip as I stumble from my post in the garden towards the common room.

The noise of the party has me clutching my temples as I draw closer, but I'm so thirsty, I keep walking, straight through the open doors and into the pit of hell.

Fire roars in every direction and the boom from the bass is so violent it reverberates right through my body.

The place is even fuller than it was the day of the theme announcement. Hot sweaty bodies are rammed together. Swaying and gyrating together, hands and mouths exploring warm flesh.

Most of House Venus is topless, including the girls, their bodies smeared in red paint that gleams like blood in the flickering firelight. Some wear magnificent horns that curl like antlers on their heads. But the most magnificent pair, of course, rests on Tristan's. Black like jet, filed to deadly points. His eyes are piercing scarlet and his pants hang low on his hips, made from the hide of a black sheep, the fur fine and tightly curled.

He's sitting on a raised throne, surveying all around him, a girl balanced on each knee, one sucking on his neck, the other pawing at his body.

For a moment, I just stand and stare at him.

He looks like something otherworldly. Like maybe he really

is the prince of darkness. He looks like every woman's fantasy and nightmare rolled into one.

As I stand frozen, his head slowly turns and he meets my eyes, his scarlet gaze like poison in my blood. The pain in my head thumps more forcefully.

"If it isn't a fallen angel," he cackles, his voice somehow amplified above the noise.

If anybody else hears, they don't seem to notice. They're too entranced by the music, by the sway of bodies around them.

It's only me who seems to hear.

He stands, knocking the two girls off his lap and into the throng of dancers below him.

"What is it you want, fallen angel? Are you lost?"

I feel like I'm in a dream. My vision swims. The noises rise and fall in my ears.

"Water," I gasp, "I need water."

He looks at me, his expression unreadable.

"You want water, Pig Girl, then water you shall have."

He waves his hand and, too late, I see a bucket rise from the floor and fly towards me. I try to jump back, attempt to duck away. But I'm too late. The bucket tips above my head and ice cold water crashes on top of me, flowing down my head, over my face and down my body.

I gasp from the cold.

The music halts. Now everybody turns to look as if released by their trance.

They see me standing there soaked to the skin, Winnie's thin night dress clinging to my body.

At first there's silence. Then the first smile cracks across a face. Then another and another, like a wave across the ocean. Someone cackles. Someone giggles. First one. Then two. Then three. Until the room erupts with it. Loud and vulgar.

They point. Someone snaps a photo. Others follow.

I peer down at my body.

My nightdress is see-through, completely see-through.

They can see everything.

I raise my gaze and glare at Tristan.

I lift my hand. He knows what I'm capable of now. He knows what I can do. I could do it again. I'm certain I could do it again.

He lifts a painted eyebrow, daring me to try, daring me to do it.

Rage licks through my body, begging me to. Commanding me to.

Magic crackles in my fingertips. The hook in my belly scrapes at my insides.

I'm going to show him. I'm going to show him he can't hurt me like this.

My brow hardens, the tendons in my neck stiffen.

My fingers sizzle.

I'm going to do it. I don't care about the consequences.

But then something bumps against my leg.

Something warm.

Followed by a snort.

I jerk.

I jerk as if I've been woken from a dream.

I glance down towards my feet.

It's Pip, bumping his snout against my calf.

"Pip," I whisper.

It makes the crowd laugh harder.

I don't care,

I scoop him up and step out of the common room, slamming the door behind me.

39

R^{hi}

I WAKE EARLY the next morning to the sound of humming.

I creak open an eyelid.

My head isn't as sore as it was last night but it still hurts, especially when my vision is met by bright sunlight.

"Woah, Winnie, did you open the curtains?" I ask, slamming my eyes shut.

"Oh, yes sorry, it's just such a beautiful day."

I hear her crank the curtains shut and I venture to open my eyes again.

"You're in a good mood this morning," I observe as she floats round the room, scooping up clothes and rearranging books. She nods and smiles to herself.

"Can I conclude that last night was a good one then?"

"He kissed me!" she blurts out. "Well, actually I kissed him. Or maybe it was more like we both did it at the same time."

"And?" I ask, propping myself up on my elbow so I can get a better look at my best friend.

"And," she clutches her stomach and spins around. "It was so good. So seriously good."

"How long were you kissing for?" I laugh. "You came in really late."

That crimson color creeps up her face. "It wasn't only kissing," she admits. "We went back to his room ... and let's just say that man is very talented with his hands."

"Winnie," I shriek, flinging my pillow over my head. "I don't want to know," I mumble into goose feathers, ignoring the pang of jealousy that gnaws in my stomach.

Am I really jealous? Do I really care? I don't want that, do I? Do I?

What happened with the man in black was a distraction. A mistake. Nothing more.

And as for that kiss with Spencer ...

I peek my head out from under the pillow. "Actually, I do want to know."

Winnie grins and climbs up into my bed, recounting everything in miniscule detail until we're interrupted by her phone beeping.

"It's him," she says, almost dropping her phone. "He's not meant to contact me for at least three days."

"Why not?" I ask, frowning.

"Never mind," she says with a wave of her hand. "He wants me to go hang out with him tonight."

"I bet he does!" It sounds like the two of them had a very good time last night. Winnie on more than one occasion.

I have a feeling my best friend and her long-term crush may now be a thing.

Her gaze flicks up to mine. "He is going to make tacos. You can come too, hang out with us."

"I don't think that is what Trent has in mind, Winnie."

"That doesn't matter. You're my best friend. I'm not about to dump you for a dude and leave you on your own on a Saturday night."

"Winnie, it's fine. I have *Puzzle Master* and Pip remember. I'll be just dandy."

Winnie chews on her lip. "I'll tell him I'll be over at ten, that way we can–"

I snatch the phone from her hand.

"No, you will not. You've liked this guy for forever, haven't you?" She nods. "Then you're not going to blow things on my account."

"Trent's a nice guy, Rhi. He'll understand."

"Winnie, you need to go get some for the both of us, okay. I need to live vicariously through you."

Winnie giggles. "I promise to tell you all about it afterwards."

"You'd better," I say, knocking my elbow against hers.

We spend the rest of the morning eating the cookies Winnie's mom sent her this week, and swapping gossip about the evening. Eventually, I tell her about the bucket incident, although something keeps me from disclosing my encounter with Stone. I haven't told Winnie about my attack on Spencer, about his wound or what Spencer and Tristan told me about scarlet magic.

The secrets I'm keeping from my best friend are stacking up, the pile growing ever higher. But I didn't tell her right at the start and now I'm nervous about how she'll react when she learns I've kept so much from her. Not to mention what she'll think of me when she hears I've wielded scarlet magic.

Winnie's my first ever friend – apart from Pip and the chickens – and I don't want to lose her. Especially when she's prepared to share homemade double chocolate cookies with me.

"I can't believe that jerk did that to you," she says with a frown.

"Really? Those dickheads seem to live for torturing me. Have you forgotten the pig's trotter?"

Winnie turns a shade of green.

"Do you want me to check social media?" Winnie asks softly. "It's likely someone filmed the bucket incident."

I groan. "Shit," I mutter, "I didn't think of that."

Winnie picks up her phone and after a few minutes of scrolling, cringes.

"Is it bad?"

"You weren't wearing a bra."

"No, it didn't really work under the night dress."

"Well," Winnie attempts to say cheerfully, "on the upside at least you have a very good pair of tits."

I groan a second time. "And now I suppose the whole academy has seen them."

"No doubt about it."

"Let me see."

Winnie holds her phone to her chest. "Are you sure? The comments are pretty gross."

"I'd rather know what they're saying about me."

Gingerly, Winnie passes me the phone, her gaze locked on my face as I take a peek. It seems more than one person has posted a photo of me, soaking wet in my see-through nightie. Surprise, surprise though, Aysha's post seems the most liked and has the most comments – all of them derogatory and mean.

It hardly registers. What captures my attention the most is my face. Deathly pale, my eyes red-rimmed. I guess most people will assume it's from the shock of an entire bucket of freezing cold water thrown over my head, but I know it's not. I know it's from Stone's intrusion of my mind.

I swallow, the pain in my head still there as a humming reminder.

For a moment, I consider reporting him to Principal York. I may not be a walking embodiment of the rule book, I may not have actually read it, but I'm pretty certain he isn't allowed to torture students in that way. Although then again torture does seem to be a daily occurrence in this stupid academy.

However, if I reported him, Principal York is bound to ask questions about what he was searching for in my mind and if I wasn't prepared to tell Stone, I'm definitely not divulging that information to the principal.

No, this is better left between me and Stone.

※

IN THE EARLY AFTERNOON, I help Winnie pick out her outfit for her date with Trent.

"Are you nervous?" I ask her, as she pulls a casual black dress over her head.

"About what?"

"You know ... doing it."

I know they didn't go all the way last night. I also know Winnie is dead keen to rectify that situation.

"A little, I guess." She tugs the tight material down her body and admires herself in the mirror, before her eyes meet mine again. "Oh ... wait ... you didn't think ... Rhi, I'm not a virgin."

"Oh," I say, feeling my cheeks turn the red Winnie's so often do. "I didn't mean to assume. I'm sorry if ... really? Who?"

"This guy back home. Before I left for the academy. We weren't in love or anything like that but curious and ... well... we decided it might be a good idea to practice." She smiles. "We ended up doing quite a lot of practicing. I guess that's why I'm so desperate to do it with Trent. I know how good it can be. And, oh god, it's such a long time since I got laid."

She flings her head back and groans.

I thought Winnie and I were alike. Just as clueless when it came to men and sex. I've misjudged my friend and as usual, it turns out I'm the ignorant one who knows nothing.

Winnie must read this on my face. Because she takes my hand.

"You don't need a man, Rhi. But if you wanted one you could get one. I mean if I can–"

"Winnie don't you dare," I warn her.

"Well, in the meantime we could get you a vibrator."

Maybe a vibrator is what I need. Maybe it would stop me feeling things about people I shouldn't. People like Stone.

That moment we'd had before the fucker invaded my mind had been thrilling, had made my skin come alive, had made everything in my core spin.

Of course, then he'd had to go and ruin it all. Reminding me exactly why he is not the man for me.

"A vibrator sounds interesting," I venture. Definitely preferable to a fucker like Stone. "Maybe I'll do some research while you're out."

She leaves me later and I consider a dinner of more cookies, anything to avoid the dining hall alone.

In the end, I decide I'm braver than that and not cowered by a bunch of kids with too much money and oversized egos.

However, I needn't have worried. The hall is almost empty. There isn't a bouncing bunny in sight. In fact, their usual table is completely empty.

Everyone must still be sleeping off their hangovers. Or like me wanting to avoid scrutiny after whatever humiliations they encountered the night before. A little perusal on social media shows me I'm not the only one who's had my photo and name pinned up for public ridicule.

I grab a plate of pasta and head for our usual spot in the

corner. I'm halfway through my dinner when the bench on the other side of the table scrapes along the floor.

I look up and find Andrew taking a seat opposite me.

"Hey Rhi," he says with a hint of caution.

Although we're talking again, things aren't entirely back to the way they were.

"Hey Andrew, on your own too?"

"Yeah, Dane's still puking his guts out. He claims he has food poisoning but I think it has less to do with rancid food and more to do with the barrel of beer he consumed last night." He shakes his head, grinning. "Is Winnie suffering too?"

"No," I shrug, "she just has other plans tonight." I'm not sure how public I am allowed to go with Winnie's new liaison.

"Trent?" Andrew asks with another grin.

"Hmmm, how did you–"

"They were making out right in the middle of the Neptune common room."

"Really?" That doesn't sound like Winnie but good for her. I twist spaghetti around my fork. "How was your night?"

"Yeah, it was all right. How about yours?" I cringe. "Ahhh ... yeah ... sorry."

"You saw the post?"

"Yeah, if it makes you feel any better, you were one of many."

"It does a little."

"Tristan Kennedy is an asshole."

"Shush," I laugh. "You can't say that. It's like sacrilegious around here."

"But true!"

"Yeah, definitely true."

Andrew leans back on the bench dropping his fork. "Sometimes this place sucks."

"I thought you preferred it to your old school."

"Yeah, I do. That place sucked as well."

"Maybe all schools do."

"Yeah." He picks up his fork and pokes at a fat-looking sausage on his plate. "You wanna get out of here?"

"Now?"

"Yeah, I was thinking of heading into Los Magicos, but if you don't fancy–"

"Hmm," I say, considering the offer. It's been weeks since I've been allowed off this campus and I'm definitely beginning to show the signs of cabin fever. Besides, I've only been into Los Magicos once and I'm still curious to explore the place. "I'd really like to get out of here but I'm not sure I could go see Tristan Kennedy right now without scratching his eyes out, and without a permission slip ..." I shake my head.

"Ahhh, you don't need to worry about that. Most of the school – including the teachers – are comatose. You could raid the kitchen and vandalize the library today and nobody would even notice."

"Hmmm," I say, severely tempted. "I can't leave Pip."

He frowns at me. "Your pig?"

"Yeah." I tell him about the pig's trotter. Just like Winnie did earlier, he turns a shade of green.

"We could ask Dane to babysit him. The dude will not be leaving his room."

"Do you think he would? And do you actually think he'd be conscious enough to pay attention?"

"The dude owes me a favor. I put him to bed last night and sat up to make sure he didn't choke on his own vomit."

"Ewww," I say.

"Yeah." Andrew grimaces. "He'll do it and he's a good guy. If he knows it's important to you, he'll watch that pig like a hawk."

"Hawks eat little pigs," I point out.

"You know what I mean."

I chew, thinking about it.

"Okay," I say. "Where did you have in mind? I'm not sure I

have the energy to get all dressed up." I gesture to the outfit I'm wearing: my jeans and my old hoodie.

"Pool hall?"

"I've never played."

"I'll teach you."

I study his face. I don't know if he still has feelings for me. "That sounds fun but just so we're on the same page here, this isn't a–"

"Date? Yeah, yeah, I know," he says, dismissing my concerns with his hand. He peers at his wrist watch. "Campus bus leaves for the city in thirty minutes. Can you make that?"

"Easily," I tell him, my shoulders already feeling lighter and my head clearer.

I can't wait to get out of this place.

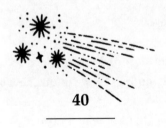

40

T he man in black

I'M SEARCHING for information on a fugitive. A man who eluded the authorities when they came to arrest him for smuggling banned magical substances into the republic.

The occupants in this part of the city, down by the docks, are tight-lipped. They don't want to tell me anything. They know the old adage: snitches get stitches. But there's always someone who's willing to talk. Someone who's prepared to risk a beating for a purse of gold, or who's nursing a grudge they can finally avenge.

It can take a while to seek that person out. Usually, they'll make themselves known to me. All I have to do is make myself visible. Ask the usual questions, knowing the majority will feed me misinformation or stare at me blankly like I'm talking a different language to them.

So I stroll through the docks, my cloak drawn closed against the cold mist that rolls off the water, ducking inside the odd bar, ordering a beer and watching as people shift uneasily around me.

Most people can't do this job, not because it's physically demanding – months on the road, chasing down the worst in this world. Not because of the dangers involved. Not because several powerful people would like to see me dead. No, they couldn't do it because of the way people react to my presence. The way they slide away from me. The way they shift uneasily on their feet. Most people can't stand to feel like a pariah. They can't stand to be hated. Most people want to be loved.

I adjust the hood of my cloak, that cold mist nipping at my nose, and head to the dock's edge where a few remaining fishermen unload their boats among the monstrous tankers, stacked high with crates – some on their way across the ocean, some having been sent from there.

There are usually some women and young men hanging about this area, hoping to snag business from a sailor or two. They're usually as tight-lipped as anyone else. But today's fugitive has a reputation for using women as punch bags and they may be more than happy to see him off the streets.

I turn a corner, smelling the salt from the sea, listening as the tall metal ships groan in the water.

I walk along the waterfront, ignoring the way people side eye me, pretending not to see me, continuing with their every day. I swerve around a pile of barrels and stop.

A bike stands directly behind the barrels, hidden to anyone coming from the direction I just have.

A sleek, modern thing. Black and red. A sprinting wolf painted along its side.

I know who that bike belongs to.

Shit, probably everyone in this part of the city does.

The question is: why the hell is he here?

※

Fuck the fugitive. Fuck my assignment. Fuck the fact I'm going to be in the shit with my employer.

Fuck all that.

I spin on my toes and walk briskly in the opposite direction, wishing now I hadn't made myself so damn obvious.

Not that it matters. Renzo won't assume I'm searching for him. He'll have heard I'm after some smaller fish.

I stride quickly through the alleyways of the docks, trying to stop myself from running. The man in black doesn't run. Not unless he's in pursuit. If I start sprinting now, I'll have tongues wagging.

So I keep my pace fast but constrained, all the way to my own damn bike. As soon as I'm seated on the thing, I hit the gas, speeding away, not caring who looks my way now, not caring about the speed limit, heading in the direction of Arrow Hart Academy.

I'm thumping on Stone's cabin door 45 minutes later. They gave him this place out on the perimeter of the campus as some kind of sweetener to convince him to take up the position. The school board and the authorities both saw how useful a magical like Stone would be teaching at the school. They pretended to court him, although he never really had a choice. And the cabin, sold to him as some kind of luxury because it has a semblance of privacy the other teachers don't enjoy, is run down and seriously crappy.

I don't know if he'll even be here or locked in his office up at the mansion.

I hammer again.

"Stone! Stone! Are you in there?"

I hear the floorboards within creak and then hear the locks on the door click back, and the door swing open.

"Shit!" I mumble when I get a look at my friend. Dark rings

circle his eyes, his hair's a mess and his jaw covered in untrimmed beard. He also stinks to high heaven of booze. I wave my hand in front of my face, noting the bottle of whisky he's clutching in one hand and the way he sways on his feet. "What happened to you?"

"Bad night," he mumbles, glaring at me.

"Wasn't it Founders' Night last night?" I ask with suspicion.

"What do you want?" he asks, rubbing at his temples.

I stomp inside his cabin, eyes swinging around the place.

"Where's Blackwaters?"

Stone takes a swig straight from the neck of the bottle. "Not here. You didn't seriously think she would be–"

"Where is she?"

"Why the fuck should I know?" he says with aggression, and my suspicion that his current state has something to do with the girl is only confirmed. I don't have time to fuck about trying to uncover what's happened though.

"We need to find her."

Stone rests the whisky bottle onto a tabletop and leans against it. "You want to tell me why?"

"Renzo Barone."

Stone blinks and a sobriety flickers across his face. "You think ..."

"Why else would he be here?"

"For any number of reasons, man."

"I've been strolling around downtown for the last two days. Showing my face. Letting the locals know I'm there. You think he'd show up in the city for just any old job when he knows I'm here?"

"And you think this job is special?"

"Of course it damn well is, Phoenix. This is personal."

Stone scrubs his hands down his face. "Shit! Shit! We need to let York know."

"No time. We need to find the girl. You know where she'll be?"

"I thought you had a tracker on her phone."

"It's switched off. Do you know where she is?"

"Unlike you, I'm not tracking her around the school," he says tersely and I raise an eyebrow at him. "Fuck off," he mutters, because we both know he is.

He strolls to the sink and turns the tap on. He holds his palms under the flowing waters and leans forward, scrubbing the cold liquid over his face and his scalp. Then he stands up, shaking his head, water droplets flying through the air. "Come on, there are a few places she might be."

We try her dorm first, but the lights are out and there's no sign of her, her roommate or even the damn pig.

"Where the hell has she gone with that pig?" Phoenix mutters.

"You said we should check the library."

"Pigs are not allowed in there."

"We should try it anyway."

"Fine. You head there. I'll go knock on some doors. See if she's hanging out in any of the dorms."

I nod and jog along the path. It's always strange being back in the place. It's like I never left. Like time never passed. Like I'm still the young man who attended here and not the man I've become.

It gives me the creeps and I shake off the sensation and focus on the job in hand. Finding the girl before Renzo fucking Barone does.

The library is completely deserted – even the librarian is not sitting at her usual post. It's hardly surprising. I remember Founders' Night clearly. A night full of frivolity and raucous behavior. No wonder the campus is deadly quiet tonight. Which makes me even more uneasy. Why isn't the girl in her dorm, nursing a hangover like every other student here? Where the hell is she?

I walk the library stacks anyway, and circle the upper story balcony. In case, she's hiding out somewhere.

I know she's not though. I'd know if she was here. I'd feel it.

I call Stone.

"Any luck?"

"No, I'm assuming you've had none either."

"Library's empty."

"I did find her roommate."

"And ..."

"She doesn't know where she went. She says as far as she knew, Rhi was staying in their room tonight."

"You don't think she's ..."

"All her stuff is still in her room."

"The pig's not though," I point out. That pig is the only thing I think Rhi would take if she did run. She brought hardly anything here. I doubt she'll take anything when she leaves. "Get her friend to call her."

"I already have it's still going to voicemail."

"Fuck, Stone," I snap, "she can't have vanished into thin air!"

"Keep calm, man," Stone says, although I have no fucking clue how he can. Renzo Barone. She's as good as dead. She won't stand a fucking chance. Why the hell haven't we been more careful? Why the hell haven't we been guarding her?

Because I never expected Marcus Lowsky to make a move like this. Damn stupid.

"She has a couple more friends. I'm on my way there now."

"Hurry the fuck up!" I snap, switching off the call.

Maybe Stone was right. Maybe we should have gone straight to York. We could have had the entire faculty searching for her by now.

I decide it isn't too late. Leaving the library, I sprint along the corridor and up the staircase heading towards the principal's quarters. I'm a foot away from her door, when my cell rings.

I pick it up.

"Yes?" I bark.

"Bingo," Stone says down the end.

"What the fuck does that–"

"I found the pig. The student who's watching it said she went into the city with another student. The friend says they caught the campus bus. With any luck we can intercept it. Catch them while they're still on it."

"Good," I say. "Then let's go."

My friend's already there waiting for me on his bike when I reach mine.

"You know the route the bus takes?" I ask him, jumping up on my bike and revving the engine.

"Main one," he answers and we fly out of the academy grounds and out onto the country roads.

I try not to think of the last time I drove this way – from the academy to the city – with the girl on the back of my bike, her arms curled around my waist, her thighs flush to mine. I try not to think about how different she is from every other person. Not shrinking away from me, not stepping away. No, if anything she's drawn to me, just like I am to her.

It's foolish. She should be as wary of me as everyone else is. She knows what I am. What I do. She's seen me kill.

Is her reaction to me genuine? Or is it something beyond her control? Something she is unaware of? Something she couldn't stop if she wanted to?

I focus on the road in front of me. The mist from the sea hasn't rolled in this far and the night is a clear one, the stars scattered across the sky like rice for birds and the moon barely there, only a slither of silver. But the beams of my headlights are enough to bathe the road in a ghostly white.

We speed along the roads too quickly, skidding around

corners and veering towards hedgerows; I grip the handle bar and stare straight ahead. Where is that bus? Where the hell is that bus?

The road becomes more sturdy. Widens. We meet other traffic. Another bike. Two cars. The first houses on the outskirts of the city appear. Then more. Denser and denser, lining up to create neat rows. I see the towers of the financial district, the cranes from the dock, the great dome of the Council building.

The traffic is dense now, despite the late hour. It's a Saturday night. The road is jammed with taxis and trams. Not a bus in fucking sight.

We should have caught the thing by now. She should be perched behind me safe and sound. Her warm body pressed to mine. That strange scent of hers filling my senses.

I glance towards Stone and he points down the road with his gloved hand. In the distance, tucked between two trucks, its indicator flicking, is the campus bus, the name of the academy painted down its side like a fucking neon advertisement. It should be more discreet. It shouldn't be announcing to every lowlife in the city that a bus load of innocents have just pulled up.

I nod to him and we speed past the traffic, cutting in and out, and coming to flank the bus on either side. I thump on the side of the bus, catching the driver's attention.

He goes to lean on his horn, but when I turn and glare at him, he falls back against his seat. He knows who I am.

I signal to him to pull over and Stone and I follow, parking up in front of the bus.

Then together, we walk to the doors. They swing open for us.

"What's wrong?" the driver starts anxiously.

I don't bother answering, I climb up inside, my gaze swinging along the rows of seats and the students who perch there with mouths agape. There aren't many. Four or five.

I stare at them. They stare back, shifting on their seats.

"She's not here!" Stone mutters.

"Rhi," I yell, hoping on the off chance he's wrong. That I'm wrong. That there she is, sitting on the seat right in front of me. Safe. "Rhi Blackwaters."

No one answers and the blood pounds against my eardrums. Thump. Thump. Thump.

"Do any of you know where Rhianna Blackwaters is?" Stone growls.

The students glance among each other like this is the most challenging question they've ever been asked.

"Well, do you or not?" I bark, making one girl leap in her seat.

"Pig Girl?" a boy with more pimples than face asks, his brow wrinkling.

Stone growls again. "That what you call her?"

The boy gulps and decides not to answer that question.

"She got off at the first stop."

I spin and march to the driver.

"Where was that?"

"Downtown."

I look at Stone.

What the hell is she doing there?

41

Rhi

"So I'm assuming this is the shitty part of the city," I say, tugging up the hood of my sweater. There's a bite to the air and a sea mist hangs around the rundown-looking buildings.

"Yeah, I guess so," Andrew says, peering around. "Why? Is it not up to your standards?" he asks, with a humor that sounds a tad defensive.

"No, you should have seen some of the places I've lived in. This is like a paradise compared to some of those towns," I say, with a smile. Although, if I'm honest, those places may have been rundown, they may have lacked money and taste, but they didn't have this aura of threat about them. Unlike this place with its poorly lit alleyways, and eerie creak of distant machinery. "How far's the pool hall?"

Andrew continues to swing his gaze, ignoring my question.

"Are we lost?" I tease. "I thought you were a regular."

"What?" he snaps.

"I thought you were a regular," I repeat. "Are we lost?"

"No, I mean, yes, I am a regular. It's just around this corner."

"There?" I say, frowning as he points to what looks like a dead end. "I can't see the entrance, Andrew. Are you sure you got this right? Maybe we should retrace our steps, or ask someone or–"

"It's right there," he says, pushing me towards the dark street.

"Andrew?" I say.

I don't like this. My magic tingles in my fingers.

Suddenly I don't like this at all.

What am I doing on a lonely, dark street with a man who has already proven himself to be untrustworthy?

"You're frightening me, Andrew," I say, lifting my hands.

Andrew shakes his head and I suddenly see he's as uneasy as I am; his face drained of color.

"It's not him you need to be frightened of, little mouse," a sinister voice says from behind me.

I jump.

Andrew steps away.

"I'm sorry," Andrew whispers, "I'm really sorry, Rhi, I had no choice."

"Ahh look at that. He's sorry," the voice says, now dripping with sarcasm. "Beat it kid, before I ..."

Whoever the man stood behind me is, he doesn't need to finish his threat. Andrew turns on his heels and sprints away, soon lost in the shadows and the swirling sea mist, his footsteps dying away on the sidewalk.

I turn around.

The man behind me is bathed in shadow but I can see he's tall and broad. Easily twice my size.

"Who are you?" I ask, strangely calm. "And what do you want?"

The man chuckles and steps into the light of the flickering lamp above him. "You don't know?"

He's younger than his deep voice suggests. In his mid-twenties perhaps. His hair is jet black, swept back from his face, and his skin is olive. Several scars cross his face, one running the length of his cheek, another slicing his eyebrow in two.

A heavy silver chain rests around his neck and underneath it crawls tattoos, many more scribbled all over the skin of his hands and his arms. Hoops hang in a line along the lobes of his ears and his fingers are covered in heavy silver rings.

"Marcus Lowsky," I say and the man shakes his head and chuckles.

"No, little mouse. Not him. Want to guess again?"

"No, I don't."

"Shame." He steps forward, his gaze flicking down my form, his tongue sliding along the rim of his lower lip. "I like to play games. I was hoping you did too."

"Who are you?" I repeat, taking a decided step backwards. "And what do you want?"

From the corners of my eyes, I assess my surroundings. The road I'm standing in is a dead end; the man in front of me blocking my exit. There are two doors on this street though, one on either side of the road. If I could blast him, perhaps I'd have enough time to run. But am I better running the way I came, or opting for one of those doors?

"Ahhh you're gonna run," the man says, cocking his head to one side, an excitable smile playing on his lips. "I love it when they run. It makes things so much more interesting."

"I don't know who you are, but I'm not interested in playing any games with you. My friends will be here any minute and–"

"Rhianna Blackwaters," the man says, stepping forward another pace, "I've been watching you for some time now. Let's not pretend you have any friends. Well not if you want to count the one who just handed you over to me."

"You've been watching me?"

He takes another step closer, so we're only a foot apart.

"Watching you," he says, tipping his head to one side, then the other, "sending you gifts."

"Gifts?" I frown.

"You didn't like my gifts, little mouse?" He fakes a pout. "I put so much thought into them too. I know how much you love pigs so..." He grins at me widely and a gold tooth glints in the far recesses of his mouth.

"That was you," I whisper, fear slowly slipping down my spine. The ham, the pig's trotter. Winnie was right. It wasn't anyone in the school. It was this man.

As I stare at him, he plunges one hand into the pocket of his jeans and tugs out an object. For a moment, I don't understand what it is. Then the lamplight catches it and a blade glints silver. My knife.

"You work for the Wolves of Night, for Marcus Lowsky."

"I am the Wolves of Night." He takes another step towards me, spinning the knife in his fingers, and I realize I'm frozen to the spot, that his words have weaved a magic around me without me even noticing, and now I'm held here, unable to move, unable to run, unable to fight. "I am their knife, slicing through the night, silent and deadly. I am their angel of death, delivering vengeance swiftly and ... well ..." he chuckles, flicking his thumbnail against the blade, "sometimes not so swiftly. Sometimes I like to take my time."

He runs his tongue along his lower lip for a second time, slowly as if he's teasing me, and though I'm frozen in place, I feel that hook in my stomach, tugging at me.

The man frowns.

"Lowsky wants you dead, little mouse."

"I know," I say.

"Says you killed his little brother." His gaze swims all over me and he scoffs. "I don't see how that's possible, a scrawny little thing like you."

"Maybe I'm stronger than I look," I hiss at him, struggling against the confines of this magic he's wrapped me in.

He frowns again and, squeezing his free hand into a fist, tightens the binds. It's like nothing I've experienced before. Powerful and solid.

"Are you now?" he says. "Then do you want to play after all, little mouse?"

He's toying with me. He thinks he's caught me and like a cat with its prey, he'll let me run, then stomp on my tail.

But I've had enough games. I haven't endured all the crap I have this term, to end up another toy for some psychopath in a dark alley. No way.

I close my eyes, take an inhale, and focusing with all my might, blast through his magic with everything I have.

The force of it blows us apart, both of us stumbling backwards.

If he's shocked by my display of power, if he's in any way impressed, he doesn't show it on his face. If anything the psychopath looks excited, as if this was just what he was hoping for.

"Ahhh, well, shit, little mouse, maybe there is more to you after all. And you're not going to make it easy for me?" He grins, his eyes twinkling with amusement. "Come on then little mouse, let's see what more you have."

It took a considerable chunk of my magic to break through his powerful binds and now I'm seriously depleted; my legs feel like jelly and my head thumps again from the assault it took last night.

But I'm not giving up. I'm not giving up without a fight. My aunt gave her entire life to keep me safe. She endured more pain than one person ever should.

I won't let her down now by succumbing to this man. I

won't allow my own stupidity in trusting Andrew to be my downfall.

No.

No way.

I delve deep inside my body, calling on all the energy I can muster from every nerve and every cell. I draw it out with all my might, roaring with pain as I send it all thundering towards the man before me.

His eyes grow wide with shock but it doesn't last for long. He manages to dodge some of the assault, some of my magic hitting him hard on the shoulder and making him hiss. His eyes and his face darken and he sends a volley my way in retaliation.

I block some, holding my arms in front of my face and shielding myself. His magic bounces and splinters on my arm and I scream as my flesh burns.

"Seems there is more to you than I realized," I hear him taunt through the swirling mist. "Maybe Marcus is a fool to want you dead. Maybe he could make use of you instead."

"I'm not going anywhere with you!" My arms fall to my sides, hanging limp. My legs shake. I want to collapse to the ground, curl up in a ball and sleep.

"In that case, you don't need to fight," he whispers, his words seeming to swim through the air and curl around me. "I could make it quick. With the knife. You wouldn't feel a thing."

My eyes fall shut. His words are like a lullaby, soothing and seductive, lulling me into sleep.

I struggle to open my eyes and see him pacing toward me, closing the gap between us.

I lift my fingers, willing magic from my body with everything I have. A few sparks splinter into the air, hissing, fizzing and dying by his feet.

He comes closer still and this time I feel the cold tentacles of his magic curling around my body. He peers down into my face, my eyes forced upwards to meet his.

"You put up a good fight, little mouse," he says with a smirk. "Would you like to beg now, plead for your life. I always love it when they beg."

"Fuck you," I mumble, my body so exhausted I can hardly remain upright.

He hooks a forefinger under my chin, the metal of his ring cold against my skin.

"Now that isn't very nice, is it? And here I was, promising to be nice to you. To make this painless. I can change my mind."

He sweeps his thumb along the line of my jaw and peers deep into my eyes. His are a mixture of colors, one eye more green, the other more brown. I stare up into his and I feel like I'm falling. That hook in my stomach is the only thing tethering me to the ground.

I watch as the pupils of his eyes blow wide, swallowing up the myriad colors.

I don't want to die. I don't want to die like this. But my body has nothing left to give. I remember the man in black, kneeling in the clearing, the gun poised to his temple. The way he'd closed his eyes ready for his death, accepting its arrival. I remember the way the knife had flown from my hand before I'd even realized what I was doing, before I'd had time to think.

All I knew was that I had to save him. That I couldn't let him die.

There'll be no one to save me. Once upon a time there was. But she's gone now. She left me all alone.

I wonder if I'll see her again. If she'll be waiting for me.

I close my eyes like I saw the man in black do, I wait for the blow. I wait for my knife.

"This isn't possible," the man who is going to kill me says.

And then magic collides with my body.

42

R^{hi}

I GRUNT as I'm flung backwards, landing on my back.

My breath catches in my chest. For a moment I don't breathe. Then oxygen rasps into my lungs, my heart beats in my chest. I'm still alive.

Magic thunders in the air above me, bright sparks of it crashing through the dark. I try to lift my head to see what the hell is going on, but the pain is too great and I cry out as my head falls back against the hard sidewalk.

"Rhi!" I blink open my eyes, staring up into the concerned face of Stone. He turns his head. "She's here. Hurt but alive."

Boots thunder on the ground. More magic crashes against buildings. Male voices yell above the noise but I can't make out the words.

Stone ducks low, then lifts his hand to send a stream of fire roaring through the air, the heat of it vivid against my skin.

Then as quickly as it starts, it stops.

The street is suddenly silent.

"Azlan!" Stone yells, stumbling to his feet. "Azlan." He holds up his hands, ready to attack.

"I'm here," a voice thunders, and then the man in black steps forward, out of the choking smoke.

"Barone?"

"Gone."

"Fuck." Stone steps towards his friend, resting his palms on his shoulders. "Are you okay?"

The man in black shakes him off. "Fine. The girl?"

Stone looks down at me, contempt spreading over his face. "She'll live."

The man in black walks towards me, crouching down and hooking his arm under my shoulder, helping me to sit.

"Rhi," he says softly. "Are you hurt?"

"I ... I don't know."

His gaze flickers over my face, and down my body as if he's searching for any signs of an injury.

"What happened?" he asks.

"She fucked up, that's what," Stone snaps. He's standing with his hands on his hips, his shoulders rising and falling. "I told her, I told her so many times. Stay at the academy."

"Stone," the man in black warns.

"I was with my friend Andrew."

"Your friend? Where is he now?"

I shake my head. "He left me here. It was ... it was a trap."

"Andrew? Andrew who?" the man in black demands.

"Andrew Playford."

"I know the one," Stone says darkly.

"The name means nothing to me," the man in black says. "What's the connection?"

"I don't know." He shakes his head in frustration, then glares at me. "What the hell did you think you were doing?

Leaving campus? Wandering around this part of the fucking city?"

I close my eyes, his words a painful barrage to my head.

"Stone," the man in black growls.

"She's a liability," he mutters, pacing now, rage rolling off his body in waves. "He was going to ... He was so close to–"

"Stone, I know."

The professor glares at his friend, then disappears into the smoke, leaving the two of us behind.

I push myself away from the man in black, rolling onto my side. My body shakes, nausea brewing in my stomach.

"I'm fine," I say, gritting my teeth against the pain that spirals through my body, every part of me in agony.

"You're not fine," the man in black says, resting his palm on the small of my back. Warmth radiates from his touch, swimming through my body and making me groan with relief. "Your magical reserves are almost depleted and your ..." I peer down at my right leg, twisted into an ugly angle. I gag.

"Can you fix it?" I ask, my voice trembling.

"Yes," he says, "if you want to end up with a permanent limp. It needs to be done professionally. I'm going to take you to the hospital."

I groan. "I can't afford a hospital."

The man in black takes no notice, scooping me up into his arms as gently as he can, careful not to jolt my injured leg. He'd needn't have bothered. There's something about his embrace, the warmth of it, the solid protective wall of his strength, that has the pain seeping away. I melt against him, my eyes heavier than ever, my head falling to rest on his shoulder.

"You're safe now, Rhianna."

"Who was he?"

"It doesn't matter," he whispers and I close my eyes, feeling his warm mouth against mine, feeling him kiss me with a tenderness I don't understand, feel his lips move against mine, feel his tongue sweep against my mouth, taste him, sink further and further into him.

※

I DON'T KNOW how he transports me through the city because when I open my eyes again, I'm lying out on a mattress, under the bright lights of a clinic, the smell of antiseptic strong in my nose and the man in black's hand in mine.

He reaches forward, stroking a strand of hair from my face.

"How are you feeling?"

"Still exhausted," I mumble, stifling a yawn. I search my body for signs of pain but everything feels numb and blissful. Numb and blissful and humming with magic. "My magic," I say in astonishment. "It's ... it's back."

I've never pushed my magic that far before, never used every last ounce of it, but when I have used large chunks of it, it's always taken days and a fair bit of sleep for it to replenish. How is that possible?

The man in black nods. "The doctor should be here soon to fix your leg. It's a bad break, Rhi, but they said it will be good as new."

I peer down at it, instantly flinching and darting my gaze away. My eyes land on his face. He looks exhausted. Soot marks his cheek and a cut runs along his brow.

"Your face," I say.

He lifts his free hand, touching the slash and peering at the blood on his fingers. "Ahhh yeah," he mutters.

"Shouldn't you fix it?" I smile at him. "It's simple magic, you know."

He smiles sheepishly. "I'm pretty depleted on magic myself," he confesses.

"You are?" I say, surprised. "Well then, let me. I owe you after all."

I lift my hand and he catches it in his own.

"You should save your energy," he smirks, "besides I'd rather like to keep my face scar-free."

"I have actually learned some stuff at the academy," I say with a mock frown that quickly turns real. "That man, his face was covered in scars. Why, when he could–"

"I gather he wears them as a badge of honor," the man in black says, his lips curling in disgust.

"Who was he?" I ask again.

"You really don't know?"

"I can guess. He had my knife. He belongs to the Wolves of Night, doesn't he? He works for Marcos Lowsky."

"Yes, he's his assassin." He squeezes my hand. "Not many people have crossed his path and lived to tell the tale."

"I wouldn't have," I hold his gaze, my hand still warm in his, "lived, if it hadn't been for you."

"And Stone," he corrects.

I frown a second time. I don't want to think about Stone right now. Stone and his harsh words. Stone who tried to force his way into my mind.

"How did you know? How did you find me?"

"I saw Barone's bike earlier today. I knew he was in the city. I had my suspicions that he was–"

"Looking for me."

"Yes. He wouldn't usually risk turning up in the city when he knows I'm here."

The man in black's eyes darken.

"The two of you have history."

"You could say that."

"Is he dead?" I ask, peering into the man in black's eyes. I've seen him kill before.

"No." He shakes his head. "I'm sorry, Rhi. He got away."

"There's no need to be sor–"

"He'll be back," he says, his jaw tightening.

I consider these words for a moment. I've had this price on my head all this time. Hanging there. But I never knew who was coming for me, how they'd strike. Now I have a name and a face. Somehow it makes me feel less afraid.

"Good," I say firmly, "because I want my knife back."

The man in black opens his mouth to respond, but the curtain, drawn around my bed, rattles and then swings back. A young doctor steps through, a nurse following behind her.

"Azlan, a word please," the doctor says, motioning her blonde head towards the gap in the curtain. She's beautiful, her long blonde hair tied back in a bun, her eyes a bright green.

And she knows his name.

Azlan.

Is that it? His name?

Azlan. The name hums around my ears.

"Is it necessary, Lucinda?"

"Yes," she says, their eyes connecting in a way that makes me uneasy, my skin pricking and bile sloshing in the back of my throat.

She doesn't just know his name. She knows him.

The man in black stands, leaning forward to kiss the crown of my head. The press of his lips is brief, lasting barely a second, and yet it sets butterflies fluttering in my stomach. Which is stupid. Really stupid. He's only showing fatherly concern. Nothing more.

And as for that kiss ... kiss? Did he kiss me? Or was I dreaming?

His hand slips from mine and he disappears after the doctor, her hips swaying seductively.

A growl rips from my throat as all the pain that had been colliding through my body out there on the sidewalk slams back into me.

I writhe on the bed, clutching my stomach, my eyes screwed shut against the agony.

A cool hand rests on my forehead and a voice floats in the air.

"What's wrong?"

"No!" I gasp, "no, please."

"Where does it hurt?"

"My stomach!" I cry out, forcing open my eyes to stare up at the nurse.

She peers down at me with compassion. "Your stomach?"

Sweat runs down my neck, I clench my teeth together moaning.

"Please, please," I beg her. "It hurts." It hurts like nothing I've ever experienced before.

"Oh gosh!" she says, her hands flying to her mouth, "he didn't say ... we didn't realize ... but with the transfer of magic we should have ... gosh we shouldn't be separating you like this right now. I'll go fetch him right away," she says, patting my arm, "it's okay, I'll go get your mate."

I catch her hand, her face swims through my tears.

"Mate?" I croak out, her words making no sense.

"Yes, it's okay, I'll go fetch your fated mate right back here. We should never have separated you."

I release her fingers and she pulls her arm free, scurrying away through the curtains.

The hook in my stomach twists deep and relentless as if attempting to scrape out my insides.

I pant through the pain.

I try to make sense of her words.

The world spins dangerously out of control, unconsciousness begging to claim me.

And then he's there again. The man in black.

He rests his hand on my shoulder and it all melts away. All that pain just vanishes.

It's more than magic.

What the hell?

I glare at him, tears racing down my cheeks. "F-f-fated mate?" I stutter.

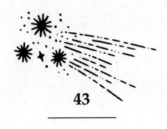

43

The man in black

SHE STARES at me as if she's seen a ghost, her face deathly pale, tears streaming down her cheeks, her dark hair damp around her temples.

The words slip from her lips again.

Half question. Half accusation.

"Fated mate?"

I close my eyes. My heart thumps in my chest. The hook in my stomach thrums. Her magic flickers against mine.

Fated mate.

Perhaps I'd known it the very first time I caught a whiff of her scent in that shack of her house. Or perhaps it was the very first time I'd laid eyes on her. The first time I'd felt that tug deep in my gut. One I'd never felt before. One I will never feel again.

"Is it true?" she asks when I say nothing.

I take a deep breath in and open my eyes.

The dark pupils of her eyes bloom as her gaze connects with mine.

"Yes," I say. "Yes, it's true."

She shuffles on the bed and regretfully, I remove my palm from her shoulder.

"How do you know?"

I can tell it pains her to ask the question. Her ignorance grates her. She's a proud little thing.

I place my hand over my stomach. "In my gut."

She scoffs, shaking her head. "Your gut tells you this."

"No, that's not what I'm saying. It's a sensation in the pit of my stomach, constantly pulling me towards you, straining at me whenever we're apart."

What little blood she had remaining in her face, drains before my eyes.

"You feel it too?" I ask her, although the answer is written all over her face.

"How long have you known?" Her voice trembles as she whispers.

I don't answer.

"As long as I have …" she says, her words trailing away as understanding dawns across her features. She frowns. "But you didn't say anything."

"Neither did you."

"I didn't understand what it meant."

"And I didn't know that."

"So you just thought, what? That I was ignoring it?"

"I didn't know what to think, Rhianna. This took me by surprise. Fated mates are rare. And you're younger than me. I didn't know if it was real."

"Or," she says, holding my gaze, "you didn't want it to be me. You didn't want me to be your fated mate."

Shame floods through my body and that hook in my stomach aches.

"I didn't know you then," I whisper.

"You still don't know me now." She leans forward on the bed. "You never even told me your name."

"Azlan," I tell her. "My name is Azlan."

"I know," she says, the tears cascading down her face, "because I heard that other woman call it you." I lift my hand to her face but she bats it away. "Don't. Don't touch me."

I can't pull my hand away from her so it hangs there in the air between us.

"Please just leave," she whispers.

"I can't," I say firmly.

"Why not? You left me before. You've left me over and over again."

"The pain would be too much." I dip my head, finding her gaze again. "For you."

Her body stills.

"What have you done?"

I hesitate. I still don't know why I did it. Except that she was waning, waning in my arms, becoming weaker and weaker, her magic so low I could not find it. And in that moment the cold fingers of fear gripped my throat in a way it never had before. All those times I'd faced death unafraid. Never frightened. Never fearful. Never with anything to lose.

And yet, the idea of losing her, of watching her drift away in my arms, had paralyzed me with terror.

I did the only thing I could.

Damn the fucking consequences.

"I gave you my power."

Her forehead crinkles. "What does that mean? What does that mean you gave me your magic?"

"It means the fated mate bond between us is sealed." She's still too weak to feel it, the thread connecting us, vibrant and alive, binding us together. "And now it's unbreakable."

Read Book Two next, *Twisted Ties*

For sneaky previews, spoilers and all the latest news, join Hannah's reader group

THANK you so much for reading. If you enjoyed this book, please consider leaving a review or rating — it's a great help to indie authors like me!

ALSO BY HANNAH HAZE

All available on Amazon and Kindle Unlimited.

Paranormal RH romance

The Arrow Hart Academy

Fractured Fates

Twisted Ties

Shattered Stars

Contemporary RH omegaverse

In With The Pack

In Deep - Rosie's story

In Trouble - Connie's story

In Knots - Alexa's story

In Doubt - Giorgie's story

In Control - Sophia's story

The Rockview Omegaverse

Pack Rivals Part I

Pack Rivals Part II

Pack Choices

Pack Gamble Part I

Pack Gamble Part II

Contemporary MF omegaverse series

The Alpha Rock Stars

The Rockstar's Omega

Rocked by the Alpha

Fourth Base with the Alpha

Contemporary MF omegaverse standalones

Oxford Heat

The Alpha Escort Agency

Omega's Forbidden Heat

Contemporary MF omegaverse novellas

The Omega Chase

Online Heat

Christmas Heat

Alien omegaverse MF romance series

The Alpha Prince of Astia

Alien Desire

Alien Passion

ABOUT THE AUTHOR

A recovering cynic, Hannah grew up swearing she would never marry. Then in 2001, she met her husband and has been a card-carrying romantic ever since. Despite being an avid writer and reader, Hannah decided to do the sensible thing and study science at university, putting authoring ideas to one side. This all changed when she discovered the joys of a good romance book and came to the realisation that love stories are always the best ones.

She now uses her knowledge of chemical bonds and reactions to ensure her books are full of sparks. In fact the electricity between her characters is sure to set your pulse racing and your heart fluttering.

Hannah loves reading to her three children, including doing all the silly voices, and going for long walks in the countryside (the muddier the better). Her head is always full of new story ideas and you are most likely to find her avoiding the demands of her very naughty cat as she attempts to write them all down.

Sign up to my newsletter:
www.hannahhaze.com/about

Join my reader groups:
https://www.facebook.com/groups/hannahhazehotromancereads

https://www.facebook.com/groups/softandsteamyomegaverse

Visit my website:
www.hannahhaze.com

Catch me on TikTok:
www.tiktok.com/@hannahhaze_author

ACKNOWLEDGMENTS

Firstly, as always, a huge thank you to my readers. This book is something a bit different from me and I'm so pleased you gave it a chance. I truly hope you enjoyed it!

I have a massive team of beta readers to thank for their help — Jessica, Chelsea, Leandri, LeeAnne, Tara, Jenna, Aimee, Sara, Courtney , Alanys, Nancy, Naomi, Jessica, Sara, Lili, Melissa, Morgan and Kiki. I am grateful for all your thoughts, comments, ideas and encouragement.

Thank you to Christian for this very awesome cover, to Marie for bringing Rhi and Pip to life, and James for a wonderful editing job.

To my Mr D and Stephy — I will always be eternally grateful for your encouragement. Writing is scary and sometimes you need someone to hold your hand or kick you up the backside. Lots of kisses to you both.

And lastly, to my wonderful children: you inspire me with your awesomeness and crazy imaginations every day. Love you all!

Printed in Great Britain
by Amazon

b5bf2e1c-7438-4c6e-9d5c-e1af6f63b5ccR01